THESE FOUR WALLS

THESE FOUR WALLS

SUSAN CAMERON

McArthur & Company
Toronto

Published in 2007 by
McArthur & Company
322 King St. West, Suite 402
Toronto, Ontario
M4V 1J2
www.mcarthur-co.com

Library and Archives Canada Cataloguing in Publication

Cameron, Susan M. (Susan Micheline), 1946–
These four walls : a novel / Susan Cameron.

ISBN 978-1-55278-666-6

I. Title.

PS8555.A522T44 2007   C813'.54   C2007-904154-X

Printed in Canada by Friesens

The publisher would like to acknowledge the financial support of
the Government of Canada through the Book Publishing Industry
Development Program, the Canada Council for the Arts, and the Ontario
Arts Council for our publishing activities. We also acknowledge the
Government of Ontario through the Ontario Media Development
Corporation Ontario Book Initiative.

10 9 8 7 6 5 4 3 2 1

For Lila
and
For Hope

Guide to Map of Halifax

GOVERNMENT AND MILITARY BUILDINGS

Armouries	D5
City Hall	E4
City Market	E4
Cold Storage	E1
Court House	E3
Customs House	F4
Federal Building	D4
Grain Elevator	E2
North Barracks	E5
Post Office	F4
Province House	F4
Provincial Annex	F4
R. A. Park	E4
South Barracks	E4
Union Station	E2
Wellington Barracks	D6

THEATRES AND AMUSEMENTS

Capitol Theatre	E3
Casino Theatre	D5
Community Theatre	D5
Family Theatre	E3
The Forum	C6
Garrick Theatre	E3
Orpheus Theatre	E3
Theatre Arts Guild	C4
Empire Theatre	D6
Gaiety Theatre	E5
Oxford Theatre	B5

HOTELS

Carleton Hotel	E4
Elmwood Hotel	E2
Halifax Hotel	E3
Hillside Hall	E3
Lord Nelson Hotel	D4
Nova Scotian Hotel	E2
Waverly Hotel	E3

CHURCHES (Anglican)

All Saints Cathedral	D3
Old Dutch Church	E6
St. Augustine's	B3
St. George's Round Church	E5
St. James	A6
St. John's	A7
St. Mark's	C6
St. Matthias	C5
St. Paul's	E4
Trinity	E5

CHURCHES (Miscellaneous)

First Baptist	E3
Central Baptist	D6
West End Baptist	C5
Christian Church	D6
Church of the Redeemer (Univ.)	E5
Church of the Resurrection (Luth.)	C5
First Church of Christ (Chr. Sc.)	D2
Full Gospel Church	D5
Jewish Tabernacle	E6
St. David's (Presbyterian)	E3
Seventh Day Adventist	D5
Zion African	D5

CHURCHES (Roman Catholic)

Holy Heart Seminary	C5
St. Agnes	A6
St. John the Baptist	A5
St. Joseph's	D6
St. Mary's Cathedral	E3
St. Patrick's	E5
St. Theresa's	C6
St. Thomas Aquinas	C5

CHURCHES (United)

Bethany	A6
Brunswick	E5
Fort Massey	D3
Memorial J. Wesley Smith	E5
St. Andrew's	C4
St. John's	C6
St. Matthew's	E3
United Memorial	D7

COLLEGES

Dalhousie University	C4
Kings University	C4
Maritime Business College	D4
Nova Scotia College of Art	E4
Nova Scotia Technical College	E3
Pine Hill United Church College	C2
St. Mary's College	C5

MUSEUMS

Nova Scotia Archives	C4
Provincial Museum	E3

CLUBS AND SOCIETY BUILDINGS

Elks Club	E3
Gorsebrook Golf Club	E3
Ashburn Golf Club	A7
Knights of Columbus	E3
Masonic Temple	E3
North West Arm Rowing Club	D3
Royal N. S. Yacht Squadron	D1
Waegwoltic Club	B4
Wanderers A. A. Club	D4
Y. M. C. A.	E3
Y. W. C. A.	E2

Historic Sites in Halifax

Province House	1811-9	F4
Government House	1801	E3
St. Paul's Cemetery	1749	E3
Provincial Museum		E3
Archives Building		C4
Maroon Tower	1756	D1
Gorsebrook Golf Club House	1820	C3
St. Paul's Church	1750	E4
Citadel	1828	D4
Old Town Clock	1801	E4
Ordnance Wharf	1810	F4
St. George's Round Church	1800	E5
Old Dutch Church	1755	E5
Admiralty House	1814	D6
H. M. C. Dockyard	1759	E6
Melville Island Prison	1808	A5
Memorial Tower	1908	B3

Halifax to Boston 442 miles
Halifax to New York 599 miles

HALIFAX
NOVA SCOTIA
Founded 1749
By Hon. Edward Cornwallis

E MARI MERCES

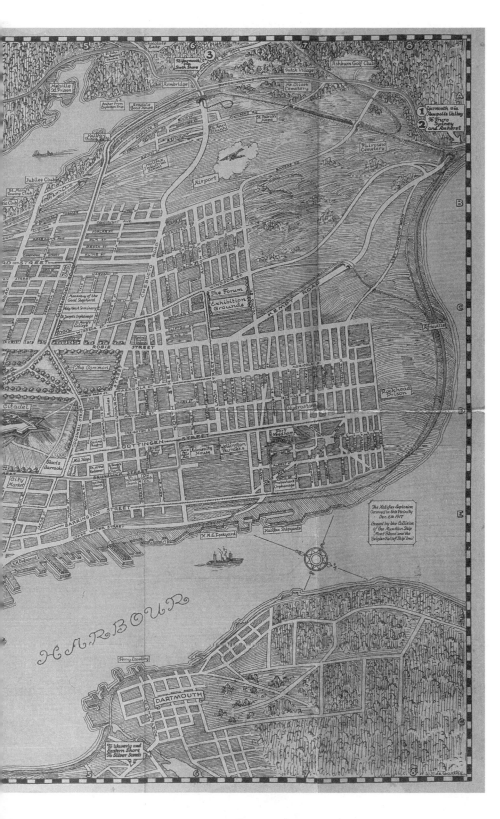

THESE FOUR WALLS

FAMILY TREE

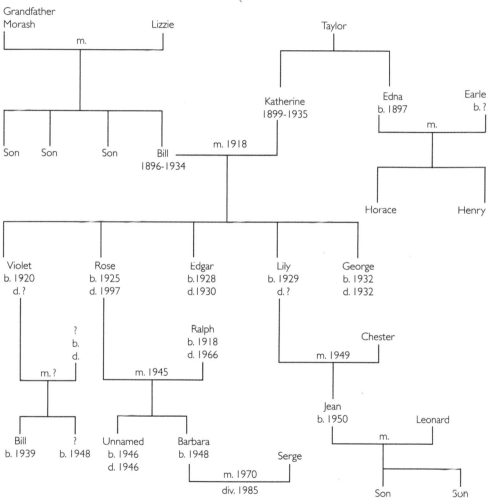

Grandfather
Morash   Lizzie
     m.

Taylor

Son   Son   Son   Bill
1896-1934

Katherine
1899-1935   m. 1918

Edna
b. 1897   Earle
b. ?
m.

Horace   Henry

Violet
b. 1920
d. ?

Rose
b. 1925
d. 1997

Edgar
b.1928
d.1930

Lily
b. 1929
d. ?

George
b. 1932
d. 1932

?
b.
d.
m. ?

Ralph
b. 1918
d. 1966
m. 1945

Chester
m. 1949

Bill
b. 1939

?
b. 1948

Unnamed
b. 1946
d. 1946

Barbara
b. 1948
Serge
m. 1970
div. 1985

Jean
b. 1950

Leonard
m.

Son   Son

Solo

Day 1

A ringing telephone wakes Barbara at seven in the morning. It is the hospital calling, informing her that her mother has lapsed into a coma. There has been no kidney output for hours, her vitals are steadily slowing.

"How much longer?" Barbara asks, fighting to control the lump in her throat.

"Difficult to say," a woman's voice replies. "Several hours perhaps; probably less."

"I'll be there as soon as I can," Barbara says.

At eight-thirty she is hurrying into the hospital lobby, pressing the button for the fourth floor.

Please, God, let me get there in time. Please.

Her heart contracts, skips a beat, when she arrives at the nursing unit. In the room at the far end of the corridor, an overhead light has been switched on and two figures in white are bending over the bed. She can see the doctor's hand moving, the glint of the stethoscope's disk on her mother's chest.

No, don't tell me! Don't!

Barbara breaks into a run, the soles of her leather boots echoing off the tiled floor. The young resident hears her, steps back from the bed, removes the stethoscope from his ears. "You're the daughter," he says.

"Yes."

"There's no heartbeat—no pulse," he says softly. "She's gone, I'm afraid. I'm sorry."

It's not fair. Just a few more minutes, that's all I needed.

Another voice, addressing her. "It was a peaceful end. Just a gradual slowing down. Very, very easy."

Easy for you.

Barbara nods, not trusting herself to speak.

"I'll get you a glass of water," someone says.

Barbara blinks, rubs at her forehead. Water? Water, for God's sake. I'm already drowning—in all the unfinished business between us.

"Thank you." Her voice wavers.

"There are a few papers," the young doctor explains. "I'll see to them, if you'll excuse me—"

Of course.

"If you like I'll call for the chaplain," the nurse offers. She finishes pulling up the sheet, smoothes out the coverlet.

"Chaplain," Barbara repeats. Her tongue feels thick, her head stupid. "Yes, all right. Thanks." How polite she is in the face of death, this death. *Act like a lady, dear. No matter what the circumstances.*

The nurse dims the light, leaves her alone. Barbara picks up her mother's still warm hand, touches the wedding ring, surprised that it hasn't been whisked into a secure place. Perhaps the fingers were so swollen they couldn't get it off. Perhaps. Perhaps she should have noticed such things before, when it might have made a difference. Instead of now, when it is too late, when nothing is at stake.

She gathers up her courage, bends down, kisses the pale forehead. "Bye, Mom," she whispers. "Love you." Her mother's face is thin, the skin over the cheekbones taut, almost transparent. The eyes are closed, the lips slightly parted. There is no expression, either of peace or of pain, on the slack mouth. Nothing to help Barbara understand those last moments of leaving, when she should have been there, and wasn't.

The young resident returns with a form. "Permission to release the body," he says. Already her mother has ceased to be a person.

The chaplain is next, arriving with the glass of water in one hand, a Bible in the other. She is a middle-aged woman with a kind expression and tired eyes. She reads the sentences, says a prayer, asks if there is anything more she can do.

"Nothing, really," Barbara replies. "I think I can manage."

Afterwards, the chaplain walks with her to the elevator. "Peace be with you," she says, touching Barbara's wrist.

"Yes, I hope so," is as much as Barbara can muster. She must get away from this place, these people. Their infernal calm unnerves her, their efficiency makes her feel useless. In the main lobby she pauses to button her coat, tie her scarf around her neck, shift the overnight bag onto her left arm. The bag contains her mother's personal items—toiletries, slippers, two nightgowns and a robe, a hand-painted china clock. How meagre, these last few things of her mother's life.

Under the portico, Barbara hesitates. By rights she should go straight back to the house, start phoning people, making arrangements. But she can't, not yet. She needs space, a place to sit, walk, think. She needs the hill.

Ten minutes later she is parking near the Citadel's main gate. There are no other cars in the lot. It is well past tourist season and the museum has been locked up tight for another winter. She gets out, crosses the pavement to the look-off platform, and, sucking in great gulps of cold air, surveys the downtown skyline.

What was once a spectacular panorama of old city and harbour is now largely hidden by modern office buildings and apartment towers. Her eyes search for the familiar landmarks of her childhood, glimpse the flag on the old post-office building, the spire of St. Mary's Basilica, off to the right; and, in a space between two tall buildings, a bit of blue water with the barren hillock of George's Island rising out of it.

The dome of St. Paul's is there too, tucked in behind a concrete structure that faces Brunswick. A black-on-white sign reads Government of Canada. How ugly, she thinks. Her father, if alive, would agree. "It's a crime to pull down fine old buildings and stick up those damn things," he used to grumble. "They'll be falling apart inside of twenty years."

He wouldn't be happy with the new sports complex, she was sure of that. A solid supporter of local hockey and ice shows in the old days, he always bought the best front-row seats at the Forum. Now, the hockey enthusiasts trooped downtown to see the games, making a beeline for the popular watering holes—Ginger's, Maxwell's Plum, The Lower Deck—immediately afterwards. A dissecting of the play over raised tankards and swilled beer.

A powerful gust of wind whips hair across her face, flattens her trench coat against her legs. At this height the wind is a reckoning force, but she likes it. She likes all the winds up here—the icy blasts that roar down from the north, the damp, sea-tinged sou'westers that blow in from the harbour mouth, the gentler breezes that waft across the Central Commons and meander their way upwards.

Tightening her belt and pulling her collar up, Barbara starts along the driveway loop. From this side of the hill she can see the flat playing fields of the Central and North Commons. She grins, thinking of the countless ball games she's watched down there, cheering her favourite team, her special guy, from a top seat on the bleachers. Today though, the ball diamonds and rugby fields are deserted, save for a lone man, head lowered against the gusts, striding along a diagonal pathway.

On the lower side of North Park Street a row of older houses and seedy-looking tenements stretches along the block to the Armouries. She has never been inside the massive, turreted sandstone structure, can only imagine what the legions of soldiers must do there year after year, with their rifles and jeeps, their shouted orders, their combat drills.

She keeps on, determined to walk the entire perimeter of the fort. On the lee side of the hill the wind is less brutal and she pauses for a moment. The southern slopes conjure up more memories—of winter tobogganing, Canada Day fireworks, Natal Day concerts, and other, less public escapades. In her first year of high school she and her best friend often sneaked over at lunchtime to smoke pilfered cigarettes. Right there, under that tree, she thinks. That's where we sat.

By the time she arrives back at the car her ears are like ice, her fingers numb. She fumbles with her keys, slides gratefully onto the driver's seat, turns the ignition, shoves the heater up to high. She sits quietly, feels the tingling sensation in her fingers and toes. Outside the car window a flag flaps violently.

That's it, then. No more visits to the hospital. The days and weeks of sitting in the hospital room, watching, waiting, are over. Her mother has become "past-tense." By now they would have wheeled the sheet-covered body down to the morgue, tagged it for transport to the funeral home. Already, the hospital visits seem oddly remote; as distant as those summertime visits of Aunt Lily and her girl, Jean.

Aunt Lily enjoyed coming to the hill; liked to sit on the grass with her binoculars and watch the movement of ships in the harbour; declared that the Citadel's tearoom, with its checked tablecloths and oatmeal cookies, was "just a dear spot." Barbara's mother was less enthusiastic, much preferring a band concert in the Gardens and tea in the Lord Nelson dining room. "I think we've seen enough, Ralph," her mother would say. "It's the same old view—buildings, water, treetops. Let's move along. Girls, you can run on ahead. We'll see the exhibits in the museum, and take some pictures of you by the cannon."

Such an active, busy woman, her mother; always on the go, full of a nervous energy that couldn't be contained, as if sitting still was suspect when there were things—cameras, picnic hampers, sun hats—to see to. And if not something, then somebody.

Me, for instance. My clothes, my piano lessons, my skating class, my bloody life.

At sixteen, resentful, Barbara would often lash out in self-defence. "Don't be at me all the time! Just leave me alone."

Not that talking back got her anywhere. "You don't need to be like that, Barbara! I'm only trying to help, for goodness sake. Get a move on, girl. Life's too short to be mooning about, wasting time."

The summer between high school and university Barbara had managed to get hired on as a greeter here at the hill. The uniform and the badge had won a grudging approval from her mother. "Thank goodness you've got a real job at last," she'd said.

Barbara is sweating now, from exertion, the car's heater, memory. She reaches across the steering wheel, turns back the heater, loosens the scarf at her neck. *Jack and Jill went up the hill / To fetch a pail of water.* What does she hope to fetch—or find—here? The stream has long since dried up, hasn't it? The bucket is empty.

In the spring of her eighteenth year her father was killed in a train crash on the South Shore line. The suddenness of his death had left her reeling, but she'd managed to get through the first bad weeks, had written her final exams, was looking ahead to university in the fall.

Her mother's grief was a different matter; a lingering process that alternated between quiet rage and dark despair. Barbara's job at the hill had been her own salvation, a welcome relief from her mother's silences, the awful bitterness. It had paid well, too; so well that Barbara felt half-guilty every time she cashed her paycheque. She'd been able to bank most of her wages, and to impress them enough to be rehired the following year.

Barbara shakes her head, runs her hands through her hair. Enough already! Get a move on. There are things to do. Your mother just died—remember? Your mother, who believed in action.

She shifts into gear, maneuvers the first curve. In the distance she can see the spire of St. George's Church, the span of the harbour bridge, the stern of a freighter heading for the Basin. She noses the car over the crest of the northern slope, coasts down the incline. Eleven months since I was last up here, she thinks. I threw snowballs at the flagpole, made a snow angel.

On that January day her mother's second small stroke had prompted a consultation with the medical team. They were pushing for a nursing home placement. "She can't live alone," they'd said.

"Don't put me in an institution," her mother had pleaded.

Barbara had tried reasoning, reassurance. "We'll get you a nice room with a view, maybe at Northwood. We can fix it up just the way you want. You'll soon get used to it."

"No, no, I won't!" her mother had cried, clinging to Barbara's sleeve with her one good hand. "You don't understand."

"It's a difficult transition," the social worker had said. "So much to give up."

"They're terrible places, those homes." Her mother's voice had risen to a shrill pitch. "I'm not going; I'm not."

"Mom, Mom, don't get so upset. They're not terrible places."

"They are. I know, believe me." Her mother had pulled the blanket over her face, refused to speak to her for days afterward.

At the bottom of the hill Barbara turns right, waits for the green light, accelerates, heads north. There are no cars behind her at the Armouries intersection, but she can't rid herself of a mounting disquiet, a panicked sense of being pursued.

Nerves, she tells herself. Emotional fatigue. She forces herself to face a new and growing realization. There is no getting away from it; she is at another crossroads. No more mother to watch out for, to fret over. Now—too late, too soon—all that is finished.

She will draw some sympathy, the standard condolences, for a few days. But once the funeral is over, the rest of the world will revert to normal, will expect the same of her. After all, most people outlive their parents, and become orphans. It's a mid-life reality, a new passage, whether or not you're an only child.

You'll get used to it. You'll get used to it.

The first year is the worst year. Then you'll get used to it.

The lyrics of the old navy showtune pop into her head, follow her to the next corner. What a kick her father always got out of the song. She can see his big frame shak-

ing with laughter at a solitary man in a sailor suit, swab-
bing an imaginary deck with a mop, his sad-sack face cast
into half-shadow by the stage lights.

   . . . You gotta get used to it.
   And when you're used to it,
   You'll be twice as happy as you were before.

Barbara is crying now. Her ragged sobs fill the car. A car
honks and speeds past, but she does not hear it. Instead, the
voices of her mother and father echo down the corridors
of her mind.

By all means, be sad. Throw yourself into grieving for a
little while. Then let it go, girl; let it all blow away on the
wind. Face the crowd, and the music, as the solo act you are.
You need to accept it. Get used to it. For when you're used
to it, you might be twice as happy as you were before.

Late Morning—Day 1

The Locket

Barbara drives to her mother's house, unlocks the door, throws her jacket over a chair, proceeds to the kitchen to plug in the kettle. While she waits for it to boil she looks up the funeral home number.

A male voice—polite, subdued—introduces himself as "the director." He extends brief condolences, and then gets on with business. The morgue has contacted them; the remains are expected shortly. Barbara draws in her breath at "the remains." The label reduces that complex, vibrant woman who was her mother to something less than human. Akin to leftovers; table scraps.

The director agrees to meet Barbara at three that afternoon.

"Kindly bring the clothing that you wish to have the remains dressed in," he says. "Also any jewellery."

"Certainly," Barbara says. "I'll have everything ready."

She replaces the receiver, jumps up to get the kettle. Her head feels light, her legs rubbery. She pours boiling water over the instant coffee, suddenly aware that she hasn't eaten since last evening's supper. She opens the fridge and takes out a loaf of bread, inserts two slices in the toaster, cuts a piece of cheese. When the toast pops up, she butters it, puts it and the cheese on a plate and takes the lot to the dining-room table.

The house is quiet. No ticking clock or rumbling furnace; nor, through the closed windows, muted swish of cars going by in the street. While she eats, the silence builds.

She is used to being alone in the house; has flown down from Toronto every six weeks over the past year, making a long weekend of the trip, visiting her mother at the nursing home. She has slept in her old bed, read in the living room, cooked in the kitchen. It's been quiet, always, but never like this.

Barbara swallows, fighting the lump in her throat. I should scream and wail, she thinks; hang black crepe at the windows. They used to do that in the old days; announce the departure so that the world would know what to say, how to behave. She doesn't scream though; instead, she takes her plate and mug to the sink, runs them under the hot water.

No time to cry. There's work to do.

Upstairs, in her mother's bedroom, she opens the closet door and surveys the rack of dresses, the shelves of hats, bags, shoes. Next week she will need to clear it out; but now her task is to select a suitable outfit to take with her to the funeral home.

She rifles through the clothing, pulls out three possibilities, checks buttons and zippers, eliminates two of them. A long-sleeved blue crepe with an overjacket is the clear winner. She lays the dress on the bed, paws through suits and sweaters for the mink jacket. It is at the right, on a padded hanger, covered with a crocheted shawl. A hat and handbag are next. Barbara settles on a blue cloche, and a black patent bag with a gold clasp. She gets down on her hands and knees to inspect the shoes, chooses a pair of patent pumps that match the bag.

She lays the hat, bag and shoes next to the dress and walks to the dresser. She knows that her mother's underwear drawer is at the top left. The slips, girdles and panties, all folded neatly, many of them with their sales tags still on, bring tears. Until the stroke, her mother had loved shopping, buying constantly, almost compulsively. Barbara could never fault her mother for the buying binges, though. She knew that they were compensation for the long years of hard work, the losses, and the loneliness.

Hesitantly, she opens the top righthand drawer. Inside, arranged in little boxes and special zippered pouches, is the jewellery. Barbara considers several brooches and earrings, settles on the cultured pearl set. She tries not to think about the white box at the back. Time enough for that later.

Toronto, September, 1992

Barbara has just arrived in from work and is sitting with her feet up, sipping her first gin and tonic of the weekend when the phone rings. She curses, considers not answering, and then wearily picks up the receiver.

"Hello," says a man's voice. "Are you the daughter of Rose Varner?"

"Yes, I am. Who's speaking?"

"Head of Security, ma'am. Eaton's—Halifax."

She sits up straighter, sets her drink on the table. "Yes. What is it?"

"There was an incident today, ma'am. Involving your mother."

"An incident?"

"Yes, ma'am. Mrs. Varner was looking at some of our better necklaces in the jewellery department. Our floorwalker found her actions somewhat suspicious so he kept her under observation—" There is a pause.

"Yes, yes. Go on," she says.

"A piece of jewellery is missing, ma'am. A silver locket."

Goddamn it all, she thinks.

"Mrs. Varner was apprehended in the parking lot, brought back inside for questioning."

"Did you find it, then?" she demands, trying to keep her voice calm.

"No. We searched her handbag, pockets, her satchel. There was a box of candy and several items of underwear. She had cash register slips for the underwear."

Chocolate-covered nuts, no doubt. Her mother adored them.

"So?"

"We couldn't detain her without evidence. The manager said to let the candy go."

What could she say to that; I'll be happy to send a cheque for the candy?

"Where is my mother, now?" Barbara manages instead.

"She was escorted out. She was upset. Talked a little wild; said we'd hear from her lawyer."

"I see." To her own ears, her voice sounds like a frog's croak; a very weary frog.

"We can't press charges without evidence," he continues. "But, given her age, management said to alert the family. You might want to monitor her; perhaps have her seen by a doctor."

"Yes, of course," Barbara replies. "Thank you."

She makes herself another drink after she hangs up; sits considering her options. Sociologists did research, produced statistics on this sort of thing. Percentages of the elderly who stole for kicks. Surely to God her mother hadn't come to that.

Two weeks after the call Barbara flies home for the

Thanksgiving weekend. After the Sunday evening meal—turkey, dressing, the works—she brings up the phone call.

"Mom, I got a call from Eaton's last month. Some upset about a missing locket. Want to tell me about it?"

Her mother looks wounded. "I had nothing to do with any missing locket. The nerve of them; me, one of their best customers. The clerk probably took it, or lost it. They're so careless these days."

The suggestion of a medical check-up is met with out-and-out resistance. "I don't need to see any doctors. There's nothing wrong with my head, if that's what you're getting at. It's theirs that need examining."

Barbara chooses to let the incident go. Too far away to be her mother's keeper, she consoles herself with the thought that, if her mother had tried to pull a fast one, the interrogation had probably scared her enough that she wouldn't attempt any repeat performances.

Otherwise, their time together is pleasant. They go to Simpson's for lunch, take a stroll in the park; drive out to the look-off at Herring Cove. On their last evening, they sit in the front room, sipping freshly steeped tea and eating the remaining two pieces of apple pie.

"I shouldn't be drinking tea," Barbara moans, mopping her face with a napkin. "It sets off my hot flashes, especially at night."

"You poor dear," her mother says. "My silk fan was a godsend. I'll bet I used it every day for over five years. I'm glad all that is over with."

"Maybe I should get a fan," Barbara replies. "Or move to the North Pole."

"Oh, you young things have hormone pills now," her mother says. "But if you want a fan, mine's still in my bureau—second drawer down."

"You know, I think I'll give it a try."

In the second drawer Barbara finds two neat piles of lace-edged hankies, several unopened packages of hosiery, and a row of gloves—white, tan, beige, and black. Each pair is laid flat, with palms facing inward. There is no sign of the fan.

Guess I'm out of luck, Barbara thinks. Unless—

Perhaps her mother had meant the dresser, not the bureau. Barbara moves across the room, opens the righthand drawer. A satin-lined tray is filled with costume jewellery. There are several distinctive blue Birks boxes as well; and, at the back, poking out from under an old concert program is a white one. It bears the maroon and black stripe of the T. Eaton Company.

Barbara's heart starts to race, and a wave of heat radiates up the back of her neck and across her scalp. From the kitchen, the kettle whistles.

Another cup of that damned tea and I'll be able to swim back to Ontario.

Her hand moves to the white box, pulls it out, lifts the cover. A silver oval, nestled in a bed of cotton wool, gleams in the lamp light. The oval has a fine link chain, a delicate clasp. It is, obviously, very expensive.

From the bottom of the stairs, her mother's voice is merry. "Did you find the fan? Come on down; let's have another cup before we turn in."

"Coming!" Barbara shouts, her hands fumbling at the cotton wool. She shoves the box back in place, eases the drawer shut. Her neck is clammy now and she's shivering. Why hadn't she left well enough alone?

She starts down the steps slowly. The man on the phone said they'd searched her purse, the shopping bag, her pockets. Where could she have hidden it? In her shoe, perhaps? Or—

In a cubicle of the Ladies Room you could pull down your drawers, do your thing: void, wipe, insert, as needed. No way would they strip-search a dignified, elderly lady.

Her mother has always been a smart, capable woman; able to think of just about anything. Even of that.

Afternoon—Day 1

The Funeral Home

Barbara makes it to the funeral home by three, is ushered into a wood-panelled office. The man across the desk is quiet-spoken and sombre-faced. He is dressed in the regulation black suit, white shirt, and black tie of an undertaker.

She waits, tense in her chair, for him to consider her request. She knows it is an unusual one; knows, too, that it must be granted. This is what her mother wants, and she must honour her mother's wishes. As must this man in black: JC Wilcox, Director.

Her mind reels, lurches.

JC. For Johnny Cash, the other man in black.

For Jesus Christ, too. The Holy One, who wouldn't be caught dead in black. White, for Him, always. Even when dead and unburied. A white loin cloth, a white shroud. White, for purity. For love.

Barbara blinks. This man in black appears to be studying the green baize blotter on the burnished mahogany desktop. His hands intrigue her; forefingers raised in an inverted *v*, the others interlocked. *Here's the church / and here's the steeple / Open the door / and here's the people.*

The fingers unfold, drop to the desktop, pick up a gold-topped pen. When is an undertaker mortified? The impertinence of the silent question amuses Barbara and she bites her lip, resisting the urge to giggle.

Mr. JC slides a sheet of paper into place, uncaps the fountain pen, clears his throat. "It's not our practice to present the remains in hats and fur coats."

"Perhaps not," Barbara replies. "But my mother's instructions are very clear."

She watches him wet his lips, knows he'll agree. After all, customer satisfaction is his bread and butter.

"However, if it is so important—"

"It is," she repeats. "Thank you."

Barbara gives him the zippered garment bag and the hat box. The blue dress has been freshly pressed; the patent leather pumps wrapped in tissue paper.

He suppresses a sigh. "We'll do what we can," he says. "But I do recommend that the hat be left till after the viewing. As for the shoes, I must warn you that ankles often swell, in which case we'll have to slit the backs."

"Of course." Whatever it takes, she thinks. Better the shoes than the throat. Aloud she murmurs, "I know you'll do your best. My grandfather was a shoemaker."

"Ah," he replies. His eyes are pale green, with flecks through them. Just like the wallpaper, she thinks.

She deals with the florist next, has supper at a little place on Quinpool, returns to the house to make phone calls; a dozen or so names from her mother's address book; cousin Jean, on PEI; a few of the Varner relations, a couple of Barbara's closest Toronto friends. Knut, who she's been seeing lately, asks what he can do to help. "Nothing, really," she replies. "I can manage. It won't be a complicated affair."

Later, in her old bed, the dream is vivid. Accompanied by a winged navigator, her mother floats across a cloudless sky. A breeze ruffs the curls that peek from underneath the blue cloche, and sends ripples through the skirt of the blue dress. The patent shoes haven't a speck of dirt on them. Well, why would they? Air travellers rarely get their feet dirty.

Barbara attempts to call out, but is unable to make her lips move. She is annoyed, wanting to remind her mother of the comb, mirror, and lipstick that she's placed in the handbag. There are four quarters, as well, for emergency telephone calls. Girl Guide prepared, just in case.

Evening—Day 2

After the visitors leave, Barbara kneels at the open casket. In the thirty-six hours since she's last seen it, her mother's face has changed. The essence has departed, leaving the death mask behind.

"I'm sorry I didn't know you better," Barbara whispers. "I tried. Honest." She waits a moment, half-expecting a response. There is none. The mask remains intact, harbouring its secrets.

Barbara consoles herself with the effect of the blue dress and the fur jacket. The Lodge ladies had been impressed.

"She looks lovely, Barbara dear. Just lovely. Doesn't she, Peg?"

"Yes, indeed. Wearing her mink is a splendid idea. I'm going to insist they do the same for me when I go."

Lord God, Barbara thinks. *Just steps this side of the grave, and Mom may have started a new trend.*

The room is empty when Barbara gets up from the bench. From the corridor, she can hear Cousin Jean's voice, engaged in a discussion with the assistant about donation cards.

Right, she thinks, reaching for a tote that she's brought along. *The coast is clear.*

She removes her mother's handbag from the tote and leans over the still body. Positioning the handbag below the folded hands, she slides the strap under the left one and pulls it through. Barbara knows very well that her mother would never set out on a trip without her handbag. Inside the bag she has placed the brush and comb, lipstick and change purse. She has also added the velvet box containing the locket. After all, the ancient Chinese and Egyptians did this all the time. Sent both the necessaries and the spoils along on the journey. Just in case.

"There you go, Mom," she whispers, touching the marble-cold wrist. "You're all set. There's nothing more I can do for you."

She stands still for a moment, then backs away slowly, turns, and walks out of the room.

ROSE

PART ONE

The Home

Ending

June, 1936

Rose had just put the jampot and butter dish away in the pantry and was wiping off the tabletop when Mrs. McGinn called down from the landing.

"Rosie, luv, there's a big black car at the curb and a lady's getting out. You show her in while I brush up Lily's hair."

Rose paused, wet dishcloth in her hand. She knew she should hang her apron behind the stove and hurry to open the front door, but her feet had suddenly taken root in the worn patch of lino, and the queer thudding sensation was back in her chest. She stared at her white ankle socks and black patent shoes for a moment, and then looked up at the clock above the icebox.

It had just gone nine on a Thursday morning. By rights she should be at school now, standing beside her desk in the classroom at the top of the stairs, singing "O Canada," saluting the flag, reciting the Pledge of Allegiance and the Lord's Prayer. That was the pattern she knew and she wanted it. She wanted to be there with her classmates; doing her arithmetic and her spellings, taking her turn cleaning erasers, stacking the writing workbooks in the cupboard at the back of the room; anything but here, in her good dress and shoes, dreading, waiting.

Mrs. McGinn had told her the previous evening. They were alone in the kitchen, with the supper dishes put away and a fresh pot of tea steeping on the back of the stove. Mavis, the oldest girl, was upstairs putting little Bridget to bed and the big boys were outside playing a game of hide-and-seek with Lily and the twins.

"Rosie, come and sit down with me. I've got something very important to say and you must listen close."

Rose braced herself. She didn't need Mrs. McGinn's worried look to know what was coming. She'd known the minute she'd arrived in from school and spied her pink dress and Lily's yellow one hanging on the wash line. Mrs. McGinn did the washing on Mondays, not Wednesdays, and there were no other clothes on the line, just their two dresses. Mrs. McGinn had baked a fruit pie, too, and put a clean white cloth on the table even though it was nobody's birthday, just a regular night for doing lessons.

"Wish to the dear Lord it could be different, Rosie." Mrs. McGinn's big fingers picked at a thread in the hem of her dress. "It's not that I don't think the world of you and Lily. And I told your mother, God rest her soul, that I'd do what I could to help. But Father Hanrahan says this is the way it must be and I trust him to know what's best. 'The girls need to be looked after by their own.' Those were his very words."

Father Hanrahan again, always Father Hanrahan. The McGinn children clustered around him on his visits, clamouring for one of the pink mints that he kept in a pocket of his suit jacket, but Rose had always hung back, suspicious and uneasy, even before their mother's death. Her sister Violet had never trusted him either. "He's got no time for Protestants like us," Violet had told her more than once. "One step higher than dirt, that's his opinion, Rose—and don't you forget it."

After she had climbed into the bed she shared with Lily,

Rose lay awake for a long time, going over things in her mind. She knew that Mrs. McGinn could never disagree with the parish priest. In her eyes he was every bit as powerful, and his word as much the law as Moses, as the Ten Commandments.

Of course, he wasn't the only one to have meddled. The minister from St. Paul's had put in his two cents' worth, and the doctor, too. Why couldn't they mind their own business and leave them alone! Mama had wanted more than anything else for them to stick together. "You three girls are to stay in this house, you hear," she'd said when she was still able to talk. "Violet will be in charge. She's old enough." It hadn't worked out that way, though. Violet had been sent away and the bank had taken the house for taxes. It wasn't fair, it just wasn't.

Rose turned over and closed her eyes but she couldn't settle into sleep. After tomorrow she'd be gone from here. There would be a new, strange house to live in, people they had never met to get used to. She fought back a sob, afraid she might disturb Lily. She didn't want to go away; she wanted her mother back, she wanted Violet. As for Father Hanrahan, he could go to the devil. She would never forgive him for his part in breaking up her family—never.

A rap at the door sent Rose into a panicked flurry. Dropping her wet cloth into the dishpan, she untied her apron and dashed to the front hall mirror. A pale, worried face stared back at her as she ran her tongue over her lips and fiddled with her hair ribbon. It was too late now to go back upstairs and clean her teeth, but she'd brushed her dark curls till they shone nicely and she was wearing the pink dress that Aunt Edna had sent for her birthday. Mrs. McGinn had reminded her to put an apron over it earlier, and Rose was glad she had, for little Bridget had chosen this morning to throw a tantrum, spitting a mouthful of soggy bread into her lap less than ten minutes ago.

A tall woman in a drab navy suit, felt hat, and no-nonsense brown oxfords was standing on the verandah. She had a satchel over her arm and a brown envelope in her hand. "I'm Miss Stoddard," she said to Rose. "Mrs. McGinn is expecting me."

"Come in," Rose replied. "She'll be right down." Her mother had taught her to say "please come in" but she couldn't be polite, not this morning. She showed the woman into the parlour and retreated to the bottom of the stairs. It's not a social call, Rose told herself. I don't have to be friendly. Her heart had started its familiar thudding and a new knot was forming in her stomach.

On the floor near her feet sat the two valises. You're going away, girl, they seemed to be saying to her. There's no getting out of it.

Don't think. And don't cry. Crying will just make things worse.

Mrs. McGinn was coming down the stairs now, with Lily at her heels. "Sorry to be keeping you, ma'am," she said over the top of Rose's head. "The girls are ready, aren't you?"

"We'll be on our way, then," Miss Stoddard said, reaching for one of the valises. "You look a sturdy girl," she said to Rose. "You can carry the other bag."

Rose stood by the trunk of the car while the driver stowed the bags. The packing last evening hadn't taken long. They each had a school skirt and blouse, a sweater, a pair of brown shoes, three sets of underwear, two thin cotton nightgowns, socks, and a hairbrush. There was an old prayer book, as well, along with Lily's rag doll, and, wrapped in a piece of white tissue paper, a silver locket containing the only picture Rose had of her mother.

"My doll. I want my doll," Lily was whining, refusing to let go of Mrs. McGinn's hand until Rose had dug into the bag and produced it.

Rose waited until Lily and Miss Stoddard were installed in the back seat before she climbed onto the running board. Arranging her face in a smile, she turned and gave a gallant wave. "Bye," she called out to the twins who were standing wide-eyed at the verandah railing. "Be good for your mother."

"Bye, Rosie," they shouted back. "Bye, Lily."

Goodbye. Be good. Her mother's last words to them on that cold, dreary January afternoon. Rose noticed the crow just as the car was pulling away from the curb; he was perched on the edge of the verandah roof, surveying the scene with two black, curious eyes. One crow meant sorrow, so Mama used to say.

At the end of the street the car stopped, waiting for a coal wagon to go by. The big bay horse pulling the wagon was in no hurry, giving Rose time to look out the rear window. She had a final glimpse of Mrs. McGinn, still waving from the verandah, before the driver turned into the traffic on the main thoroughfare.

Gottingen Street, one of the city's major shopping districts, was alive with its usual Thursday morning bustle. Merchants were sweeping in front of their shops, delivery men and their helpers were unloading wagons and trucks, trundling crates and boxes on wheeled carts from curbside to entrances. The sidewalks were crowded with shoppers too, most of them women like Mrs. McGinn, out to make their purchases. In front of Murphy's Barber Shop the regular huddle of older gentlemen had already gathered to smoke and share their newspapers. Her father's old shop was next, with drawn blinds and a For Rent sign in the front window. Rose averted her eyes as they drove by.

"You're eleven now, aren't you, Rose," Miss Stoddard said, breaking the silence inside the car. Lily had come out of her sobbing spell and was watching the traffic, her doll clutched tight to her chest.

"Yes. On the twenty-sixth of June."

"Old enough to understand that this is for the best."

No. I'll never be old enough to understand that.

"I liked it at Mrs. McGinn's," Rose said aloud. "She's kind. She helped out a lot when Mama was sick."

"I'm sure she did. But it's important to concentrate on the future now. You'll be well looked after in your new home, and you'll see things in a new light soon, mark my words."

Rose looked down at her hands. She had no intention of marking anybody's words, or seeing things in a new light, either. People like this woman had a lot of nerve. Not one of them could possibly know how she was feeling or what was best, yet they'd be in charge just the same, lording it over her from now on, making her do things that she didn't want to do. She'd have to put up with them until she was old enough to get out on her own.

The hollow feeling was washing over her again. Where was Violet? She needed Violet to come and rescue them, to take them home. Hadn't Violet kept house just fine when Mama was sick, and after Mama died, too. Even though she was only fifteen, Violet could cook and clean and do the shopping. Why, Violet could handle anything; when the money in the tin box was used up, Violet found a man to buy Mama's silver, and later on another man came to take the mirrors and the dining-room chairs. They'd managed like that for most of the winter.

The one mistake Violet had made was to ask one of the ladies at St. Patrick's if they could help with a bit of money for food and some oil for the stove. The woman had run straight to Father Hanrahan and he'd wasted no time getting onto the Anglican minister. Both men, in their sombre black suits and equally sombre faces, had come one afternoon to tell Violet it was impossible for three young girls to continue on their own and that other arrangements would have to be made. An angry Violet had insisted that she was old enough, but they'd ignored her and got on the phone to Aunt Edna in Chester to see if she could take them. Aunt Edna had said they couldn't; they were sorry but they had a business to run and their own boys to feed and an elderly mother to see to, and surely no one could say they didn't have their hands plenty full.

By the following week Violet was gone and Mrs. McGinn had come to take Lily and her next door. "I would have made room for Violet, too, but Father said no," Mrs. McGinn had explained. "There'll be a spot for her at St. Paul's Home after a bit. And next year, when she'll be old enough, they'll help her get a job."

"When will we see her again?" Rose had asked over and over. "When?"

"In a little while, dear," Mrs. McGinn kept telling her. "You must be patient and keep saying your prayers."

Rose dared not admit that she had precious little time these days for patience, and even less for prayer. All the praying they'd been doing for their mother's recovery hadn't helped one bit. She realized that when she heard the doctor talking to Violet in their front room.

"I'm afraid there's nothing left now but to wait," the doctor was saying.

"How long will it be?" Violet asked, her voice husky from crying.

"Not long. Several days, possibly a week. Keep her comfortable."

Six days was all it took.

During the funeral service, in the front pew of St. Paul's with Aunt Edna beside them, they were obliged to sit through a new set of prayers. This time there was no mention of St. Luke's failed healing power. Instead, an invisible God was petitioned to receive and keep their mother's soul. "Hear us, O Lord," the mourners chanted in unison.

"Such a laugh, all of it," Violet said afterwards. "Mama's finished, simple as that. End of the line. That's what death is, Rose—an ending. No angels, no harps, no trips beyond the clouds. Just a lonely ride to the cemetery and a dark hole in the cold ground."

They had left the shopping district now and were travelling north, past tall Victorian dwellings interspersed with long lines of flat-roofed row houses. There was a Temperance Hall on one corner, with a blacksmith's shop next to it. Directly across from the blacksmith's was the main gate of the naval base with two sailors standing guard at the sentry box. Their black boots made Rose think of her father and his once-thriving business. Over the years his biggest orders had come from the military. He'd got started in the boot and shoe business as a young lad during the latter years of the Great War, apprenticing with old Mr. Connors, down on Buckingham Street.

The walled enclosure of the base stretched on and on, finally giving way to an open field and the lower slopes of a steep hill. "Where are we?" Rose asked. She didn't remember ever being in this part of the city.

"Coming into Richmond," Miss Stoddard replied. "That's Fort Needham up there. This is the area that was destroyed by the explosion."

"Oh," said Rose. "Yes." With her own world in tatters, she couldn't muster much interest in an explosion that had taken place years earlier. Not that she didn't feel badly for the people who'd been blinded by it (their father always warned them not to stare when they saw the white canes); but at the moment she had much more important matters to deal with.

"Where exactly is the house we're going to?" she persisted. No one had told them the address. It was as if they were cattle, too stupid to know or care.

"The orphanage is at the bottom of the hill. We turn at the next corner."

Orphanage. The word sent a small shiver through Rose. St. Joseph's on Quinpool Road, a long, brick building with a statue on the front lawn, was home to the poor, parentless Catholic children. They were a common sight during the summer months, at ball games on the Commons and picnicking at the Dingle Park. Usually in groups of six or ten, herded like sheep by two or three nuns in long black habits and veils.

We'll be just like those children from now on in, Rose thought. Herded and controlled, with not so much as a pot of our own to pee in. She used to giggle, half shocked, when Violet used that expression, but any humour it had once held was now gone. They no longer had a pot or a pan, or two red cents to rub together. Just a few clothes, Lily's rag doll, and Mama's locket, wrapped in a piece of white tissue.

"There's your new home," Miss Stoddard said, leaning forward and pointing. "The last one on the left."

A tall, grey-shingled house stood off on its own in a hollow, with an open grassy field on its north side and a triangle of overgrown bushes and scrubby trees sloping down to the harbour road on its south.

"It's so big," Rose said, counting four stories in all and more than a dozen tall, narrow windows facing the street.

"It needs to be," Miss Stoddard replied. "With nearly thirty of you."

Thirty! Rose didn't want any part of thirty strange children, all crammed under the one roof. She wanted to live in a little house, with people she knew and cared about. On the seat beside her, Lily was sliding closer, seeking contact. Rose laced her fingers through Lily's and held her hand until the car stopped.

"Here we are, then," Miss Stoddard said, gathering up her gloves and satchel. "Out you get. Miss Crooks will be waiting." Three wide, brick steps, each set with a clay pot of geraniums, led up to a massive oak door. Rose looked with distaste at the blooms. Her mother always claimed that geraniums were a poor man's flower.

They watched Miss Stoddard ring the bell, heard the sound of chimes echoing from inside the house.

"Is this a church?" whispered Lily, staring at a stained-glass fan light above the door.

"No," Rose said. "Just a big house with a fancy window, that's all."

A small woman in a floral print house frock answered the bell. Rose was quick to notice the darns in the woman's cotton-ribbed stockings and the bristle of bobby pins that held her nondescript brown hair back behind her ears. She can't be the head lady, Rose concluded. She must be the maid.

"Good morning, Greta," Miss Stoddard said. "I'm here with the new admissions."

The woman looked Rose up and down, glanced at Lily, then stood back and motioned them through the foyer and into a centre hall. Black-and-white floor tiles gleamed with fresh polish and there was a faint scent of lemon oil off the dark wood banister and wainscoting.

"The girls can wait on the window seat while you see Matron," the woman said to Miss Stoddard. "She's in her office."

The window seat at the end of the dark passageway looked out over the inner harbour. A small vessel was making for a jetty on the far shore and a loaded freighter was steaming along the centre channel, heading for the outer waters. Lily kneeled on the cushions and pressed her nose against the glass. "Oh, Rosie, look at all the boats," she exclaimed. "Just look!"

"Yes, I see them," Rose replied absently, less interested in ships than the conversation that was taking place beyond the half-open door of the office.

"Everything's on file," Miss Stoddard was explaining. "We had to contact St. Paul's for new copies of their baptismal certificates. In the upheaval of the past few months, the originals had gone missing."

Rose frowned. Mama had kept all their certificates inside the back cover of the Bible. Surely Violet hadn't sold it, too.

"I gather that these girls came from means," said another voice.

"They did, yes. The father had a successful shoe repair business at one point, but with his illness the family fell on hard times."

"TB, I suppose."

"Yes."

"And the mother?"

"The same. She died January past. She responded well to bed rest initially but insisted on going home far too early. And then there was another child on the way, if you can believe it. They took the baby, but the damage was done. She never did get back on her feet."

A baby? Another baby after little Edgar who was buried in the cemetery. Rose had gone once with her mother; had left a bouquet of wild flowers on a bit of grass under a huge oak tree.

"...TB is rampant. We have seven or eight children here because of it." There was pause, the rustle of paper. "What about bills of health for these two?"

"Clear, both of them," Miss Stoddard replied. "Reports are in the file. The older sister had some worrying results earlier on but she's been cleared since."

"Placed, then, is she?"

"Yes, temporarily, as you might appreciate. She'll go to St. Paul's Home on Tower Road after her confinement. The rector has it all looked after."

"Sad, that."

"I should say. She's only fifteen."

"Goes to show the importance of proper guidance. Trouble has a way of moving in quickly otherwise."

It distressed Rose to hear them speak about Violet like this. Violet, the big sister who had taken care of things when Mama was so sick.

"Rosie, there's another big boat," Lily cried, tugging at her arm. "Where's it going? Tell me."

"I'm not sure, Lily," she replied. "Probably far away—to England or France. Maybe even to Spain." Well, wasn't that where the ships in their history books sailed to, taking fur pelts back for the Kings and Queens.

". . . very little in clothing," Miss Stoddard was explaining. "They've both grown, and their allotment won't start until the first of next month."

"We're used to making do," the other woman replied. "And St. Mark's has just sent a box of things. No shoes, mind you; they're always the hardest to come by. We've decided to let the children go barefoot outdoors for the summer. They'll be content enough, and it hardly matters once school's out. They wear socks in the house, so it's only on Sundays that shoes are necessary."

Rose looked down at her feet for the second time that morning. They'd always had lovely shoes: black or white patent for dress up and brown leather with buckled straps for school and play. Twice each year their father would take them to his shop to help pick out pieces of tanned hide from the strips hanging out back. They would climb up on the high seat he used for polishing and he'd measure their feet, and within a week or two their new shoes would be ready to wear.

That routine didn't change until he got sick and had to leave Ben, his helper, in charge. Rose had heard her father tell Mama and Violet more than once that he was worried at Ben's inability to manage the business side of things. "I guess hanging onto him for dear life was a mistake," her father eventually admitted. Later, she'd asked Violet to explain "for dear life" and Violet had told her that it was about saving your hide and staying afloat, and that didn't mean shoe leather or a swim at the beach, either.

". . . they've no valuables, then. Jewellery—brooches, necklaces, that sort of thing?" the woman was asking Miss Stoddard.

"No, nothing like that."

Rose's eyes went to the two valises that the driver had set at the bottom of the stairs. She must hide the locket! Otherwise, it might be taken away from her. She ran to the bag and knelt on the floor, her hands fumbling with the buttoned flap, feeling through the contents for the tissue-wrapped package. It was at the bottom, underneath one of her nightgowns. I'll tuck it under the waistband of my underpants till I can find a hiding spot, she told herself, managing to pull her dress back in place and button the flap of the valise before the two women appeared at the door.

"Rose, Lily—" Miss Stoddard said. "This is Miss Crooks. She's the Matron here."

"Welcome," said the Matron, a tall, thin woman dressed in a white blouse, a tweed suit with a pleated skirt and lace-up brown suede shoes. Her grey-flecked hair was pulled back in a tight bun on her neck, and she had a cameo brooch pinned on her lapel.

"I'm sure you'll fit in and be part of us very soon," she went on.

"Yes," Rose murmured, struggling to contain her anger and her disappointment. Why did these people assume that they would fit in? She already knew she wouldn't be fitting in, that she would despise every day she had to spend in this place and would be happy again only she was able to leave for good.

The dark thoughts were interrupted by Greta's return. "Take the girls upstairs and get them unpacked," Matron said to the little woman. "They can amuse themselves outside until dinnertime. Miss Duffy will be back by then and she'll go over the rules. The sooner they know them, the better."

Greta picked up the two valises and started up the stairs, beckoning them to follow her. "Come, Lily," Rose murmured. "Bring your doll and we'll go see our new bedroom."

"My best to you both," Miss Stoddard said. "Make Matron proud of you." Rose did not reply.

Beginnings

Greta led them to a large, sunny room at the back of the house. Eight single beds, spaced a few feet apart, lined two of the walls. Each bed was covered with a plain bleached spread and had a white card taped to its footboard. There were no lamps or clocks, nor any bedside tables to put them on, and no sign of any toys or books. The windows were covered with plain cotton panels and raised green blinds, and the walls were bare, save for a framed print of Jesus with the children gathered around him. Rose recognized the picture from her Sunday School days. *Suffer the little children to come unto Me.*

Greta stopped at the third bed. "This is where you'll be sleeping," she said to Lily, depositing her bag on the coverlet.

"Am I beside her?" Rose asked.

"Why no," Greta said, looking surprised. "This is the little girls' room. Matron told me that you're eleven, so you're in with the older ones. There'll be seven altogether, counting you. Crowded for sure, but that's what happens with so many of you needing a spot to lay your head."

Lily was looking alarmed, prompting Rose to say, "But we've been together in the same room for a long time, ever since—" The lump was there again, making her throat as tight as it had been when she'd come down with the mumps.

Greta's voice softened. "Well now, try not to feel too bad. I know that home must have been a lot different for you. But that's the rule and there's no point arguing. You'll get used to it after the first couple nights. So let's get you both put away."

"What are the cards for?" Rose asked, blinking and taking a deep breath. She would not cry, not in front of Lily.

"Every child here gets a number." Greta stood with her hands on her hips and looked at Lily. "Yours is twenty-three, missy. It's marked on your card along with your name, and tomorrow when Mrs. Durnford comes, she'll sew it on all your clothes."

"Twenty-fwee," Lily repeated.

How like school, Rose thought. Numbers and names to learn, every bit as important as arithmetic, or the Kings and Queens of England. Miss Crooks, Mrs. Durnford, Greta, Miss Duffy.

"You've got number nine," Greta said to Rose, consulting a bit of paper she'd taken from her apron pocket. "That's Millie's old one. You take your bag to the front bedroom—through there—and you'll find it marked on one of the bed cards. It's on your section of the wardrobe, too. Put your clothes away and stow your empty bag on the top shelf."

Bed Nine. Millie's old number.

Rose wanted to ask what had happened to Millie. Was the poor girl dead from pneumonia or scarlet fever? Or was she one of the lucky ones, with family coming to retrieve her and take her away.

"Nightgown gets folded and put under the pillow, like this," Greta was explaining to Lily. "After you take your good dress off, put it on the middle hook. There's room for your school blouse and skirt next to it. Socks and underwear go on the shelf below. Shoes stay downstairs; there's a rack inside the basement door. Only socks indoors, summer and winter. And don't you forget, or you'll have Greta to answer to."

The floor creaked under her feet as Rose made her way along a narrow connecting corridor. Sunlight poured in through an east window, casting a honey-coloured glow over the dingy plastered walls and reflecting on the brass corner pieces of a large travel trunk that was sitting on the floor next to the radiator.

Rose eyed the trunk, pausing to run her hand over its metal lid. It wasn't new by any means. The top was scratched in several places and there was a bad dent directly below the left hinge. A Cunard Lines sticker clung in shreds to one end. Curious, she peered at the name card in the leather-bound slot on the lid's top. R.B. Crooks, 72 Robie Street, Halifax, NS, had been neatly printed in bold, black letters.

Crooks; why that's the name of the Matron, Rose thought. Could it be that the stern-faced woman in charge here had once sailed on an ocean liner; had managed to salvage many of the things from her own family, packing them carefully in this trunk and bringing them with her? Rose tried to imagine the trunk's contents: taffeta ball gowns and crocheted shawls; glittery shoes and evening bags to match; perhaps a fur-trimmed cape. There might be fine linens, too, and perhaps a silver tea service. Miss Crooks would be wanting—and needing—them all when she saw fit to leave this horrid place for a home of her own.

A quick survey of the front bedroom did little to lift Rose's flagging spirits. Eight more beds, each covered with a bleached cotton spread and a precisely folded woollen blanket, confronted her. She sank down on one of the coverlets, unable to stop a new, advancing wave of dread. Eight girls packed into this drab, stark space, would be like living in a sardine can.

She breathed deep, longing, despite her best efforts, for the room that she used to share with Lily. Their mother had made the tufted comforter for their spool bed, as well as the braided mat on the floor. They had a wooden chest for their toys and games, a long shelf for story books, and a little corner under the sloping ceiling for their dolls' crib and carriage. There was a tall bureau, too, and a bedside lamp with a Bo Peep scene painted on its china base.

Don't remember. And don't be feeling sorry for yourself. It won't do one bit of good.

Rose wiped the wet from her eyes and stood up. Violet would be so annoyed if she saw her crying. Violet, who wouldn't be caught dead blubbering like a baby, no matter how terrible things were. Besides that, crying usually left Rose with a dull headache, and she didn't need that on top of everything else.

Surveying the room for a second time, Rose noticed that there were no religious pictures on any of these mustard-coloured walls. No gentle Jesus holding a lamb, or triumphant Jesus on a donkey, or boy Jesus talking with the elders in the temple. The only wall hangings were two small samplers, worked in simple cross-stitch on squares of cheap linen.

That girl can't cross-stitch to save her soul, Rose thought, eyeing the crooked lettering in the words of *Bless This House*. Even Lily, can do a better job than that. Beside it, *Home, Sweet Home,* was a far better effort. The sewer had worked three colours—pale pink, yellow, and mauve—into the tulip petal border, and had gone to the extra effort of adding her name and the date.

Wonder if she's my age, Rose mused, lingering over *Ora Jefferson March, 1935* in the lower-lefthand corner of the linen square. Her thoughts spun on. Surely the new school would have a Sewing Circle for the girls in Grade Six. She loved taking a plain piece of fabric and making an apron or a dresser scarf, adding crocheted edges, doing cross-stitching.

The Wednesday Sewing Circle had been a highlight for her; an escape from the tedium of multiplication drills, spelling bees, and poetry recitations.

By now Rose was well aware that she was never going to be a top student; her performance in arithmetic and science was mediocre at best; nor did she fare much better in grammar, history, or social studies. Her strengths were her nimble hands and her eye for colour and shapes, so it was in art and sewing where she shone.

When she'd won the Grade Five Needle Woman prize she'd run straight home to show her mother. And, sick as her mother had been by that point, she'd struggled to sit up in bed, exclaiming over the velvet pincushion and packets of embroidery thread. "Your stitches are so fine and even, my love," she'd said in a voice scarcely above a raspy whisper. "You'll make a living from your hands one day, I'm certain of it."

Rose bit down on her lip and turned abruptly away from the samplers. The memory of the prize was a bittersweet one; less than a month later her mother was gone forever. The day of the funeral Mrs. McGinn had brought a bowl of corned beef hash for their supper, arriving in the kitchen to find Rose, frantic and desolate, searching the house for the pincushion. "I can't find it," Rose had sobbed. "I've looked everywhere. I need it. I have to find it!"

"Rosie, luv," Mrs. McGinn had pleaded. "Try not to be so upset over a pincushion. We've just buried your mother. You'll get another pincushion one of these days."

Rose had run out of the kitchen, making her escape to the bathroom and sitting on the edge of the tub with a cold cloth against her face. How could she expect anybody to understand? A hundred other pincushions could never have the same meaning; they hadn't been part of that last afternoon when, between bouts of coughing, her precious mother had praised to the skies the handiwork of her middle daughter.

"Mercy, aren't you finished yet?"

Greta, with Lily at her side, was standing at the bedroom door. "I'm showing little missy the girls' washroom. Get into your play clothes and meet us there. And don't dawdle, for goodness sake. I got work to do before dinner."

Rose reached for her valise. There would be no sympathy in this house, and the sooner she accepted that fact the better off she'd be. She unpacked quickly, hanging her good dress and school outfit in the armoire and arranging her other clothing in two neat piles on the shelf. One for her blouses, camisole, and extra nightgown, a second for her bloomers and socks.

The prayer book that Aunt Edna had sent for her eighth birthday was in the bottom of the valise. Rose hadn't wanted to bring it and had packed it only because Mrs. McGinn kept reminding her not to forget it. Dear Mrs. McGinn. She meant well, of course; was a devout woman who said her Rosary every day, a woman as sure in her own faith as Rose was not. Too many bad things had happened for Rose to have any time for such empty, hollow words. She stuck the prayer book on the window ledge; if one of the other girls took it, she would be just as well pleased.

Her locket was last. She pulled the tiny packet furtively from the waistband of her bloomers, undid the tissue, and held the silver oval against her chest. There were times when she felt half-guilty about snitching it, unbeknownst to Violet; but she knew very well what its fate would have been if she hadn't.

The secondhand dealer had been to the house twice previously, and they were getting low on things to sell. That particular day a desperate and angry Violet was methodically searching every room, opening dresser drawers, checking closet shelves, gathering up the last of their mother's things and laying them out on the quilt: a silver-backed brush and comb set, a pretty blue alabaster dish, the little cranberry glass bud-vase, and the framed needlepoint pictures of Blue Boy and Pinky.

Rose had slipped into her mother's room ahead of Violet, taken the locket out of its satin-lined box, and hidden it under a loose board in the sewing nook. "No," she'd lied when Violet asked her if she'd seen it. "Mama kept it in a little box. I thought it was still there."

Now, once again, she was obliged to hide the locket. But where? The sparsely furnished bedroom offered few prospects. Under the mattress didn't seem a very good idea, nor in the wardrobe either. One of the other girls might snoop through her clothes and find it or, worse still, steal it.

Well, if not in the wardrobe, what about behind it? The thought prodded her into action; she eased her arm into the narrow recess, gingerly feeling the rough wooden backing with her fingers, smiling when they came in contact with a protruding screw. That'll do nicely, she thought, looping the chain of the locket over the screw's head. No one will find it back there, not if I'm very careful. I can sneak it out, look at Mama's picture, at night after the others are asleep.

"I thought for sure I'd have to send out a search party," Greta said when Rose finally made her way to the girls' bathroom at the top of the stairs. Lily was standing at one of the stained enamel sinks, making faces in the mirror above it. Greta handed Rose a frayed washcloth and a thin blue hand towel. "Here, put these away. Slot nine. Lily's done hers already." She pointed to a wall of small receptacles directly across from the sinks. "You'll have to wait for a toothbrush. Friday is drugstore-order day."

Rose did as she was told. She'd been in this house less than an hour and already she hated the numbering system. *I'm not a nine!* she longed to shout. *I'm Rose! Rose! You hear me!*

A deep, claw-footed tub stood under a frosted glass window at the far end of the narrow room. Opposite the tub were two toilet stalls separated by a half-wall. There was no privacy door on either of the openings.

"Where are the doors?" she asked Greta, motioning toward the toilets.

"Doors!" Greta chuckled. "Pardon me, Your Highness, but this isn't Buckingham Palace and you aren't Princess Margaret Rose. Stalls with no doors will have to do." She locked the linen cupboard and put the key in her apron pocket. "You'll get a clean set of towels after your bath on Saturday. Miss Duffy will have your name on the list by then."

From below a grandfather clock chimed, its deep bongs reverberating up the stairwell.

"Mercy on us," Greta exclaimed. "Eleven o'clock already. I've got to shake a tail. You two can play outdoors till dinnertime."

She whisked them down two flights of stairs and out onto a back stoop. "Go to it," she said. "Just make sure you stay inside the fence. That's a rule." With that, the screen door slammed behind her.

Two small girls were making castles in a sandbox and, beyond it, a boy of about the same age pushed a red truck in the dirt. The girls glanced up without speaking and went back to their play. Lily, ignoring them, headed instead for a rope swing that hung from the lower branch of a giant elm.

"Watch me," she called out to Rose, hoisting herself onto its seat. "Watch how high I can go!"

Rose stood for several minutes; then, reassured that Lily could keep herself amused, she set out to explore the property. A high wooden fence blocked out a ready view of the shore road, but Rose could hear the rumble of a tram car passing by on the other side of the fence. She could hear voices, too—the high-pitched voices of children singing. They seemed to be coming from the open windows of a long, one-storey building at the southeast tip of the yard. The song was a familiar one she knew by heart.

Flow gently sweet Afton
Among thy green braes
Flow gently I'll sing thee
A song in thy praise—
My Mary's asleep by thy
murmuring stream.
Flow gently sweet Afton
Disturb not her dream.

That's a school, she thought, perplexed, for it was unlike any school building she knew. She was used to red-brick structures with high transom windows, wide cement steps leading up to double-doors, and plaques with the school's name mounted above the entrance. By comparison this structure looked like one of the warehouses that lined the waterfront, or, worse still, an old cow barn.

Not wishing to be noticed, Rose avoided the open windows and picked her way through tall grass to the far side of the building. Overgrown bushes grew thick and dense here, blocking her way. Undaunted, she pushed the foliage away from her face and found herself in a dank, shaded enclosure, bordered on one side by a length of moss-covered fence and on another by a crumbling stone wall.

Clay pots, some cracked, others filled with rootbound earth, were piled in one corner of a rickety lean-to, and a long-handled spade rested across the rim of a rusted wheelbarrow. An old push mower was shoved in beside the wheelbarrow, half-hidden under a piece of tarpaulin.

Tiny pools of rainwater had formed in folds of the sagging tarpaulin, and, in one of these pools, two drowned spiders floated, their legs entwined in a grotesque death grip. Repulsed and shivering from the sight of the dead insects and the overpowering smell of leaf mold and musty earth, Rose backed away, scrabbling through the bushes and out into sunlight again.

Doctor Foster went to Glouster
In a shower of rain
He fell in a puddle right up to his middle
And never got home again.

Suddenly, unexpectedly, the innocent words of the old nursery rhyme took on a new and darker meaning. We'll never get home again either, she thought. There's no home to go to. This house will never be home, not for me. Lily might get used to it—she's young enough that she won't remember much of what it was like before. But I can.

They knew it was dinnertime when a group of children and a youngish woman in a dark skirt and a white blouse emerged from the out-building and started up the gravel driveway toward the house. The three little ones in the sandbox had apparently been waiting and watching, for as soon as they spied the others, they raced across the grass to meet the older children in a crush at the back door.

"I'm hungry," Lily whined when everyone had disappeared inside. "Don't we get our dinner now?"

"Of course," Rose replied, doing her best to hide her own confusion over what to do next. "Come on, let's go."

The chatter of voices and the scraping of chair legs across the wooden floor helped them find their way up the stairs and along a central corridor. When they reached the threshold of a big room at the back of the house, Rose motioned to Lily to stop. There was a momentary hush in the room, followed by a woman's voice. "Let us pray."

Lord, for this and every other gift
Our grateful hearts to Thee we lift. Amen.

On the Amen, a team of serving girls wasted no time moving into action. In pairs, they distributed the plates of buttered brown bread, ladled soup into bowls from a crockery pot, filled the metal serving trays with the steaming soup bowls, and carried the trays to the six tables. Within five minutes everyone except Rose and Lily was eating.

"Don't I hate Thursdays," groaned a boy at the nearest table. "When I get out of here I'm never having pea soup for the rest of my life. Never."

"I'll eat it, then," his seatmate said, reaching for the bowl. "I'm starved! Any more bread up there, Sam? Come on, pass it down this way. You're the worst hog, honest to Pete."

"I like soup," Lily was saying, tugging at Rose's arm. "I want some."

Greta's voice, over the clatter of aluminum mugs and spoons, rescued them from their dilemma. "Gracious, I clear forgot about you two," she said, hurrying over to them, her little bird face flushed. "Come, sit here by Dorothy. Girls, this is Rose and Lily, just arrived this morning. Pass along the rest of that bread; and Mary, go get two more bowls of soup."

Rose slid into the empty space and drew Lily down beside her. The soup arrived promptly and she picked up her spoon. Pea soup wasn't her favourite, either, but it was hot, and the brown bread was fresh, and she realized how long it had been since the untasted breakfast at Mrs. McGinn's.

"I'm Dot," said the girl in the next seat after a minute or two. "I came last month. Uncle Buck brought me in his coal truck. I sat in the cab all the way 'cross town. I heard you two came in a car. What kind was it, anyway?"

Rose thought quickly. She had no idea what kind of car they'd driven in, nor any interest in finding out. For her, the car was a hateful thing, whisking them away from their old life, dumping them here and driving off again.

"A Packard—a black one," she replied smoothly, giving Lily's leg a warning kick under the table. "It belongs to my aunt. She's sick, so cousin Henry brought us."

Well, it wasn't a total lie. The car had been black, and they did have a cousin Henry—he was Aunt Edna's son. Rose couldn't remember how long it had been since she'd seen him, or his older brother, Horace. Violet hated both of them; said they were snots, and ugly ones at that.

"My father comes to visit when he's not out to sea," said another girl. "You got any folks?"

"No, not now." Rose felt her throat tighten at the words.

"Did they die or fly the coop?" the girl went on.

"They died," Rose shot back. *Really! Mama and Daddy never flew any coops.*

"What'd they die from?"

Careful! Don't mention the sickness.

48

"My mother had a bad heart." That wasn't exactly a lie. Violet always claimed that Aunt Edna had broken their mother's heart when she turned her back on them.

"Mama coughed, too," Lily said. "All the time."

No!

Rose had been counting on Lily to keep quiet. It was safer that way.

"Sounds like she had TB," the girl said. "You'll probably come down with it next. Pops says it runs in families."

The sight of Lily's face—confused and fearful—angered Rose, and she was about to deliver a sharp retort when a freckle-faced girl cut in. "Stop it, Flo. You don't need to be like that."

"Shut-up your mouth, Ora," the girl replied. "I can say what I want, so there!"

Any further argument was squelched by Matron's curt voice. "Please rise for our final grace."

Chair legs scraped and spoons and mugs clattered on the tabletops as everyone got to their feet. "For what we have received, Lord, make us truly thankful; and may we be ever mindful of the needs of others. Amen."

This is so weird, Rose thought—giving thanks twice for the same meal. At home, the saying of Grace had been reserved for Sundays and special holidays like Christmas and Easter, and even the McGinn's, for all their Catholic ways, often dispensed with it at noon, and sometimes at supper, too.

The room emptied quickly, leaving only Greta and the girls on clean-up duty.

"Miss Duffy wants to see you two," Greta said to Rose. "She's our Assistant Matron. Come with me."

She led the way through a play area and ushered them

into a sunroom filled with plants. With a mumbled, "Our new girls," she left quickly, closing the French doors behind her. From a wicker arm chair, Miss Duffy waved them toward a chintz-covered settee. "Sit there," she said. When they were seated, she continued. "Greta tells me that you're unpacked and settled." Rose nodded. They were unpacked, certainly. As for settled, that was a whole different story.

Miss Duffy leaned slightly forward in her chair. "Life here is not complicated," she said. "As long as you know our rules and abide by them, you'll be fine."

Rose sat very still. She'd heard more than a few of them already.

"We expect you to be obedient, honest, and clean," Miss Duffy began. "In return, you'll be treated kindly and fairly. There are no special favours; with thirty children, there can't be. You're to help with chores, be punctual for all meals, behave well in school, and do your lessons willingly. As for church, we attend in a group every Sunday morning. Unless you are sick or we plan a special outing, there is no reason for any change in our routine. Do you understand?"

"Yes, ma'am," Rose and Lily replied in unison.

"There is time for play, of course; in our yard if it's fine—we believe that fresh air is good for children—in the playroom if it's raining. You are forbidden to leave the property on your own, or to go to the homes of other children. We have all you need right here. Puzzles and games never leave the playroom. We keep all books in our library; they can be taken to the playroom to read, or to the dining room in the evenings if you need them to do your lessons, but they must be put back each night. Nothing is to be taken upstairs. Bedrooms are for sleeping only."

"Yes, ma'am."

"Now, about the plants—" Miss Duffy gestured expansively toward the window ledges. "The older girls take turns watering them," she explained. "We post a list on Mondays. A good watering takes at least half an hour. You'll find watering cans over behind the door."

Rose could see why the watering task might take so long. The window ledges and tabletops were crammed with greenery and flowers: geraniums and azaleas, broad-leafed ivies and wispy ferns, African violets, cyclamen, and begonias. There wasn't so much as a square inch of space remaining.

Supper that evening consisted of more brown bread, cold sliced ham, and a dish of stewed rhubarb for dessert. Rose ate the food without tasting it, sneaking constant glances toward Lily's table.

"Try not to worry about your sister," murmured the freckle-faced girl. Her name, Rose had found out, was Ora. "The younger ones always sit together. It's a rule."

Of course, thought Rose. As if there aren't enough rules already. Later, while the others did arithmetic, spellings, and grammar, she tried to kill time with a book. It would be a relief, she realized, to go to school in the morning. Too much time to think, to brood, wasn't good.

Lights out at nine o'clock put an end to a long, lonely, unsettling day. Rose was burying her head into the pillow—longing for the feel of Lily's body beside her, for Mrs. McGinn and anything connected with home—when she heard Ora's whisper from the next bed.

"'Night, Rose. You sleep tight, okay? I'll see you tomorrow."

Impressions

A clanging bell cut into Rose's sleep early the next morning. She sat up, confused, wondering for a moment where on earth she was.

"Last one dressed is a rotten egg," Ora said from the next bed. She pushed back her covers and plunked her feet on the floor. "Come on; let's get to the bathroom before the slow pokes. Breakfast's at seven-thirty sharp and we need to be ready, with our beds made. Dot's duty this week and she'll report you if you're not."

Ora was right about the bathroom. Rose found herself waiting ages for a wash basin and had just enough time to splash warm water over her face and run a brush through her hair before a second warning bell sounded.

"Next week I'm on the roster for cutting bread," Ora explained as they edged past a couple of small boys tussling on the landing. "We get up earlier when we're duty for breakfast. Miss Duffy shakes you awake at six-thirty. You'll see."

Lily, already seated at a table with four other little girls, waved, and Rose blew her a kiss. She felt badly that she hadn't been able to say goodnight the previous evening, but when she'd gone upstairs after study hour the lights in the back corridor were already switched off and the door to the little girls' room was closed.

"Can I talk to Lily for a few minutes," she asked Greta now. "No, you can't," Greta replied in her sharp-edged way. "Lily's doing just fine. Best thing you can do is leave her be and don't fret so."

The hurriedly mumbled Grace was followed by bowls of thick oatmeal porridge. "Is there any brown sugar?"

Rose whispered to Ora. There were two enamel jugs on the table; a large white one of milk and a smaller blue-speckled one filled with dark molasses.

"You kidding? There's never any sugar." Ora reached for the molasses jug. "We're lucky to get this, let me tell you. Here, pour yourself some, but be careful you don't take too much; there'll be war if there's not enough to go around the table."

They ate quickly and efficiently, with a minimum of talk. Rose helped herself to a second piece of the brown bread and was finishing off the crust when Greta tapped her on the shoulder. "I'm putting you on stairs with Dot," she said. "Sooner you learn the ropes the better."

"Let's go, then," Dot said. She shoved her chair back and grabbed Rose's arm.

"You have to get here quick as you can," Dot explained when they reached the broom closet on the second floor. "There's only five mops and always six of us on cleaning, so whoever is last has to wait, and that can make you late for school. Here's your mop. And grab a dusting rag. You need it, too."

Dot stuck one of the dusters into the front of her skirt and Rose did likewise. "The boys live on third," she continued, leading Rose up yet another flight of stairs. "It's out of bounds for girls unless you're cleaning. Remember that."

"Oh—okay." Dot's air of authority both irritated and amused Rose. She's like another Greta, Rose thought. Full of rules and regulations.

"Now, watch me," Dot ordered, running her mop along the top step. "Back and forth twice, like so; then take a clean rag and wipe in between the railings. And don't poke; there's just enough time. Shake your mop out the side window when you're done, then put it back in the closet on its hook. There's a string at the top of the handle." Rose tried to work quickly but was interrupted every few minutes by a boy with school books scrambling past her, and by the time she had stowed her cleaning things away, it was past eight-thirty and Ora was calling anxiously from the lower hall. "Hurry, Rose! We have to go. The bell rings at quarter to nine."

She passed a worn leather bookbag to Rose. "Here, take this. It's Millie's old one, I think. Greta put two new pencils and a clean scribbler in it for you."

Rose accepted the bag reluctantly, trying not to notice the broken buckle and the frayed shoulder strap. How horrified her father would be if he knew. He'd made such lovely bookbags for Violet and her—brown leather, with a separate zipped pouch for pencils. She'd had hers at Mrs. McGinn's, but in the turmoil of packing yesterday it must have been left behind.

They left by the side door and started up the hill. The June morning was perfect, with the trees in full leaf and the scent of lilac in the air. Children walked in clusters of three and four, but Ora made no attempt to join any of the groups, choosing instead to keep close to Rose's side.

"You're so quiet," Ora said. "Are you nervous?"

"A little," Rose replied and left it at that.

She didn't know Ora well enough yet to let on how much she hated the house and its dozens of stupid rules; and how lonely she was feeling now that Lily, too, had been taken from her. "Lily will go to school on the property," Greta had told Rose the previous evening. "We have our own teacher for Primary to Three."

"I'll show you where the office is," Ora said when they reached the schoolyard; and she was as good as her word, depositing Rose at a door marked Principal.

"Keep your fingers crossed that you get in my room," she said. "If not, I'll see you at recess."

Rose tapped on the frosted glass and stood waiting. She would miss her former school friends, of course, but otherwise this new setting wasn't worrisome. The routine of school was a predictable one: the smell of chalk dust, the tap of the teacher's pointer on the blackboard, the buzzing of insects at the windows in spring, the sizzle of hot radiators on cold winter days.

What was going to be far more difficult and strange was her new life in the big house. It would be a very long time—years, in fact—until she was old enough to leave it and make her own way. "We can go when we're sixteen," Ora had said.

Sixteen. When she could live where she liked, go where she wanted, work at a job, buy things for herself and for Lily. A magical time, when there'd be no more house rules to put up with. She'd be free to make her own rules; live by her own code.

Sixteen couldn't come soon enough.

If, after three days in the house, Rose thought she could cope with anything, she was wrong. She hadn't yet faced the Sunday routine. The wake-up bell roused them a full hour later than usual, and with no floors to sweep or stairs to dust, breakfast was not quite so rushed.

Greta, however, was still at them, nagging everyone to be ready at nine-thirty; girls in their good dresses; boys in white shirts and dark pants. Then, like sheep, she herded them out the front door and onto the sidewalk. They walked in strict formation over Albert and up the Russell Street hill: Matron in front, the younger children directly behind her, and the older girls next. Miss Duffy and the three big boys brought up the rear.

"This is like Noah's ark," Rose whispered to Ora, humiliation welling up inside her. Were the people in these Sunday-quiet houses looking out their front windows, clucking in sympathy at the sight of poor children on the way to worship? Or were they laughing, there behind their net curtains? Either way, Rose wished that the ground would open and swallow her.

Their arrival in the church foyer was no less embarrassing. A black-garbed minister greeted them, making a great fuss over the little ones. When he spied Lily he actually leaned down to her and said, "You're new, aren't you? Welcome to the Lord's house, my dear."

Rose took an instant dislike to the smiling, beetle-like man. *Just like Father Hanrahan,* she thought in distaste. *Doling out blessings, patting our heads like we're pet dogs. It means nothing, though; not when all's said and done.*

She was relieved when Matron led them directly into a back pew. The last straw would have been to parade up the aisle like the waifs they were, on display to the entire congregation. The interior was, she saw instantly, very different to the Anglican church she had known; different, also, to Mrs. McGinn's church. There were no flickering candles or kneeling benches, no Stations of the Cross, no chancel steps, and no high altar table.

Instead, a raised platform, rather like the stage in the school auditorium, took up the space where the chancel steps should be. In the centre of the platform was the pulpit, draped with a gold-fringed, maroon hanging, and a high-backed, ornate arm chair. A basket of spring flowers sat on a low table in front of the platform. *It's Pentecost* now, Rose thought, bemused. The hangings are supposed to be red, not maroon and gold.

Also missing was the brass eagle lectern and the altar table. A solid wall of organ pipes, topped with carved wooden frescos, took up the space where the stained-glass window should be.

"This can't be an Anglican church," Rose murmured to Ora.

"No," Ora whispered back. "It's not. It's United."

"Why do we come here?" Rose persisted, ignoring a warning look from Miss Duffy. She had assumed that all children at the Home were Anglicans, like Lily and her.

"We take turns. Next week it'll be St. Mark's."

"But why?"

Ora shrugged. "I don't know why. Just because. Sometimes it's better not to ask too many questions."

The service went on for a very long time, and Rose could sense everyone around her getting more and more fidgety; but it did finally come to an end in a rousing recessional hymn that startled a half-dozing old man across the aisle, much to the amusement of the older boys and the accompanying frowns of Miss Crooks at the muffled sniggering. Afterwards, they formed a line-up for the return walk, waiting impatiently for Matron to finish her conversation with a tall man in an ill-fitting brown suit.

"Yes, the Board has voted to continue with alternating Sundays," Matron was saying.

"It's not my place to question the Board's decision, of course," the man replied. "But when fall comes I think we should discuss Sunday School again. And we sincerely hope the children will attend our picnic. It's only two weeks away."

"Transporting thirty children isn't that easy. You remember the problem we had last year."

"Yes I do, but not to worry. That mix-up won't happen again. Superintendent Wamboldt is making his truck available."

"I see. Well, I'll have Miss Duffy phone. Hopefully, a suitable arrangement can be worked out."

Rose's table talked nothing but picnic all through dinner.

"It's a lot of fun, Rose," Ora said. "There's races and prizes and we have sandwiches and ice-cream. You'll love it, and Lily will, too."

Rose had her reservations. The idea of a picnic with dozens of noisy children didn't sound very appealing. She supposed that she and Lily would have to attend, though. If everyone was going, there'd be no choice in the matter. Deep down, however, she would gladly have traded six— no, ten—picnics for one Sunday dinner with the McGinns; or for one visit, one letter, even one phone call, from Violet.

Flight

By late October Rose was tired of waiting and wondering. After much scheming—on her own and with input from Ora—she settled on a Friday afternoon to try and find Violet. She and Ora dawdled as long as they could after the noon meal, waiting until everyone else had left for school before setting out. They walked arm-in-arm until they reached the vacant lot on the lower side of the street.

"Nobody's behind us," Ora said, glancing as nonchalantly as she could over her shoulder. "Better take off."

"Okay," Rose replied. "Wish me luck."

"I do," Ora said. "Now, go!"

Rose climbed over the sagging wire fencing and made her way to a stand of straggly birches in the lot's far corner. Behind the trees the jagged cliff face dropped away sharply, ending at a high cement retaining wall. She inched down the treacherous incline to the retaining wall and hesitated, surveying the gully below. She couldn't afford to cut herself on a shard of broken glass or a jagged bit of discarded metal. Reassured that the ridged earth and tufts of matted grass held little risk of either, she took a deep breath and jumped, landing awkwardly in a spray of loose stones and dry earth.

Her objective, the tram stop, was directly opposite. She darted across the deserted road and ducked behind a telephone pole, counting on the angle of its shadow to help conceal her petite, upright figure. A long minute passed, then another. She shaded her eyes with one hand and peered south, anxiety mounting. If she was to make any headway today, she needed to make every precious minute, every second count.

Supper on Fridays was later than on school nights; but, still and all, she knew she had less than four hours before her absence would be detected. One of the girls at her table—nosey, blabbermouth Dot, most probably—would see her vacant seat and ask "where's Rose?" Ora, primed with their carefully constructed answer, was to say that she'd taken sick on the way to school and was probably in bed in the infirmary.

Of course, the stall tactic would work only until Greta missed her and came over to inquire. Someone would be sent upstairs to check, and when it was clear that Rose wasn't in the infirmary or in the older girls' dorm, a full-scale search of the house and the yard would be mounted. By that point it would be six o'clock, and dark outside.

Matron would be alerted next. Rose knew how displeased she would be that quiet, obedient Rose Morash, in her care for such a short while, was lost, injured, or (the unthinkable) a deliberate runaway. She would waste no time calling Lily and Ora into her office. Rose could see the girls standing at Matron's big desk, having to look her directly in the eye.

"Do you have any idea where Rose is?" Matron would ask each in turn. "Would she have gone into someone's house after school, perhaps? You must tell us; it's very important that we find her and bring her back."

Lily wouldn't know, of course. She'd be scared, perhaps even cry; afraid of Matron, afraid that her big sister was lost or hit by a truck, like little Alfie had been back in the summer; or worse still, that Rose had gone away and left her behind. The image of little Lily being grilled by a stern-faced Matron bothered Rose, but she tried to ignore the niggling guilt. She mustn't lose her nerve, not now;

she must stick to her guns and go through with her plan; so much counted on it.

Ora, on the other hand, was a different kettle of fish. Her friend's cheerful smile and sunny disposition hid a tougher, more cunning side, and Rose knew that she could count on Ora to keep her mouth shut and her expression innocent, no matter how long and hard she was grilled. Ora, with an impish grin, had admitted to Rose that she would relish the opportunity to pull the wool over Matron's eyes. "The old biddy will be wetting her pants over you skipping out," Ora had predicted. "It'll be so funny, watching her sweat."

More precious minutes passed. Where on earth was that tram? Just her luck that it would be running late, today of all days. She could see their big house over the treetops, acutely aware that anyone looking out a back window—Greta, Cook, or Matron, in the sunroom with her beloved ivies and begonias—had an almost unobstructed view of the shore road and of anyone walking—or waiting—on it.

After what seemed like an eternity, she detected a low, rumbling noise and, as she peered into the distance, she caught sight of the tram rounding the shipyard turn. Excited now, she dug into her jacket pocket for the two nickels that Ora had coaxed out of her father during his last Sunday visit. "For my friend, Rose," Ora had told her dad. "She needs to go and see her sick sister."

Rose gave the driver a bright smile as she climbed on and deposited her coins in the fare box. There was an empty spot beside a heavy-set woman in a woollen sweater, and Rose slid into it.

"Nice day," said the woman, shifting a shopping bag on her lap.

"Yes, very nice," Rose replied.

"School out early?"

Rose's heart did a skip, but she was prepared. "No," she replied, arranging her face in what she hoped was a concerned expression. "I'm going to see my sister Violet. She's sick in the hospital. My mother can't go, so she's sending me instead."

"Aw, what a shame," the woman said. She thumped on her shopping bag as if giving it a good beating, like a carpet on the line, would get rid of the dust and germs. "Such a lot of sickness about and it's not even winter yet," she continued. "I don't know what'll become of us if it's a hard one."

"Oh, we'll muddle through somehow," Rose replied. "We're tough." Violet often said that, especially in those last awful months.

"I sure hope so," the woman replied. She adjusted the shopping bag again, draping her arms across its wooden-handled top. The old-fashioned watch on her wrist had a large, square face and black Roman numeral markings, giving Rose a clear view of the time. It had just gone one-fifty.

By now, the teacher would have called the roll, recording "absent" in the register next to Rose's name and today's date. "I'll tell her that you took sick," Ora had promised. "Don't worry. They never call to check unless you're in the dumb-bell row."

The waterfront warehouses and fish plants were giving way to the brick-fronted offices and shops of the commercial district. Ahead, on the lower side of the busy thoroughfare, Rose could see the distinctive green awnings of the Jewish clothing shops and, in the distance, the spire of St. Paul's. As soon as they reached the Cogswell corner she would get off and walk straight up the hill, past Trinity Church. Her old street was a mere block and a half beyond the church grounds, and the the McGinn's house was five in from the corner on the lefthand side.

"My stop's next," murmured the woman beside her. She yanked on the cord and got to her feet. "Hope you'll have a nice visit with your sister, dear," she said.

"Thanks. I will," Rose replied, returning the woman's parting nod, idly watching as the woman climbed heavily down the exit steps and onto the pavement.

It was then that Rose saw the hat. Beige felt, small brim, with a brown-and-white feather stuck into the front of its band. Its wearer was a tall, thin lady in a beige three-quarter coat.

No. It can't be! Rose turned her face away from the window and bent down, pretending to pull up her sock, her heart pumping at double speed. Matron was tall and thin. Matron walked briskly. Matron had a hat exactly like that one. She wore it to church, with a three-quarter coat, a dark serge skirt and lace-up, brown oxfords. The girls loathed the outfit, agreeing that it made Matron look like a two-legged giraffe.

Rose waited until the tram had pulled away from the stop before raising her head. It might not have been Matron, of course, but Rose couldn't afford to take any chances. She had no intention of being stopped, questioned, and possibly prevented from continuing her journey. For today was the day she was going to find Violet, and that was all there was to it.

Cemetery

"Mary, Mother of God, it's Rosie! Come in, my love, come in."

Mrs. McGinn's strong arms encircled her in a crushing hug and Rose hugged back, savouring the feel of the big woman's body against her own. She missed Mrs. McGinn's warmth and affection, the dozens of little endearments that she used, not only with her own brood, but with Lily and her as well. The grown-ups at the Home never called you "love" or "dearie" and certainly never hugged you. Greta was kind enough in a gruff, no-nonsense way, but both Miss Duffy and Matron were remote, distinctly undemonstrative women. For the lucky children with family—a sister or father, sometimes a brother—it didn't matter so much; they were able to stock up on hugs and kisses during the all-too-brief Sunday afternoon visits. But in the four months they'd been at the Home Rose and Lily hadn't had one visitor, let alone a hug.

"You're taller and thinner," Mrs. McGinn said when she finally released Rose and stood back, appraising her with a knowing eye. "I can tell. They better be feeding you right or there'll be trouble."

She looked past Rose to the open front door, "Don't tell me you came all by yourself—where's Lily?"

"Yes, I came by myself," Rose said, the words tumbling out in her rush to explain. "On the tram. Lily's at school."

"I see," said Mrs. McGinn, closing the door with a decided push. The good woman asked nothing more for the moment, instead putting her arm around Rose's shoulder. "Come along to the kitchen with me, lass. I just put the wee one down for a nap, so we'll have a nice, quiet cuppa together before she wakes up. There's a bit of pudding left, too, thank the Lord. You surely do need some fattening up or my name isn't Bridget Eileen."

While Mrs. McGinn got cups and plates from the shelf and ran water into the kettle for the tea Rose took off her coat and draped it over the back of a chair. It felt so good to be back in the bright, cozy kitchen. She loved the red-and-white checkered wallpaper, the dented porridge pot on the stove, the crucifix on the wall over the table, even the stained enamel drain board and the worn lino by the sink. The room had such a homey, lived-in feel to it, so different to that other kitchen, up "there."

The older girls at the Home had their own name for the big, antiseptic room in the back corner of the house. They called it The Olive Pit, after Olive Pittman, the leather-faced Newfoundland woman who cooked for them. Olive talked with an accent so thick Rose couldn't understand half of what she said, but it made little matter when it came to following orders. A list on the wall by the stove told you what your duties were for the week.

"Listen here," Olive liked to say, "—a tight ship's what I run. And I won't be putting up with any kid who's not quick, neat, and quiet." Every duty girl soon learned what Olive meant if you didn't measure up. "Tuck that flappin' tongue back in your mouth or I'll cut it right out," Olive would shout from the stove if you talked too much. Or, if you didn't move as quickly as she wanted, "What's the matter with you? Got a broomstick up that arse of yours?"

She was a stickler on cleanliness, too. The floor had to be mopped daily and the long wooden table that she used for chopping vegetables and making bread scrubbed with a stiff brush. She checked the deep sink after supper each night, sending one of them back to do it over again if she found any trace of white residue from the dried disinfectant. And three times a week the stovetop had to be scoured with steel wool.

To be fair, she had her good points, too. Despite her tough talk and her pickiness, everyone agreed that Olive was a pretty decent cook. She didn't do fancy cakes or puddings, but she did make excellent brown bread and good corn chowder, and her white fish on Fridays was pan crispy, just the way Rose liked it, with green peas mixed into the hash browns.

It was just too bad that The Olive Pit would never be a relaxed place; a place where you could enjoy the preparation, and the eating, of food. The food cupboards were a prime example. Rose was horrified when she found out they were locked between meals. "Matron's orders," was the way Olive put it. "We can't afford to let you help yourselves. This way, nobody's tempted and nobody gets into trouble."

So unlike the McGinn's where you could help yourself any time. Mrs. McGinn kept molasses cookies in a glass jar on the sideboard and heels of bread under a clean dish cloth in the pantry, and in the autumn there was always a big basket of apples on the back stoop. You weren't supposed to swipe six cookies at a time, or leave milk rings and molasses drips on the cupboard; but if you did "swipe" or neglect to wipe up your spills, you weren't hauled into the office to explain or given smacks with the pointer. It was a kitchen where food wasn't rationed and spills weren't considered sinful.

Mrs. McGinn set a mug of tea and a dish of the promised pudding in front of Rose. "Don't talk till you eat this," she said.

The pudding smelled of cinnamon, with fat, juicy raisins

swimming in a thick, brown-sugar sauce. Rose tucked in without hesitation. She'd had raisins only once in the past four months. A man from United Memorial had donated four pies on Thanksgiving—three pumpkin and one raisin—and Rose had been lucky enough to get a piece of the raisin. Olive sometimes made puddings for Sunday dessert, but they were usually rice, with a sprinkle of nutmeg on top. Today they'd had the usual Friday fare—green and red jelly, cut into cubes.

"Now then, let's hear it," Mrs. McGinn said when Rose had finished the dessert and downed the last of the tea. "You'll be in a heap of trouble over this, I figure. But you knew that and came anyway, so there must be a darn good reason."

"I have to find Violet," Rose said. "I don't know where she is and I need you to help me. Matron won't tell me. I know she knows but she keeps on saying that I must have patience. It's not fair! I want my sister—now. Lily does, too."

"Oh, Rosie luv, I feel so bad for you." Mrs. McGinn pulled a hankie from her apron pocket and blew her nose. "You've been such a brave lass, too—you remind me of your mama that way. Why, my Mavis wouldn't have stood up half so well and she's older than you."

Rose sat, silent, staring at the bottom of her empty mug. It was all very well for Mrs. McGinn to feel badly, and to admire her, too, but there were so few hours in this bright, fall afternoon. Barely enough time for action, not nearly enough for talk. What would she do if Mrs. McGinn refused her; what on earth would she do?

"Rosie, I know you want your sister," Mrs. McGinn said. "And you should have her, too. Family needs to stick together, through thick and thin. I never did agree with Father Hanrahan's sending you two away. It was a terrible mistake. Your mother will be turning over in her grave, I'm sure of that."

She got up and carried the two mugs over to the stove. "I wanted to visit you," she said as she poured more tea and brought the mugs back to the table. "Wasn't for lack of trying, believe me. Twice I packed a basket and went up on the tram, and both times the little woman who answered the door wouldn't let me in."

Mrs. McGinn stirred her tea, took the spoon out and laid it on the table. "The first time, she told me that the only visitors allowed were family. She wouldn't even take the basket of goodies. I tried again a few weeks later, hoping that maybe somebody else would answer, but she was there again, just like a soldier standing guard. After she shut the door on me that day I walked along by the fence, hoping I might see you or Lily in the yard, but there was only one little fellow playing in a sandbox. I called out to him, trying to get his attention. I thought if he would come over to the fence I could ask him to take the basket in to you. I called and called, but he didn't even look up.

"We're not supposed to speak to strangers," Rose said wearily. "It's a rule."

"Well it's a sad, silly one, and that's my honest opinion. When I told my Paddy, he was mad. "Stay away, Bridget," he says. "They don't want the likes of you nosing around and that's all there is to it.""

It was close to four o'clock when Rose and Mrs. McGinn finally set out. "Get the supper started at five," Mrs. McGinn said to Mavis as she and Rose buttoned up their coats. "Everything's ready in the pantry. You can feed the baby ahead, but I want the rest of you to wait till we get back."

They crossed North Park at Cogswell, followed the footpath along the central Commons, and then headed south. Mrs. McGinn's stride was purposeful and Rose quickened her own pace in an effort to keep up.

They walked without speaking, and for that Rose was grateful. She wouldn't be seeing Violet today after all, and that in itself should have left her crushed and horribly disappointed. But the news that Mrs. McGinn had shared was so startling, quite beyond anything she might have imagined, that Rose needed time to absorb it. All these weeks of worrying, lying in the dark night after night, fearing the worst, convinced that Violet had come down with TB and was deathly ill, perhaps even dead, wasn't the case at all. Violet wasn't dead. Indeed, she was very much alive; alive and waiting for her baby to be born.

It was difficult for Rose to picture Violet as a mother. Violet, who never cared a hoot for babies; who, as far as Rose knew, didn't even have a steady fellow.

"Her baby's due next month, Rose," Mrs. McGinn had said. "She'll have to stay quiet until then, but once she's on her feet again, I'm sure she'll come to see you two."

"And then we can live together, like we used to? Violet and me and Lily and the baby?" Rose had persisted.

"I don't think so, luv. Violet's still too young, and she hasn't any money. She won't be able to keep the baby, not without a husband. She'll have to give it up for adoption and go out to work. There's no other choice."

They had reached the hospital grounds. Opposite, on the upper side of the boulevard, the sturdy wooden houses stretched on for several blocks. Houses with fences and porches, and front doors that led into living rooms, and kitchens where real families ate together. Rose tried to imagine Violet, thick and heavy, sitting in a rocking chair in one of these living rooms, waiting for the baby to come. A baby that would be whisked away from her and taken in by strangers. A baby who would not be baptized in the smocked christening dress that their mother had made, or the tiny crocheted sweater and bonnet either.

"Why doesn't Violet get married?" Rose asked. Surely marriage was the obvious answer. Marriage would solve two problems—Violet's need for a husband and their need for a father-provider. "Other girls do and they're not nearly as pretty as she is," she went on. "With a husband she'd be able to keep house and look after the baby. Lily and I would be at school in the daytime but we'd help when we got home. That way, we'd all be together again."

"It's not that simple, my lass," Mrs. McGinn replied. "When you're older you'll understand."

They walked on for another block, stopping finally at the gates of the cemetery. "Let's go and see where your parents are buried, Rose."

A canopy of crimson and bronze blotted out the weak late-afternoon sun as they made their way along a rutted path. Fallen leaves rustled against their shoes; otherwise, there was no sound; no sighing wind, not even the distant sound of traffic from the street. The row of gravestones, many of them covered with moss, eventually gave way to a neglected patch of turf. It was here that Mrs. McGinn halted.

"There they are, your mother and father," she said, pointing toward two rough-hewn wooden markers. There was no money for real stones, so Paddy did what he could. If you go closer, you'll see their names."

Rose took three steps and dropped to her knees on the damp turf. A flat metal plate was lashed with leather twine to the centre of each cross. *George William Morash 1896–1934*, on the left; *Eva Katherine Morash — 1899–1935*, on the right.

Mrs. McGinn's voice was soft behind her. "The two

babies are buried here, too. Over near that tree, I think. I came with your mother for each of them, but it's hard without a marker to guide you. With the angels now, all of them, God keep their souls."

Rose knelt until her knees were numb from the cold earth. When she got up, she walked to a maple tree, broke off two branches, retraced her steps, and laid the scarlet leaves at the base of each cross.

"They'll be knowing you've been, lass. The dead always do," Mrs. McGinn murmured, reaching for Rose's arm and pulling her close.

Rose pressed her face against the rough wool cloth, grieving for the baby brothers she had never known and for her mother and father, all of them so terribly still and lonely in their pauper-like graves.

"A thin place is a graveyard. My granny always said so," Mrs. McGinn whispered reverently.

"Thin?" Rose asked, looking up in surprise. For her, the cemetery was not at all thin, but thick and wide, filled with all kinds of people; soldiers from long ago wars; rich people from the mansions of the south end; railway men and sailors; little babies like her own two brothers. There were rows and rows of graves; marked with white crosses and grey slabs, marble urns and granite columns.

"Yes, thin places," Mrs. McGinn replied. "It's an old Irish legend. Thin is the veil between sacred ground and the heavens. Angels like it here because it's so quiet and peaceful. They sit in the grass and hide in the bushes and swing from the tree branches. If we were to sit very still and quiet for a very long time, we might be able to catch a glimpse of them. Oh yes, they're all around, if only we had the eyes to see them."

"Oh," Rose murmured.

It was a pretty, if far-fetched story, but she didn't want to hurt Mrs. McGinn's feelings by saying so. Her father used to laugh at the Irish and their superstitions, and she suspected that this angel business was just one more example of their fanciful ways. For if they could find leprechauns and pots of gold at the end of rainbows, and fairies in glades and dells, they would certainly have no trouble at all seeing angels in cemeteries.

Such foolishness wasn't for her, though. Angels and fairies, like Santa Claus and the Easter Bunny, were part of the make-believe world of childhood, a childhood that she had left behind forever. It had disappeared in the same way as the Bo Peep lamp from her old bedroom; was as dead as were her parents, lying here in this cold ground.

What she needed was to keep her wits about her and her head screwed on straight. She was twelve now, with no parents and no money, a big sister who was having a baby that she couldn't keep, an aunt and uncle who could have helped out but had turned their backs on them. No, Rose didn't have any time to waste on fairies and veils. The world outside this cemetery was a tough place: unfair and complicated. Life wasn't thin and filmy at all; it was thick and messy, with people she must deal with and obstacles that she must do her best to overcome.

Return

The autumn dusk had descended by the time Rose and Mrs. McGinn arrived back at the house. Mavis had the supper ready and they sat down immediately to eat. The fishcakes and fried bread were standard Friday night fare, but to Rose the meal seemed feast-like. Seated around the square wooden table were the twins and Mavis, the two older boys, and Mrs. McGinn, with Bridget's high chair drawn in close. It was a noisy half-hour, with the twins squirming and poking each other, little Bridget banging on the tray of her high chair with a spoon, and Sean, the sixteen year old, teasing Rose like he'd always done. Mrs. McGinn added her two cents' worth, never once shushing them or reminding them not to reach or squirm; and the Grace mercifully short.

Determined to enjoy herself while she could, Rose tucked in, asking for an extra piece of "pan bread," dipping her spoon into the pickle jar for more of Mrs. McGinn's green tomato chow. Its tangy smell brought back the aroma of tomatoes and onions simmering in a big pot on her mother's stove. She'd loved helping mama and Violet at pickling time.

Violet, deemed old enough to use the sharp knives, did most of the cutting and chopping, but Rose's tasks were every bit as important, as her mother was quick to emphasize. She washed the tomatoes in salted water, carried the peelings out to the garbage bin, and had the honour of filling the gauze pouch with spices, tying it with waxed string and dropping it into the pot. Later, when the mixture had come to a slow, steady simmer, she took her turn stirring, using the blackened wooden spoon that was brought into service each pickling season.

"Where's Mr. McGinn?" Rose asked, suddenly conscious of his absence. She liked the big, ruddy-faced man who had been their neighbour for as long as she could remember; who talked with her father over the hedge on summer nights, fixed the swing when it broke, built a treehouse in the big elm, and sat in the wood shed after the first snow, sandpaper in hand and a can of wax on a stump, polishing the sled runners until they shone like new.

"Dadda won't be home for an age, Rosie," Mavis said. "He plays cards at Uncle Jimmy's on Fridays—remember."

Of course. Uncle Jimmy. A carbon-copy of Mr. McGinn; the same red hair and bushy eyebrows, the same lilting voice. Mr. McGinn had brought Uncle Jimmy and his fiddle to see her ailing father one rainy March evening two years ago. Setting themselves up in the front room, with her father wrapped in a quilt on the settee, they'd sung and played for the longest time. Rose had hung over the banister, listening to their deep, rich tones floating up the stairwell. She'd been thrilled when her father joined in, managing to get through the first two verses of "The Mountains of Mourne" before he was overcome by coughing spasms.

Her mother had cried afterwards. "Bill had such a beautiful voice," Rose heard her telling Violet in the pantry. "He sang tenor. The three of them were as good a trio as you could hear anywhere in this city." Rose would never forget the sight of her mother's head on Violet's shoulder, the look of utter anguish on Violet's face.

As soon as the dishes were washed and dried, Mrs. McGinn told Mavis to get her coat on. "Go to the Glebe house and ask permission to use their phone. If Father's not there, ask his housekeeper. Say your mother sent you and it's important. You'll have to get the number from the operator. When you get through, tell the Matron at the Home that Rose is with us and ask if she can stay the night—say I'll bring her back tomorrow on the tram."

When Mavis had gone, she turned to Rose. "I hope they haven't reported you missing, my luv. Better if we don't have any policemen landing on our doorstep."

Rose lifted Bridget out of the high chair and stood with the sleepy child in her arms. "I don't want to go back," she said, burying her face in Bridget's neck. "Can't we please live here again?"

"Rosie, Rosie—" Mrs. McGinn's voice sounded weary. "I'm just as Irish as I was before and just as Catholic too, so they aren't about to agree to that." She reached over and cupped Rose's face in her hands. "But I do have an idea— came to me in the cemetery."

"What is it?" Rose asked. "Tell me."

Mrs. McGinn just smiled and shook her head. "You wait, luv. 'Til later."

Rose was perched on the edge of the twins' bed reading *Peter Rabbit* when she heard Mavis come in. "I have to go now," she said. She handed the book to Paddy, trying hard to ignore his pleas of "stay, Rosie, stay!"

"The lady at the Home said to tell you that she's sending a cab right away," Mavis was explaining to her mother, her face shiny with sweat from hurrying back in the cold. "Rose is supposed to be ready. And Ma—she didn't sound any too pleased."

"Didn't she! Well, isn't that just too bad!" With her hands on her hips and her jaw stuck out, Mrs. McGinn reminded Rose of a bull waiting to charge. "She should be thankful Rose is all right instead of getting her nose out of joint."

Resigned to the inevitable and realizing that co-operation was her only alternative, Rose was ready when the cab tooted. "I'll be okay," she said, giving the tearful Mavis a quick hug. For added courage, she linked her arm through Mrs. McGinn's and together they hurried out into the October night.

In the cab she sat close to the kindly woman, drawing comfort from Mrs. McGinn's solid frame, thankful that she didn't need to play the big sister role; that this time she could rely on an older, braver person.

Greta was waiting under the portico light when they pulled up, a shawl thrown around her bony shoulders. Before the driver could get the meter turned off she was at his window, fare money in her hand.

"Matron's in her office," she murmured, leading them indoors. "Rose knows the way."

I know the way all right. And what to expect, too.

What Rose hadn't expected was the quick pat that Greta gave her on the shoulder. It was a surprising yet strangely reassuring touch; a rare and fleeting hint of emotion from an odd little woman not given to such gestures. A woman not so much unkind as unwavering and unquestioning; who scurried about the house hearing plenty, seeing much, saying little; who seldom let her feelings get in the way of the job that needed doing.

Matron was sitting at her desk, her arms folded across her chest. Later, Rose would describe her face to Ora: "Dark and darkening; like a thundercloud over the harbour." In front of her lay an open file folder.

She waited a moment before speaking and when she did, her words were slow and deliberate. "I can't believe that you, Rose—of all our girls—would do such a foolish thing. Do you realize the upset you've caused?"

"I'm very sorry," Rose replied. She had made up her mind that she would not—absolutely not—buckle under the weight of Matron's displeasure. "I had to see if I could find Violet. She's my sister and I need her."

"I believe that we are the better judges of when your sister should be contacted," Matron said. "Children can hardly be expected to know what's best for them."

Rose stared at the toe of her shoe, resentment mounting.

No, you don't know what's best for me! How could you? You hardly know me. All you know is what's in that file folder—words, sentences, paragraphs.

Hadn't Mama told her that talk was cheap? And words on paper weren't much better. What counted was action— the courage to do what was important; and what was important now was to find Violet. Surely anybody who had the least bit of common sense could understand that.

Mrs. McGinn cleared her throat, her hand tightening on Rose's shoulder.

"The girl's not asking for a lot, Missus. Just a chance to see her sister; and us folks, too. I don't see how you've got any right to stand in the way."

"I beg your pardon!" Matron leaned forward, her fore-finger jabbing the file docket. "I have every right. This file gives me that right; to do as I see fit for this girl, and for every other child in this house."

She looked down at Rose. "We're not keeping you apart, as this woman chooses to call it. Your sister is a minor and has serious problems to deal with at the moment. If— and when—she straightens her life out, you may be put in touch with her. Meanwhile, you'll have to be patient. We do our best for all of the children here. As for other visitors, the committee has set the rule and I abide by it. Immediate family only. It's as simple as that."

Rose could feel the chill of defeat spreading through her,

and with it a sickening nervousness thud in her stomach. If Matron remained unrelenting, hiding behind her infernal rules, the trip to find Violet would be a wasted effort, one that Matron wasn't soon likely to forget or forgive.

Mrs. McGinn, however, wasn't giving up that easily. In the harsh glare of the overhead bulb, Rose could see the fight in her eyes.

"Well, it's downright cruel," Mrs. McGinn said, "keeping this girl away from her sister, and from us, too. Sure, Violet's got herself in a bad way, no question. But she's no more a sinner than any of the rest of us. Let him who's without cast the first stone. That's what the good book says."

"I wasn't suggesting any such—" Matron began.

"Father Hanrahan was at our house today," Mrs. McGinn cut in, ignoring her. "I told him all about Rose's plight. He was upset, let me tell you. Said he'd step in and try to get things put to rights. He even mentioned the Bishop."

She reached for Rose's hand. "Rose was so happy to hear it, weren't you, Rose? He'll do what he says, too. He's a man of his word, is Father."

Rose nodded in dumb, amazed agreement. Mr. McGinn wasn't the only one playing cards tonight, it would seem. Mrs. McGinn also had a game on; at this very moment playing the one ace she had up her sleeve. It was a gamble, though. What if Matron called her bluff?

Matron sat quietly, her face impassive. Then she reached for a pen, took out a sheet of paper, and began to write. Rose watched the nib glide purposefully over the paper; one sentence, then two, three, four. What on earth was she writing—a letter to Father Hanrahan? If so, Mrs. McGinn would soon enough be caught in her lie.

Matron replaced her pen in the inkwell, folded the paper and closed the file docket before looking up. "I've made a note of your concerns," she said in a controlled voice. "They'll be sent on to our Board. How soon they'll be tabled is out of my hands. However, should there be changes to the visitation rules, you'll be notified. That's the best I can do."

She stood up and gave Mrs. McGinn a frosty bow. "We appreciate your bringing Rose back safely. Rose, you are to go upstairs immediately. Greta will be waiting for you. Tomorrow will be time enough to discuss suitable penalties. Goodnight to you both."

Rose mumbled a hasty response and found her way, almost shell-shocked, to the stairs. To think that Father Hanrahan of all people, a man she disliked so intensely, was a pawn in this little game. Well, he'd done enough damage in the past; this time let him be put to good use.

Violet would have no problem with what had taken place, Rose knew that. "Life's never simple, Rosie," she'd said the day she bartered the silver candlesticks for a load of coal. "It's not a case of black and white, good and bad. Candles won't keep us warm this month, will they? I do what needs to be done."

Mrs. McGinn obviously shared Violet's view, doing what was needed to achieve the objective. On this occasion, Father Hanrahan was the means to the end. Father, the black and white man. Black when he walked the neighbourhood, talking to regular people, doing his deeds and misdeeds; white during Mass, when he was pure and holy and talked to God. "I am but a servant of the Lord." Rose had heard him say that plenty of times. Well, let him be her servant for a change.

Ora was still awake when Rose slipped into the darkened bedroom, groped her way to the wardrobe and pulled out her nightgown.

"Any luck?"

"Maybe. I'll tell you about it tomorrow."

"Okay."

A rustle from Ora's bed, followed by a mumbled, "I said a prayer for you."

"Thanks." Rose tiptoed to her bed, got in, pulled her covers up. There was another rustle, a small sigh and silence.

She's fallen asleep, Rose thought. Dear Ora, who was still willing to give God a chance. Rose had given up on Him, viewing the time spent in prayer a useless waste. God, if He was up there at all, was a remote Being, as formidable and disinterested as Matron herself, and Rose had lost faith in both of them.

It was December before Rose knew the full verdict on her flight. Miss Duffy called her into the sunroom on a cold, snowy afternoon.

"Your family friend, a Mrs. McGinn, has received special approval from the Committee for one visit a month. Matron asked me to inform you."

"Starting this Sunday?" Rose asked, trying to contain her excitement.

"Indeed not! She'll begin sometime after the new year," Miss Duffy replied.

"But that's weeks away," Rose protested.

"Correct. Matron says it's part and parcel of your penalty."

Of course. The penalty. Hot seat and cold shoulder.

"What about my sister—Violet?" Rose persisted. "When will she come?"

"I have no idea. Nothing was said about your sister. Nothing at all."

Christmas

School finished early on the twenty-third of December. To her credit, Miss Duffy had organized things so that everyone was kept occupied with assorted scissors, crayons, and pots of glue. They spent the afternoon in the playroom, happily drawing pictures of winter scenes, fashioning link-chains from leftover wallpaper and cutting snowflakes from pieces of used tissue. The older girls were undaunted by the wrinkles in the tissue, quickly getting out the iron and pressing it into renewed smoothness between two towels.

"What a good idea," said Miss Duffy, obviously impressed. She disappeared into the sewing room and returned with several balls of twine and a paper bag filled with loose beads. "You can string these, like so," she said, demonstrating at Rose's table. "They'll make garlands for the tree, and we'll loop a couple of strands through the wreaths on the doors. Should look very nice, don't you think?"

The three oldest boys were assigned the task of putting up the paper chains, running them diagonally from the corners of the dining room and the front parlor. The finished effect pleased everyone, even Greta, who let up on her dire warnings about the risk of fire and her refrain of "what a lot of foolishness this Christmas business was."

Mr. Everett, the man who saw to the furnace and the yard, delivered the fir tree early on Christmas Eve morning, causing a great commotion among the little ones. To keep her sanity Rose gave into the pleas of six-year-old Joey and opened the parlour door wide enough for him to see Mr. Everett wrestling the tree into its pot. Her attempt did little to calm the excited boy, however; and long after Mr.

Everett had driven off, Joey was still chanting, "Our twee is here. Our twee is here. Santa's coming."

Much to Ora's disgust and Rose's disappointment, it was Dot who made the tree-trimming roster. "We'll never hear the end of it, you know," Ora said under her breath. She wasn't exaggerating. During supper Dot related in elaborate detail the vital role she seemed to have played.

"I can't wait for the day when she turns sixteen and they boot her out," Ora grumbled afterwards. "It'll be so peaceful around here, we'll think we died and went to Heaven."

Seven o'clock was the appointed time for them to gather in the parlour. A chorus of delighted oohs rippled across the room when they were finally ushered in. The tree stood in the corner by the French doors, as fine a specimen of nature's greenery as any on a Woolworth's greeting card. There was no fire lit in the grate, but the mantel had been decorated with spruce boughs and silvered pine cones, and two grand fir wreaths hung on the front windows.

And the window ledge! Tiny carved wooden houses nestled in soft mounds of cotton-wool snow; there were little shops, too, a wooden horse and sleigh, and a miniature snowman in a cotton-wool field. Clothespin people, dressed in winter coats, muffs, and hats, dotted two cinder paths. One path led up an incline to a painted white church; the other path sloped down to a pond on which tiny stick people were skating.

The children ignored the prim sofa and the uninviting chairs, choosing instead to sit in two semicircles on the floor in front of the tree. The old upright piano from the playroom had been called into service, and Matron sat at it now. The piano was in rough shape—from her dusting, Rose knew that Middle C was badly cracked and High D was missing altogether—and it hadn't been tuned in a dog's age, but that didn't deter Matron.

"Let's have a bit of singing, shall we?" she said. Rose was surprised at the animated expression on her face. Why, Matron looks almost pretty, she thought.

They started with "I Saw Three Ships" and "Deck the Halls." Despite the piano's shortcomings, Matron played quite skillfully, and Rose was impressed.

Olive opened the playroom door as soon as they'd finished "The First Noel." The crafts table had been pulled into the centre of the floor and on it sat two huge metal pitchers and a tray heaped high with molasses cookies.

"Treats," she said, gesturing toward it. "Cookies and hot apple cider. Help yourself. Merry Christmas."

They gorged on the cookies while Matron read "The Night before Christmas." Their plea for "another story—just one more," was firmly declined. "Eight-thirty," she said, clapping her hands in her annoying way. "Bedtime—and that means everyone."

Joey ran over to Olive and tugged at her apron, his small, thin face a study in determination.

"What do you want, little guy?" she asked.

"There'll be turkey tomorrow, won't there?"

"Turkey—for a bunch of rascals like you?" Olive winked at Rose. "I was planning to chase those two hens I got from the prison farm the other day into the pot. Soon as I chop off their heads, that is."

Aghast, Joey looked at Rose. "We can't eat hens," he wailed. "Hens are for laying eggs. I want turkey—turkey drumstick."

Olive laughed and headed for the kitchen with a tray of empty mugs, leaving Rose to console him. "Don't worry," she said, taking his hand. "Olive's only fooling. There'll be turkey for dinner, just you wait and see."

It was close to midnight before Rose tiptoed across the darkened bedroom and retrieved her locket from the back of the wardrobe. She fumbled with its clasp, her fingers shaking from nervousness and the room's chill, fastened the chain around her neck, and then crept back to the warmth of her bed.

A winter moon shone in on the still forms of her sleeping roommates. Rose lay in the arc of light, her head swirling in memories. There was Violet, making snow angels in the front yard; Daddy helping an unsteady Mr. McGinn down the front steps after they'd toasted the season; and Mama tucking them in on Christmas Eve.

If only she could have her mother back! Mama in the flesh, sitting on the side of the bed and singing "Silent Night" in her clear soprano voice. "Just like a lark, is my Kate," her father used to say.

Rose thumped at her pillow but her thoughts wouldn't go away. Was Violet awake and restless, on this, their first Christmas apart? Was she lonely, too; or so busy with the new baby that she hadn't a moment to think, let alone be sad? Rose hoped that Mrs. McGinn was wrong about Violet keeping the baby. Perhaps Violet would surprise everyone by getting married after all. In which case, she would surely come for Lily and her very soon.

Breakfast was an obligation; a necessity to suffer through. "Who in their right mind bothers with brown bread and porridge on Christmas morning," Ora said to Greta.

"Quit complaining and eat!" Greta ordered. "The presents don't start till everybody's finished. That's the rule."

Rose figured as much. In this house, not even Christmas Day was exempt.

The little ones were all eyes and whispers when they finally did parade into the parlour and saw a tall man in a Santa suit standing by the tree.

"Why isn't he back at the North Pole!"

"He hasn't finished delivering yet, silly goose. He's got the whole world, you know."

"That's not Santa! That's a man pretending."

All commentary evaporated the minute he began digging into his sack. Everyone got an orange, a bag of ribbon candy wrapped in cellophane, and a pair of home-knit socks. The wool socks were thick and warm but decidedly plain, knit in dark colours: brown, navy, wine, green.

The sack contained dolls, trucks, and building blocks, as well; and it wasn't any time before the swapping began, a practice that was overlooked for once by both Matron and Miss Duffy. Lily was delighted with her present—a Shirley Temple doll with flaxen ringlets and blue eyes that opened and closed—and, despite being approached with three or four offers of barter, managed to hold onto her treasure.

"We'll get a book or a game—you watch," Ora whispered. "The men from the church look after the Santa sack, and they don't know a thing about shopping for girls our age."

Rose's gift, a colourful edition of the latest *Girl's Annual*, proved Ora's prediction. Rose flipped hurriedly through its pages. The adventures of faraway British schoolgirls held little interest for her. A brush-and-comb set, or a small clock—something she could use every day—would have been much more to her liking.

After Santa left, Matron took over, distributing one wrapped present to each of them. "It'll be clothes," Ora explained. "The girls always get sweaters or good dresses, and the boys get shirts or long pants." Matron or Miss Duffy bought the gifts with money donated either by family members or by the Ladies' Committee.

Lily and Rose both received dresses: pale green, with three-quarter sleeves and a detachable pinafore for Lily; and blue corduroy, with a pleated skirt and a white collar edged in lace for Rose. The card on the package contained a thoroughly impersonal message: "Merry Christmas to a fine young lady."

Rose tried on her dress before putting it away that night. It was a good fit, no question, and she knew that she would have to wear it. But she so wished it had been given in love, not duty.

On Boxing Day, they trooped to the bottom of their hill and caught a number nine into the city's centre. Barrington Street was a downtown winter wonderland with snow piled high on the curbs, fir wreaths adorning every lamp post, and a massive tree standing in the middle of the Grand Parade. Most stores had Christmas scenes painted on their front windows: snowmen with carrot noses; carolers with lanterns; kneeling Wise Men with their camels.

The marquee at the Capitol Theatre announced their arrival in large, black letters. *Season's Greetings to the Orphanage Children. From Wood Brothers ~ Your Quality Clothing Store.* Rose cringed, anxious to get inside as quickly as possible. She loathed the curious glances they got whenever they were out in public. Knowing looks that spoke volumes. "She's got someone's secondhand coat on, poor thing. Isn't it a shame."

The matinee was preceded by free packets of popcorn

and a magic act. Joey was picked from the audience to hold the rabbit, and they all cheered when a man from the newspaper took his picture. The main feature, a musical romp with Shirley Temple and John Boles, was a fun-filled hour and a half. When it was over and the house lights came back on, the floor underneath their seats was completely covered with soggy popcorn wrappers, many of them in tatters from the melted snow off their boots.

Rose couldn't get Shirley Temple off her mind during the tram ride return. What a happy, smiling kid she was! Who wouldn't be, though, when you were the world's best-paid little darling, with plenty of money for tap dancing lessons, and hairdressers to curl your ringlets, and one shopping spree after another. Yes, little Shirley's life had to be just about peachy-cream perfect; a carbon-copy of the charmed life she portrayed in her movies. A winsome Curly Top dances and sings, plays matchmaker, helps her big sister land the handsome millionaire, and they all live happily ever after.

"That's it for Christmas," said Ora as they filed off the tram and made their way uphill against the biting northeast wind. "Turkey soup, squabbles over broken toys, then back to school and lessons. What a grind. Nothing much going on from now till Easter."

"Yeah," Rose said, shoving her hands deeper into her pockets.

Nothing much. The thought was a discouraging one.

Violet's First Visit

Rose leaned against the window casing and stared out at the leafless trees. Heavy rain earlier in the week had washed much of the snow away, but the temperature had dipped again overnight, leaving patches of ice dotting the frozen grass of the backyard. One of the boys had slipped and sprained his ankle going up to church that morning, prompting Matron to announce at dinner that outdoor play was cancelled. Those without Sunday visitors would have to amuse themselves inside instead.

The contrast between this Sunday and the previous one howled, dampening Rose's spirits, making her feel as bleak as the landscape outside the window. This time last week, she and Lily had been part of the Sunday excitement, sitting in the crowded front hall with Mrs. McGinn, catching up on the news, eating the treats that the good woman had brought for them. The twins had drawn pictures, too; and Mavis, bless her, had made a greeting card with a hand-printed verse inside it.

"Won't be long till my next visit," Mrs. McGinn had said when she left at four. "Give me a kiss, now, and don't be looking sad."

Rose stifled a sigh. She knew they could count on Mrs. McGinn: she was a woman of her word. But at this very moment on this January day, next month seemed farther away than next year. An endless succession of weeks; days and nights lived in the company of strangers.

For that was exactly how Rose viewed life here. Greta, Matron, Miss Duffy, and Olive were all strangers; women to be tolerated. People who "saw to" you; fleeting looks at the surface, never beneath it.

Greta, for instance, saw to your clean clothes; and Olive saw that you had three meals a day. Miss Duffy—or Matron if she wasn't too busy—saw to it that your report card was signed (a distinctly unpleasant experience if your performance had been unsatisfactory). But not one of them saw the real you. They didn't braid your hair in a special way or hear your spellings after supper; couldn't tell stories about the summer evenings when your father wheeled you up and down Gottingen Street in the carriage till you fell asleep. Here, you were a blur at best; at worst, invisible. Little more than a brief essay, filed in a folder and locked away in the metal cabinet in Matron's office.

About you, but never you.

Beyond the hedge at the back of the property Rose could see the water of the harbour and, closer in, a stretch of the lower road. A tram had pulled into its stop and two people—a man and a woman in winter coats and hats—were getting off. They stood side-by-side on the shoulder of the road, the man pointing with one gloved hand. A moment later he touched his hat in a farewell gesture and headed north, leaving the woman, a woollen scarf pulled up around her face, to cross the street on her own.

Rose watched the man's receding figure until he'd disappeared from view. He was probably going home; to a cozy front room, a hot cup of tea, a wife and children.

She visualized three children—all girls. Sisters, two of whom cuddled beside him on the sofa while the third stretched out on a mat by the hearth, a sleeping cat curled in her lap. Lucky girls who knew nothing about Sunday afternoon visitation, sitting on straight-backed chairs in the front hall, a picture of *Nelson Dying at Trafalgar* staring down at them from the opposite wall. Girls who would never be required to make the Sunday hugs and kisses last all week.

From behind her, Donny's voice broke into her reverie. "No! I want it! You get your own!" She turned to see him scowling at Herbie and clutching a battered red dump truck tight to his chest.

"Hey, you two! No fighting," Rose said. She hadn't the will to scold Donny, marvelling that he was actually alive after his bout with scarlet fever. During the first crucial weeks of his illness, Matron and Nurse Gregory had allowed him to keep a stuffed bear that he'd cried out for; but once the fever had broken and he was officially out of danger, the bear had been taken away and burned. She had seen it—a brown teddy with blue button eyes—covered with potato peelings in the garbage bin. "Don't touch," Olive had warned the boys in charge of burning trash in the backyard. "It's filled with germs."

"I'm gonna be a truck driver when I grow up," Donny announced to Rose. "Then I can drive far, far away. To Africa."

"Good idea," she replied gently. Leaving, getting away, was a common theme here in this house. The question was when. And how.

Lily, kneeling on the floor by the piano bench, was busy sorting through a box of doll clothes that had been sent over by the church ladies. Castoffs from girls who'd either outgrown their dolls or received new ones. Privileged girls.

"We're going out for a walk today," Lily was explaining to her adopted Shirley Temple baby. "And you need to look decent." Lily struggled with the lace-edged bonnet, wrestling to secure it over the doll's stiff, artificial ringlets. Rose, watching, smiled. *A lady wears a hat for an afternoon outing.* Echoes of their mother's early teaching.

On the floor next to Lily, Sara, the youngest girl, was patiently winding a ragged strip of flannelette sheeting around a doll with empty eye sockets. Blind Mona, the doll was called. Rose knew the story. Herbie, in one of his tantrums, had poked her eyes in with a stick. "They're in her stomach," he'd solemnly told her. "If you hold her upside down and give her a shake, you can hear them rattle."

Rose would have avoided the doll at all costs. In addition to its empty eye sockets, the china face was mottled with ugly green blotches, and a tuft of hair at the back of its head was missing. Sara, surprisingly, seemed to overlook its shortcomings, having chosen it over two others still on the shelf.

It had gone three by the grandfather clock in the parlour when Greta appeared. "Rose, Matron wants you and Lily in the small sitting room," she said. "Go along, now. I'll get somebody else to keep a watch on this lot."

The summons was unusual, but Rose did as she was told. She'd learned that there was no point in querying Greta. "Go" meant go and "stop" meant stop, and you'd better be prepared to respond instantly to either command.

With Lily's hand in hers, she proceeded along the back hall to the central passageway. It was packed, as usual, with Sunday guests: fathers, grown-up sisters and brothers, aunts and uncles, occupied every chair that the boys had set out. The children—perched on laps or on the floor beside their guests—were talking and laughing, devouring the candy treats that were a Sunday trademark.

"I like chocolates," Lily whined, eyeing one of the open boxes. "You know I do."

"Shush up, Lily," Rose admonished, embarrassed at the child's pleading. Morash girls weren't brought up to beg. "And mind your manners."

The sitting room, situated at the left of the front entrance, was a small, rarely used chamber. The sympathy room, Ora called it. "Matron put the minister and Pa and me and my oldest sister in there when my mom died. I cried all through the prayers. It was awful. I told Greta I hated that room and didn't want to go there ever again, but she said I was being silly and I needed to get over such nonsense."

Rose shared Ora's distaste for the gloomy chamber, and was always relieved when her turn to dust and sweep it was over for another month. The furniture was old and smelled of mothballs and mold. Chairs with spindly legs, a love seat upholstered in a shiny, slippery sateen; a sickly looking fern that shed dead bits on the carpet; and a brass bellows, propped up against an unused fireplace.

Two pictures, both depressing, hung on the floral patterned wallpaper. One, above the mahogany secretary, was a large painting of a peasant couple standing in a ploughed field. They were leaning on their hoes, with their hands folded in prayer. In the background a church steeple rose against a grey, threatening sky.

The second picture was a smallish black-and-white photograph. *Orphanage Children—1917* was written in the white space above the frame. "They died in the explosion," Ora had explained. "Every single one of them. Trapped in the basement when the house fell on top of them. Pa remembers it. He said they probably burned to a crisp."

At the panelled oak door, Rose tapped hesitantly and waited. *Nothing sad, please. Nothing sad. Nothing sad.*

"Come in," Matron called out. Rose, with Lily in tow, stepped inside.

Matron was seated at the mahogany secretary, facing them. A dark-haired woman, her back to them, sat opposite, her white woollen scarf flung carelessly over the arm of the chair.

"Hi Rosie. Hi Lily," the woman said, turning. "If you don't look like a couple of surprised little monkeys."

"I knew you'd come," Lily shouted, hurling herself into the outstretched arms. "I just knew it!"

"Visiting finishes at four. No exceptions."

Was that Matron's voice? It seemed very far off, like the church steeple in the painting. Rose's face was buried in the green woollen coat, and, beside her, Lily was squealing, "You came. You came."

Violet—their sister—was laughing. The old, familiar laugh that Rose knew so well.

An hour simply wasn't enough time. There were a hundred questions to ask; a hundred more to answer.

"I've been so worried," Rose said after they'd calmed down a bit. "I thought that you'd died from TB after all and they weren't telling us."

Violet shook her head and laced her fingers through Rose's. "Not me, Rosie. I'm too young to die, and too bad. I'll be around for a good long while. Trust me."

"What about—you know—the baby?"

"He was born healthy," Violet replied, her face sombre. "But he's gone now; they took him from me when he was a week old."

"You'll get him back, won't you? When you get married?" The baby couldn't be gone for good. There had to be a husband on the horizon, ready to make everything right.

"No, Rose. The baby's gone forever. You mustn't think about him anymore. And there's no husband, either. At least, not the kind that I'd want."

"When you're older you'll get married," Rose persisted.

"You're pretty, and smart, too. All the boys liked you at school. You know they did."

Violet shrugged. "Yeah, they liked me all right. Liked me too much. Nope—there won't be any husbands for a good long time, believe me. I'm holding out for a rich old geizer—someday." She flashed Rose a short, hard smile. "It's the money train that counts from now on, Rosie. No money, no kissy."

She leaned down and nuzzled at Lily's ear.

"Right, Lily mine? No candy, no kissy?"

Giggling, Lily jerked her head away. "I want to go on a train," she said, pulling on Violet's sleeve. "Let's."

"You don't want much, do you?" Violet replied. "But sure, I'll take you on a train trip someday."

"When's someday?" Lily demanded. "When?"

"When you're older," Rose replied. Her voice sounded falsely cheerful, even to her own ears, and Lily, her head resting against Violet's shoulder, looked doubtful.

"Enough about trains," Violet said. "We haven't got a lot of time today. That sawed-off little runt who answers the door will be chasing me out before you know it. I want to hear more about you two. Do you get enough to eat? Are they treating you okay?"

Rose did her best to tell Violet how it was. The meals were all right, even though there was never any lemon pie and no brown sugar for the porridge. Yes, it was noisy and crowded. Lonely, too, especially at night after the lights went out. It bothered her that Lily wasn't allowed to take her rag doll to bed with her. School? It wasn't so bad. Rose liked music and sewing class best.

"I hear Mrs. McGinn's been to see you," Violet said.

"Only once," Rose replied. "She had to get special permission. She's coming again next month, though. She promised."

"Salt of the earth, that woman," Violet said, looking pensive. "I've got a lot of time for her, even if she is a Mick. She was good to Mama, and I won't be soon forgetting it."

Rose nodded, watching a grey-haired man down the line of chairs who was bouncing a little girl on his knee. I'll bet he's her grandfather, she thought in envy.

"I wish we three sisters could be together again." There, she'd said it out loud. Her last waking thought of the day; her recurring dream at night.

"That's not likely to happen very soon, Rosie," Violet replied quietly. "Not without a small miracle."

Rose bit down on her lip. Why did it require a miracle? Couldn't they make it happen, if they wanted it enough? She wished she could say so, but something in Violet's face prevented her.

"Do you have a job?" she asked instead. Violet's beret and her green wool coat looked new. She must be making decent wages, Rose thought. If she saves up, surely we can get a house and be together.

"Yeah, I work," Violet replied. "In a uniform factory. It's a drudge job but it pays the bills. I'll stay till something better comes along."

"Do you live in a house like this?" Rose ventured next.

"I did for a while," Violet said. "Till after the baby. They had in mind to send me out as a maid, but I squashed that idea. Scrubbing floors and cleaning up other people's dirt isn't my cup of tea. After I got the sewing job, I looked for a room and found one not far from the factory. It's clean and cheap. I give the old lady a hand on the weekends to help with the rent. It'll do for now."

A factory job and a rented room. It was a long way from Rose's dream of a house together.

"I'll be back in two weeks," Violet said when the buzzer sounded. "The battle-axe told me twice a month, providing I follow her stupid rules." She pulled on her mitts and bent down to hug Lily. "You be a good girl, you hear? Next time, treats."

To Rose, "Brrr—" she said. "It's cold as the dickens out there. I don't relish waiting for a tram, let me tell you."

"If only you could stay the night," Rose replied, knowing how silly the words sounded, even to her ears.

"Ye Gods! I don't think so," Violet said, grimacing and adjusting her beret on her glossy, dark curls. She pointed to a plaque on the vestibule wall. "I couldn't handle any joint that sticks up verses like that one," she said. "These places are all the same, so help me. Long on talk and short on action. They might actually get past the Pearly Gates if they would practise what they preach. But they don't, so they won't."

When Rose could no longer see the back of Violet's green coat, she closed the outer door. *Good thing Greta's not around,* she thought. *She'd have my hide for letting in the cold air.*

The murmur of voices and the clinking of china wafted along the empty corridor from the back of the house. The duty girls were starting to set up for the evening meal and would be wondering where she was. She didn't feel like joining them, yet, however. Instead, she stood reading the verse that had caught Violet's criticism and her scorn.

Visit, O Lord, this humble habitation and keep safe all who dwell herein. Bestow upon us Thy bounty and blessings, and help us live in peace and joy all the days of our lives. This we ask in the name of our Savior, Jesus Christ. Amen.

Violet was right. Flowery words, but what did they really add up to? Rose couldn't imagine any of the Founding Fathers wanting to stay the night in this ark of a place; not if they had grander houses awaiting them, beyond the Hill, in the rich part of town. Certainly, the committee ladies who arrived once a month for their two-hour meeting and a cup of tea with Matron soon scooted away afterwards; off the hook, so to speak, for another thirty days.

Peace and joy. Well, that was debatable. As for bounty, if it came at all, it was in the form of making do, marking time. A pervasive sense of waiting for something better, later on, beyond this place.

Violet Tells

Violet arrived with a box of chocolates and two knitted caps on her second visit.

"Cute, don't you think? I bought them from an old woman at the market," Violet said. She tied the red woollen toque under Lily's chin and laughed, watching as Lily admired herself in the glass insets at the side of the front door.

"Oh, Violet, you don't have to bring us presents," Rose said, distressed. "We haven't got anything for you."

"I know I don't have to; but I want to," Violet replied. "And, since the only thing better than chocolates is a new chapeau, I brought both." She grabbed at the pompoms on Lily's cap and gave them a twirl. "Right, missy?"

"Yes," Lily agreed, nodding vigorously. Squatting on the floor with the chocolate box on her knees and her cheeks bulging, she looked like an overgrown squirrel in a nightcap.

"Lily," Rose said, irritated. "Don't stuff your mouth like that! It's not polite."

"Oh, let her be," Violet said. "If I had the Warden's bunch rationing sugar like you say they do, I'd be the same way."

"Do shush," Rose whispered nervously. "We'll be in trouble if Matron hears that you were calling her names."

"Too bad," Violet said. "If the shoe fits, wear it, I say."

"Do you like my new dress?" Rose asked, eager to steer the conversation onto safer ground. Violet was wearing new snowboots with fur-trimmed tops, and, under her green wool coat, a cardigan trimmed with pearl buttons.

"Yeah, I do," Violet replied. "Pretty shade, that deep blue. Bet a dime it didn't come from a box of hand-me-downs."

"No, it didn't," Rose said. I got it for Christmas. Lily got one, too. From Aunt Edna and Uncle Earle. Matron said they sent the money for them."

"Kid me not!" Violet replied. "Old tight arse Edna. I find that hard to believe."

How blue Violet's eyes were! Deep cornflower blue, like their mother's had been.

"Must be his doing, the old goat," Violet went on. She leaned in closer, her voice lowering. "Listen here, Rose. I want you to keep your distance. From both of them, and especially him. Got it? Take it from me, he's no Santa Claus, and no Easter Bunny either."

They talked about clothes and school and what was playing at the movies and, for the remainder of Violet's visit, things seemed fine. But Rose could sense an underlying tension in Violet. Her voice took on an edgy quality and there was a strain in her laughter that made Rose nervous.

The unsettled feeling stayed with her after Violet had departed. Rose helped with the supper clean-up, sat with her books during study period, and still the feeling persisted.

Memories of Aunt Edna and Uncle Earle flooded over her. Of their lives in the "before" time.

In those days their aunt and uncle drove into city every other Sunday during the good weather, arriving in time for dinner at noon and staying until after four o'clock tea. Once the meal was over, the men made for the front room and Violet took Lily up for her nap, leaving Rose in the kitchen with their mother and Aunt Edna. The women talked while Rose cleared the table and stacked the dishes for washing. Or, more precisely, Edna talked and their mother listened. The stories were endlessly boring. Who was about to be married in Chester; who was sick, and who'd died.

Rose stayed just long enough to complete her task before escaping to the front room. She didn't much like her aunt, a bossy, opinionated woman who loved ordering people about. Rose, however, followed her mother's example in dealing with Edna, realizing early that diplomacy worked far better than confrontation. Not so, Violet. Edna infuriated Violet, and Violet didn't mince words in telling her off.

"I don't have to do what you say," Violet would retort if Edna started on her. "I'm not your property." Her refusal to put up with Edna didn't help their mother, who was then obliged to listen to the tiresome lectures.

"That girl's impossible, Kate. Bill's more to blame than you, of course. He indulges her; you know very well he does. What she needs is a firmer hand. If she were my daughter, I'd soon see to it that she changed her ways."

Violet always flounced off in a huff, unwilling to hear the standard pronouncement. Later, to Rose, she would mutter, "She'll never lord it over me, the fat old cow. Never."

Uncle Earle, on the other hand, was big, jovial, and easygoing. After he'd eaten—two helpings of everything and three cups of tea—he invariably settled on the sofa in the front room and, with his feet up on the hassock, prepared to indulge in his after-dinner cigar.

"One of my few pleasures," he would say with a wink and a grin, unwrapping the cellophane and slicing off the cigar's tip with his penknife. "Edna can't stand these things, but I'm not about to give 'em up, supposing I have to sit out in the snowbank."

Rose, watching the familiar procedure, waited for him to pass her the embossed gold seal from the wrapping. She liked to slip it onto her finger and pretend that it was a wedding ring.

Until he took sick, her father joined in, savouring the tobacco as the thick, bluish smoke and pungent odour filled the room. But, when his coughing spasms worsened and, he was no longer able to tolerate tobacco, he would make for the front verandah or the hammock in the backyard, leaving Rose alone with her uncle.

It was Earle who came up with the game he called Circus Rider. Privately, Rose thought she was too big for such silliness, but he was so insistent that she didn't have the heart to say no. "Up you come," he would say, patting his knee, and she would climb on, doing her best to keep from toppling off while he jigged her up and down, increasing the pace until he was panting, his breath coming in little gasps. The game was short and always ended in the same way. He groaned and fell back against the cushions while she slid, giggling, onto the sofa beside him.

"Such a good girl," he would say afterwards. "Really sweet." He was perspiring by then, rivulets that ran down his neck and soaked into his shirt collar. He would mop his face with his handkerchief and then get up awkwardly and head for the stairs. "Need a drink of water," he would say to Rose. "Be right back."

He came back down after ten minutes or so, looking no less hot and rumpled, and made straight for the kitchen.

"Where's Bill?" he would usually ask her mother. "The girls are tired of entertaining an old fellow like me."

His words puzzled Rose. After all, *he* was the one who got so tired, not her. And Violet was always upstairs minding Lily and never got to play with them. As for a drink of water, it would have made far more sense for him to go straight to the kitchen and get one. Her mother kept a full pitcher on the top shelf of the icebox.

She didn't complain, however, having learned that there

was money coming her way. Usually a couple of quarters, slipped into her hand as he was leaving.

"For a treat, my Rosie," he would say in a whisper. "And no telling, or your mother will say that I'm spoiling you."

Early on, she made up her mind not to spend her money on treats. Instead, she put the coins in the small change purse that she kept in the top drawer of her dresser. She knew exactly what she would do when she had ten dollars saved. She would buy a silver locket. They had lovely ones displayed on a blue velvet tray in the window of a jeweller on Barrington Street.

After their father's death, however, and with their mother's health deteriorating, things grew steadily worse. Edna and Earle stopped coming to the house, and money was tight. The full gravity of the situation hit Rose when she came home from school one day and found the empty money can on the kitchen counter. Upstairs, a frantic Violet was checking the pockets of every garment in their mother's clothes closet.

"What are you doing?" Rose asked from the doorway, dreading the answer.

"Oh, Rosie," Violet said, sinking onto the bed. "We're out of medicine for Mama and we need groceries, too. There's no money in the tin box, and I can't find a cent anywhere in this house. I've been through everything. I already sold Daddy's gold cufflinks, and his watch went to a man in the pawnshop months ago. Lord God, I never thought it would come to this."

"Don't swear—please," Rose said. "I've got money we can use."

"Money? How much?"

"Over six dollars. In my change purse. I'll go get it."

She came back with the money, pressed it into Violet's hand. "Go get the medicine. Please. For Mama."

"How'd you get all this," Violet demanded, counting the coins and looking up at her.

Rose hesitated. She wasn't supposed to tell, but surely it wouldn't hurt. After all, Violet was her sister.

"Uncle Earle gave it to me. He said not to tell."

"Uncle Earle?" A strange look came over Violet's face.

"Yes. For playing Circus Rider."

"Circus Rider?"

"It was a game we used to play on Sunday afternoons," Rose said. "You were upstairs minding Lily or you could have played too. I hope he gave you money. Did he?"

Violet's laugh was like gunshot in the still room.

"Yeah, I got money all right. Not enough for the job I was doing, though. Not nearly enough."

It seemed a strange answer. Violet didn't have a job; she was only fourteen. But then Violet often said things that Rose didn't understand.

Rose Remembers

On the last Sunday in Lent Violet arrived with a battered cardboard photo-holder stuffed into her satchel. "You wanted to see pictures, so here they are," Violet said after they'd got settled. With Lily clamouring to "see the babies," they sat and looked through the assortment together.

There were several black-and-white snapshots: the family feeding the ducks in the park; Rose and Violet making a snowman; Lily in her carriage; their father in his garden; their mother in a new spring hat. The back of each was dated in their mother's fine, neat script.

The other pictures were formal photographer shots. A wedding photo of their parents, with their two faces staring solemnly into the camera lens. There was one of Rose in a long christening gown, and another, badly waterstained, of Violet in the same lace-edged dress and bonnet. The last was of Aunt Edna with Lily, her goddaughter, on her lap.

"Where's the silver frame the wedding picture was in?" Rose asked. It had always stood in its place of honour on the lefthand side of the mantel, flanked by two candlesticks.

"Gone," Violet said. "We needed the money, so I sold the frames along with the other silver."

Always the same reason. No money, no money. Rose hated being poor.

"There must be more pictures," she insisted, a catch in her voice. "The big album—where is it?"

"There are no more pictures, Rose," Violet replied firmly. "The album was real leather; Daddy had made it for us. It went with the other things in the sale. I took the pictures out and put them in a box for safekeeping. I don't know what became of the box, though. I looked and looked after Mama died but I couldn't find it."

"It's not fair—all our pictures gone, too. It's like we never existed."

Violet shoved the photos back into her satchel, a grim look on her face. "Fair or not, that's the way it is," she replied. "Better get used to it. We might've had silver frames once upon a time, but we've got squat now. The pickings are slim and the path's pretty rocky. So be careful and watch your step."

Rose did try, but she could not settle down to her lessons that evening. The teacher was giving them a geography test in the morning and Rose needed to do well on it, but the Dominion of Canada and its major waterways would not stay in focus. The St. Lawrence River, the Great Lakes, Hudson Bay, the Bering Sea, all took a back seat to what Violet had said earlier.

Watch your step. If the shoe fits, wear it, were expressions that Violet would have picked up from their father. She'd spent a lot of time at the shop with him on Saturdays, happily sweeping up the cuttings, putting the finished boots and shoes on the rack, running little errands.

Sometimes Rose went along too, but the shop didn't hold the same appeal for her. It smelled of leather and boot black, and she had to edge between the machines to avoid getting her dress mussed or her hands soiled.

No smells and no amount of dirt or grease seemed to bother Violet, though. In fact, she told everyone that she'd like to learn the trade and work with her father when she was old enough. Rose thought the idea of a woman shoemaker very weird. Who but Violet would come up with such an odd notion? It was fine to wear pretty shoes like the ones their father made for them, but the last thing in the world Rose could imagine would be to make them.

Certainly, none of the maidens in her fairy-tale books—Rapunzel, Snow White, Cinderella—had ever hankered to be shoemakers. On the contrary, each of those girls wanted to escape lives of drudgery and dirt. Rose's plan was to follow in their footsteps; success measured in glass slippers, a pumpkin coach, and a dashingly handsome Prince Charming. Anything less was a mark of failure; it just wouldn't do.

Rose blinked and shook her head. She *must* get back to the map of Canada in her geography book. What a huge country Canada was, stretching north and south, east and west, for thousands of miles, making her feel very small and insignificant. Where would Lily and Violet and she end up, with no parents and no money? Sharing a teepee (or was it a wigwam) with the prairie Indians? Or in an igloo—Lord help them—on the shores of Baffin Island?

Almost everything from their old life, including the family album, had now been lost or sold. Only their mother's silver locket and a handful of pictures remained. Who, or what, could they claim to be with such slim pickings? A person needed to come from somewhere, from something, to become *somebody*. Didn't they?

Pushing the map away, Rose opened one of her scribblers to a blank page and wrote the following names, one under the other: Rose Mildred, Violet Katherine, and Lily Edna.

In the beginning, they *were* somebody. In the beginning, there was a white house, two parents, three sisters, and a cat. A complete life. A visible existence.

Rose Mildred was the middle girl born to Eva Katherine and George William Morash. She loved her name, Rose, but had never cared for Mildred. Her mother told her she was named after a cousin from Windsor Forks who'd gone out West, married a well-to-do rancher, and then chosen not to keep in touch. Such a waste, carrying around a stranger's name. That's how Rose had always thought of Mildred—as a faceless, uncaring stranger. Not part of Rose's life in any way.

Violet got Katherine, after their grandmother, Katherine Taylor. They had never known Gramma Taylor; she'd died a year or so after their own mother was married. As for Grandfather Taylor, he'd been killed during the last year of the Great War.

Lily was Aunt Edna's namesake. Poor, unlucky Lily, saddled with the burden of living up to (or down to, according to Violet) the name of a woman they disliked so much. Violet always chanted "Ed-na, na, na-na, na," behind their aunt's back.

Their father had chosen the flower names. Lily, after the plants on the altar table at Easter; Violet for the little patch that grew in the shade of the backyard hedge; and Rose because she'd arrived the week that the June climbers were starting to bud. "You were less than a day old when I took you out to the rose trellis," her father told her. "I tucked one of the buds into your blanket."

There had been two brothers, as well. Both died when they were babies. George came down with pneumonia when he was three months old, and little Edgar got whooping cough before his first birthday. They lay in unmarked graves near their mother and father's plot, graves that had, over the years, become completely obliterated by the wild grass that grew there.

Rose had made a vow to herself that when she was out working, with money saved, she would have white marble markers erected for her parents and for the two little boys. That their resting places were hidden by scrub grass and marked only by wooden crosses that could not possibly withstand years of rain and snow and neglect was horrible. Nobody should be forgotten, overlooked, like that. Nobody.

On the day of their mother's funeral, her legs and feet numb from the cold, Rose stood, shivering, beside the open grave. The minister, his black cloak swirling around his legs from the wind, sprinkled ashes on the casket. "Ashes to ashes and dust to dust," he said. He nodded to Violet, who stepped forward and placed a single white carnation on the casket's lid.

The white petals fluttered in the wind, reminding Rose of angel wings. Was it too early for their mother's soul to have left her body; to have found its way up, up, into the clouds and beyond? How long would it be until their pretty, dark-haired mother, now lying so still and white in an ivory lace dress, was reduced to ashes? Months—or years?

Once the casket was lowered into the waiting wooden box, Rose knew what the next step would be. The gravediggers would nail the box shut and begin the task of filling in the hole. Would the box keep out the worms and the beetles? Violet would know the answers, but Rose wasn't about to ask her. She was too afraid of what the answers might be.

As soon as the other mourners had departed, Uncle Earle took Violet aside. "I think we can work out an arrangement," he'd said, one of his paw-shaped hands resting on the sleeve of her blouse. "You just leave it to me."

"No, thanks," Violet replied, pulling her arm away and rubbing the spot where his hand had been. "I can keep house fine. We can manage."

"Don't be so hasty, my girl," Uncle Earle murmured, his florid face paler than Rose had ever seen it. "You haven't any money, and you're not old enough to be in charge. You know that."

"I'm old enough for plenty," was Violet's reply. "And that's something that *you* know about."

"If I get asked to recite the nine-times table, I'm in trouble," Rose moaned to Ora when study hour was over.

"Hey, don't you worry a thing about it," Ora replied. "I don't know it either. Anyway, there's more to life than school. Why they even bother with most of what they teach us is beyond me. It's not as if we need maps or the nine-times table to keep house. We'd be a lot better off with a good cookbook. Pa always says that."

Rose hoped that Ora's father was right. It was a gamble, though. Supposing they came to find out that the nine-times table was darn important after all.

Exit One for Violet

"Don't go! Please don't. Stay here with us."

Rose knew she was begging, but she couldn't help herself.

"Stop it, Rose," Violet said, her voice a blend of impatience and anger. "It only makes it harder. I have to—can't you see that?"

Why couldn't she see that? Was it because she didn't believe that Violet *had* to.

That, deep down, she suspected the real reason Violet was going was because she wanted to. Violet, the restless one, was bored and needed a change.

It was a beautiful spring day and they were outside, seated side-by-side on a bench in what was known as the pavilion but which was, in fact, little more than a grassy knoll on the north side of the house. The younger girls, Lily among them, were amusing themselves on the swings, leaving the boys jostling for a turn at the wheel of the old jalopy that someone had hauled to the property and parked by the upper fence. Around the World the boys called their game, pretending, when their turn came, that they could drive the car wherever they chose.

Rose stared at the boys, blinking back her tears. The little fellows were hollering like banshees, quite unaware that Violet—the sister that Rose had counted on—was leaving. Going far away. To Boston. Without Lily and her.

"But what about our plan? Our house—being together?" Even as she spoke, Rose knew that the plan was always hers; never Violet's.

"Someday, Rose. Someday. But first, I've got to make real money. And the States is the place for that."

Violet's friend, Maureen, had sold her on the plan. Maureen knew a fellow who worked in a big hotel on Cape Cod. He could put in a word for them, get them on as chambermaids or, better still, waitresses in the coffee shop. The money was fantastic, he claimed. Rich people everywhere, ready to throw dollar bills at you just for serving them breakfast, making beds, holding doors open.

"We've got hotels here," Rose said.

"Here! Don't kid me. I don't stand a snowball's chance in this hick city. My only hope is to go where the action is."

"How long till we see you again?"

"I dunno, Rose. Honest I don't. It might take me a year to get worked in, till I get a vacation."

"A year!"

Don't even sigh. Violet will be mad if you do.

"I'll write you, Rose," Violet said. "I'll send a postcard on the way down. And letters as soon as I'm settled. I promise."

It would have to do. Violet had made up her mind.

Lily had finished on the swings and came running over, plopping herself down at their feet. With a quick look at Rose, Violet eased herself off the bench and sat on the grass beside Lily.

"Missy mine," she said, ruffling Lily's hair. "Your big sister's going away for a while. On a trip."

"A trip? Where?"

"To Boston."

"Where's Boston?" Lily demanded.

"In the States."

"Is it far?"

"Quite far. Hundreds and hundreds of miles."

"Oh," Lily looked from Violet to Rose and back again. "On the train?"

"Yes. Two trains, in fact."

"You said you'd take me on a train," Lily said.

"I know I did. And when you're big, I'll do just that."

"Rose, too?"

"Rose too."

Maybe, Rose thought. When Violet makes enough money to suit her. Meantime, we wait and wait. Till our ship comes in; till the cows come home.

Violet had first visited them on a cold January afternoon, nearly four months earlier. She'd come to see them half a dozen times since then. Rose had kept track, making a pencil mark on the back of the wardrobe after each visit. Seven pencil marks, recorded meticulously as the snow melted, replaced by crocus and hyacinths, pussy willows and daffodils, forsythia and mayflowers. Lucky number seven.

In a few days, Violet would be celebrating her sixteenth birthday. Rose had discovered a patch of mayflowers in the vacant lot next door; had wrapped them in a piece of wax paper, and was planning to give them to Violet today. It was her small way of continuing the tradition that their father had started. A pot of lilies on April 30th; a bunch of violets on May 15; and, on June 26th, two roses, placed in a cut-glass vase on the dining-room table.

How life had changed them since those happy, safe times. Violet had grown into a defiant young woman who had every intention of doing as she pleased. Even as a child, Violet had never been one to hang back, uncertain. She'd always gone ahead and done the things that she considered were necessary; fitting people into the plan if it suited her, tossing them aside if they didn't. Now Rose and Lily were to be added to her casualty list.

Rose tried not to think of the dream she'd been having lately; a dream that refused to go away and leave her alone. In the dream, Violet walks along a narrow dirt track that snakes through a great, dark forest. With Lily pulling at her skirt, Rose hurries to catch up. But her feet are heavy and she cannot make any headway. She reaches out, desperate to grab hold of Violet's arm, and stumbles. When she rights herself, Violet is gone; swallowed up in a swirl of mist.

Each time, Rose has awakened from the dream trembling, straining to hear a cry, a sigh, an echo. But there is only the sound of her own ragged breathing mingling with the steady inhaling and exhaling of girls in the beds around her.

Matron's Marriage

Rose came down the stairs hurriedly. It was her week on breakfast duty and she was late, having lingered too long at a back window, watching as an outward-bound freighter made its way through the Narrows channel. She wondered if it was heading across the ocean for England. Since war had been declared, the activity in the harbour and the Basin had steadily increased. Although ships came and went at all times of the day and night, more often than not they slipped their moorings under cover of the darkness and were gone when you woke up in the morning. The news-papers were filled with worrying reports of advancing German forces and of Hitler's plan to conquer all of Europe; and the casualty lists were appearing with grim frequency.

A sailor went to sea, sea, sea / To see what he could see, see, see / But all that he could see, see, see / Was the bottom of the bright blue sea, sea, sea.

Rose had never shared Lily's enthusiasm for the child-hood chant, or for the hand-clapping that went with it. To her, any sailor who could see the bottom of the bright blue sea was a drowned sailor.

As she rounded the newel post, preparing herself for the tongue-lashing she'd be bound to receive from Olive, she saw Ora beckoning to her from the dining room.

"Rose! Come here. I've got something to tell you."

"What is it?" Rose asked. "I'm late. Olive's going to throttle me."

"Oh bosh on Olive," Ora exclaimed. "This is important. It's about Matron."

"Matron—" Rose asked. "What about her?"

"Hold onto your hat at this—she's leaving!"

"Leaving?" Rose tried to process this information, to see the logic in it, like the theorems they were doing in Geometry.

Matrons are fixtures.

Matrons don't leave.

Miss Crooks is a Matron.

Therefore, Miss Crooks doesn't leave.

"You hoo!" Ora was snapping her fingers in front of Rose's nose. "Come back, come back!"

"What do you mean, she's leaving?" Rose asked.

"Leaving, leaving! Like 'toodles,' bye bye, so long."

"But why?" Rose asked. "Is she sick?"

It was the best Rose could do. The only people who left this house were the children: those that were old enough to be placed in work; the few who ran away and couldn't be found; the unfortunates who got into trouble and were banished to the Industrial School or the School for Wayward Girls in Truro. Occasionally, one died; like little Sara, last year; wrapped in a white sheet and carried out of the infirmary room by two men in dark suits.

"No!" Ora was almost at her bursting point.

"She's getting married!"

"Married?" Rose's head whirred. Married meant a husband, family. People related to you, not cast-offs from other families. Your *own* children. No! That could never be—not the children part—not for Miss Crooks. She was too old, too remote. She wasn't "mother." She was Matron. Period.

They got through breakfast, after a fashion; and later, lunch and supper. But the whispering and conjecture ran rampant all day. Olive finally gave up on her "shush up, girls" and "get a move on." As for Miss Crooks, she appeared oblivious to the rumblings and glances. She ate her meal, drank her tea, and led the same two graces as though the world was turning on its axis as it should.

Miss Crooks, personification of non-change. *I will not change. You will not change. We will not change.* But change, like a sudden windstorm, had caught Miss Crooks in its vortex. It was blowing her away.

The conjecture continued unabated into the next day, and the following one. Leah had known first, from an aunt who'd picked up the tidbit at her church group. There were no details as to who "he" was, but it didn't stop the older girls from imagining.

"She's such an old maid. Who'd want her?" was the general consensus.

"He's probably as ugly as a toad."

"Maybe he *was* a toad. Maybe she kissed him and he turned into a real man."

"I'll bet he's ancient. With a long white beard that's stained from his chewing tobacco."

"Think of the babies they'll have. Little prissy missy girls who sit still all day long."

"And nasty, ugly toad boys with warts. Hopping around, getting underfoot till Matron goes after them with the broom and whacks their ugly little behinds."

Each ludicrous suggestion was followed by sniggers and stifled laughter. To Rose, though, the idea of Matron being married was difficult enough to wrestle with, but the thought of her sleeping in a marriage bed, engaging in the activities that produced babies, was too much of a stretch.

"She's too dignified, Ora. Too proper."

"Oh, I don't know," Ora replied. "You'd be surprised what an old-maid might do when the lights are out. I'll bet you Matron will be mighty happy to lift up her nightgown and oblige after all these years of sitting on the shelf."

"Oh Ora, do stop!" Rose begged, putting her hands over her ears. "I can't stand it!"

Miss Crooks announced her departure on Thursday evening. A hush descended upon the room as all eyes turned toward her. As usual, she was sparing with words. "I wish to inform you that I will be leaving you tomorrow."

Herbie, as clumsy as ever, took that very moment to knock his spoon on the floor, and hung his head in shame as it clattered against the floorboards. Matron waited till the noise subsided, and then went on.

"I am to be married this coming weekend, and will be moving to Windsor with my clergyman husband." There was a small pause as her eyes swept about the room. "Miss Duffy is to be your new Matron. She will take excellent care of you, as I have always tried to do. She deserves your continued obedience. Make her proud of you." With that, she pushed back her chair and left the table.

Rose dreamed of Miss Crooks that night; a smiling Miss Crooks who ran down a circular staircase and into a waiting golden coach. Rose couldn't make out the prince's face, but she could see Miss Crook's triumphant expression as she leaned out of the coach's window. She waved and waved her lace hankie until she and the coach were swallowed up in the clouds of dust kicked up by six magnificent white horses.

The prince arrived to claim his prize after dinner on Friday. Miss Duffy granted them permission to stay and wave goodbye, and the entire household stood on the front steps, watching two of the older boys wrestle Matron's trunk onto the roof of the old Ford.

Everyone strained for a good look at the bridegroom. Neither prince nor toad, he was a slightly built, unremarkable-looking man, in a black suit and clerical collar.

"It figures that he'd be a minister," Ora murmured. "After all, where else does she ever go to meet a man." She grinned and lowered her voice. "I heard my Uncle Fred tell my brother that ministers are men, too. They can get their pants down and their peckers up, just like anybody else."

The girls standing beside her tittered and Miss Duffy, hearing the laughter, threw them one of her dagger looks.

"I bet he's a widower with a backload of kids," Leah whispered. "Needs a woman to look after them, and she's the ticket."

Rose refrained from comment. A marriage of convenience, people called it. One wants a husband; the other needs a wife. Put the *want* and the *need* together and—presto—you've got a marriage.

They clapped when Matron emerged, dressed in the same navy suit and hat that she wore to church. Rose was appalled. She should have bought a new outfit to go away in, Rose thought. After all, how often does a person get married.

There were no farewell kisses. At the car, Matron turned and waved, and then climbed quickly into the front seat. One of the boys closed the door, the minister (Rose could NOT think of him as Matron's fiancé) started the engine, and the car pulled away. It was only then that they saw the shoe. It dangled from the back bumper, below a cardboard sign on which someone had printed: *Getting Married. Finally. Yippee.*

Olive laughed, and even Miss Duffy smiled. "I wouldn't want to guess which of you came up with that idea," Olive said, wiping at her eyes with her apron.

"Off you go, then," Miss Duffy said, regaining her usual bland expression. "You'll be late for school if you don't hurry."

Ora had the rhyme worked out before they reached the schoolyard.

There was an old woman / who lived in a shoe
With so many children / What else could she do?
Please send me a husband, / She prayed from the pew
God answered / She grabbed him
After all / Wouldn't you?

"Matron was getting past her prime," Leah said. "She couldn't afford to wait too much longer."

"Yeah," Ora replied. "Beggars can't be choosers. My mom used to say that a leftover piece of pie is better than no pie at all."

Pie, applied to the selection of husbands. Hmm—that was something that might be worth remembering.

Leaving Veith

Ora left the Home a month after Matron's departure. Rose wasn't surprised. They got rid of you pretty quickly, once you were sixteen. As Greta was fond of saying, "You go when you're old enough to earn your own keep. Plenty of others to take your spot. One thing this place never lacks is a new mouth to feed."

"It'll be so awful without you in the next bed," Rose moaned on Ora's last evening. They were in the older girls' dorm, with Ora's battered cardboard suitcase open on the bedspread. "I'll be bluer than blue. You know I will."

"Now, now—" Ora consoled as she stuffed underwear, her extra skirt, and the school blouses into the case, "—you'll be just fine." She scrunched her one pair of good shoes on top, spread a rumpled rainjacket over the lot, closed the case, and snapped the lock.

"Besides, you'll be going soon, too," she added. "Think about the fun we'll have when we're both out of here. We can do what we want, whenever we want."

She was gone when Rose got in from school the following day; and a new girl was sleeping in Ora's bed by the next night.

Rose's birthday fell on a Tuesday that year. There were no presents, of course, nor any cards. Aunt Edna had long since given up on sending gifts, and there'd been nothing from Violet in over three years. The year she left, Violet had sent a couple of postcards from Boston, and, that Christmas, a parcel. None of the correspondence had included a return address. After the parcel, there was nothing more.

Rose appealed to Matron to locate Violet, and Miss

Duffy had obliged with two letters of inquiry. One went to General Delivery in a place called Concord and the second to a resort in Cape Cod. Both came back weeks later, stamped "Return to Sender. Addressee Unknown."

Rose did her best to explain Violet's silence to Lily; tried also to convince herself that she didn't care any longer; that, except for visits from the loyal Mrs. McGinn, she and Lily were alone.

Rose celebrated her birthday with a piece of plain cake, shared with the three others who had also been June babies. She didn't mind the sharing, actually; Olive's cakes were always a mastery in the art of skimping. Too few eggs, too little white sugar, not enough butter. Pale, fluff-like imitations of what a birthday cake should be. Olive did what she could with what she had on hand; Rose realized that. But it wasn't good enough. Rose craved richness and substance; real pound cake, like the ones her mother used to make.

The following Thursday afternoon Miss Duffy summoned Rose to her office. As she stood in front of the massive desk, watching Miss Duffy pull papers out of a manila folder, Rose was reminded of the October evening, four years earlier, when Miss Crooks had done the very same thing.

"You're now sixteen, Rose," Miss Duffy said.

"Yes, ma'am. On Tuesday."

"I've been looking at your file, trying to decide on the best course of action, now that you're of working age."

"Yes."

"One thing is very clear. You're not meant for the halls of higher learning."

Rose flushed. Her lacklustre performance at school had been a constant source of embarrassment. "Satisfactory" was the best she could do in English and Social Studies; "Fair" in Arithmetic. Art and Domestic Science were her only shining stars; she was proud of the consistent "Very Good" grades she received in sewing and pattern design.

"There seems little reason to keep you in school next fall; and no indication that you'd make a suitable candidate for business college."

Rose shifted her weight to her right foot. She knew better than to interrupt.

"However, a good placement opportunity has just become available," Miss Duffy said. "A family in the South end is looking for a girl who is quick-witted and hard-working, mannerly and neat. I've decided to recommend you."

Rose's heart skipped a beat—excitement, mingled with anxiety.

"The Browne family is very highly regarded by our committee. They are stalwart members at the cathedral."

Rose could feel the disdain welling up, as it always did, at the supposed virtues of the outwardly religious. Hanging around churches didn't necessarily mean you were a good—or even nice—person. Father Hanrahan was a prime example of that. Piety, prayer, and preaching did not a Christian make. Amen.

"—and with both their daughter and her husband in delicate health, Mrs. Browne is very much in need of an extra pair of hands."

Rose shifted her weight again. *Just the facts, lady. I don't need the sob story.*

The facts were simple enough. She was to be placed as a maid; obliged to live in someone else's house, clean up their messes, and do their bidding. "In-service" was how the genteel committee ladies put it; and it was a common enough fate for girls at the Home. Maid service and factory work were, after all, the only real options, if you weren't going on to high school.

Dear Ora, who hated cleaning anything, had, luckily, escaped this placement. She was working in an overall factory, and living with an aunt who had an extra room in her boarding house.

Miss Duffy was at full cruising speed, now: Rose could hone her homemaking skills; learn new ones. She would be wise to apply herself; to follow orders, work diligently, blah, blah . . .

Yeah, right. Thanks to living here, I'm an expert at following orders.

. . . in time, a suitable young man could be found for her.

Found. As if he was lost in the dark forest, like Hansel and his sister, Gretel.

. . . The Brownes would probably assist with marriage arrangements. They'd done so for their last girl. Miss Duffy had it on very good authority.

"They'll help you get started, I expect," Miss Duffy concluded. "Since you haven't any family of your own, you should consider yourself very lucky."

Lucky, eh? In the space of ten minutes, not only had this woman sentenced her to the scrub-bucket brigade, she was also plotting how to get her married off. What a nerve!

"You're very quiet," Miss Duffy said, having run out of steam.

Quiet is right. You haven't given me a chance to get a word in edgewise.

"What about Lily?" Rose asked. "She'll be so alone here without me."

"You're to have every second Sunday off," Miss Duffy replied. "You can come over on the tram to visit."

They'd worked it all out, then. Rose would go along with their plans and be grateful. There was no choice.

Miss Duffy closed the manila folder. As Matron, her day was crammed with important matters. The future prospects of one less-than-distinguishable girl could not consume too much of it.

"Tomorrow, after breakfast, the Brownes are sending a car for you. You can spend the rest of today getting your clothes in order. I've already told Greta. Feel free to take your needlework, if you like, and the prayer book you got from St. Mark's when you were confirmed."

The car arrived, as promised, at ten in the morning. The youngish driver introduced himself as Harris Dunlop, Mrs. Browne's nephew. Lily, allowed to stay home from school to see Rose off, cried.

"I'll be back to see you in two weeks, Lily," Rose whispered. "I promise."

Why did she say "I promise"? She shouldn't have. The words echoed of Violet, and they both knew how empty her promises had been.

Arms around each other, Rose and Lily watched the young man stash the old valise in the trunk. "Right, then," he said. "Done. Might as well be on our way."

Miss Duffy moved toward Rose and offered her hand. "Goodbye, Rose. My best wishes to you."

Rose shook the older woman's hand, gave Lily a last quick hug, and climbed into the back seat. The engine started, and the car moved forward. She managed one brief wave before Lily, the house, the life she had known for the past four years, were left behind.

The car purred down streets and around corners, past the Armouries, the western slopes of the Hill, the Central

Common—but Rose paid no attention to the familiar landmarks. She was deep inside herself, head resting against the plush upholstery and hands crossed against her quaking stomach.

Aunt Edna and Uncle Earle had driven away from them in a black car very much like this one. A long black under-taker's hearse had taken their mother's body to the graveyard and dumped it there; and a black taxicab had spirited Lily and her away from the warmth and safety of the McGinn's.

Rose hated black cars.

If I had the money I'd buy a silver roadster. Maybe maroon. Never black.

Black cars were for endings; for death.

ROSE

PART TWO

The Brownes'

The Brownes' Place

It wasn't until they'd turned onto a wide avenue lined with very grand-looking houses that Harris broke the silence. "See—over there," he said, pointing to an imposing three-storey house set well back from the street. "That's where my aunt and uncle live." A moment later he'd swung into a cobblestoned driveway and brought the car to a smooth stop.

"Wait while I get your bag," he said. "Then we'll get you in and introduced."

How nearsighted he is, Rose thought, noticing the bottle-thick lens of his spectacles. At school, fellows like him were called "four-eyes" or "Squint." His spectacles, and the way he peered when he looked her way, reminded her of an owl dazzled by the daylight.

She stepped from the car as confidently as she could, smoothed her skirt, and followed him up the walk. Two huge stone urns filled with luxurious red begonias stood on either side of the oak door. The plants gave off an earthy, just-watered scent as she brushed past them.

Harris used a key from his chain to unlock the door, and then stood aside and allowed her to enter the foyer ahead of him. The welcoming area was truly impressive—a far cry from the narrow front hall at the Home. Standing to the left of the door was a mirrored hall-tree and an ornately carved umbrella stand; on the right, a longish oak table flanked by two brocade-covered reception chairs. Two large paintings hung on the wall above the chairs.

"Hello, Aunt Ethel," he said to a tallish woman coming down the wide, carpeted staircase. "Bringing your new girl, like you asked."

New girl. Maidservant.

"Hello," the woman said to Rose. "I'm Mrs. Browne and I'm pleased that you've come to give us a hand."

What should she say to that? "I'm pleased to meet you?" Or, better still, "Don't get too used to me. I won't be sticking around long?" Rose settled for the safe route. "Thank you. I'm pleased to be here." It was a lie, of course; but, really, what did it matter.

Harris didn't linger long. "Must get to the office," he said, giving Mrs. Browne a quick kiss on her cheek. "See you for Sunday dinner."

Left alone, Rose felt awkward and suddenly very shy.

"Come along to the kitchen to meet Mrs. May, our cook," Mrs. Browne said.

"She'll show you about. It's a big house, but not an impossible one. In any case, your Matron assured me that you're a smart girl, so you'll get the hang of things in no time."

The next few hours were a blur, filled with impressions and instructions, sights and sounds; and it was past two in the afternoon before Rose had a bit of time on her own.

"We usually can squeeze a half-hour to ourselves around this time," Mrs. May explained, leading Rose up to her room on the third floor. "Unless Mrs. B is entertaining or out, she likes to have a cat-nap about now. Now then, I'll leave you to get settled. Come down the back stairs at three. There's ironing to finish up, and then you can help me with the vegetables for supper."

She paused at the doorway. "Oh, and by the way, you can call me Minnie May. Everybody does."

Rose nodded. She was feeling too overwhelmed to tackle her unpacking and was relieved to have a chance to sit quietly and collect her thoughts. This was a big house, no question, with beautifully furnished rooms full of love-ly things. There was an elegant, yet comfortable-looking parlour at the front of the house, with a long velvet sofa and matching wing chairs done in blue brocade. The china lamps and delicate porcelain vases on the tables were hand-painted; and, filling two shelves of the corner curio cabinet, was an entire collection of cranberry glass.

In the dining room, a full silver service tea set graced the top of a massive mahogany sideboard; placed around a matching mahogany table were ten high-backed chairs. The chair seats had been exquisitely crafted in fine needlepoint, with a different floral scene on each of them.

Minnie's May's territory was at the back of the house. She had a large, well-equipped kitchen and a little den tucked under the back stairs. The den was a cozy room, with wicker furniture, a sewing machine, and a tabletop radio. "I love my shows in the afternoon, dear," Minnie May told Rose. "Rain or shine. I wouldn't miss them for the world."

The bedroom to which Minnie May had taken Rose was on the top floor. "Our help stays up here," was her only comment. It was a small room, with slanting walls and one low window that looked out over the front lawn. Placed in front of the window was a single rattan-backed straight chair. A three-quarter bedstead and a small, painted night table with a brass lamp on it took up the longest wall. A four-drawer bureau (far too much space for my few things, Rose thought) and wash basin and stand stood opposite the bed. The planked floor was bare, save for a small oval mat made from multicoloured cotton remnants.

Rose suspected that the room would be plenty hot on warm summer nights, and more than a little chilly on cold winter ones, even with the chimney in the corner. She was, however, quite satisfied with the space. It was simple and quiet; and most important of all, it was hers. For the first time in over five years, she had a room of her own.

She could do as she pleased here: keep the lamp on as late as she wished; toss her hairbrush on the dresser and not be scolded by Greta. If, on her days off, she wanted to lie in bed late, she could do that. Or she could go out—on her own— to see Ora, take in a movie, visit Lily, walk in the park.

Here then, at last, was the freedom she'd been longing for. She was sixteen now; grown up in the eyes of the world. Ready (she hoped) to tackle whatever people and events it might bring her way.

That evening, under the summerweight covers of her new bed, Rose was still sorting out her impressions, trying to make some sense of the people who were living under this roof. Minnie May wasn't a live-in. She came by the day and went home to her family at six each evening. "Unless there's a dinner party, dear. Then I'm here till all hours. You'll see."

The three people who comprised the family were polite, remote—and odd—individuals. Mrs. Browne, an attractive, middle-aged woman, had a definite tension about her, a strain that was evident in her eyes and in the lines around her mouth. Mr. Browne, who appeared to be much older than his wife, had a pleasantly vague and apologetic manner, as if he were sorry for something, or everything. And the daughter, Adele—how to describe her? She was like a half-wilted flower; a delicate orchid, left too long without a good watering.

Rose was still awake when the thunder started. In the distance at first, but gradually getting louder, closer. She considered getting up to close the window but decided against it. It was too muggy and hot; she needed the air, even if a bit of rain did come in.

She lay on her back, her eyes open, thinking about her new life; wondering how Lily was doing without her; and when she would be able to contact Ora.

In the semidarkness of the room, she could see the outline of the dresser at the foot of the bed. She'd put her few clothes away in it, had set her brush and comb on the top. When she got paid, she would buy a few things at Woolworth's: a calendar and a framed print for the wall, perhaps a little trinket box, a second small mat for the floor. She needed to take away the starkness; make the room "hers."

She'd buy a necklace, too; a pretty costume piece. And later, when she had enough saved up, she would replace it with a real silver locket. It still hurt terribly, thinking about her mother's locket. She had discovered it missing one dreadful day about six months earlier. She knew immediately who had taken it; knew, yet was unable to do a blessed thing about it. It wasn't just a coincidence that the locket's disappearance occurred the very week that Dot was placed out.

"Sure she took it," Ora said. "Nasty little bitch. She always was a sneak and a cheat."

A downpour followed the thunder and lightning. Rose didn't hear when it finally let up. After ten minutes of steady drumbeat on the roof, her weary mind was lulled into a deep and much-needed sleep.

Oxford Street

Rose sat on the back steps, savouring the warmth of the August day, lulled by the soft sounds and smells of summer. The aroma of the sweet-pea trellis drifted her way on a gentle breeze, insects hummed in the hollyhock border, and, two houses along, a young fellow whistled as he painted the gable trim.

It was early afternoon and Rose was weary. Up at six-thirty every morning, she had come to appreciate this one bit of respite in an otherwise crowded workday.

"It's about the only time I get to myself until after the dishes are done at night," she'd said to Ora over sodas. A pleasant little café, just two blocks from the Gardens, was doing duty as a Saturday afternoon meeting place.

"Those folks are running you ragged," Ora replied, swirling the strawberry froth around in her glass. "You should get proper breaks, just like we do. Fifteen minutes, morning and afternoons, and a half-hour for lunch."

"Yeah, I suppose," Rose said. She hadn't meant to sound so critical. Her days were busy, yes, but the work wasn't difficult, and the Brownes were not unpleasant people. Odd, definitely; but not nasty. As for breaks, the back stoop (or, on rainy days, the little den at the back of the house), had to be a darn sight better than any factory lunchroom; sitting shoulder-to-shoulder at a table with a dozen other shift workers, most of whom would be getting in a quick smoke before heading back to the shop floor. Not that she'd dream of saying so, and risk hurting the feelings of her best and only friend.

Rose pushed at curls on the back of her neck. She'd spent the better part of the morning over a hot stove and the collar of her housedress was still damp from sweat. Minnie May had left directly after breakfast to attend a funeral in the country, leaving Rose to deal with the meals by herself.

Harris had joined the family for lunch, making a foursome around the table. The feeding of four didn't seem like a very tall order but, as Minnie May was fond of pointing out, it meant just as much work as feeding a dozen.

The meal itself had consisted of cold roast beef, creamed cucumber salad, pickled beets, and a crusty loaf from the French Pastry over on Quinpool. "Bakery bread will have to do," Minnie May had said to Rose. "I haven't got time to think about bread this morning, let alone bake it." She had, however, rolled out piecrust and prepared the cherry filling while Rose was seeing to the boiled eggs and breakfast tea.

"Needs a hot oven," she warned before heading out. "Be careful not to let the syrup bubble over. Looks so messy if you do." Rose followed her instructions to the letter and was delighted when the pie came out browned to perfection.

Harris wolfed down his first piece and wasn't shy in asking for seconds. "Next to Minnie May, Rose is the second best pie cooker in town," he said in the teasing way she was beginning to get used to. Mrs. Browne nodded in agreement. By now, Rose knew that Mrs. Browne also had a sweet tooth. Minnie May made a point of keeping a tin on the sideboard filled with squares or fudge. "One of her few pleasures, poor woman," was Minnie May's cryptic comment.

The reference intrigued Rose. She wouldn't have described Mrs. B as "poor" at all. In fact, to Rose, her employer appeared to have just about everything, and in goodly abundance, too. It was Mr. Browne, who was the "poor old soul" in Rose's books. He rose late, went to bed early, and seemed to have no purpose to any of his days, spending the better part of each in an armchair by the dining-room window, with Laddie snoozing at his feet.

"Is he sick?" Rose had asked of Minnie May.

"No, not really," she'd replied, somewhat curtly. "He just needs a lot of rest. Leave him be if he doesn't answer when you knock on his door in the mornings. And leave his room till last to make up."

That he had his own bedroom also struck Rose as odd. A man and a woman were supposed to share a bedroom when they got married, unless, of course, one of them got very sick, like her father had done. But Minnie May had said that Mr. B wasn't sick; well, if he wasn't sick, what the dickens was the matter with him?

At the table he dithered with his utensils and often did little more than peck at his food, watching the others with a vague smile. Sometimes he spilled his peas or knocked over his glass, forcing Rose to run for a cloth to sop up the water. He was unfailingly polite, however, and always said "please" and "thank you" when she served him.

"Mr. Browne doesn't go out to work, then?" Rose had asked Minnie May.

"No," Minnie May replied. "He doesn't. Harris looks after the business now."

A sudden movement followed by three decidedly unmusical squawks startled Rose from her reverie. In a whirr of wings a blue jay emerged from the foliage and edged along a low-hanging branch to the newly installed birdhouse. It poked its beak into the tiny doorway, backed away, and tried again. Rose watched in amusement at the bird's futile attempts to look inside the miniature dwelling.

Mrs. Browne had arrived home with the birdhouse two weeks earlier.

"A man out on the Cove Road was selling them," she'd said, showing her purchase to Minnie May and Adele. "He looked so down on his luck, I felt I just had to buy something. We'll get Freddy to put it up when he comes to cut the grass."

Which was exactly what Freddy had done yesterday, although not without his own brand of editorial comment.

"Poorest excuse for a birdhouse I ever saw," he grumbled, uncorking his Thermos and pouring hot tea into its top. "The missus has a mania for the damn things. I must have put up three or four of 'em in the past couple of years." He dug into his lunchpail and pulled out a healthy slab of cheese, two thick wedges of cornbread, and a hard-boiled egg.

Rose placed a spoon and a dish of chow in front of him. "I noticed one in the big larch outside my window," she said.

"That's right," he replied, his mouth full. "And I'll bet there's no sign of a bird in it." He jabbed a gnarled forefinger on the tabletop. "This one won't be any different, either, mark my words. Stupid contraptions. Even a blue jay's got more sense than to nest in 'em, and a better sniffer, too. That cheap varnish is enough to make a seagull puke."

Minnie May laughed. "She means well, Fred. And the man made a few dollars."

"Hey, I got no quarrel with that." He cracked his egg on the table edge and peeled it. "Anyway, it makes no nevermind to me. All in a day's work." He shook salt onto the egg and popped it into his mouth.

"If that's lunch, then I've had it," he said, washing the egg down with the last of his tea. "Better get at the hedge. It's been growing like a jungle vine, what with the rain and that manure I got from old man Penny. Good manure, his. I never get it from anybody else."

At three o'clock Rose poured herself a glass of lemon-ade and sat down to tackle the silver. The church ladies were coming on Wednesday, and she'd promised Minnie May that she would do the silver today, leaving Tuesday free to wash and iron linens. Thankfully, the radio was calling for clear, sunny weather. Her plan was to have the linens on the line by ten, dried by two, and ironed before supper.

She had impressed Minnie May by her quick mastery of the wringer-washer. "You sure know how to work smart-like," the older woman said, watching with a practised eye. Rose finished guiding a sheet through the wringer and let it drop into the basket on the floor before replying. "I like things done right," she said, switching the lever to the Off position. "Just like you."

"No doubt about that. And Mrs. B knows it, 'cause I told her," Minnie May said. "Not everyone's cut out for housework. It takes a clear head, as well as willing hands. You've got both, which is more than I can say for the girl who was here last."

Minnie May spread a newspaper on the kitchen count-er and dumped turnips onto it before continuing. "Not that the girl didn't try," she said. "But, lord love her, she was as clumsy as an ox and more stupid than a cow. I told her to be careful of the lever on that wringer. Might just as well have saved my breath, though. Didn't she up and get her arm caught! I came on the tear when I heard her scream-ing. Broke her wrist bad; had a cast on it for six weeks. Mrs. B was upset, let me tell you. But who's the one who got stuck with the extra work—me!"

Rose was buffing the handle of the teapot when Mrs. Browne came into the server's pantry. "How are you mak-ing out with the silver, Rose?" she asked.

"This is the last piece," Rose replied. "I put the others

over there." Lined up on a shelf under the west window were the pieces she'd finished: a sugar bowl and cream pitcher, the hot water urn, and a large, fluted tray. Each piece sparkled in the rays of the afternoon sun.

"They look good," Mrs. Browne pronounced, having picked up several to examine. "The guild meets here on Wednesday and I like to use the complete tea service."

"Yes," Rose replied. "Minnie May told me."

"Ah, right. Well, then, I must go and see to a couple of telephone calls. If Mr. Browne asks for me, tell him I'm not to be disturbed."

"Certainly," Rose replied. Mrs. Browne spent a great deal of time alone in her study; and when she wasn't closeted in the study, she went out. It seemed as if she couldn't bear to be in the house with only her husband and Adele to keep her company.

The day of the meeting Minnie May baked non-stop from early morning until noon. Mrs. Browne dithered and fussed, asking Rose to adjust doilies, and shift chairs, and move end tables from one place to another. Mrs. Browne's fussing was nerve-wracking enough, but Rose hadn't counted on having Adele underfoot. She was playing the piano when Rose wanted to sweep the grate, and was reading in the wing chair by the window when Rose wanted to water the pedestal fern.

"She's like a lost sheep," Rose muttered to Minnie May as she hurried out to the back stoop with her mop.

Minnie May, frosting the sides of a layer cake, looked up and frowned. "Never been any different. I wonder what's to become of her. I really do."

Thankfully, Harris had come by earlier to spirit Mr.

Browne and Laddie away. "Don't worry," Rose heard him say to his aunt. "We'll be gone the entire afternoon."

All was in order by one-thirty, giving Rose enough time to dash upstairs, comb her hair, and put on a clean apron. Back in the kitchen, she grabbed a quick cup of Minnie May's tea and two of the sandwich triangles deemed not uniform enough for the glass serving tray.

The ladies began arriving at two. Rose helped them off with their wraps, hung the damp garments (it had started raining soon after dawn and hadn't let up) in the hall wardrobe, and propped the assorted umbrellas against the radiator to dry.

By the time she'd seen to the latecomers, the opening hymn and prayers had begun. Rose hovered out of sight in the hall, ready to alert Minnie May as soon as the business portion of the meeting was underway. "After all these years, I got it down to a fine art," Minnie May had explained. "There's just enough time to get the water good and boiling before they finish up."

The proceedings were an interesting lesson in the conduct and manners of these privileged women. Madame President—a large woman in a mauve dress—was installed in the wing chair by the piano, with the marble-topped end table pulled in front of her knees. Placed on the table's top were her gavel, a brass bell, and her sheaf of papers. From the chair by the fireplace a fat lady in a printed day-dress read minutes from a tapestry-covered notebook.

There were three "all in favour" calls from Madame President. Each request received a chorus of "ayes." A tedious discussion ensued on whether or not they would donate Bibles to some mission or other overseas. Then, suddenly, it was over, and Madame President was declaring the meeting "adjourned."

Such a lot of fuss and bother, Rose thought as she uncovered the trays of sandwiches and sweets and disappeared into the pantry. A lot of talk, too; over not much of anything. But, then again, who was she to pass judgement? A slip of a girl who knew precious little about the ways of society ladies. Their schooling would have been so different to Rose's own. As would their upbringing have been. There was just no question of that.

War

Although the country was at war, its impact on Rose's daily life was minimal. Like everyone else, she had to put up with ration books and heavy blackout curtains, tedious air-raid drills, and crowded tram cars. But these were irksome inconveniences rather than worrisome events.

Just my luck, she would sometimes think when she went out to do the errands. I get clear of the Home, with all its shortages—the hand-me-down clothes and corn chowder suppers—and then a war comes along and we all have to scrimp again. It's not fair. Besides, it's stupid war. All wars are.

She had to give credit to Minnie May, though. The woman had a knack for getting the things she needed. Sugar, eggs, a good-sized roast for Sunday dinner, Minnie May knew all the right people.

Rose would often hear her on the phone, talking to one of the local merchants. "Tell him it's Minnie May and I'm calling for Mrs. H.G. Browne." Before too long, a delivery van would be nosing into the service lane, and the young helper would be knocking on the back door, a carton balanced on his shoulder.

"Don't ask questions," she would say to Rose after the van had driven off. "Less known, the better."

Rose was sure that Harris had a part to play. After all, supplying ships was the family business; and, war effort or not, Harris had a direct line to whatever they needed.

On the Friday before the family was to leave for their summer cottage, Rose headed down Spring Garden with her shopping list: thread, a yard of lace edging, a length of medium-width elastic for herself; and, for Mrs. Browne, a tube of insect repellent, a bottle of iodine, and a roll of gauze. "I always go to the shore with a well-stocked first aid kit," Mrs. Browne had told her. "The girl at the druggist's knows the sizes and brands I prefer."

At the grocer's, just two up from the drugstore, Rose stopped for a minute to read the newest banner pasted on their front window. The slogan, *Better potluck with Churchill today than humble pie under Hitler tomorrow,* nettled Rose. She was willing to bet a quarter that Mr. MacDonald, the grocer, would never eat much humble pie, supposing he lived to be a hundred. He lived in a fancy, three-storey place down near the hospital, and owned a big car, too, along with the delivery van. She'd heard Max, at the dinner table, joke about him. "Old man MacDonald sure isn't suffering. He's got the first nickel he ever made, and plenty more since."

As for Prime Minister Churchill, Rose was certain he was as wealthy as he was fat. Plenty of roast beef dinners, Yorkshire puddings included, and precious little potluck, was her private assessment. Nor did he suffer from lack of smokes, either. In the newspaper pictures, and on the newsreels, he was either holding a cigar or smoking one.

"Where does cigar tobacco come from, anyway," she asked Minnie May one day.

"Cigars?" Minnie May pondered the question while she filled a pot with water from the tap. "From one of those islands down south, I'd say. Jamaica or Cuba, maybe. Same place the rum comes from, I'd say."

Across the street from the grocer's, the bank's War Bonds campaign was going full tilt. Rose had opened a savings account soon after starting work at the Brownes' and was pleased with her progress so far. Her pay wasn't high—not as much as Ora got at the plant—but she didn't have board to pay out, and her little nest egg was steadily building.

Each time that Rose made a deposit, the teller pointed out the benefits of buying a war bond or a savings certificate, and each time, Rose declined. Their own posters, *Buy Victory Bonds* and *As long as Jack is at war, we'll eat hash and like it*, did not instill in her any patriotic fervour. She didn't have any Jacks in her family, and the only family she did have—Lily—was eating her share of hash already. It had been standard Monday-night fare up at the Home for years now.

No one in the Browne family was involved in active service, either. Uncle Max held an administrative post with the ARP, but Mr. B was far too muddled to do volunteer duty. As for Harris, he poked fun at his own status. "I tried to enlist," he'd said. "But the Recruiting Office sent me packing. The old Colonel told me I was as blind as a bloody bat, and to get the hell out of there."

Which was just fine with Rose. She didn't want Harris shipped overseas, like the sailors in the park. She looked forward to Sundays, when he and his parents came to dinner. Harris kept everyone at the table entertained, sparring with his father on all kinds of topics: war and politics, shipping and sports, cars and business.

The conversation—and Harris—was lively, interesting, and fun.

Second Summer

Minnie May baked a cake for Rose's seventeenth birthday. Rose discovered it when she went into the dining room to set the table for breakfast. There it was, at the end of the table, sitting beside two wrapped packages. Taped to the longer, flat box, was a card: *Hope you will enjoy these. Sincerely, The Brownes.*

"Hurry and open them, Rosie," Minnie May urged from the kitchen doorway, apron gathered under a wooden spoon coated with pancake batter.

Rose ripped the paper off the round box and lifted out a brimmed sun hat: white straw with plaited yellow ribbons wound around the crown. She placed it on her head and pivoted, catching a bit of her reflection in the sideboard's mirrored top.

"Snazzy, that," Minnie May pronounced. "Looks real good on you, too. Now, for mercy's sake, let's see what else you got!"

A yellow and white gingham sundress lay nestled in the tissue paper of the second box. Lifting it out, Rose took in every detail: the eyelet shoulder straps, the row of daisy-shaped buttons down the front, the flounce around the hem. It was exactly like the ones she and Ora had been drooling over in the Simpson's catalogue.

"You'll be the cat's meow in that outfit," Minnie May said with a chuckle.

"The boys'll go wild."

Rose didn't trust herself to speak for a moment. *They don't have to do this*, she was thinking. *After all, I'm only the maid.*

She served the cake at lunchtime. Still feeling overwhelmed at the gifts, she wrote a note of thanks and placed it next to Mrs. Browne's napkin. Harris arrived just as she was pouring the tea.

"Fe, fi, fo, fum, I smell c-a-k-e," he said, licking his lips and rubbing his hands together. Both Adele and Mrs. Browne laughed, and even Mr. Browne came out of his mealtime stupor long enough to smile.

"You did, indeed, Harris," Mrs. Browne replied. "Do have a seat. If you're a good boy, I'm sure Rose will serve you a piece."

"Minnie May baked it," said Rose, placing a cup of tea and an extra thick slice on a plate in front of him. "It's very good."

"I don't doubt that for one minute," he replied. "Minnie May's the best cake baker in town, bar none." He raised his tea cup. "Here's to the birthday girl. May the year be good to you."

"It was nice of them to remember me," Rose said to Minnie May when they were on their own in the kitchen.

"Oh, they're good folks, really. Got their moments, mind you, but so's everybody." She skimmed froth from a shank of ham she was boiling on top of the stove. "I never had any complaints, and I've been with 'em for over twelve years."

Rose folded carrot peelings into a piece of newspaper and carried the bundle out to the bin on the back stoop. Twelve years! She had no intention of being here that long. The Brownes were fine people, but they weren't her people. Surely to God the war would be over soon, and the boys back from overseas. In twelve years, she expected to be married, with a family, a home of her own.

Inside the pocket of her apron was a card she intended to put into her keepsake box. Not Mrs. Browne's card, but the one that Harris had left by his teacup. Under its printed verse he had written: *To Rose ~ Hoping that all your wishes will come true. Yours, Harris.*

Rose put the lid back on the garbage bin and wiped her hands on a damp tea towel. She'd so love to meet someone thoughtful and family-centred. A fellow who was established, with a good job and enough money. Not just anyone, mind you; but a fellow just like Harris.

By midafternoon, it was too warm for comfort outside. If the weather keeps like this, I'll wear my new hat and sundress on Sunday, when I go to see Lily, Rose thought, getting out the ironing board.

She was looking forward to the change that summer would offer her daily routine.

With the family due to leave for the cottage directly after Dominion Day, Rose expected that she'd be sent, once again, to the home of Harris' parents, who wanted to give Madeleine, their own maid, extra time off this year so that she could lend a hand with her ailing father down in Cape Breton.

Rose had enjoyed her stint with Gert and Max last year. Aunt Gert, a lively woman who shared Harris' easy, cheerful disposition, was often out with friends, and Uncle Max was away a good deal on business trips, making Rose's workload much lighter than she was used to at the Brownes'. Once she'd seen to the laundry and the main meal, she was free to do as she pleased. As a result, she and Ora had taken in all the latest movies downtown, and had got to most of the Saturday-night dances at the Pavilion. And, before the family's return on Labour Day, she and Ora had taken the train to Windsor for a week with Ora's sister and her husband.

Rose was ironing a fresh cloth for the dining-room table when she heard Mrs. Browne's bell. She left the cloth draped over the ironing board and hurried along the hall toward the study. Hope I put enough sugar in the iced tea, she thought. She'd taken in a pitcher at two-thirty, placing it quietly on the teawagon, so as not to disturb Mrs. Browne, who was working on the accounts at her rolltop desk.

"It's me, ma'am," Rose called out, tapping on the half-closed door.

"Come in," Mrs. Browne replied.

If she wants more ice, she's out of luck, Rose thought, stepping into the wood-panelled study. The ice man hadn't made his delivery, and Minnie May hadn't been able to find out what the problem was.

"Sit down for a moment, Rose," Mrs. Browne said. She finished addressing an envelope and sealed it.

Bet a dime she'll be going out to the post office, Rose thought, eyeing the pile of envelopes on the blotter. Mailing letters was the one task that Mrs. Browne did not ask of Rose, choosing to walk the three blocks to the post office herself. It didn't matter if the weather was stifling hot, freezing cold, or pelting rain, Mrs. Browne went just the same, her brown satchel tucked firmly under her arm.

Minnie May shrugged when Rose commented on the daily ritual. "She's one of those folks who likes writing letters, I guess. Me, I never write letters. Too busy cooking and cleaning."

Mrs. Browne pushed a wisp of hair back from her forehead. "Rose, we're leaving for the shore earlier than planned. It's been so hot we need to get near the water as soon as possible. I've arranged with Harris to drive us down on Sunday."

Sunday! That gave Rose less than five days to get the summer things packed and ready.

"Shall I start the clothes tomorrow, then?" she asked.

"Yes. Check with Adele on her things. She needs new beachwear, but her other outfits will be fine, I should think. Oh, and make sure you use fresh whitener. The old box should be thrown out."

"Certainly. Is that all, then?"

"Actually, no," Mrs. Browne replied. "You're to come with us this year."

"Me?" Rose replied. *Why?*

As if reading Rose's mind, Mrs. Browne went on to explain. "Adele wants to concentrate on her painting. Last year's fog was such a disappointment. She plans to take her sketchbook and a hamper and go off on her own most days. I have friends to visit in the afternoons, but Mr. Browne is quite happy to sit on the sun porch or have a little stroll along the cove when the tide is out."

So that was it, then. Mrs. Browne and Adele wanted to be free to do as they liked and they couldn't leave Mr. Browne alone. Speaking of fog, he'd become decidedly more foggy over the past few months. Rose could see a real change in him since Easter. With the war escalating, Harris was too busy to come and take him out. Which left the poor man either sitting forlornly or wandering about the house, with Laddie as his sole companion.

"Mrs. Boutilier from the village comes each day during the week to do sandwiches and salad for lunch, and for the main meal at night," Mrs. Browne went on. "We book Sunday dinner at the hotel, and on Saturdays there are invitations to friends. Your main chores will be to help her in the kitchen, as you do here with Minnie May, and tidy up each day. Mrs. Boutilier does the laundry at her house, once a week. We don't stand on ceremony at the shore. A bit of sand tracking in is part of the charm."

When Mrs. Browne smiled, Rose was always struck by the change it made in her face. Suddenly, she was years younger; the image of Adele: the same even, white teeth, with dimples crinkling the corners of her mouth.

"It sounds very nice," Rose replied. She'd never been to the ocean; had never felt waves washing over her feet, or seen the ripples they left in the sand. Her childhood outings to the Basin, or to Point Pleasant, at the mouth of the harbour, didn't count in the same way. The water was salty, true; but the waves were subdued and the seaweed sparse. The sea that she'd only read of, or heard about from schoolmates who were lucky enough to get away from the city's heat, would be, at last, hers to experience. She couldn't wait to tell Ora and Lily.

There was precious little time to think about waves and sand dunes over the next few days, however. Instead, there were clothes to wash and iron, suitcases and cabin trunks to air out, dust covers to get ready for the furniture, and Laddie to take to the vet's for his summer clipping. Each time that Rose thought she'd finished with the dresses, Adele brought another to her. "Rose, I think I'll take this one, too. If you'll just freshen it up for me."

"How many dresses does a person need at a cottage?" Rose asked Minnie May on the day before they were due to leave. On the clothesline, three more summer frocks fluttered in a light breeze. "I thought Adele was going to paint most of the time. Wouldn't she be needing smocks and old shirts instead of all those dresses?"

"Rosie, dear, Adele in an old shirt! That wouldn't happen in a month of Sundays. For what it's worth, there's them that paints and parties, and them that does the work. Always been like that—always will."

How true, thought Rose. Things hadn't changed much since the days of Cinderella and her ugly stepsisters.

Harris arrived at ten on Sunday morning.

"Going for a year, Madame Renoir?" he teased as Adele came down the steps with a hatbox over one arm and a summer shawl over the other.

"Oh stop, Harris," she pouted. "We're not like you men. We can't just go without our things. Can we, Rose?"

"I guess not," Rose replied. She was trying to make a nest under the jump seat for the cold drinks satchel, thankful that the big suitcases and Adele's cabin trunk had been sent ahead by train.

"All aboard," Harris called out in a mock conductor's voice. "Departing this platform in two minutes. Station stops at French Village, Ingramport, and Hubbards. All aboard."

They piled in, Mr. Browne and Laddie up front, Adele and Mrs. Browne in the back seat, with extra cushions for armrests, and Rose in the jump seat ahead of Adele.

Minnie May stood on the front steps to see them off. She would do a final check before pulling the drapes and locking up the house. Tomorrow she, too, would be heading out; taking the train to Folly Lake, for a week's visit with her sister. One of her married sons would come by every couple of days to check on the house, and Fred would tend the lawn and flower beds each week until their return.

Adele

Rose watched intently as the city streets slipped past the car windows. After ten minutes or so, they had skirted the headwaters of the Northwest Arm and were following the winding hill road that would take them to the ocean. Houses, with ragged children playing in the front yards, dotted the landscape for several miles. These tapered out, finally, replaced by long stretches of dark forest, interspersed with ridges of granite rock, little lakes, and low, swampy, marsh land.

The scrubby, uninteresting terrain was not very appealing and Rose could understand why the others, used to the trip, were not paying it any attention. Mr. Browne and Laddie had both fallen asleep. Rose could see the tip of Laddie's nose on Mr. Browne's lap, and Mr. Browne's head, lolling forward, his mouth slack and open.

It was awfully good of Harris to do chauffeur duty, she thought, catching a glimpse of his face in the rearview mirror. His eyes, behind his thick wire-rimmed glasses, were intent on the road, and she could hear him whistling softly. Not many nephews would be so obliging, giving up an entire day off to cart their relations down to the country. And he wouldn't have the luxury of resting up the next day, either. According to Adele he would unload the car, have a bite of supper, and be on the road back to the city before dark.

"Next weekend, he'll be bringing Aunt Gert and Uncle Max down," Adele had told her. "They're planning to spend about six weeks at their place, out on the point. I'm glad, for it'll seem like the old days. My brother and I used to have such good times down here with Harris."

Rose was surprised to hear of a brother. Up until now, there had been no mention of a son and there were no photographs of him, anywhere in the house. She was sure of that, for she dusted every room. She didn't ask for details, though; and Adele didn't elaborate.

It was Minnie May who filled her. "Oh yes, dear. H.G. Junior. He was three years younger than Adele. Such a fine lad. His father was never the same after he died."

"What happened?" Rose asked.

"He drowned, dear. Went out alone in his canoe. They didn't find him for nearly three weeks. You daren't so much as mention boats to Mrs. B, ever since. Not that Adele is much for going near the water—or in it, either. It was Junior who was the sports-minded one. He was a champion paddler. There used to be two rows of medals on the wall in his room. They're all put away somewhere. In the attic, most likely."

Rose thought of him now, as the dark spruce forest blurred past the car windows. Perhaps every family was broken, one way or another. Split apart by death and absence; with those left behind so deeply shattered, so wounded that it took years for the scars to heal. If, in fact, they ever did.

Adele's brother, lost and gone.

My sister, lost and gone, too. Maybe dead.

In that respect—and only that—Rose felt a tiny affinity with Adele. Except, of course, that Adele knew where *her* brother was.

"What's Adele like, anyway?" Ora had asked Rose. "Stuck up, I suppose."

They were window shopping on Barrington Street. Inspecting the spring and summer fashions on the mannequins in the windows of Eaton's and Wood's.

Rose thought for a long minute before answering. How did you describe a girl like Adele?

"No, I wouldn't call her stuck up."

"What, then?"

"Oh, I don't know. Kind of dreamy, I guess. Like she's not paying attention. Sad, too."

"Sad! What's a girl like that got to be sad about, living in luxury, with you to wait on her. I suppose she's got a closet full of clothes, too."

"Yes. And a big bureau crammed full. Sweaters, blouses, gloves, scarves. Some that I've never seen on her back. But it doesn't stop her from buying new."

"That's what it's like to have money," Ora said.

She had stopped and was admiring a three-quarter length coat—gabardine—with a shawl collar. The mannequin's hat, set at a ninety-degree angle on her coal black hair, was a jaunty little number; flat as a plate, with an oversize bow sticking off its rim, and held in place with two pearl-tipped hat pins.

"Cute, isn't it?" Ora said, pointing to the hat. "I love how it fastens onto her hair without flattening it." She turned to Rose. "I'd love to get my hair permed. The curly look is very in."

"Not me," Rose replied. "My hair's curly enough. Actually, I kind of wish it was straighter. You should see how Adele's got hers."

"How?"

"Just like Veronica Lake's."

Adele had, in fact, managed to imitate the popular movie star's alluring look, pulling her pale blonde hair across the left side of her face so that her eye and part of her cheek were hidden. Although it did not quite turn Adele into *Modern Screen* sultry, the effect was, nonetheless, dramatic, making her seem slightly mysterious, even tragic.

"Does Adele have a steady?" Ora asked.

"I don't think so," Rose replied.

"I wonder why not. If she's pretty, with lots of money and loads of nice clothes, she should have a fellow."

"I think she might be waiting for someone overseas."

"Oh," Ora said, eyeing a serviceman who was standing at the corner, waiting for the light to change. "Well, she doesn't want to be two-timing; not if he's fighting for all of us. Does he write her a lot?"

"I'm not sure. She never mentions letters. Mrs. Browne sorts them, so I never get to see who they're addressed to."

"You should take a peek, just out of curiosity."

"Oh, Ora, I wouldn't dare. Mrs. Browne doesn't want anyone going through the mail. She made that clear right from the beginning. I'm to take them in a pile and put them face down on her desk. She'd be really mad if she caught me looking through them."

"Oh, bosh," Ora said, wrinkling her nose. "You could have a quick look at the names on the envelopes. She'll never know the difference, for goodness sake."

Rose did check the mail a few times after that. There were bulky, brown business envelopes, with return addresses printed in the upper-lefthand corners; notices from the church and other charities that Mrs. Browne supported; and notes from her women friends, on monogrammed stationery. A couple of long white envelopes, addressed to E.J. Browne in bold, upward handwriting, were the only unusual ones. Nothing for Adele; and, of course, never anything for Rose.

Adele's lack of men, and friends in general, puzzled Rose. The only phone calls she got were from a couple of former schoolfriends, both married, and her two female cousins. And the only people who came to the house regularly were the four youngsters that she had taken on as piano pupils. It seemed a very strange state of affairs for a nice-looking, well-heeled young woman.

In the year since she had come to their house, Rose had become quite well acquainted with Adele's daily pattern. She rarely came down to breakfast much before nine-thirty. The one exception was Thursday; she and her mother visited the wards at Camp Hill Hospital in the mornings, and then continued on to the Red Cross Lodge for an afternoon of rolling bandages and packing care parcels for the boys overseas.

On Friday evenings, she and a cousin went to a show at the Capitol, downtown. And on Sundays, after an early supper, a car arrived to take her to church group. "Going to Young People's," she would call out. "Back by ten."

Rose thought Adele was a little old to be going to a youth group, but, as Minnie May said, beggars couldn't be choosers. "Better than mooning about in her bedroom or playing those dreary pieces on the piano, day after day. Enough to drive a person stark-raving mad."

"Why doesn't she help out at the canteens," Rose asked. "There's lots of chance to meet people and have some fun. She could play the piano and sing for the fellows. They'd adore it."

Minnie May raised one eyebrow and kept on kneading her bread. "Rosie dear, I wouldn't be knowing, nor guessing. The meals is my job. I keep my nose out of the rest."

Rose kept quiet about Adele after that. The canteen crowd probably wouldn't be classy enough for a girl like

Adele. She'd be looking for at least two stripes on a guy's sleeve; the common ranks just wouldn't do.

Standing on Adele's bedside table was a framed photograph of an RAF flyer (Rose could tell from the wings on his cap badge). He was a rather handsome-looking, older man with a Clark Gable mustache and a serious expression. Rose had picked up the frame, expecting to see an inscription. Something along the lines of *To Adele, With All My Love.* There was nothing. Not even a stray speck of dust.

The Cottage

The car hummed along, effortlessly taking the twists and turns of the winding shore road. Lulled by the smooth motion, Rose felt her eyes getting heavy. Behind her, both women had lapsed into silence and, up front, neither Laddie nor Mr. Browne had stirred. She must have dozed off, awaking with a start as the car came to a stop.

Directly ahead, across a wide gravelled driveway, was a weathered-looking building with a wooden sign over its doorway. *Doreen's Diner. Fish Our Specialty.*

"Time for lunch," Harris announced. "You folks nab one of those picnic tables while I give the girl our order." By the time Rose had spread a cloth over the rough planked tabletop and uncorked the two Thermos jugs, he was back with five funnel-shaped paper containers, a shaker of salt and a small jug of white vinegar.

"Dig in," he said. "While it's good and hot."

The food was delicious; healthy servings of white, flaky fillets dipped in batter and deep-fried, and plump, crispy-brown wedges of potato.

"This makes the long drive worth it," Harris said, reaching for the vinegar jug. "They meet the boats every day, you know. Why, I'll bet the fellow we're eating was still swimming in the ocean last night."

Everyone perked up during the final leg of their journey. By now, they had emerged from the miles of dark forest and were travelling parallel to the water. Serene little coves, with fishing boats moored to buoys and wharves, gave way to breathtaking stretches of open ocean, its surf pounding against hard-packed sand. At one hairpin turn, Rose

gripped the edge of her seat, fearful that, despite Harris'
skill at the wheel, the car might swerve and plunge them all
into the sea.

Mr. Browne was fully awake now, watching the road
ahead with an intensity that Rose had not thought him
capable of. "Over there," he announced suddenly, sitting
bolt upright and pointing. "We used to hike around that
headland when we were lads. Yes, sir; we did so."

They turned off the main road moments later, and
bumped along a rutted lane so narrow that the wild roses
brushed against the sides of the car.

"Smell that sea air," Mrs. Browne murmured. "I can
never get enough of it."

Just past a stand of tall spruce trees the lane widened, and
a sloping roof and red brick chimney came into view. "Final
station stop, ladies and gentlemen," Harris announced,
braking the car and switching off the ignition. "All out
what's going out."

He helped unload the car and agreed to have a bite of
Mrs. Boutilier's salad supper before readying himself for the
drive back to the city. "I'll just about make it before the sun
sets," he said. He placed a hamper of Mrs. Boutilier's goodies on the rear seat before turning to his aunt. "And, no,
Aunt Ethel, I won't forget to bring the mail on my next
trip. That's a promise."

They went to bed early, tired from the journey and the
unpacking. Rose slept soundly, awaking at first light to the
cry of gulls in the distance. She jumped out of bed quickly, tiptoed over the creaking floorboards to her window, and
pulled back the curtain. To the east, a rising sun was creat-
ing sparkles of light on the rippled surface of the bay. Below
her, at the edge of the lawn, a flight of wooden steps led
down a steep embankment to a crescent strip of pure white

sand. The incoming tide lapped gently, persistently, against the shore, and, a few yards out, a lone gull skimmed across the shimmering surface of the water in search of a morsel or two for his breakfast.

Rose felt she should give herself a pinch, to see if she might still be dreaming.

Perhaps, like Alice, she had fallen down a rabbit hole into another world. That might be it, she thought. I'm in wonderland, and I don't ever want to wake up.

The interior of the cottage was certainly like something out of a fairy tale. "A fishing family lived here, once upon a time," Mrs. Browne had explained the previous evening. "But it's belonged to the Brownes for over fifty years. My husband used to come here when he was a boy."

"Indeed I did," he'd said. "I know every nook and cranny of this property. Blindfolded."

To help chase away the early morning dampness, Rose lit a fire in the kitchen stove. Before she'd gone home the previous evening, Mrs. Boutilier had laid out the kindling and newspaper. "An old Scouts method," she'd said to Rose. "Never fails."

Once the flames were licking around the dry wood, Rose put the kettle on for tea. While she was waiting for the kettle to boil, she had another look through the rooms on the main level. The kitchen, a large square room with a low ceiling, was situated at the back of the dwelling. Under a latticed window that opened outward, toward the ocean, was a long wooden table and six cane-bottomed chairs. The table and chairs had been painted a bright blue to match the wainscoting and the old-fashioned china cabinet. Red and-blue checkered wallpaper covered the walls, and, attached to the exposed ceiling beams, were three oil lamps.

A massive brick fireplace took up the better part of an inside wall, its blackened hearth hung with huge iron pots and old kettles. Beyond it, a low door led into the scullery. Mrs. Boutilier had shown Rose how to draw water from the pump, and had pulled up the trapdoor to show her the six stone steps that led to an earth-walled cold room underneath the scullery floor. "Take it from me, dear. This cold room's a far better place to keep butter and milk than any icebox I know of."

The sitting room was a bright, airy place. Three of its long windows faced the ocean and a huge fireplace built of beach rock took up one complete corner. The light pine furniture pieces were a refreshing change from the heavy, burnished mahogany of the house in the city. There were two chintz-covered sofas to loll on, with plenty of plump cushions for your head, and several wicker arm chairs, with matching chintz-covered footstools.

Shells and beach stones served as table decorations, and the east wall was draped with fish netting. A cluster of painted buoys lay on the floor next to a retired lobster trap, and, propped on its lid, was a life-ring bearing the name *The Eleanor Margaret* in bold, black lettering. In the corner opposite the fireplace stood a tall bookcase. Three of its four shelves were crammed to overflowing with books and magazines; the other was stacked with boxes of games and jigsaw puzzles.

A steep flight of crooked stairs led to the bedrooms, on the second level. Rose stood for a moment, listening, but there was no sign yet of anyone stirring. Mrs. Browne had taken the larger front bedroom, and Mr. Browne the smaller one next to it. Adele's room led off a little landing, next to the bath. There was a fourth room, too, for overnight guests. Each of the bedrooms had slanting walls and a planked door that opened and closed with a metal latch. Inside, there was just enough space for the bedstead and a small washstand with its china pitcher and matching bowl. Hooks on the back of the door served as a clothes rack; and, in place of a night table, a rough-hewn shelf had been attached to the wall beside the bed.

Rose had been happy enough to claim the loft for her quarters. Although she had to climb a ladder to get to it, and the trundle bed wasn't especially comfortable, these were small inconveniences compared to the delight of having an ocean view from the small gable window.

That Adele and Mrs. Browne were so willing to put up with the cramped bedrooms was intriguing, but Rose heeded Minnie May's advice and kept her thoughts to herself. It wasn't her place to question or be surprised. She was there to help and to serve. Period.

A creak in the floorboards above her head sent Rose hurrying back to the kitchen. She fetched milk and butter from the cool room and picked out several brown eggs from a bowl in the pantry nook. As she sliced bread and spooned jam into a dish, she contemplated what the coming days and weeks would mean for her.

That she'd been brought along to help with the meals and the general tidying up was obvious. Even more important, though, was the role she was bound to play in looking after Mr. Browne. Last evening's conversation at the supper table had made that clear. Mrs. Browne had a full slate of outings planned; an extension of her social life in town, Rose thought, but with the added bonus of sand dunes and ocean overlaid by the screech and soar of the gulls. As for Adele, she was ecstatic over the painting projects she'd mapped out in her head. "I'll get an early start in the mornings, Mother," she had announced.

We'll see about that, Rose thought as she placed the eggs into the water. Miss Adele wasn't a morning person. Mrs. Browne would be the first one down, as usual. In the city she was always the early bird, impeccably dressed and groomed, composed, polite, distant.

Rose had struggled for words to describe Adele to Ora, but Mrs. Browne was a far greater challenge. What could you say about a woman who was not old, but not young either; who was civil but decidedly lacking in warmth; who was less than beautiful, but certainly far from ugly. Her colouring was fair and her hair brown, with faint streaks of gray at the temples. She chose clothes that suited her age and her activities: cashmere sweaters over neat white blouses, tailored suits for business outings, tea dresses for afternoon gatherings, a fur jacket and matching hat for church in winter. All of which was more a sketch of what Mrs. Browne *looked* like than the kind of person she *was*.

After five minutes, Rose lifted the eggs from the water, wrapped them in a clean tea towel and placed them in a crockery bowl. She set the bowl in the centre of the table, next to the teapot. If they're not down soon, she thought, the tea will be cold and the eggs too hard.

Hmm. Perhaps that was the best way to explain Mrs. Browne. Cool, with a solid core, and a shell that was extremely hard to crack.

Paradise

By her second week, Rose had, as Minnie May would say, things down to a fine art. Her chores, such as they were, were easy: getting the breakfast, helping Mrs. Boutilier with the other meals, washing the dishes, sweeping the floors, gathering up the badminton racquets and the croquet balls at the end of the day.

In her free time, she found all sorts of places where she could amuse herself, happily and alone, for the longest stretches. She explored the sandy beaches and the rocky ones, climbed the bluff on the point, followed the rabbit warren of paths that led inland from the cliffs, finding wild strawberries, and, later, blueberries.

After her first few excursions along paths so overgrown with fern and wild grasses that she scarcely knew where to put her feet, she took a little dipper to hold the berries she'd picked. Back in the kitchen, she washed them off and stored them in the cold room for Mrs. Boutilier to make into pies or muffins.

The crescent beach below the cottage remained her favourite spot. She loved watching the pipers at play in the salt water, delighted at the rippled patterns left in the pristine sand by the ebb tide, and adored searching for new shells and sea urchins to add to her collection. She placed her treasures in an old pillow case, careful not to bundle it too tight for fear of crushing its delicate contents.

On the window ledge of her loft room, her collection steadily grew. From Adele she learned to tell one shell from another: the large white half-moons were the abandoned homes of scallops and oysters, the smaller purple-tingled ones were clam, and the black, whiskered ones were mussel.

She had lobster claws, starfish, and periwinkles, too, as well as sand dollars and mermaid's purses. In the evenings, she liked to rearrange them, trying out various formations, quite delighted with her artistic endeavours.

Eager to share her new knowledge, she wrote a long letter to Lily, describing her sea treasures in great detail. *I'll put them all in a shoebox and bring them over for you to see. Maybe we can make you a necklace out of the smaller shells. Won't that be fun? We'll just have to be careful that Greta doesn't see it.*

How she wished Lily could come down, for just a day; and Ora, too. What fun they could have together, splashing in the surf and climbing the rocks.

Breakfasts, just after eight, were leisurely affairs. Mrs. Browne lingered, sometimes in her dressing gown, over several cups of tea, making an extra effort to draw her husband into the conversations, and listening to his stories of the old days. "When I was a boy," he'd begin, and Mrs. Browne would settle back with a second slice of toast and a third cup of tea and listen attentively.

Rose suspected that Mrs. Browne had heard most of the stories a thousand times, but she didn't cut him off, or display any outward signs of boredom. Instead, she listened patiently; not until the tale began to circle back on itself did she deftly move to divert him. "Oh my, Hal—" she might exclaim, pointing toward the ocean. "Look—there's old Mr. Misener, heading out in his lobster boat." On other occasions, she used Laddie as the diversion. Using a crust of her toast, she would beckon to him. "Laddie, come, boy. Father has a treat for you." When Laddie came bounding over to the table, she passed the toast to Mr. Browne and watched as he fed it to the dog.

Adele, true to her promise, was up early most days.

Unless it was raining, she took off with her painting gear by midmorning, reappearing around three, in time for iced tea and cookies under the sun umbrella.

As soon as lunch was over, Mr. Browne settled into his deck chair for a siesta and Mrs. Browne disappeared to her room to change her clothes and fix her hair. "I'm off, then," was her standard farewell. "Back by supper." And she was gone, walking up their lane toward the village.

"It's little wonder she keeps in such good shape," Rose wrote in a letter to Ora. "She walks everywhere she goes."

In the city Mrs. Browne's figure hadn't been obvious, underplayed by her choice of tailored suits and full-cut day dresses. But here, under the light summer blouses and cotton skirts, her small waist was noticeable, as was her full, firm bosom, and her neat, trim ankles. She would tuck her blouse in and cinch her skirt with a bright sash, tied at the side in a double knot. On her feet, she favoured crepe-soled, canvas walking shoes, with open toes.

Rose worked cross-stitch on aprons or crocheted doilies while Mr. Browne dozed. Laddie, good as the gold of his coat, curled up in the shade of the elm and snoozed away the hour, occasionally opening one eye if an insect buzzed too close to one of his ears.

They both roused themselves, as if by magic, precisely at three o'clock. "I could time a pie in the oven by them," Rose joked to Mrs. Boutilier.

Adele arrived back by the time Rose had prepared the snack, and they sat together in the shade of the verandah, contentedly soaking up the remainder of the summer afternoon.

Mrs. Browne returned last, often looking flushed, as though she'd been hurrying in the heat, and often with her hair mussed. Perhaps she goes swimming with her friends,

Rose thought, although she'd not seen Mrs. Browne take a swimsuit with her, nor a beach towel, either.

Mr. Browne played on the grass with Laddie while Rose prepared the supper, throwing ball after ball for the dog to chase, while Mrs. Browne and Adele sat and discussed the scene or the shading of Adele's newest sketches. Unless it was rainy, they played croquet in the early evenings, and, at Adele's coaxing, Rose joined in. "It doesn't matter if you've never played before," Adele insisted. "We'll show you. It's more fun with four."

Once she'd got the hang of it, Rose enjoyed the game, and came to look forward to the soft summer evenings, with the sun setting, and the hum of insects mingling with the sharp crack of the mallets.

"Nice one, yes siree," Mr. Browne shouted, whenever Rose hit a tidy ball through the wicket. Mrs. Browne and Adele would smile, making Rose feel, for a moment, like she was one of them.

During their first month, they saw Harris only on weekends. But, once Grace and Max had been installed next door, invitations to join them for lunch or tea arrived regularly. Adele often accepted, taking her father with her, seemingly quite happy to spend time in the company of older people. Rose would watch them set out, arm-in-arm, through the birch grove that separated the two properties.

Mrs. Browne declined all afternoon invitations. "I can't go today," she'd say to Adele. "I've made plans with other friends." She never invited her friends to the cottage, however, leaving Rose to conclude that she wasn't willing to risk being embarrassed by Mr. Browne's odd behaviour.

Only one incident, in late July, marred their otherwise idyllic existence. Mr. Browne, down on all fours, was frolicking with Laddie on the verandah, teasing the dog with a piece of driftwood. Laddie, ears back and head down, growled playfully, swiping repeatedly at the stick with one of his paws. "Get it, boy. Get the stick," Mr. Browne coaxed, jabbing the stick toward the dog and then withdrawing it a moment later. "Come on, you can do it."

Feeling sorry for Laddie, Rose was about to intercede when she heard Mrs. Browne's voice, sharp and irritated, coming from the verandah steps. "Stop it, Harold! You'll have the poor animal worked up into a total lather."

Sensing that she'd be better off out of the way, Rose nudged open the screen door with her foot, anxious to make a hasty retreat.

"Give me the stick," she heard Mrs. Browne say. "Honestly, you do try my patience at times. I'm ashamed of you."

Rose couldn't see Mrs. Browne's face, but the disapproval in her voice sent goose bumps up Rose's arms. Memories of the playroom at the Home on rainy Sunday afternoons flooded over her. Matron and Greta, scolding one of them; fed up at having to deal, yet again, with another tedious and frustrating child.

The weather on the third Wednesday in August was cool, with a stiff breeze blowing off the water. There had been thunder through the night, and flashes of intermittent lightning; and, in the hour before dawn, it had poured buckets. But, by midmorning, it was starting to clear, and Rose was eager to get lunch over with so that she could do her errands in the village. Twice weekly she made the mile and a half trek, picking up the paper and the mail from the postmistress, and treating herself to a milkshake at the local diner.

"Should I run out and lower our flag," Adele asked, peering out the window at the flagpole. White caps dotted the water in the cove, and they could hear the surf pounding on the beach below the embankment. "I think I can work the ropes, really I do."

"I'd leave it," Mrs. Browne replied. "Gert and Max haven't bothered to take theirs in; I can see it flapping like mad."

"The Smiths are coming on Saturday," Adele continued. "Claudia got back last week. It's the last big gathering of the summer. We're invited for evening dinner; don't forget."

"I haven't forgotten." Mrs. Browne replied. She finished arranging a bunch of sunflowers in an earthenware vase and set it down on the hearth.

"These are really outdoor flowers, but I must admit, I do like them."

"I suppose we'll have to be on our best behaviour," Adele said. She took her mug over to the sofa and sat down. "First impressions are so important."

"Yes, I suppose we will," her mother replied, frowning. "Harris is so easygoing, though; I doubt he's too worried about impressions."

"No? Well, we'll see." With that, Adele buried herself in her favourite fashion magazine.

"Will you be home this afternoon?" Rose asked Mrs. Browne as soon as she'd finished the last of the lunch dishes and put them away. "I'd like to go into the village. Shouldn't be too long, though."

"I'm not sure," Mrs. Browne replied. "But you go along. Adele plans to stay put, so there's no need to hurry back."

Rose set out shortly after one, taking a canvas shopping bag to put the newspapers and parcels in. She so hoped there'd be a letter from Ora, and a note from Lily as well. Getting mail made her feel important, like she really did exist beyond her lowly role. After the rain, the air was heavy with the cloying smell of moist earth, the fresh scent of wild roses, and the pungent odour of spruce. She stepped gingerly around puddles and over deep ruts, walking as close as she dared to the fenced pasture of a neighbouring dairy farm. One of the cows raised its head, staring blankly in her direction as she walked past.

Rose didn't have much time for cows; they were, in her opinion, stupid, lazy animals. The horses in the upper paddock were much more appealing. On her last trip, the newest colt, a sweet little fellow with a diamond-shaped marking on his nose, had been brave enough to leave his mother and come trotting over for a pat. *I must remember to ask for a sugar cube at the diner,* she thought. *He'll love a treat like that.*

Mrs. Croft, the postmistress, was alone at the counter when Rose got there. She had a bundle of letters waiting, and three days' worth of newspapers.

"Dreadful, the news from France," she said, pointing to one of the headlines. "The Allies landed at Dieppe the other day. It was a disaster, though. Outright slaughter. Hundreds and hundreds killed."

"How awful," Rose replied. "I didn't know anything about it. The Brownes don't have a radio at the cottage."

"Well, there's plenty to read, and wonder about, in them papers. If they don't put the run to the Germans soon, I don't know what'll become of us all." She passed the bundle to Rose and watched her put them in her bag.

"What's the latest down on the point, anyway?" Mrs. Croft went on. "I hear the mister isn't doing so well. Such a shame, him failing in his head like that. Why, he can't be much older than me, and I'll be fifty-three next birthday."

Mrs. Boutilier's mouth must be going a mile a minute, Rose thought. Well, she had no intention of adding to the gossip mill, not with the likes of Mrs. Croft. The better part of valour was discretion; they'd memorized that saying when she was at school.

"Actually, he's doing fine," Rose replied. "He walks the dog every day, and visits the relatives next door. Likes to play croquet, too." That much was true, she thought. Mrs. Boutilier couldn't say otherwise.

"I hear that the daughter paints a lot."

"Yes, she does. Watercolors. They're very nice. Sea scenes and landscapes, too."

"Any fellas on the horizon? She'd be quite the catch, I'd say, with all that money."

Rose's reply was deliberately lighthearted. "Slim pickings, with so many of the men away fighting," she said. "I'm not hitched yet, either. But then, maybe I'm playing too hard to get."

Mrs. Croft laughed. "Pretty thing like you shouldn't have any trouble. You just have to go to the right places. Sticking down on that point night after night ain't any good. You need to come to the dances on Fridays. The Iona's a sure place to meet fellows. Everybody says so."

"Maybe I will one of these weeks," Rose said, picking up her basket. She knew very well that she wouldn't be showing up at any dance hall by herself. It wasn't that she didn't like dancing; but to arrive alone, not knowing another soul—she just couldn't bring herself to do that.

The soda fountain in the village's only eating place was her next stop. "Turned out nice, after all, eh?" said the fellow on the gas pump as she approached.

"Yes, grand. How's everything with you?" she asked. "I didn't see you last time I was here."

"Hunky-dorey," he replied with a lopsided grin. There

was fine fuzz covering his upper lip and chin, and his mop of pale blond hair had been bleached white from the sun.

"I just joined up," he informed her. "Me and two of my cousins. We report to Aldershot on Monday."

As his words sunk in, her smile faded.

"You enlisted?"

"Yeah; in the army. My dad was with the Halifax Rifles. Three of my uncles, too. We figure it's our turn now."

She wanted to cry, "No, no, don't!" He was so young. So very, very young. Judging from the baby fuzz on his lip, he hadn't even started to shave. What on earth would the army, and battle, do to him?

At the soda fountain counter, Rose couldn't get him out of her mind. You were supposed to be eighteen to enlist, but she knew that many boys lied, or got relatives to swear false affidavits, counting on the recruiting offices to turn a blind eye.

Would this fellow be okay? Would he make it through; return in one piece to his family? Would his mother, his sisters, understand that he was no longer the young boy they once knew?

Too many questions; too few answers. If you thought about either too much, you could drive yourself crazy.

She took a few sips of her drink and pushed it away.

"I'll see you in a few days," she said to the girl behind the counter.

A few days. That was about as far into the future as anyone could sensibly plan for.

The Cove

It had just gone three when Rose reached the fork in the dirt road. She didn't feel like hurrying back, and in any case, there was no need to rush. Mrs. Boutilier had done a potato salad this morning, and there were biscuits and cold roast left from yesterday. Adele was keeping a watch on things, and she could, surely, find the lemonade in the icebox and the cookie tin in the pantry. She might be delicate, but she wasn't totally helpless.

Think I'll go the shore way for a change, Rose decided, eyeing the path that would take her through a dense, wooded grove and out onto the top of a rocky bluff. The shale beach below the bluff had yielded many of the lovely shells in her collection; perhaps today, she'd find a delightful new one to add to it. And, if she found a sheltered spot, she could sit for a while and read her letters. Ora might have news of her brother, Joe. He'd been in England at last report, waiting for new orders.

Rose paid little attention to the blue coupe parked in the clearing. She knew that local people came down here, too; couples in particular, looking for a deserted spot where they might tryst for an hour or two. She picked her way through tall grass, and climbed over a fallen tree trunk. The half-hidden, mossy path was still wet from the rain, and her shoes were soon soaked through, but she wasn't worried. She could take off her shoes and socks when she reached the beach; prop them up against a rock to dry in the breeze.

Above her head, birds were calling to each other and squirrels chattered. A large brown rabbit startled her when he hopped over her foot and disappeared into the underbrush on the other side of the path. She walked steadily on for ten more minutes, hearing the roar of the surf get louder and louder, and emerged onto a windswept promontory. Ten feet ahead, the land ended, dropping off abruptly to a shale beach thirty feet below.

From this height, the view was magnificent. She could see the long stretch of rocky shore, with the headland in the distance, and out on the water, a fishing boat riding on the long, slow swells. A dark figure on its deck was bending low, stringing nets. Closer in, a flock of seabirds circled a craggy jut of rock; and to her left, a stunted evergreen, its roots exposed, grabbed at the cliff face like a desperate, falling man.

She advanced cautiously, scanning the cliff edge, searching for a way down. There was only one spot that looked like a safe descent route and she'd need to watch her footing, for the slightest stumble could mean a twisted ankle, or worse.

It was then that she saw the two figures—a man and a woman—sitting together in the lee of a craggy boulder, farther up the beach. The man had one arm around the woman's waist, and she was resting her head on his shoulder.

Their obvious intimacy made Rose feel a bit like an intruder and she paused to reconsider her plan. Perhaps she should carry on home. After all, she could go for a walk here another time. As she stood in hesitation at the top of the bluff, the man got up, helped the woman to her feet, and they embraced. When, after what seemed to Rose an eternity, the kiss ended, they linked arms and began to walk slowly in the opposite direction.

Rose watched, almost spellbound, as their figures receded into the distance. There was something almost familiar in the way the woman walked, in the filmy material that trailed out over the brim of her hat.

It was past four-thirty when Rose got back to the cottage. Mr. Browne was sitting alone on the porch, with Laddie at his feet.

"All by yourself?" Rose asked. "Where's Adele?"

"I don't know," he replied. "I had a nap, and when I woke up, no one was around. We had some cookies, didn't we, boy?"

He had indeed. There were crumbs all over the counter in the pantry. And the cookie tin, half-full after lunch, was empty.

Rose was in the kitchen slicing bread when she heard the slam of the screen door and the voices of the two women. Adele and Mrs. Browne must have arrived home together.

When it was quiet again, Rose went into the front room. Hanging on the rack by the door were two hats: a white canvas one that Adele wore when she was painting, and a straw sun hat that both liked to wear. The organza ties of the sun hat were designed to do double duty. You could tie them under your chin, or push them back and let them trail out behind you. On a breezy day, they fluttered grace-fully, beautifully, in the wind.

Harris

Saturday dawned bright and clear, with the sun climbing steadily in a cloudless sky. In the cove, the light shimmered on the surface of water. Little diamond sparkles, moving gently, gracefully, with the tide. *It's like a dance,* Rose thought as she hung tea towels on the line to dry. A minuet—rhythm patterns of one-two-three, four-five-six, repeated again and again.

Once lunch was over, she was planning to have a nice stroll along the sand. It would be her last chance to put her feet in the water, for tomorrow they would be busy packing up, in readiness for an early departure on Monday morning. *All good things must come to an end,* their mother used to say when she and Violet were small. Rose could hear their little-girl voices, pleading, begging to stay awhile longer in the park. "Please, Mama. Can't we? We love it here."

No time, now, though, to be thinking about the past. A full workday lay ahead; Harris had already been over to ask for her help.

"I come asking favours," he announced, pulling an extra chair up to the breakfast table. "We've got a thundering big bag of corn to husk, not to mention a dozen other things to get ready." He took a biscuit off the plate and spooned jam over its top, nodding his thanks to Rose for the cup of tea she set down by his place.

"Mother was wondering if we could borrow Rose," he said. "Our woman's been a busy beaver since yesterday and she's still up to her elbows in pie dough. She could use an extra set of hands in the kitchen."

"Of course she can borrow Rose," Mrs. Browne replied. "Your mother asked for my big platter, as well; and extra dessert plates. Rose will bring the lot when she comes."

Borrow me is about the size of it, Rose thought. *Like I'm another plate, or a cleaning mop.*

"It's a done deal, then," Harris said. "Mind you, I'd be quite happy eating corn and blueberry pie off a tin plate. But that won't suit you gals, will it?"

"Goodness me! I can't imagine anything more unappetizing than eating off a tin plate."

Nor could Rose. With Mrs. Browne, every picnic was turned into an elegant eating occasion. The picnic hamper was testament to that fact. It was a marvellous contraption, fitted with padded bags to hold the china mugs, special compartments for plates, and, sewn into the lid, separate pockets with button flaps for the knives, forks, and spoons.

"Are my husband's clothes ready, Rose?" Mrs. Browne called out from the landing after they'd eaten lunch.

"Everything's laid out on the bed, ma'am," Rose replied. "Shirt, dark jacket, and white trousers, like you said. I pressed them this morning."

A faint "lovely," drifted back down the stairs, together with the sound of the door latch clicking shut.

You're welcome. I'm glad you appreciate the fine job I did.

Rose glanced at the clock on the wall, doing a quick calculation in her head. It was now one-thirty and she wasn't expected next door until three, which gave her enough time for a little stroll along the shore. She needed to say goodbye to the cove—and to summer—on her own.

She didn't have the cove to herself for very long, though. She was standing knee-deep in the water when she heard her name, and looked up in time to see Harris toss his towel down on the sand and head toward her. "Last one ducked gets the booby prize!" he yelled. He dove out of sight, surfacing five yards farther out, and floated on his back for several minutes before swimming in to shore.

"Do you swim, Rose?" he asked, wading toward her in the shallow water.

"No," she replied. "I never learned. But I love the surf, and collecting shells."

"Ah," he said, wiping water from his eyes. "We'll have to find you one, then." He dug his foot into the wet sand and reached down. "Here you are," he said. "Add this to your collection."

"Thanks," she said, delighted at the perfect little spiral which lay in his open palm. "I haven't got one quite like that."

He plunged into the chilly water again, swimming swiftly and surely the entire width of the cove before re-emerging. "I'd better get a move on," he said, picking up his towel and draping it around his neck. "I promised Dad I'd help him get the wood ready for the firepit."

Afterwards, several images remained etched in Rose's mind. The feel of his hand, wet but warm, on her fingertips as she took the spiral shell from him; the fine, reddish-blond hair that grew on the back of his wrist. His eyes were different, too, without his thick glasses. Crinkled at the corners, their pupils shot with amber flecks. Strange, how you didn't notice the colour of a person's eyes when they had their glasses on.

Strange, too, how different a man looked without his shirt. Transformed, somehow; rather like the Greek God statues in the Gardens. Broad shoulders, muscular chest; sun-browned back and neck; neat, trim waist; and, below the drawstring swimming trunks, long, straight legs, and bare feet caked with sand.

There was plenty to do when Rose arrived at quarter past three. "Do the corn for starters, there's a good girl," Myrtle said, pointing to a huge burlap sack. Rose took the sack out to the back step and sat husking three dozen ears while Myrtle got out the cooking kettle and readied it on a grate over the open firepit.

The silverware and napkins were next. "Wrap the silver inside each napkin," Myrtle said. "Keeps the flies off."

She set a carton down on the grass. "Missus wants these on the serving table," she said, pointing to the coloured-glass candleholders inside. "Stick a couple on the porch railing while you're at it. Shove the empty box under the stoop when you're done. Nobody will see it there."

"When are the guests arriving?" Rose asked, fitting the small white candles into their holders.

"Around six. Some of 'em took a drive down the shore this afternoon. Now, let's hustle on indoors. Still plenty left to do in the kitchen."

While Myrtle stirred mayonnaise into the potato salad, Rose cut the pies into serving pieces and covered them with wax paper.

"Here, take the bowl and put it in the cool room," Myrtle said, rubbing her shoulder and grimacing. "I can't mix another second. My arm feels like it's coming off, honest to Pete."

When Rose returned, Myrtle was testing the tomato aspic in their molds. "We'll leave them till the very last to turn out," she said. "Then they won't melt and drip all over our nice clean table cloth. Right?"

"Right," Rose repeated. She had to give Myrtle credit—the woman was totally organized.

With each of them holding an end of the pan, they slid the cooked salmon onto Mrs. Browne's platter. "There you go, you little kipper," Myrtle said, poking gently at his tail with her finger. "Last night, you were swimming; tonight, you're supper. Never know what a day'll bring, eh?" She grinned at Rose and mopped the sweat off her face with a corner of her apron.

"How many are coming?" Rose asked, setting the platter on top of a pan of sea water to chill.

"Oh, about a dozen, I figure." Myrtle looked over at Rose. "Think we got enough grub?"

"Goodness, I'd say!" Rose replied. "There's enough here to feed an army."

By eight that evening the party was in full swing. If "party" was the way to describe it. There were no games—not even a round of croquet—and no music, either; which was a shame, for Adele could easily have sung a few numbers. She had a fine, clear voice, and wouldn't have needed any piano accompaniment.

The guests themselves were pleasant, civil people. In addition to the three Brownes, the group included the elder Smiths and their daughter, Claudia; a Mr. Thompson, who was in the shipping business; a youngish army officer with his arm in a cast, and a distinguished man in the gold braid and brass buttons of a naval captain.

There was no shortage of liquor. The men helped themselves from a wide assortment that Uncle Max had set out on a large wooden tray. Flasks of hard spirits, several bottles of chilled wine for the women, and a full keg of ale, with a spout on the side of the barrel.

"Nice beer, that," Myrtle whispered to her. "I had myself a little drop, earlier."

During the early evening, the men clustered together, talking war and politics. Rose caught bits here and there, as she went back and forth with the dishes of food.

"Churchill's holding onto his trump cards," Mr. Smith insisted, jabbing his finger against Max's blazer.

"Damn it to hell, man," Max protested, "—when's he going to play them, then? First, Dunkirk, and now, Dieppe. And where are our boys? Running England's hills and dales, that's what. Like a troop of bloody Boy Scouts."

"I agree with Max," the naval captain said. "Either we're at war or we're not." He turned toward Mr. Thompson, a quiet-spoken, ruddy-faced man in civilian clothes. "Russ, explain to these chaps the point you were making to me, earlier."

"As I was saying on the way down here—" Mr. Thompson replied, "—the Merchant Navy needs ships. With two more sunk this week, it seems to me the company's in a great position to offer two—maybe even three—on a lease arrangement . . ."

"Is war all that men want to talk about these days?" Rose said to Myrtle when she went into the kitchen for clean plates. "Oh, I dunno about that," Myrtle replied. "Seems to me they still like sports and their cars, too."

The women were another story. Clustered around Claudia, who was holding court under the striped canopy, they seemed content to be hanging onto her every word.

". . . so pretty, isn't it, all along the shore . . ."

". . . we wanted a table on the terrace . . ."

". . . very expensive, of course . . ."

". . . you can always tell who the summer people are . . ."

Everyone had eaten their fill by the time the sun dipped below the stand of fir on the west side of the cottage. At Gert's signal, Rose and Myrtle gathered up what was left of the food, and Harris lit the candles. This had an almost magical effect on the assembled guests, quieting their voices and softening their faces into shadowed orange hues.

Even Claudia seemed less abrasive and more attractive. Rose had been quick enough to pass judgement, finding little about Claudia that was attractive. She was a large girl, with a prominent nose and a square jaw. Only her expensive clothes and her hair, glossy black and thick, rated any points in Rose's books.

Rose tried to ignore the lost, empty feeling she had whenever she looked in Harris' direction. For the past half-hour he'd been sitting next to Claudia, his shoulder not quite touching hers. Each of them seemed relaxed, in the comfortable way of two people who knew each other well. She might not have made anything more of their companionship if it hadn't been for Myrtle's comment.

"Be a match, that Smith girl and Harris," Myrtle said. She and Rose were taking a breather at the kitchen table, their plates heaped with potato salad and pieces of the leftover fish.

"What makes you say that?" Rose asked, a twinge of jealousy darting through her.

"His folks want it; badly. The families have been friends for years."

"Why does he have to do what they want?" Her throat felt tight and she reached for the water jug, half filling a glass and drinking it down.

"There's money involved, girl," Myrtle said. "And money talks."

Myrtle chattered on, and Rose pretended that she was listening. Deep down, though, she was struggling, trying to come to grips with her doubts, and her sense of betrayal.

She could not believe that Harris would stoop so low; had taken for granted that he, of all people, would adhere to the highest of standards when it came to choosing a wife. She did a mental tally of what she considered to be the essential qualities a man like Harris would look for. Someone who was gracious and beautiful, intelligent and accomplished, well-spoken and kindhearted, loving and compassionate. An ideal of womanhood, in fact; somebody perfect. Somebody quite out of reach.

The party came to an end soon after midnight.

Rose led the way back through the birch grove, shining the flashlight over the tree roots so that Adele and her mother, on either side of Mr. Browne, could find their footing.

Rose firmly declined Harris' offer to accompany them. "I know the way like the back of my hand," he said. "I'd feel really badly if one of you tripped and sprained an ankle."

"I can manage," she insisted, reaching for the flashlight. "You'd better be seeing to your guests. They're a good deal more important than we are."

In the yellow arc of the flashlight's beam, she could just make out his expression. He looked startled and uncertain. As though, for the life of him, he couldn't figure out what he'd done—or said—that was wrong.

War Comes Home

Rose was in the kitchen, sorting the soiled clothes into separate piles, when the phone rang. Getting back to rights after "a simple vacation at the shore," involved a mountain of laundry to wash, iron, and put away.

"Rose, the phone's for you," Adele called from the front hall. "I think it's important."

Turning off the tap in the sink, Rose hurried to answer it. She never had phone calls. Perhaps it was the Home. Perhaps Lily was sick, or there'd been an accident.

It wasn't the Home calling, though. It was Ora. Sobbing over the phone wire.

"He's gone, Rose. My brother's gone."

It took a minute for her words to register. *Joe, gone? Where was he, anyway? Oh yes, somewhere in France.*

"Where's he gone?" she implored, not wanting to understand. "Back to England?"

"No! He's dead! He was killed—at Dieppe. I guess it was awful. Hundreds and hundreds of them, all dead."

Rose's head reeled. Surely there was a mistake.

An image surfaced of the cemetery where her parents lay. Four words, engraved on a granite stone. *Gone, but not forgotten.*

Ora, on the other end of the wire, recited the facts like a veteran news reporter. "Pa got a telegram last week telling us he was missing. Then a second one came. He was killed in action, it said. I had to call and tell you. You're my best friend. I've been trying your number for the past three days. The lady who cooks finally answered and told me when you folks were due back."

Rose found her own voice. "Ora, I am so sorry. I don't

know what to say. He was special—a special big brother. Your father, is he all right?"

"I guess so. He doesn't talk much. He's been sitting in the front room by himself a lot. Says to leave him alone. The minister came over. They're reading Joe's name out at Sunday's memorial service. Will you come? Sit beside me?"

"Of course, if you want me to. Mrs. Browne will give me the time off. She's pretty good that way."

"I better go now, Rose. I'm on my break. I'll see you on Sunday, then."

"Yes, Sunday, sure . . ." And then, because Ora meant so much to her: "Ora—"

"What?"

She tried to form the thought, get it out. "Ora. I just feel so bad for you. Be brave."

"I will, Rose. We're not the only ones. But it's hard. Bye."

Rose put the phone down slowly and went back to her washing. How dreadful it must have been for Ora's father to answer the door and be handed one of those yellow telegrams. She tried to imagine his despair, to conjure up the hurt and loss Ora must feel over the loss of her older brother. It was difficult, though. Rose had no experience in saying goodbye to a father or brothers; had not watched them wave and march off, to board troop ships under cover of darkness and sail away before dawn's light. As far as she knew, she didn't have an uncle who'd gone over, either. No one to get letters from, or worry over.

Possibly, one or both of Uncle Earle's boys—hazy figures from long-ago Sunday afternoons—might have enlisted; might be serving as soldiers or sailors. But, so what if they were. She hadn't seen or heard from any of them for years; they were strangers to her.

After she'd cleared up the dishes that evening, she looked up the reports on Dieppe in the papers. Minnie May had saved the last week's worth, knowing that Mrs. Browne would want to go through them. Joe's name was there, along with dozens of other local boys. The list indicated that he'd been attached to an Ontario unit. Engineers, so it said. Building bridges and repairing roads. Weird, that. Ora used to say that Joe loved to make and fix things. Well, he wouldn't be fixing things any longer.

Rose caught an early tram car on Sunday morning, choosing a seat at the back, away from the other passengers. She wasn't looking forward to the service. It had been a long time since she'd attended church, longer still since she'd been inside St. Mark's. The children from the Home might be there today, actually. Lily and the others, crowded into the back pews; and Miss Duffy, puffed up with her own importance as she'd always been, riding herd from her spot, near the centre aisle.

Dear God, how could you ever predict the way things might turn out, the cards that you might be forced to play? Did Ora's brother ask for a transfer to the Engineering unit, or had he been sent? And, if he hadn't gone, would he still be alive?

She gathered up her bag and put on her gloves. Her stop was next, just outside the Regimental Gate, a block north of the Base's main entrance. Tears blurred her eyes as she waited to cross the street. She'd thought that war, with its battles and its casualties, would never touch her. She was wrong, though. Because of Ora, the war had found its way home.

Clotheslines

By the end of September, Adele and Mrs. Browne had picked up the threads of their city activities and, on the surface at least, life seemed to be falling into its familiar pattern. Adele's piano pupils came back and forth, and Mrs. Browne was gone a good deal, often not returning until late in the evening. Mr. Browne spent more and more time on his own, and appeared to have lost all the spark that he'd displayed during their weeks at the cottage. He was much duller, less interested in taking Laddie out for his daily walk, and tended to doze off in his chair immediately after he'd eaten.

"He'll sleep himself into an early grave, that's what," Minnie May muttered to Rose one afternoon. "I can see it coming."

His behaviour worried Rose, who had been thinking much the same thing as Minnie May. She might have mustered the nerve to speak to Harris about Mr. Browne, had she seen him. However, since their return from the shore, Harris had visited only once, claiming increased demands at the office as the chief reason for his absence. Rose wasn't about to be fooled by that line, however. Now that Claudia was on the scene, he was, undoubtedly, being kept very, very occupied.

On an early October afternoon Rose took her basket out on the stoop to gather in the clothes. "I should get a job in a Chinese laundry," she joked to Minnie May on her way through the kitchen. "Honest to Pete, it seems like I spend all my time washing and ironing."

The pillow slips flapped in the brisk autumn breeze as

she struggled with the groaning pulley. The wind had played havoc with her neatly pegged linens, and she was irritated, for she prided herself on a perfectly hung wash. All the darks together, then the whites, in graduated lengths, and, lastly, the cleaning cloths.

"If there's ever a contest for hanging out laundry, you'd be a sure winner," Minnie May had told her. "And I know what first prize would be—a wash bucket and a big box of Rinso." Rose had laughed, taking the ribbing in stride, recognizing the compliment for what it was.

Mrs. Browne, too, had noticed the clothes. "That line of laundry is a work of art," she said one day. "If a painter could capture the light, with the clothes bobbing like that in the wind, it would make a most interesting study. I must mention it to Adele. She might like to give it a try."

People have the queerest notions, Rose had thought at the time. For the life of her, she couldn't imagine anyone wanting to paint a picture of a clothesline, let alone hang it on their living-room wall.

She reeled in the garments methodically, folding them and placing them neatly in her basket. There was a mesh bag for the cleaning rags and a canvas pouch on the outside wall for the wooden pegs.

Mrs. Browne's pink summer dressing gown was last. Rose was about to drop it into her basket when she noticed specks of what looked like dirt around the pocket. *Bother*, she thought, frowning. *If they don't shake off, I'll have to wash it over again.*

She set the basket on the floor and did a closer inspection. What she'd taken for specks of dirt turned out to be blue ink stains. She fished inside the pocket and pulled out the culprit—a damp wad of paper, folded in four. She swore to herself, casting around in her mind, trying to remember what you used to take out ink stains. Was it milk, or diluted vinegar? Perhaps a paste of baking powder?

"Mercy, I don't know what to tell you, dear," Minnie May said when Rose showed her the marks. She was settled in her chair by the den window, listening to her afternoon radio program. "There used to be a stain chart on the cellar shelf. Go see if you can find it."

Rose did exactly that, racing back upstairs to scrub at the marks with the recommended solution. She left the gown to soak in a bucket of cool water for half an hour, then rinsed it and pegged it on the line to drip dry. It wasn't until she was putting away the supper dishes that she noticed the wad of paper. It was lying on the kitchen counter where she'd tossed it earlier.

She picked up the paper gingerly, opening it along the damp crease lines, smoothing them out with the flat of her hand. If it proved to be an important document, she'd be obliged to show it to Mrs. Browne and apologize for ruining it.

It was, she saw immediately, a letter. Some of the words were obliterated from the water. A few, badly blurred, were decipherable still:

M Dea Eth
If onl how badly I   misery. can only ho
that be resolved   seems impossib
  solution to
Surely to God I towa   future
 together,   behind us.
 Our happi   should   forem
  miling my lov
  Alwa
  ur R s ll
She loves him, she loves him not.

Him? Who—Mr. Browne?

No, stupid. She loves him not.

It's the other guy she's mad about.

The man at the party.

What was his name?

Lord, lord, I can't remember . . .

Pause. Click.

The cove, the hat!

I wanted it to be Adele.

Silly girl. It never was. It was *her*.

Little wonder she didn't want anyone looking through the mail.

What would Ora say? "Hell's bells and I'll be damned."

Something like that.

The Last Straw

Rose awoke with a start. From two floors below, she could hear the faint rumble of the furnace; and, from the driveway next door, the revving of a car engine. She lay still for a few minutes, relishing the warmth of her bed, not wanting to get up. The weather had turned colder over the past week, with frost in the mornings, and the floorboards of her room felt like ice against her bare feet.

Lord, but I'm tired, she thought, staring up at a crack in the ceiling. She'd been sleeping badly these past few nights. The letter she'd found had played on her mind, and now, there was the upset over Mr. Browne.

He had slipped getting out of the bathtub the previous week. Minnie May had found him, and called for the doctor. There were no bones broken, but the doctor ordered bedrest for a week, which meant that Rose was running up and down stairs with trays of food four and five times each day. Despite Minnie May's best efforts to tempt his flagging appetite, he barely touched the hot soups, fresh biscuits, and puddings. "He'll waste away into nothing," she said, scowling, when Rose brought the trays back to the kitchen.

Two distinct thumps, followed by a dog barking, brought Rose into a sitting position. *Can't be the milkman,* she thought. *I'd have heard his wagon.* She switched on the bedside lamp, and peered at her little clock, relieved to see that she hadn't overslept. It was just twenty past six.

She was digging in the drawer for clean underwear when she heard the barking again. *That's Laddie,* she thought. *Mrs. Browne must be letting him out.* She pulled open the heavy blackout curtains and looked out into the semi-darkness. The beech tree outside her window obscured her view, but she caught a glimpse of Laddie frisking in the fallen leaves, nosing at something blue and white. Rose leaned closer to the glass, squinting for a better look.

Can't be, went her brain. She blinked and looked again. It was, though. Mr. Browne, dressed only in his blue-and-white striped pyjamas—no robe, no sweater, no coat—crouched in the leaves beside Laddie. While she stared stupidly down at the scene, he got up, brushed a few leaves off his pant leg, and, with the dog following obediently, headed down the flagstone path and onto the sidewalk.

If he gets as far as the corner, people on the tram will see him! They'll point and laugh and make jokes.

She could hear the comments.

"Look, look—over by the barber shop."

"See the silly old coot in his nightclothes."

"Haw, haw, haw!"

She had to go after him; bring him back before he became a laughing stock; a figure of embarrassment for the entire family.

The grass was still damp with frost, and she almost fell as she hopped over the lobelia border and sprinted up the sidewalk. They were at the main intersection, waiting for the light to change, by the time she reached them. Laddie's ears picked up the sound of her running feet, and he greeted her with a low, welcoming woof.

Rose gave the dog a pat before speaking.

"Good morning," she said, determined to act as if meeting them like that was nothing out of the ordinary. "You certainly are up early. I've got the tea on and steeping. Would you like a cup?"

Mr. Browne shook his head. "No thanks. No breakfast for us, yet. We're going for a swim, aren't we, boy?"

Laddie wagged his tail while Rose thought quickly.

How she wished Harris were here! He'd know what to do. He was good with his uncle.

She tried again. "I think you might find it a bit chilly for swimming. Why don't you wait till later, when the sun is up. Look, I brought your coat for you."

"No," he said, petulantly. "I'm going swimming with Laddie. Right now."

"He wouldn't budge," Rose told Minnie May later. "I don't know what I would have done without those two soldiers. He was different with them; like he saw their uniforms and knew he had to obey."

"Did they ask his name?" Minnie May demanded.

"No. And I didn't say."

"Good," she replied. "Bad enough that our dirty laundry got that far up the street. We don't need anybody reading the labels, too."

Harris, alerted by Mrs. Browne, came by before supper. "Thanks for your help this morning, Rose," he said after spending an hour behind the closed door of the study. "My uncle is not at all well."

"Yes," she replied. "I know."

He looked uncertain, uneasy. He looked like she felt.

"He'll require more attention, obviously. We'll be looking into the various options."

"Yes," she repeated.

The various options—what did that mean? Unless, of course, the doctor had a magic potion in his bag, or a new head. Now, *that* might just do the trick.

"I hope we can manage till then."

She wanted to confront him; to say, "We? What's we supposed to mean? Anyone with an ounce of sense knows that the poor man's been slipping for a long time. He needs a proper keeper, can't you see that?" But she didn't; she couldn't. Instead, she said: "We'll do what we can," leaving him to make whatever he could of that.

"He's got hardening of the arteries. No two ways about it." Ora had a way of getting to the heart of things; no beating around the bushes.

"Have they got something they can give him?" Rose shifted her satchel onto her knee to make more room on the seat. They'd caught a southbound tram, on their way to the park for the open air dance due to start at eight.

"I don't think so," Ora replied. "The person gets more and more stupid—senile, they call it. Till, finally, they're like a baby. Diapers and all."

Rose's eyes widened. She had a fleeting vision of Mr. Browne, curled up in a blanket on the sofa, sucking his thumb.

"Want a stick of gum?" Ora asked, holding out the open package.

"No, thanks." What Rose needed right now was not gum; it was answers.

"Surely Mr. Browne won't get like that."

"Well, maybe not. But it does get pretty bad. My great aunt went that way; started sneaking out in the middle of the night, sometimes with no clothes on, not even her nightgown. It got so bad that my cousin had to sleep in her room to make sure she didn't get away."

"What happened, finally?"

"She died. Which was a mercy. Everybody was relieved, especially my cousin. The poor thing was near crazy, after six long years of it."

"They're figuring out what to do now, according to Harris," Rose said.

"Well, thankfully they've got money. That always helps. He'll not likely end up like the folks who get put away in the South Street Hospital."

"They'd never do that. I know they wouldn't."

"Never say never." Ora turned and wagged her finger at Rose. "Just make sure you don't get stuck with him. After all, he's not your relative."

"No, I won't," Rose promised. "I can't. I wouldn't know how to, anyway."

Nothing startling happened in the days following the early morning escapade. Mrs. Browne stayed in, as did Adele. Harris came by each evening. The doctor made three visits, and the minister, one. Mrs. Browne received each of them in her study, and afterwards accompanied them upstairs to Mr. Browne's room. Rose couldn't help but feel badly for Mr. B. How different it must be, cooped up in his room, after the summertime freedom at the shore.

"Prayer time over, is it?" was Minnie May's comment when Rose came looking for a tray of sweets to serve to the minister. "Well, as long as it isn't the undertaker, I suppose we're still ahead in the game."

Rose's reaction was a nervous giggle. It did strike her funny, though. Mr. Browne was in a bad way, no question about it. But he wasn't dead—not yet.

Bail Out

"What do you think I should do?" Rose asked Ora. The situation at the house was getting on her nerves, and there was no way things were going to improve.

"I think you should leave, and the sooner the better," Ora replied. "Didn't I tell you that I can get you on at the plant. They need girls like crazy. There's a big order in from the army; the foreman says we'll be on overtime call from now till it's finished."

"I'd have to give notice," Rose said.

"Two weeks is plenty. They can get another girl from the Home easy enough. Anyway, you don't need to be worrying your head about it. With the dough they've got, they can hire a maid *and* a companion; or a male orderly, for that matter."

Ora was right. Why should she fret about it? If she wanted out—which she did—she'd have to take the bull by the horns.

"Why don't you ask their nephew to put in a word," Ora continued. "It'll help to have another person on your side."

"That might just work," Rose replied.

"Well, then—get a move on. There's nothing to lose by asking him. Nothing at all."

Rose nabbed Harris on his next visit.

"Excuse me, Harris. Would you have a few minutes? I'd like to speak to you about something important."

"Of course, Rose. What's up?" His usual smile belied the strain that was evident in his voice. By now, he was shouldering the bulk of the responsibility regarding his uncle's condition. Rose knew that neither Mrs. Browne nor Adele would be any good at coming up with concrete solutions.

"I've thought this over a lot," she began, trying to sound businesslike and confident. "I'm planning to give my notice to Mrs. Browne and I was hoping I could count on your support."

"Rose, don't tell me!" he said with a groan. "My aunt speaks so highly of your work, and Uncle's got so used to you. We had hoped to maintain the status quo; at least until the spring."

Rose didn't know what he meant by status quo. But, now that she'd made up her mind, she wasn't one bit interested in hanging around for another six or eight months.

"I could speak to my aunt about a raise in your pay," Harris suggested.

No way. If they think they can dangle a carrot or two, they've got another think coming.

"It's not the pay," she replied. "I've thought it all out. It's time to move on, and I need to get settled somewhere else before Christmas."

"That's less than two months away," he said. "Are you quite sure about this?"

"Yes. Absolutely."

"Well, Aunt Ethel won't wish to block you if your mind is made up. And I know she'll give you a good reference letter. Have you lined up a position with another house yet?"

There he was, assuming that all she wanted out of life was to be somebody's servant.

"I'm not looking for another domestic job," Rose replied.

"No?" He looked surprised. "What other work could you do, then?"

"Sewing," Rose said. "I'm good at any kind of needle-work. Both Mrs. Browne and your mother say so." She took a deep breath and went on. "I'd like to get on at a department store, like the one where Mrs. Matheson, who knows your mother, works. I heard her at the last IODE meeting saying that they're always short in the sewing room. If she'd put in a word for me, I'm sure it will help my chances."

Rose knew that her choices were limited, but she had no intention of working at the Dockyard, wearing coveralls and steel-toed boots and carrying a lunch bucket. And the factory sewing that Ora sweated over every day was every bit as unappealing. Sure, those jobs put food on the table and paid the rent; but they went nowhere. Better to go the route of apprentice seamstress in a high-class store. It wouldn't be glamorous work, but, if she played her cards right, it could lead to something more interesting—and better-paying—down the road. All she needed was somebody to give her a chance.

"Well, I'll give you credit," said Harris. "You seem to know what you want. I'll speak to Mother tomorrow and let you know what she says. Just promise me that you'll do your part by giving adequate notice. You owe my aunt that much."

He was as good as his word. The following evening the phone rang, and it was him. "Rose, you're to see the lady in charge of hiring next Wednesday afternoon. She said to be there at three o'clock."

"I start the first of the month," Rose told Ora while they waited in a line-up for the Saturday matinee. "The sewing room is frantic during Christmas, she says, and she's counting on me to learn fast."

"Horray!" Ora hugged Rose. "I figured they'd come through. Have you told Mrs. B yet?"

"Yes. Yesterday, when she gave me my pay."

"What did she say? Was she mad?"

"No; she wasn't mad. She was sort of—oh, I don't know—sad, I suppose."

"Yeah, right. Sad to lose a darn good worker, I'll bet. Who's to say she'll be so lucky with the next girl. Anyway, it's her problem, not yours. Have you got five cents? We can share a bag of popcorn."

The newsreel was full of the war in Europe. Churchill and Roosevelt shaking hands on a ship; General Montgomery with the troops in England. Rose tried to pay attention, but her mind wandered to the domestic events that were shaping her own little world.

No more peeling vegetables and scrubbing floors; no more polishing furniture and hanging out laundry. She was going to a real job now; nine to six from Monday to Friday, and every second Saturday. She could live her own life and not have to kow-tow to people, or be part of their troubles—and their secrets.

The newsreel wrapped up with a heart-wrenching documentary on the evacuation of the London schoolchildren. There were hundreds of them, standing on the station platforms, clutching their dolls and teddy bears close. Many—much younger than Lily was now—were being sent off to families and friends in the safer, more rural parts of the country. But, so the narrator was saying, countless others were boarding trains that would take them to the seacoast, and onto ships bound for Canada.

The sight of their faces—solemn, tearful, brave—stayed with Rose throughout the main feature. She could see Lily and herself, just as solemn and equally afraid, standing at the curb outside Mrs. McGinn's house, waiting to climb into the back seat of the black car, knowing that, whatever happened, their old lives were gone forever.

Rose picked out a new suitcase at Zeller's after the matinee was over. "I'll call it a present from me to me," she joked to Ora while the clerk was ringing it in.

"It's a dandy one," Ora said. "It'll be great when next summer comes."

"That's what I thought," Rose replied.

Summer was a long way off, but already they'd agreed on what they wanted to do. They would ask for the same week off and book a little cottage, somewhere down the shore. Maybe they could invite another girl along, to share in the costs.

In the end, Rose accepted Harris' offer to drive her to Aunt Lettie's. "I don't need to trouble you," she'd said when he first suggested it. "I can get a taxi over. It's not very far."

"Don't even think of a cab." He looked hurt, almost indignant. "It's no trouble; not a bit."

She was packed by ten o'clock on the night before her departure. Her new suitcase, as well as two cartons, were crammed with her accumulated possessions: clothes and toiletries; crocheted doilies and trinkets; two hooked mats; three framed pictures; her jewellery box and her alarm clock. Tucked inside a brown envelope were two postcards, the only mail that they'd ever received from Violet.

I'll be in Boston in a few days. Will write you then. Kisses to you both. Love, Violet. The first card had been followed by a second, a few weeks later. *What a city! People everywhere. Halifax is one hick-town compared to this burg. Am finding my way around. Cape Cod is next. Violet.*

Rose fastened the tops of the boxes with sticky tape and

looked around the room. Stripped bare of her belongings, it looked as stark and as desolate as it had on that first morning, two years earlier She'd been nervous that day, overwhelmed by the strange house and its odd people. Wanting, hoping, that things would work out for the best. As she was doing, right now, over the decision to live with Ora, at the boarding house of her Aunt Lettie.

"Aunt Lettie can use our help," Ora had explained. "Her legs are so bad from the arthritis that she can hardly move. We can have the big front bedroom. It's got a double bed and a pull-out."

Although Rose hadn't been in Aunt Lettie's house, she was willing to go along with the arrangement, at least for the time being. Aunt Lettie wasn't asking for rent, which was an extra bonus. Her only request was that they share in the grocery bill, keep the furnace stoked, and help with the cleaning.

"The Rental Board has her on their list, so she's always got three paying roomers," Ora had added. "Usually, they're navy guys, waiting to ship out. But she gets some army, too. She adores every last one; calls them all her boys."

Rose was up early, helping Minnie May, as usual, with the morning chores. Adele and Mrs. Browne said their good-byes before leaving for the hospital.

"My best wishes, Rose. I'm sure you'll do well," Mrs. Browne said. She was putting on her gloves as she spoke; a convenient way of not having to look Rose in the eye.

"Yes, good luck," Adele murmured. "Perhaps I'll see you at the store."

"Perhaps you will," Rose replied. *You won't want to speak, though. It wouldn't do, to be seen chatting with one of the sewing room girls.*

Minnie May was busy in the kitchen when Harris arrived. "I'm not much for goodbyes," she'd said to Rose over a pick-up lunch. "But I'll miss you. We've been a good team, you and me."

Rose knew that Minnie May would miss her—for a while. But, with the family to attend to and a new girl to bring up to speed, Minnie May would have precious little time to remember the former one.

Strangely enough, the last farewell came from Mr. Browne. Rose could see him, standing at the second storey window, waving. Laddie, ever faithful, was there, too, perched on the window bench, his nose pressed against the glass. So sad, that. Mr. Browne, the prisoner; confined to a life sentence in his own house.

The ride to Lettie's place, situated in the central city, opposite the North Common, was a short, silent one. Harris didn't attempt any conversation, and Rose was just as well pleased. What was there to say? One maid goes, another one arrives. Life rolls on. Amen.

"You'll love Aunt Lettie," Ora had assured her. "She'll treat you just like you're family." Rose didn't doubt Ora. Being treated like one of the family was, however, not the same as *being* family. Which was something that Ora would never understand. Sure, her mother was dead, and her brother, too. But Ora still had family: a father and three sisters, as well as aunts and uncles, and a grandmother in New Brunswick.

The car turned a corner and pulled up in front of a large brown house. Ora, good as gold, was waiting on the porch, and came tearing down the steps the minute the car had stopped. "Thank the Lord you're here," she said excitedly, reaching for Rose's arm. "I was beginning to think you'd changed your mind."

"That's everything, then," Harris said, having placed the two cartons, a canvas satchel, and Rose's suitcase on the sidewalk. "I'll be getting along." He took her hand and pressed it lightly. "Bye, Rose. All the best." It was a polite gesture, a proper farewell from a well-brought-up young man. He was behind the wheel and pulling away before Rose realized that she hadn't introduced him to Ora.

Ora didn't seem to notice, or mind. "Come on," she was urging. "Aunt Lettie's just dying to meet you."

ROSE

PART THREE

Lettie's

Lettie's Place

Rose could see right away that Aunt Lettie's place was going to be a whole new experience for her. The house itself was a large, two-storey one, full of heavy, old-fashioned furniture that hadn't seen a good polishing for years. Lettie had converted a small room off the kitchen into a bedsitting room for herself, which left four rooms on the second level for renting out.

The room that Ora and Rose shared was at the front, overlooking the boulevard. It had two deep closets for clothes, and the mahogany suite included a four-poster bed, a tall bureau, a boudoir chair, and a mirrored vanity, with drawers on both sides to hold their makeup.

Ora had laid claim to a large, square area at the end of the upper hall as well. It was a delightfully sunny spot and was big enough for a two high-backed arm chairs, a badly marked writing desk, and Lettie's treadle sewing machine.

"Sure you want to keep that old treadle?" Ora demanded, running the carpet sweeper over the once elegant Persian runner while Rose scrubbed at the window ledges.

"Yes I do," Rose replied, rinsing out her rag in a bucket of soapy water. "I tried it and it works fine. I can put it to good use."

"Better you than me," Ora said. "Doing the odd sampler is okay, but I loathe real sewing." She flicked at the writing desk with a duster, and then set a chipped plant pot containing a bedraggled ivy on its top. "How's that look?" she asked, plucking at the dead leaves. "The poor thing's dying for a bit of water and some light. Maybe the sun will revive it."

"It might come along," Rose replied. "The natural light will help. And I could get some fresh soil and a larger pot at Zeller's next week." The alcove, which they nicknamed the "hot spot," had a western exposure and, on a nice day, the sun poured in from early afternoon until after supper. Lettie had stuck a green blind up at the window, rather than the regulation blackout curtains, which helped out even more.

The only drawback was Ora's habit of yanking at the blind, often pulling so hard on it that the roller jammed. Rose knew that there was little point in nagging Ora to be more careful. Ora was dear and sweet, but she was not fastidious when it came to the small things involved in keeping a house in order. So, in order to preserve her own sanity, and prevent the problem from happening too often, Rose kept quiet, and added "check blind" to her list of daily things to do.

Use of the bathroom in the mornings was the other problem area. Five of them needed to get in and out of it as quickly as possible. Sitting on the top step, waiting, was a waste of valuable time when there was a much more efficient way to do things. A schedule was the only answer.

"Everybody gets a time slot," she explained, showing Ora the printed chart she had drawn up. "What do you think?"

"Rosie, you're a riot and a half," Ora replied. She was sitting cross-legged in the middle of the bed, hair tied back, smearing cold cream on her nose. "All I can think of is Greta and the list she used to put up in the bathroom: pee, flush, wash your hands, comb your hair—and in that order, too. Don't you remember!"

"Yes, of course I remember. But answer me. Are you in favour, or not?"

"Sure I'm in favour. As long as I get the last slot. I hate getting up any earlier than I have to." She flashed one of her impish grins. "What else can I say—I need my beauty sleep."

Satisfied, Rose posted the schedule on the wall. The guys razzed her, as she knew they would. "Private Dickson, reporting in, ma'am. Ears washed, teeth brushed, crapper flushed." The little Newfoundlander, his accent as thick as cold molasses, launched into an off-key rendition of "This Is the Army, Mr. Jones" and everyone, Lettie included, laughed.

Rose liked Aunt Lettie, a bent, wizened little woman who had Ora's red hair and easygoing disposition. Nothing seemed to fizz Lettie; not the comings and goings at all hours of the day and night, nor the ashtrays filled with the men's cigarette butts, nor the occasional empty rum bottle, left on the dining-room table in the morning.

"It's a lot of work, keeping roomers, isn't it?" Rose said to Ora one Saturday morning as she dragged out the scrub bucket and mop. "But I suppose she can use the money."

"Naw, it's not that. Uncle Bubs left her fixed okay. She just likes the company; the more the merrier. You can tell that she doesn't worry over a bit of dirt or clutter. And now she's got the two of us to whisk around, she's really in clover."

As the weeks slipped by, Rose could see that people *were* what Aunt Lettie was about. Another can of water in the soup pot was the motto she lived by. Technically, the fellows were roomers only, with kitchen privileges if they wanted them. But many evenings Rose would come in from work to find them at the long dining-room table, eating whatever was on the go—stew, baked beans, or fish, covered with tomato sauce and cheese, done in the oven.

Often they pitched in and helped with the meal, stirring chowder, or cutting bread on Lettie's nicked chopping board. "They're just youngsters, away from home for the first time," Lettie said when Ora commented about the amount of food they went through in a week. "Can't have them going to bed hungry, now, can we?"

"Oh, you don't fool me, Aunt Lettie," Ora teased. "They're more than little boys, and you know it. You're in love with their big broad shoulders and their cute little arses."

"And what's wrong with a little piece of arse now and then?" Lettie shot back with a wink at Rose. "That new sailor boy is a sweetie. Why, he can put his shoes under my bed any time he likes."

The bawdy references tended to make Rose cringe with embarrassment, but not Ora. In that respect, she was a carbon-copy of her aunt. She could banter and toss off naughty one-liners with an ease that Rose could marvel at but never emulate.

"I'd rather be a good sport than a goody two-shoes," Ora said in a moment of self-defence. "Besides, it's all in good fun. The guys brag about their flings, and talk like they hop in the sack with any skirt that comes along, but most of it's just that—talk. With a dash of wishful thinking thrown in.

Over time, Rose loosened up, becoming less offended at the rough talk and sly innuendo. The free-wheeling, say-anything-you-want atmosphere was a refreshing, almost liberating change from what she'd been used to. She tried to "let her hair down," as Ora called it, and achieved some degree of success; but she knew she'd never have Ora's easy-going way, not if she lived to be a hundred.

The Sewing Room

Rose learned a good deal about work and people in her first few weeks at the store. She learned that the customer is always right—and rich—and that she was there to produce, period. Most important of all, she learned that she might work in a fancy store, but she was no less a servant than she'd ever been.

"They know how to get their pound of flesh," Ora told her. "There's no shortage of work down at our place, either, let me tell you. Uncle Bubs used to say that somebody always profits in a war. Now I know what he meant."

There was certainly no shortage of merchandise at the store, or women to scoop it up. The customers who shopped there—Mrs. Dakin, the supervisor, preferred to call them *our clientele*—didn't seem bound by thin pocketbooks or any need to "make do." With harvest balls and Christmas just around the corner, every one of the eight girls in the sewing room went straight out, from the time the bell sounded in the morning until it rang out again at five-thirty.

"Another week at the salt mines," muttered Julia at five past nine on Rose's second Monday. Around them, girls were uncovering their machines, checking bobbin thread, and getting out scissors and tape measures. At the far end of the cutting table, Mrs. Dakin was perched on a high stool, with an open scribbler on her lap and a pencil stuck behind one ear.

Rose saw soon enough that there was precious little love for Mrs. Dakin among the girls. Julia called her the battle-axe. "She'd die if she didn't have this place to come to. It's her whole life, you know. She's first one in every morning and last one to leave at night."

"Goodness," Rose replied. "Doesn't she have family to see to?"

"Not anymore, she doesn't. Her daughter's overseas, and her old man croaked a couple of years ago. Which makes her a widow, right? And a merry one, too, if you know what I mean."

"She grinned at the look of disapproval registering on Rose's face. "Hey, I'm only telling you what everybody here knows. You should see how she is whenever Mr. Hatfield comes near."

So, the gossip mill turns, Rose thought. She'd need to be careful in future of what she said and did around the likes of Julia. Loose lips didn't just sink war ships. They torpedoed people too.

"Girls, may I have your attention!" Mrs. Dakin called out over the clatter. Instantly, all activity ceased and eight sets of eyes turned in her direction. The only sound they could hear was the steady *ping-ping* from a leaky radiator pipe.

Mrs. Dakin adjusted her glasses and looked down at the open page of her scribbler. "Bridal sent up three new wedding gowns and eight bridesmaids' dresses on Saturday." She paused, her finger running down one of the columns. "There are six more from Evening Wear, too, making a total of seventeen." She took off her glasses and looked at each of them individually. "With day dresses and coats, you know what that means, don't you?"

Every head nodded in silent unison. From the glum expressions, Rose couldn't tell if the nodding signified collective assent or private resignation; but, whatever it meant, the message from Mrs. Dakin was clear enough. Nose to the grindstone; no time for idle chatter; and don't make any mistakes.

"We'll be busy, that's for sure." Mrs. Dakin had a bad habit of stating the obvious. "So, let's get at it. Mr. Hatfield says he's prepared to authorize extra hours if it comes to that." She closed her ledger and got down from her stool. Nobody spoke. Instead, they lined up in single file at the work rack, took the garments she issued them, and went back to their machines.

"Getting at it" was an expression that grated on Rose. People used it constantly these days, to cover a multitude of lesser sins and tedious situations. Scouring toilet bowls, darning socks, polishing boots. Whatever else it meant, it certainly sent one message, loud and clear. No chatter needed; no complaints accepted.

The steady diet of hems and cuffs might have driven Rose crazy, had it not been for the Christmas rush. Mrs. Dakin came to her after lunch on Friday with an evening gown draped over one arm. "Rose, my more experienced girls are all swamped, and we need this done immediately." Mrs. Dakin pointed to the bodice of the dress. It was a low-cut affair, in a satin-like material, with a rhinestone clasp at its fitted waist and threads of silver shot throughout the fabric. One glance told Rose that it would be a challenge to work on.

"The customer was promised that we could do this for her by closing," Mrs. Dakin said. "The darts have to be let out, and the waist adjusted. It means working around that rhinestone cluster, which won't be easy. I'd like to throttle the clerk! She had no business making any promises without consulting me first."

On that point, Rose agreed. She hadn't seen the alteration

instructions, but she'd be prepared to bet a dime that the dress would involve a good two hours of work; maybe more.

"I'm going to have to use you, Rose," Mrs. Dakin said. I hope you won't run into too many snags; we've got to have this ready by five-thirty." Her voice lowered. "Friends of the manager, or I'll eat my hat." She deposited the gown on Rose's lap and hurried off.

"You'll be in her good books if you can pull that one off," Julia mumbled through a mouthful of pins. "Take it from me—" she stood up, wrestling with the mound of tulle in her arms, "—Dakin's not in the habit of giving important stuff to juniors."

"You don't need to remind me," Rose groaned, reaching for a seam ripper. "But I'll give it my best shot."

"She'll expect that, and more."

Working on the dress was as bad as Rose had anticipated. In order to get at the front and back darts, she was obliged to loosen the bodice from the waistband, open up the lining and remove the boning from under the bust. She cursed under her breath at the skimpy seams left by the factory sewers. But she found a way to do the half-inch let-outs, and was blind-stitching the rejoined waistband when Mrs. Dakin reappeared at her machine.

"Good work," Mrs. Dakin said when she'd examined the gown. "I'll be able to use you for more complicated things. Keep it up."

It didn't take Rose long to assess the sewing room's hierarchy and the people within it. Its roles were well established and its patterns of behaviour well entrenched. Change, and ambition, were frowned upon.

Hems and cuffs were the mainstay. This work required a good deal of straight stitching and very little creativity, and was assigned to the four girls who sat along the inside wall. They were constantly busy, dealing with a steady stream of day dresses and skirts, coats and suit jackets.

The bridal and evening wear was assigned to the more experienced, talented girls. Classified as apprentice dressmakers, they got a higher rate of pay, but precious little else. In reality, their jobs meant more work, more eye strain, and more stress if mistakes were made.

Darts and tucks were bad enough, but shoulder sleeves and waistbands were worse. Often, one or the other had to be re-positioned and re-attached—and done over again if they didn't pass the next fitting. Wedding dresses were, by far, the worst culprits. Entire bodices were often removed at the waist and essentially made over, and sweeping trains re-adjusted. There were hours and hours of hand-sewing, too: seed pearls, countless covered buttons, and fake gem inserts. According to Mrs. Dakin, every bride deserved to look as perfect as possible in her wedding dress. "A perfect princess," she liked to say.

Rose wasn't sure that she agreed. Some ugly ducklings would never be transformed, no matter how hard everybody tried. *We aim to flatter* would be the better motto. To her way of thinking, princesses were born, not made; which left three kinds of women in the real world: ordinary-looking girls with money, their rich (and sometimes ugly) mothers, and the servant girls who waited on the lot.

Rose knew where she fit. What worried her was the extent to which she might be able to change things.

AI

Despite the long hours of sewing and the inconveniences of a city immersed in a full-scale war effort, life overall was pretty good. Rose especially looked forward to her week-ends off. Once each month she did a half-day shift at the store (everybody did; there was no way out of it), but that still gave her three Saturdays to do exactly as she pleased.

The first Saturday in December was no exception. A blizzard had swept in from New England two weeks earlier, dumping over two feet of snow on the city. Ora and Rose loved the snow, but Lettie was less impressed. "Damn snow," they heard every time she came back from church or went out to the store. "Nearly went arse over kettle last Sunday morning. If it wasn't for Elder MacPherson, I'd have broken my bloody neck."

A cold snap followed on the heels of the snow, quickly making the outdoor rinks and ponds safe enough to skate on. Ora and Rose were eager to get out as soon as they could.

"The Poor House Pond will be too crowded," Ora said on Saturday morning. "Let's head to Chocolate Lake again. If we hurry, we can catch the twelve-fifteen tram."

The tram ride took about thirty minutes, dropping them off at the bottom of the shore road hill. With their skates slung over their shoulders, they climbed the hill and followed the trail, past waist-high snowbanks, to the shack in the clearing. Inside the shack was a bench where they could sit while they were lacing up.

The floor under the bench was piled high with boots and shoes by the time they got there. "Wow," exclaimed Ora. "Look at 'em all! Good thing we didn't come any later."

Onced laced, Rose followed Ora out of the shack and together they climbed over a mound of snow and onto the ice. They started off with arms linked, savouring the feel of the crisp winter air against their faces and the *swish swish* of their blades over the pond's frozen surface.

They'd done one complete circle of the pond when an airman tapped Ora on the shoulder. With a wave and a "See you later" the twosome sped away. Rose watched them, gliding in perfect time, until they disappeared around a little island in the pond's centre.

The ice surface was hard and smooth under her blades, and Rose skated in sure, swift strokes, relaxing into the steady, smooth motion of her body, invigorated by the total freedom, the feel of the wind feathering through her hair.

Anyone seeing her would have agreed that she was a charming and perfect study in grace; a trim little fairy figure in her bright blue jacket and white woollen cap, with her tasselled scarf wound loosely under her jacket collar. Her face, always a pretty picture, glowed in the brisk, clear air: brown eyes under thick, dark lashes, lustre of pink, frost-coloured cheeks, and dark curls peeking out from under her cap.

"*Allô, Rose! Arrêtez-vous!*"

She slowed to a stop, and turned. There he was again; her newest, most appealing skating partner.

"I thought (pronounced as *taught*) you were ignoring me," he said.

"Never!" she protested, breaking into a laugh. "I wouldn't do that to you."

"A skate, *s'il vous plaît, ma Rose?*"

"*Oui*," she said with a little curtsey, and off they went.

His name was Al, and he was doing a five-week navigation course at the Base. Once he'd finished, he expected to be assigned to one of the convoy corvettes.

"How's the course going?" Rose asked when they stopped for coffee. She liked to hear him speak in French; his accent, the way he rolled the "*r*" in her name, had a lovely musical ring to it.

"Good. A lot of . . . um . . . *mathématiques*, but I like it."

"I never did," she said with a rueful smile. "But I hated most things about school. I was glad when I could leave."

He shrugged. "Doesn't matter now, eh? You're all grown up. Got a job; all that." He drank the last of his coffee and set the cup down.

"The course is fine. *Mais*, the house—*mon Dieu!*"

"What's the matter with it?"

"Dirty, *et* crowded. I need to move. Do you know of a place?"

"I . . . might," she replied. "My friend's aunt takes roomers. We could ask her."

He came to the house that evening and Lettie showed him around. Rose could tell that the old lady had taken to him immediately.

"Handsome fella," she said after he'd gone. "Bet he's the apple of his mother's eye. What's his name, again?"

"Al," Rose replied. "Albert Doucette. He comes from a little village outside Yarmouth. His parents' names are Yvette and Guy."

The back bedroom was vacant by the weekend, and Lettie made sure he was installed later the same day.

"In plenty of time for *un joyeaux Noël*," Al said, carrying his rucksack up the stairs a week later.

"What about leave?" Rose asked. "Will you get any?"

"Seventy two hours. Last chance to see *ma famille* before I ship out. *Maman* is counting on it."

Their relationship developed steadily, and Rose delighted in it. They went for evening walks in the snow, sat in the front room and played records, caught a Saturday matinee of *Boy's Town* at the Odeon. Never a diary person, the idea of writing her thoughts in a blank-paged notebook didn't enter her mind. Her own record—a calendar—served a more functional purpose.

Each night before she went to bed she put a neat check mark next to the date. Sometimes she added a brief notation: *Pavilion dance, Lily's birthday, Ora/movie*. And, every twenty-six days, five small red crayon dots appeared. Always five, and always twenty-six days apart; regular as clockwork.

Before she went to bed on the third Friday in December, Rose made her usual check mark. Under it, she printed *Al–Walk*. She drew a small heart above his name, then put the pencil away, blew a kiss to Ora, and climbed into bed.

Life was neat, ordered, happy. Life was, in fact, very, very good.

Christmas at Lettie's

It snowed twice more before the Christmas holidays. Not nasty blizzards with howling winds, but steady snowfalls that coated the tree branches and deposited light, fluffy blankets on the streets and sidewalks.

"Look how the snow's draped over those spruce boughs," Rose said to Ora as they walked home in the December dusk. "Reminds me of the white fox stole on the mannequin in our window; and they've got her dressed in a forest green evening gown, too."

"Hey," replied Ora. "That sounds heavenly."

They walked on in silence. "How about we get a small tree for our little nook upstairs," Rose suggested. "They've got some at the market."

"Good idea," agreed Ora. "Let's."

Rose brought the tree home the next day, and they spent the evening making paper chains, silvering pine cones, and fashioning a yellow star for its top. The fellows, spurred on by a couple of rum and Cokes each, had helped to decorate the big tree in Lettie's front room, and it looked lovely. But their own, upstairs, was extraspecial.

"Here's to us and our tree," Ora said when they'd finished and were sitting with mugs of hot chocolate and a plate of Lettie's molasses chews.

"Yes, cheers," Rose echoed.

Downtown, a mighty fir stood in the centre of the Grand Parade grounds, and, at Rose's store a team hand-picked by Mr. Hatfield had laboured for the better part of two days hanging wreaths, looping garlands, and arranging nutcracker soldiers and Snow Queen figures on ledges and display tables. There was a tall pine decorated with hand-painted ornaments and dozens of twinkling lights at the foot of the stairs on the main level, and a smaller version up on fifth, outside the entrance to the tearoom.

"Battle-axe Dakin told me the other day that those tree baubles are as expensive as all-get-out," Julia informed Rose. They'd clocked in at the same time and were taking the main stairs up to Sewing. "Mr. Hatfield got them in from Germany on a special order. Must have been before the fighting started, eh? Crazy, isn't it—the way the world is?"

"Um," Rose agreed absently. "It's crazy, all right."

The state of the world had taken a distinct second place in her mind, overtaken by a determination to finish her Christmas shopping. She'd found a sweet angora scarf for Ora and a nice blouse for Lily. Her employee discount helped a lot with the cost; on Fridays, when she went to pick up her pay envelope, she made a weekly payment on the balance in her layaway account.

What to get Lettie had been the most difficult decision. "I don't need one solitary thing," the old lady had informed Ora. "You young ones spend the money on each other." Rose had wandered the aisles during her lunch break, trying to get ideas, and had settled eventually on a canister of breakfast tea and a box of assorted cookies. The biscuits came in an oval-shaped tin, with a picture of the Royal Family on the lid. Rose planned to wrap the gift in red and blue paper, with a sprig of holly tucked into the bow. After all, no one was a greater admirer of the King and Queen than Lettie. She still talked about shaking the Queen's hand during their visit in 1939. "The highlight of my life," she'd said a thousand times.

Al was the last person on Rose's list. She made three visits to the Men's Department before deciding on a pair of woollen gloves and a small silver photo frame. A snapshot of herself taken the previous summer would fit nicely into it.

She gave him his gift the night before he was to catch his train. "This is for you," she said from the doorway of his room. Strewn on his bed were packages and clothing that he was trying to make room for in his kit bag.

"*Pour moi!*" he said. "A surprise from St. Nicholas, *peut-être?*"

"No, from *me*," she said. "I hope you have a wonderful time with your *maman* and *papa*."

He gave her a light hug. "And you make sure you check under the tree Christmas morning. One of the reindeer has a package with your name on it. An elf told me so."

On Christmas Eve, two fellows from the house went to the midnight service at St. Mark's with Rose and Ora. "A blessed Christmas to you," murmured the rector on their way out.

"And to you," Rose replied automatically. It distressed her to think about the meaning of the word "blessed." People like themselves—safe at home—were blessed, no question. But what about the men and women fighting overseas; what about the people of England and France who were running from bombs, who didn't have a roof over their heads, let alone a pillow to lay their heads on. What did blessed mean, for them? The ancient story in Luke's gospel, the ceramic figures in the miniature manger, were all well and good but what did they really add up to in a world gone mad?

Back at the house, one of the guys insisted on making hot toddies.

"You'll sleep like a baby," he said with a wink, adding a shot of whisky to Rose's mug. He watched her take a cautious sip.

"Nice, eh?"

"Yes," she replied. "Very." The liquor-laced coffee had a metallic taste, but she liked the warming effect. Ora raided the basket she'd put ready to take to her father's, and came back with two chocolate bars. "We can share these," she announced, breaking the chocolate into pieces.

It was well past two by the time Rose, in a fuzzy warm haze, rolled into bed.

She didn't hear a thing until nine the following morning. Blinking at the shaft of sunlight pouring across the hooked mat, she pushed the bedclothes away and sat up, trying to ignore the dull throb at the back of her eyes. There was no sign of Ora. The pull-out bed was empty and her overnight case was gone.

"Goodness me," she thought in a panic. "I promised to help Lettie with the turkey." She hurried into her clothes and dashed downstairs.

"Bird's been stuffed," Lettie announced when Rose reached the kitchen. "If you can just give me a hand lifting it into the oven, that'll be great. Merry Christmas, dear."

"Merry Christmas to you, too," Rose replied. "Has Ora gone already?"

"Yup. Took off an hour ago." Lettie laid a piece of newspaper on the countertop and dumped the potatoes onto it. "I'll keep on with the grub if you want to set the table. Fancy it up however you like. Get yourself some tea first, though. There's bread already cut. It's under that napkin."

In the dining room Rose spread the table with Lettie's best linen cloth and set the places with her heavy, old-fashioned silverware and china. Both had been well used over the years, and there were spider cracks in several of the plates. However, the table looked grand once she'd finished, with Lettie's candlesticks and a centrepiece of pine cones and chestnuts gracing its centre.

They were counting on six for the meal. Ora was spending the day at her older sister's place, but the three servicemen would be with them; and Lily was coming, too. Matron had received the written invitation from Lettie weeks ago and it had all been approved and arranged.

"We'll send a cab for Lily," Lettie insisted. She wouldn't hear of Rose paying for it. "Nope. It's my treat, dear. Wish it was my sister coming. She would be, if she were still alive. But what can I expect, at my age."

Everyone had a merry time. Lettie had outdone herself with the meal and the men ate as if they hadn't seen food for a year. "Guess we won't need to wash the platter," Lettie joked. "You fellows licked it cleaner than Jack Sprat and the wife."

Rose helped serve the mince tarts and the War Cake. "I soaked those raisins and currents in brandy overnight," Lettie said. "Make sure you take a piece of each." While they were eating the dessert, she held up her teacup for the toast. "To good health and happiness in the year ahead. And may this war soon be over."

"Hear, hear!" they chanted. "To health, happiness, and peace."

Everyone congregated in the front room to hear the King's radio broadcast. The message, by no means original, echoed of scripture and Churchill. We'll see this through. We must keep the faith. Tyranny will die. Peace will prevail. The Empire will flourish. A new era will dawn.

There was complete silence in the room afterwards. The King was sincere, Rose had no doubt of that. He was the defender of faith, protector of his subjects. England, with the help of the Allies was still free. The Lowland countries had fallen, one after the other, like dominos, and France was occupied. The waters of the channel had saved England's bacon, but who knew how much longer they would be able to stave off the enemy.

In this same parlour, only a month earlier, they'd finished off an evening sing-song with a medley of patriotic songs: "Keep the Home Fires Burning," "The White Cliffs of Dover," "There'll Always Be an England." Lettie was in tears at the end of the singing and Ora's eyes looked wet, too.

Rose hoped that there *would* always be an England; it was inconceivable to imagine otherwise. But, in the face of the facts—the mounting casualties, the number of convoy vessels sunk and planes gunned down—a person would be a fool not to have doubts. The headline in yesterday's paper announced that there'd been another U-Boat strike, this time less than ten miles offshore.

Rose took a tired but content Lily back by tram in the late afternoon. It was no less crowded, with most of the passengers in good spirits. The one exception was an older couple in the seat opposite. The woman sobbed quietly, her head against the window; the man beside her—her husband, surely—was sitting expressionless, a hand planted on each knee.

Rose averted her eyes. It wasn't fair to intrude on the unhappiness of others. Perhaps they'd had bad news—of a son missing, or dead. Those telegrams showed mercy to no one. They were delivered every day, even at Christmas.

"I had such a good time," Lily was saying. On her lap was a shopping bag filled with her gifts.

"So did I," Rose replied. She picked up Lily's gloved hand in her own. She must be careful to keep her doubts hidden. It was important to show a positive outlook; to be hopeful.

"It's nice at Lettie's, isn't it?" Lily asked.

"Yes, it is. She's a kindhearted soul."

"Where will I go when I'm old enough?" Lily spoke in a little girl voice; uncertain, fearful, confused.

"Now, don't you go fretting," Rose said. "We'll live together. Maybe at Aunt Lettie's."

"You mean that?" Lily demanded, turning to face her.

"Yes, I do mean that."

We'll be together again. An echo of Violet. She'd promised the same thing to them, years ago; a promise that, so far, hadn't come to pass.

Now it came to pass. The story from Luke's gospel began with those very words. Rose wasn't sure how much she truly believed in the facts of the family's plight—the smelly, drafty barn, the baby without a stitch to wear, the bunch of rag-tag shepherds following a star. But, if any of it was true, you had to give the family credit. They started out with a donkey's pack of troubles but they'd stuck together, just the same; though thick and thin.

Rose knew it was up to her to see that she and Lily stuck together—through thick and thin. The two of them didn't make a complete family, but it was better than the alternative. Better, by far, than no family at all.

Dancing

Al arrived back from Yarmouth in time for New Year's Eve.

"It'll be my last night on the town," he said at the breakfast table that morning. "We're on twenty-four-hour standby now. I'll get a call anytime."

"Why don't we all go to the canteen?" Ora suggested. "The music's good, and we can have a few laughs. Jack and I love it there."

Jack was the newest man on Ora's dating roster and it was obvious that she was smitten.

"Anybody can tell you like him," Rose said. "You go starry-eyed whenever you mention his name."

"He might turn out to be *the* one," Ora said. "You never know."

Thankfully, there were no last-minute orders to deal with at work, and Rose was able to sign out at six on the dot. She was determined to get supper over early so that she and Ora would have plenty of time to do their makeup and get themselves dressed. They didn't fuss with the meal—leftover baked beans and coleslaw—and left the dishes to air dry while they ran their baths and finalized what they would wear.

They were pretty much ready by eight-thirty. "Damn these stockings," Ora complained, stuffing a foot into the toe of her new hose.

"Oh, Ora, do be careful," Rose pleaded. "If you put a run in them, we're sunk. I used the last of the clear nail polish."

It was so like Ora to be careless over her clothes. Lyle stockings weren't as fragile as nylon, but they snagged just the same. Rose was extracautious with her own, slipping her foot into the toe gingerly and easing them over the backs of her heels. She smoothed the stockings up her leg slowly, inch by inch, making sure the back seam was straight, rolling the top into double thickness so that her garter wouldn't tear the fabric.

"There—done," Ora said, standing up. She walked over to the bed and held the skirt above her knees. "Are my seams okay, Rosie?"

"Yes, they're fine."

Rose surveyed herself critically in the vanity mirror, pleased with the way her hair fluffed out over the collar of her blue crepe dance dress. She'd fiddled with it for over twenty minutes, trying barrettes on each side, removing them, and finally going back to the barrettes, angling them higher up and farther back, so that her hair swirled into neat forward curls under each ear.

Ora had spent ages on her own hair, managing to pile her fine, red mane on top of her head in a near-perfect imitation of Betty Grable's. She'd been experimenting all week, with the cover of *Screen World* taped to the bathroom mirror, and her perseverance had paid off. The style looked good on her; perky and bouncy, which matched her personality.

"Wouldn't it be awful to go bald and have to wear a wig?" Ora said, leaning into the mirror to apply her lipstick. Rose laughed. "You say the craziest things, you goof," she said. "Only men go bald."

"Pa sure is," Ora replied, blotting her mouth on a tissue and putting the lipstick tube into her evening bag. "But then, Gramps was, and they say it runs in families."

The idle comment made Rose think of her own father and what he might look like, if he were still alive. She imagined him with the same crop of brownish hair, the same bushy eyebrows and mustache. Had his hair been as dark as her own, or lighter, with coppery glints in it like Lily's? She couldn't remember. What she could remember was a pasty white face and the terrible sound of coughing. He coughed for a long, long time; years, or so it seemed. And then, there was no more coughing, and no more Daddy.

She remembered vividly her mother's beautiful, thick black hair. Remembered the lovely woman framed in the oval of the locket. A woman who had also coughed and coughed, and then was gone.

Gone, lost, applied to the woman her mother had been, the locket itself, and the little oval picture inside it. A trinity of loss. How Rose hated losing things! She always blamed herself for losing the locket. One day it was there, in its hiding place behind the big wardrobe. And when she looked again—one, two days later—it was gone. She had been devastated at the loss of it; furious, too, knowing that the sneaky, devious Dot had found it and spirited it away. Perhaps that's why Rose was extracareful—even finicky— of her things now. They were so easily lost, or taken away.

Rose gave her hair a final pat, and touched her ears. They were nicely shaped and lay flat against her head. She liked to show them off with pretty earrings, like the pair of pearl drops that Al had given her for Christmas. He hadn't yet seen them on her, and she hoped he'd be pleased with the effect. "They're not cultured pearls," she confided to Ora. "But they're pretty decent for costume jewellery."

"Hey, who can tell the difference," Ora replied. "They look real to me. The only pearls I know about are the ones in the Artie Shaw song. They played it at least three times last night on the radio. The announcer says it's on its way to the top of the charts."

Dear Ora, the "let's have a good time and not worry about tomorrow" girl. Ora wouldn't care if she never had a string of pearls, or a bracelet or a diamond ring, either. Like Lettie, she claimed that the fewer things she had to clutter up her life, the better.

Which was probably a good thing, come to think of it. On any given evening Ora's clothes could be found strewn over the bed, her shoes kicked wherever they landed. Rose had often opened her own dresser drawer to find Ora's underwear stuffed in it. Out-of-sight was plenty good enough for Ora. Best friends they were and would stay, but in household matters Rose knew that she and Ora would always be miles apart.

Al and Jack were waiting for them in the front room when they finally clattered down the stairs. Aunt Lettie, who'd come out of her den to see them off, was full of compliments. "Jane Russell and Rita Hayworth never looked any better," she said.

Ora grinned down at her aunt. "You're our biggest fan," she said.

"That may be so, but two better pairs of legs I haven't seen in a month of Sundays, honest to God. You'll be having yourselves a grand time. Wish I could still do-si-do. I'd be going with you."

"Yeah, and stealing the best fellows away. I know your tricks."

"Every girl for herself," Lettie sniffed. "I could get *any* fellow I wanted in my day. Before *and* after I was married. Bubs had his hands full, keeping hold of me."

"I believe that," Ora said, giving Lettie a hug. "I really do."

The hall was packed when they got there. Every table was taken, and there were people standing, waiting, at the coffee bar.

"Wow!" Rose exclaimed. "Look at everyone. We'll never get a seat."

"Sure we will," Jack said. "No sweat. Just follow me."

They did, making their way across the dance floor to a table in the far corner. At it were two of Jack's buddies and a girl in a WREN's uniform.

"Stand-down was earlier than we expected," one of the fellows said. He slid over on the bench to make more room. "Here, take a load off your feet." Ora and Rose sat, while Al went looking for a couple of extra chairs.

"What's up?" Ora asked. "You guys look like you've got a real glow on. Don't tell me peace was declared and we didn't hear."

"No peace tonight, sisters and brothers," one of them said. "We're celebrating 'cause it's New Year's and we feel like it." He reached under his chair, pulled his kit bag onto his lap and unzipped it. "Since this pub's got no beer, I brought along a little jazz juice to share," he whispered.

Rose didn't actually *see* a bottle. She would have sworn to that on a stack of Bibles. Just a flash of his arm when their glasses were passed to him.

"Cheers to my buddy, Light Fingers Finnigan," Jack said when everyone was topped up.

"Right," Ora said. "I'll drink to that."

After a bit, Rose and Al found themselves alone at the table, surrounded by a haze of smoke and a buzz of conversation. Out on the floor, the WREN was jitterbugging with Jack's buddy, and the other fellow had disappeared into the crowd. Jack waved as they danced past, and Ora raised her hand in a victory sign.

"Sure are having one hell of a time." Al's voice was tinged with something that Rose couldn't quite put her finger on. Sadness, maybe.

"I'll say," she replied, taking a sip of her drink. She stole a glance at his face. His usually cheerful expression had evaporated. Instead, under the thick lashes, his brown eyes looked wistful, fixed on something, or someone, beyond the room.

On the smallish stage, the pianist and the sax man were conferring. After a minute or so, they began to play a slow number. Rose recognized it instantly—"I'll Get By."

"Let's do this one," Al said abruptly, holding out his hand. She followed him onto the floor, feeling his finger-tips at the small of her back. She loved the way he danced, in smooth, sure, understated rhythm. After the number ended, he kept his arm around her waist, his cheek close but not touching hers.

When the jitterbug contest was announced, they took a pass, standing on the sidelines while six or seven couples positioned themselves, and an older woman stuck cardboard signs on their backs. Jack and Ora were number three.

"They're all very good," Al murmured to Rose halfway through.

Rose nodded her agreement. "Yeah. But I think Ora and Jack are the best."

She was right, judging from the clapping and cheering.

"Go, man, go! Go, baby, go!" Somebody started the chant, and, instantly, the entire crowd was chanting and swaying in time to the music.

Afterwards, a flushed and triumphant Ora showed them their prize. "Dinner for two at the hotel—yay!"

"Jack Be Nimble, that's my name," Jack said, kissing her on the cheek.

"Listen to him, will ya?" Ora exclaimed. "Not only can he jump over candlesticks, he can shimmy like my sister Kate, too. What a guy! What a bloody talented guy."

Al's Goodbye

Once the crowd had sung the New Year in, Al was anxious to leave. "Let's take off, *chérie*," he said to Rose. "I've had enough merry-making for one night."

There was no sign of Jack and Ora, which wasn't surprising. "Don't wait up," Ora had warned when they were in the Ladies' Room. "We might go somewhere after." Rose hadn't asked where, or why. After all, Ora was a big girl now. She could take care of herself.

She and Al walked quickly toward the bus stop, hoping to catch the last run of the evening.

"There he is," Al said, grabbing her hand. "*Dépêchez-vous!* We can make it."

They scrambled up the steps seconds before the tram pulled away, stumbling down the crowded, jolting aisle, looking in vain for an empty seat. Even at midnight the tram was filled; shipyard workers with lunch buckets; military personnel, wrapping up their evening shifts; a gaggle of assorted partygoers like themselves. The city never seemed to quiet down these days. It was the price of war, some said. Or the benefit; a debate between the opposing sides that could go on for hours.

"Amazing how many people are up," she murmured.

"*Oui*," was Al's only comment.

"Have a good one," the driver said when they got off a quarter of an hour later. "I wonder what he meant by that," Al said when he and Rose were crossing the street.

"Meant by what?" asked Rose, puzzled.

"The driver said to have a good one. Did he mean night or life? Makes one hell of a difference, don't you think?"

She groped for words to reply, found none. "I'm not sure," she said.

Inside, he helped her off with her coat and hung it in the closet. On the hall table, next to an ugly brass monkey that Aunt Lettie used as a paper weight, was a scrawled note. *Squares in covered dish in kitchen. Help yourself.*

"How about a nightcap?" he asked.

"Oh, Al—" she replied, hesitating. "The two I had were more than my usual speed."

"Don't be silly," he protested. "They weren't enough to quiet a baby. Besides, this is our last time together for who knows how long. What do you say—I've got a new bottle upstairs."

She couldn't turn him down, she knew that. "Maybe just a little bit—in some tea," she said.

The tea was brewing in a small pot when he came back down with the flask. He poured some into her teacup and a healthier shot into a water tumbler for himself, declining the offer of Lettie's squares. "*Merci, no.* I'm not hungry," he said.

"Let's put Vera Lynn on," he said, when they were in the front room.

"Sure," Rose replied. She kicked off her shoes and settled onto the sofa. The unlit tree stood in the window, a dark form against a darker background. Rose didn't suggest that they switch on the tree lights. Instead, she sat quietly while he fiddled with the phonograph needle. When he'd finished, he eased himself down beside her, his arm extended along the sofa's back, his eyes half closed.

"Do you have any idea where they'll send you?" Rose ventured after a while.

"No. And we won't till we're well out there. France, maybe, or even the Mediterranean."

She wondered if he was afraid; if he was missing his

maman and his *papa*. His father was a fisherman. He'd told her that they used to go lobstering together; that he and his brother had helped to build the new boat. There were several other brothers, and a couple of sisters, too.

"Will you be calling home before you leave?" she asked.

"There's no point," he said, his voice sombre. "They're not on the phone and the general store is over a mile down the road."

"Oh."

How terrible, she thought, to have a mother and not be able to reach her. Worse, perhaps, than having no mother, like Lily and her. With no mother, there was no wish, and no expectation. Nobody to say goodbye to.

"It'll be different," he said.

"Yes," she replied. "It will." On the turntable, the troops had joined Vera in song. *But sure a body's bound to be a dreamer / when all the things he loves are far away.* It was a haunting melody, this song about the Isle of Innesfree. Maybe he'd get to see it. Maybe, from the deck of his ship, on his way to England, to France, to somewhere.

"Aunt Lettie will miss you." Rose had heard Lettie on the phone, glowing about him to one of her friends. "Such a help around; he can do anything with his hands. Why, he even fixed the pipe on the hot water tank."

"*Ah, oui,*" he replied. "*Elle est une bonne grande dame.*"

And then, very quietly, "Will you miss me, Rose?"

"Of course I will," she said. She leaned over and gave his cheek a light pat. "We've had fun together, you and I."

He caught hold of her hand and laced his fingers through hers. "I didn't think I would like the city; I'm a real country guy. But being here, with you—it's been wonderful." His fingers tightened on hers. "When we get back, I'll be on the doorstep again, believe me."

She gave his fingers a squeeze. It'll be all right, she wanted to say. I'll be here.

He lifted her hand to his mouth, kissed her fingertips, and laid his head on her shoulder. "Getting late," she mumbled, feeling the warmth of his breath against her neck. "Time to turn in." She couldn't move, though; his head on her shoulder, the warmth of his body against hers, was too delicious.

"To hell with bed," he murmured, his voice muffled. "Stay with me. Please." He shifted position, lifting his head so that his mouth met hers. The kiss, a pleasant, moist lightness, turned quickly into something deeper, longer. Warmth spread across her shoulders and down her back. Down, down.

Someone spoke. "I don't think—" Was that her own voice?

"It's okay. Don't worry," he whispered. "You'll be fine. I've got something."

She was hot now. The perspiration was running down her back, soaking through the cotton of her bra. His hands, then hers, pulled at the buttons of her blouse and she sighed at the rush of cool air on her damp arms.

There was a rustling noise, the crackle of paper, the tickle of wool against her face. What was that? Oh, yes—the afghan. Then, a stubble of beard brushing against her breast, making her whimper.

She cried out once. After that, she forgot about crying. There was nothing to cry about. Everything was good, turning to better; and finally, at last, to best.

When she regained awareness of her surroundings, she could hear his steady breathing in the darkness, feel his body, wedged against her own. In the background, the phonograph needle was making a steady scratching noise, stuck in the grove of the record.

Her arm had gone numb and she rubbed it gently until the blood surged back. She waited until the tingling subsided, then rolled gently off the edge of the sofa. She found her blouse, slipped it on, groped for her shoes, her stockings, set them in a neat pile on the mat. She pulled the afghan over his sleeping form and gave his forehead a light kiss. Then, turning off the record player, she picked up the bundle of clothing, clutched it tight against her chest, and stole up the stairs.

There was no sign of Ora in their room. The bed was just as it had been when they'd left. Rose dropped her bundle on the stool, pulled back the covers, and got into the bed. She was asleep in minutes.

Morning Comes

Ora's bed was still empty in the morning. Rose put on her robe and tiptoed past the closed door of Al's room. She needed a little more time to reconcile what had happened between them a few hours earlier; to face him without feeling just a little bit ashamed.

Downstairs, she was relieved to find things put back to rights. He had fluffed up the sofa cushions and placed the afghan, neatly refolded, on the back of Lettie's rocking chair. The only remaining traces of the interlude were her cup and saucer and his empty glass. Rose carried them into the kitchen and ran hot water in the dishpan. She felt keyed-up, jittery, nervous.

There were no sounds overhead; only the rumble of the furnace below her, and the trickling sound of water in the radiator pipes. From the kitchen window she could see the towels from yesterday's wash hanging limply in the morning stillness. Ora was supposed to have taken them in, but she had obviously forgotten. Keeping track of towels was not one of Ora's strong points.

One of Lettie's scribbled notes lay on the kitchen table. *Went to Morning Prayer. The Base called for Al to report in. Nobody for lunch. L.*

Rose made herself a pot of tea, sliced half a loaf of bread, put four of the slices in to toast. It seemed unlikely that they would be eaten, but Rose had to keep herself occupied.

The Base called. That meant that he wasn't sleeping, as she had assumed; he had already left. Would he get back to the house, even for a few minutes? Probably not. The eventual had become the actual. Time was up. A few hours left ashore; a day at most. Did that make things easier, or harder, for him; for both of them?

As children, they used to watch the movement of the ships in the harbour from the playroom window. Once war was declared, the Basin was home to dozens and dozens of the grey-blue and black hulls. There they'd sit, silent and still on the glassy water, waiting for their orders to depart. The boys used to try and count them, arguing that not another ship—not even a canoe or a rowboat—could possibly fit into the crowded space. And then, one morning they'd wake up to find the ships had gone. No one, save for the gulls, could say just when they'd left, or where they were headed, or how long they might be away.

By noon, Rose couldn't stand being alone in the house any longer. She set out on a long walk, counting on the clear air to help settle her nerves. After two hours of steady walking, the doubts and questions remained.

Al was a sweet guy, and she cared for him a lot. But was caring for him good enough? There was no answer to that; no answer, either, on how long he'd be away, or if he would write. Sailors had lots of girls; one in every port, according to the old saying. Al was different, though. He wasn't like that.

She got back in time to eat supper with Lettie—just the two of them, at the kitchen table—and had started the dishes when Ora walked in.

"Ended up staying the night at Pa's," Ora said.

"Right," Rose replied, handing her a plate of warmed-over stew. Ora didn't need to explain where she'd gone, or what she'd done. Some things were best left unsaid.

"Do you like my Jack?" Ora asked.

"Yes, I do. He seems like a great guy," Rose replied. "Likes to have a good time, that's for sure."

Ora finished her food, licked off her fork, and brought

her empty plate to the sink. "Let's put it this way, Rosie. That Jack is every inch a sailor."

"Oh, Ora!" Rose protested, swatting at her with the towel.

"Well he is. I cannot tell a lie."

"Then don't say anything at all!"

It was somewhere between midnight and one when Rose heard the sound of muffled voices and the creak of the stairs. She lay listening, wakeful, expecting a tap on her door. There was no knock. Just the faint sound of footsteps retreating, and, from the street, the slam of a car door.

An hour went by before she finally drifted off again. Her sleep was uneasy, full of crazy, disturbing images: a rain-slicked jetty, a throng of silent onlookers, a brass band playing dirges in the background. A troop ship had cast its lines and was pulling away from the dock. She could see the sailors, standing at attention, on the main deck. She scanned the faces, trying to find Al. She wanted to wave, blow a kiss. But someone was holding her hand and wouldn't let go.

She didn't see the envelope until morning. It was on the floor, propped against the door frame. She sat down at the dressing table and turned on the lamp. The envelope contained a snapshot, tucked into a card. *With Thoughts of You,* was embossed on the face of the card; and inside, *Thinking of you and wishing you all the best, now and in the days ahead.*

The picture was a black-and-white one of Al. He was dressed in civvies, standing on what looked like railway tracks. On the back he'd written: *To Rose, A very special girl. Love, Al.*

"It was real late when they came by," Lettie explained when Rose went down for breakfast. "A man was waiting for him in the car. They were on their way to the ship."

"I hate the way they have to take off in the middle of the night," Ora said, her voice trembling. "It's so spooky. Jack'll be next. I just know it."

Before she left for work, Rose put the card and snapshot in her keepsake box. She hoped that there would be another note soon; maybe even a letter, sent by way of the Forces' overseas mail. A girl at the store, Eileen, said her guy was in England and he wrote regularly. She'd shown Rose the lace hankie he'd sent, together with a picture postcard of Westminster Abbey.

News of Al

After five weeks, there was still no letter.

"Don't be upset," Eileen consoled. "Letters can take forever. They go through the censors and everything."

She meant well, of course, but it didn't help. Ora's Jack was away, too, yet she had already received a long letter from him. "But he's only Coastal Patrol, Rose," Ora said. "That's a big difference from being overseas."

In February, they went together to the canteen Valentine party, and each of them had their pick of dance partners. The evening was pleasant enough, but it wasn't the same. Rose longed to rewind the clock; to bring back New Year's Eve. And Ora wanted Jack.

Work helped. A winter sale on coats meant plenty of alterations, and new spring merchandise was arriving daily. "We're going crazy," said a clerk from Bridal on their way to lunch on Friday.

"Everybody's getting married, I guess," Rose replied.

"I guess! Too bad we're not on commission. I could make a killing if we were."

Spring came early that year. A bright yellow profusion of forsythia and budding daffodils. "Every yard from the corner down has one of those yellow bushes," Rose said to Lettie. "Why's that, I wonder?"

Lettie laughed. "They're cheap and hardy is my guess. Bubs used to call 'em poor men's blooms. They winter pretty good and don't take much fussing. You can't kill off forsythia, once it takes root. Same with the bulbs. I leave mine in the ground from one year to the next and it doesn't seem to do 'em one bit of harm."

Rose was thinking about daffodils when she let herself into the front hall on Thursday before the Easter weekend. She checked the mail—still nothing for her—and was about to go upstairs when she heard Lettie calling. She went into the little den and found Lettie in her rocker, with an open newspaper on her lap.

"Everything all right?" Rose asked, noticing a suspicious wetness around Lettie's eyes.

"No, everything's not all right," Lettie replied. "There's another ship torpedoed—off Newfoundland. Story's on the front page."

"That's awful," Rose said. "Any survivors?"

"Some, but the casualties were heavy." Lettie put the paper on the ledge, took off her glasses and blew her nose. She got up heavily and hobbled over to Rose.

"Another bunch of our boys, gone," she said, taking hold of Rose's hand. "I can't hardly stand to think about it."

"I'll make some tea," Rose offered, patting Lettie's veined, blotched hand. "That'll make us feel better."

"No!" Lettie insisted. There was a steely—almost bitter—tone to her voice. "I'll make the tea. You sit. The list of names is on the second page."

Rose had little recollection of the evening. She must have put the paper down, helped with supper, got undressed for bed, brushed her teeth. Perhaps she also cried. She couldn't remember any of that. What stayed with her was the memory of Ora's tears. Ora, sitting on the side of her bed, murmuring over and over, "I'm so sorry, Rose. I'm so sorry. I just can't believe it. Al was your guy."

Eventually, Rose slept. When she came to, it was nearly dawn. Ora had pulled the big chair close to the bed and was sound asleep under one of Lettie's old quilts. Rose stared at

the sleeping face of her friend. How young Ora looked
without her red lipstick and her eyebrow pencil. Just like a
little girl; like the little girls they used to be when they were
together at the Home.

Despite their protests, Rose insisted on going to work
the next day. "There's no point in my staying home," she
said to Ora. "I'll go crazy, staring at the walls."

"I could call Reverend Miller," Lettie suggested. "He'll
come; I know he will. We could have prayers."

With difficulty, Rose managed to hide the anger that
welled up in her. She didn't want any ministers! They had
nothing of worth to say to her. They'd never had anything
of worth to say. Not ever.

"No, please don't call anyone," she implored. "I'll be
okay. Honest."

She wasn't being honest, though. Okay was a bland,
plateau-like emotional state, somewhere between fine and
miserable on the feelings scale. Whereas, she felt—what?
Resignation, possibly; mixed with a growing despair. A
realization that, somehow, once again, she'd failed; that it
must be her fault that the people she cared about had this
terrible habit of leaving, of disappearing from her life.
Leaving not just for a while, but for good. No—that was
all wrong, damn it! They didn't go for good; they went for
bad. Forever.

She got through the first day at work, then the next, and
the one after that. Ora cut the list of names out of the paper
and put the clipping under her jewellery box. Rose found
it there when she was dusting.

She wrestled with the idea of writing to his parents. One
minute she was sure she should—and wanted to—send a
sympathy note; the next minute she thought it was best to
leave well enough alone. She didn't know them; had never

even seen a picture. What could she possibly say that would be comforting? Sorry for your loss—our loss.

It was unlikely that they would recognize her name, in any case. After all, her romance with Al had only just begun. He might have told them that he had a new girlfriend in the city, but that's probably as much as he would have said.

On payday, she begged off her lunch date with Eileen. She wasn't in any mood for lighthearted chatter over the Friday shopper's special. Eileen understood. "My God, Rose—" she said when Rose told her about Al. "What a sad thing. My heart goes out to you."

Rose slipped into the florist's shop, made her selection, and headed down the hill, toward the waterfront. The dock area was bustling, as it always was, but she managed to find a quiet spot on the south side of the ferry wharf. The water below the wharf was dirty; oil slicks floated on the surface and bits of flotsam lapped against the pilings.

She shaded her eyes and looked out toward the mouth of the harbour. Beyond Chebucto Head, beyond the guns of the coastal defence units mounted on the cliffs, beyond the underwater netting that kept the snooping enemy subs at bay, lay the open ocean. Ploughing through that heaving, dangerous expanse of water were other convoys, steaming as fast as they could toward England, filled to capacity with their important cargoes and their precious crews. Destroyers and freighters, mine sweepers and the little corvettes that rolled and pitched like sardine cans in a storm drain. The course that Al had been taking was preparing him for the engine room on a corvette. He would have been one of the first killed, she knew that. Below deck, you didn't stand a chance of getting out alive.

She walked as far as she could along the jetty, picking

her way among the crates and netting, the coiled ropes and grappling hooks. When she reached the far end, she opened her satchel and lifted out a white rose. She unwrapped the paper from its stem, crouched down, and dropped the flower into the water. It bobbed on the surface for a minute; then, as the current caught, it swirled once, twice, and drifted away.

"Bye, Al," she said under her breath. "I think I was falling in love with you. But it was all so quick. And now it's over."

She stood, quietly, a small, lone figure, until the flower disappeared from sight.

She had contemplated bringing the pearl earrings, as well, but, in the end, had left them in the dresser drawer. She'd worn them once—on New Year's Eve; wasn't sure how she could ever bring herself to wear them again. Her mother used to say that pearls were for tears. She was right; her dear, dead mother.

At the corner of Granville and Prince, Rose paused, took a deep breath. She couldn't go back to the sewing room teary-eyed. The girls would be asking what was wrong, and she had no intention of mentioning Al's name to the likes of that crew. As soon as she got back to the store, she went straight to the pay office. They had the necessary forms to fill out if you wanted to purchase a government savings certificate. "They start as low as five dollars," the office lady told her.

"I'd like a twenty-dollar one, please," Rose replied.

She hadn't wanted to get too involved in this war. Even after Ora's brother Joe, she'd resisted. That was before, though. Before Al.

Eileen

When it came to making friends at the store, Rose played it cautious. She avoided talking about herself and didn't want or need to hear about anyone else. There was no one in the sewing room who had potential, in any case; no one who measured up to her conditions of quality, intelligence, and commitment. So, she was pleasant to all and close to none.

"Everyone thinks you put on airs," Julia said. "You should come to Bingo with us sometime. Four of us go every Friday night."

Bingo! Rose couldn't stand Bingo. They used to play it on rainy days at the Home, with marbles for prizes.

"Maybe I will, one of these days," Rose replied vaguely. Deep down, she was thinking *that'll be the foggy Friday in London town.*

Which left only Eileen, a bright, sensible girl who worked in Fabrics, on the store's lower level. Eileen had introduced herself one noon hour. Rose was browsing among the bolts, looking for a piece of floral fabric to make into cushion covers for their nook at Lettie's, when Eileen came up to her.

"Hi there," she said. "I'm Eileen. You're new, aren't you?"

"Yes," replied Rose. I work in the sewing room. My name's Rose."

Their companionship grew during the winter months. Over morning tea breaks and noontime sandwiches, they chatted comfortably about movies, clothes, and music. Eileen told Rose that her steady fellow was in the army, and that she lived with her parents and younger brother. Rose said that her older sister was married and living in Boston and that she and her cousin Ora boarded with their great-aunt Lettie.

By spring, they were going to lunch together on pay-days. Their favourite eatery, a little Chinese café three blocks from the office, was a popular spot with the down-town working crowd and the servicemen. On a balmy day in early May, Rose and Eileen hurried up the hill to Barrington, eager to get ahead of the crowd. A petite wait-ress with sleek black hair tied in a thick braid appeared at their booth before they'd got their sweaters off and their bags tucked away.

"What you like?" she asked in her singsong voice.

"Two Shopper's Specials, please," said Eileen. "We're starved."

"Sure, we hurry," the waitress replied. She placed two sets of chopsticks on their tabletop and turned to the three men in the next booth.

"Same for us, Pigtail," one of them said. "And lay on extra rice, there's a good girl."

"Did you hear that?" Rose murmured. "Calling her Pigtail to her face!"

"Dock workers—" Eileen whispered, "—who don't know any better. She's probably used to it, but it's not very nice, just the same."

The soup arrived promptly; followed by plates piled high with fried rice, chow-mein noodles, and sweet-and-sour pork.

"What's the latest with the Brides?" Eileen asked.

"Oh, the usual," Rose replied. "They're either too thin or too fat for the evening dresses they pick out."

"That's women for you," Eileen said. "We all like to think we've got a Scarlet O'Hara waist." She scooped up a piece of the pork and popped it into her mouth. "Same thing with patterns. The size fourteen girls buy a twelve,

and the twelves buy size ten. No convincing them otherwise, either. I just keep my mouth shut and ring it in."

"Must be those fairy tales we used to read," Rose
replied, trying to manipulate the chow mein noodles with
her chopsticks. "The girls in those stories were never any
bigger than a minute."

"You might be right on that," Eileen agreed. "But listen,
before I forget; I've got two patterns you can have. The covers are torn, so they're discards. One's a sweet day dress. I
can just see you in it."

They had time to kill after they'd eaten and settled the bill.

"How about a little walk?" Rose suggested when they
were outside. "It's so nice out, I hate to go back early."

"Sure," Eileen agreed. They darted across the street, hopping over the tram car rails and sidestepping a trail of fresh
horse buns near the sidewalk.

"Damn those horses," Eileen moaned when they
reached the parade square entrance. She stopped to scrape
the sole of her shoe against the rock wall. "Look at that
muck! You'd better check the bottom of your shoes, too."

The square at lunchtime was the servicemen's haven.
They were everywhere—lounging on the grass, standing in
little huddles, leaning against the stone walls—smoking,
laughing, ogling all the girls in the vicinity. "Holy shit," a
sailor shouted in a loud voice, gesturing toward a buxom
girl in a tight-fitting pink blouse. "Do you see what I see?
Eight out of ten! And give us a smoke, will ya, Les? If I ain't
getting a taste of them, a fag'll have to do."

Boob bonanza was what the men called the bawdy contest. Every female under fifty was fair game, and, now that
the weather was warm enough to leave your sweater or
jacket off, there were plenty of candidates. Rose had been
caught once before. She'd received an eight, which was, in

its own way, a compliment. It hadn't seemed like one, though. Her face had gone red in her hurry to escape the commentary, and the laughter.

"I don't think I want to barge onto that minefield," Eileen said under her breath.

"Me either," Rose replied. "Let's head for the church and up the steps. We can walk along Argyle instead. I might be a cow, but I don't need a prize ribbon to go with it."

They were almost back at the staff entrance before Rose got up the nerve to sound Eileen out on the idea that she'd been turning over in her mind. It had been a long, bleak winter. Everything—work, life at Lettie's, the canteen dances—seemed dull and lustreless. Life was flat, and it had been since the day they'd seen Al's name on the casualty list.

"Eileen, I'd like to ask you something," Rose ventured.

"Sure, what?" Eileen paused.

"It's about work," Rose said. "I don't know how much longer I can hack the sewing room. Same old thing, day after day. I don't see much future there. I really don't."

"Doesn't surprise me," Eileen replied. "It would drive me batty in no time."

"I'd love to get into sales, like you. I'd be good with the customers; I know I would. What do you think my chances would be? Who could I talk to?"

"Hmm—" Eileen's fingers played with the button on her sweater. Rose waited, hoping that she'd done the right thing by confiding in Eileen. She simply *had* to get out of the sewing room. The girls, the tedious routine, the oppressive heat, were stifling. Although it was only April, she was already having a taste of what summer would be like. By midmorning, with the sun pouring in the back windows and the machines going full-tilt, it had been so hot that they'd opened the fire escape door.

"I wondered whether Mr. Hatfield might be the person to approach," Rose added. She knew that someone of influence would need to speak on her behalf; it was the way things were done at the store. Eileen could prove useful in this regard. She'd let it drop that her father served on a church committee with Mr. Hatfield. Rose was sure that he'd been Eileen's in, two years earlier. She'd come straight from school to the store, without a bit of sales experience.

"Leave it with me," Eileen said. "I'll ask my father. He'll know."

Fashion Show

The annual Easter fashion show was running a close race with Christmas and June Birdes for the all-out promotion splurge. Rose couldn't believe it when Mrs. Dakin drew her aside two days before the show to tell her that she'd been selected to help as a dresser.

"Mr. Hatfield asked me to send you. I must confess I was surprised. New girls rarely get a chance to help with such a big event. You'll need to take an early dinner break on Wednesday and report to the fifth floor by one o'clock."

"I will, of course," Rose replied, a thrill of delight spreading over her. If Mr. Hatfield had singled her out, it must mean that Eileen's father had found a way to mention her name.

On the afternoon of the Fashion Show, Rose took the elevator to the top floor at one o'clock. According to her instructions, she was to report to the dressing area and ask for the coordinator. Rose found her in the corridor leading to the tearoom. She was an older woman, with the blackest hair Rose had ever seen. Pinned to the lapel of her very chic linen suit was a brooch in the shape of a sunburst; she wore matching earrings, and a heavy gold link bracelet on her wrist. The pin alone would have cost more than Rose's weekly salary.

"You're from——?" the woman demanded, all business.

"Sewing," Rose replied. "Mrs. Dakin——"

"Ah, right. I put you down to help with Day Wear. There's one child's outfit in that section. Do whatever needs doing. Buttons, belts, bows. Fastening jewellery. Over there—you'll see."

Signs taped at intervals along the walls indicated the categories: Beach Togs, Day Dresses, Evening Wear, Sunday Best, Wedding Party. Clusters of women milled about in each area, in varying stages of dress and readiness. At a long table in the far corner, two ladies from Cosmetics were applying makeup. Rose could see eight or ten tubes of lipstick, in various shades, and an oval tray filled with perfume atomizers.

Eileen had been assigned to Evening Wear and was already at work, zipping one of the older women into a floor-length gown with a flared skirt. Most of the models were staff, Eileen had said. The children were relatives of the department heads; a son and two daughters, plus several nieces and nephews. They were nice-looking, well-mannered children who knew how to behave in grown-up company.

Every clothing and accessory department was represented: Day Wear and Evening Gowns, Bridal, Children's, Hats, Jewellery, and Gloves. Furs also had several garments to showcase; a mink stole for the shoulders of the woman in the mauve ball gown, and a fox fur neckpiece for each of the women in suits.

The highlight, of course, was the bridal ensemble; two bridesmaids in floor-length Wedgwood blue, a mother in dusty pink, and the bride, looking—well, radiant was the only word to do her justice—in white satin. A matching satin headpiece, fashioned into six rosettes, held her three-quarter veil in place. The florist shop on Blowers Street had supplied all the flowers; pale pink roses and lily-of-the-valley for the bride's bouquet; white rose and baby's breath corsages for the other women in the party.

The groom was Mr. Hatfield himself, in full tuxedo dress. Rose was impressed. With his dark hair slicked back and his mustache trimmed, he looked like a movie star.

"He reminds me of Clark Gable," she murmured to a girl from Lingerie.

"You think?" the girl replied, removing the safety pin from her mouth. "I'd say Robert Taylor. Just like he was in *Waterloo Bridge*."

The next hour flew by at a frenzied pace. One shoulder pad needed tacking in place, an earring fell off and had to be retrieved from under the clothes valet, and the little boy in Beach Togs tripped and burst his balloon with less than five minutes to ramp call. Rose managed to dry his tears and blow up another one, giving him a reassuring hug as the coordinator moved him back into position.

"The piano player's terrific," she whispered to Eileen as the show got underway. As long as they stood well back, they were permitted to watch from the wings.

"Sure is," Eileen whispered back. "They always have live music to back up the commentator, and a reception in the tearoom afterwards."

Every chair in the anteroom was occupied. Preferred customers, including the wife of the Lieutenant-Governor, came by special invitation. There were two people from the paper—a reporter and a photographer; and Rose could see Adele and Mrs. Browne, toward the back, on the righthand side. It stood to reason that Claudia and her mother would be somewhere in the crowd, as well. Ora would call it having the whole "fam-damily aboard."

After the show, the patrons mingled and chatted over fancy sandwiches and little cakes while Rose and the others re-zippered dresses, folded scarves, matched up gloves, and sorted jewellery. Handling the furs was the one task that was not expected of them. An assistant in the fur department was standing by; and, as soon as the model had finished her walk, the fur garments were immediately whisked away.

"Stick around," Eileen murmured to Rose when they were finishing up. "Once the guests have left and we get these clothes loaded on the trolleys, we'll have a chance at the leftovers. There's always plenty of food; they never eat it all."

Revenge

The Bridal Salon was on the second floor, to the right of the stairwell. Its entrance was framed by two Doric pillars; set on top of each pillar was a terra-cotta jardiniere filled with showy artificial flowers. A red plush carpet led from the salon's foyer into a large mirrored room that was furnished with gilt arm chairs, a velvet loveseat, and a coffee table. A raised dais took up a large area directly outside the three dressing rooms. Ivory brocade drapes hung over the long windows that faced the street, and a three-tiered crystal chandelier hung from the ceiling.

It was an elegant chamber, no question; an enclosure filled with dreams and anticipation. Dreams wrapped in yards of tulle, satin, and lace, waiting for the right girl—and her father's pocketbook—to be transmuted into reality, into measured steps up a centre aisle toward a sun-dappled altar and a waiting Prince Charming. If the Salon lacked anything, it was a violinist, in white tie and tails, playing Mendelson's "Wedding March," or "Someday My Prince Will Come," from the Snow White film.

Rose spied the two women when she was shortcutting through Evening Wear, bound for Better Dresses, with four finished garments over her arm. Large as life, there were Claudia Smith and her mother, seated in two of the Salon's gilt chairs.

Rose ducked behind a rack of cocktail dresses, her heart doing an unpleasant little thrump. Claudia and Harris had set a date, then. She'd been checking the society pages, expecting to see an announcement, half-hoping she wouldn't. With Al gone and no one else in the picture, her thoughts had turned to Harris more than once. It was silly, and she was annoyed at herself, but somehow, memories of him wouldn't go away.

At eleven and twelve years old, Rose and Ora had loved to play dress up, rummaging in the boxes of cast-off clothing that the committee ladies had sent over. The worn-out shoes and gowns too soiled or limp for further service were perfect for their pretend weddings on rainy Saturday afternoons. And now, here was Claudia, the girl who had it all—including Harris—preparing for the real thing. It rankled. It really did.

"We've settled on the date," Claudia was saying in her nasal voice. "The twenty-fifth of August. It doesn't give me a lot of time, does it?"

From this distance, Rose had no difficulty hearing the conversation. Both Claudia and her mother spoke as though everyone was deaf, an unattractive habit that spoiled them both, in Rose's opinion. There was nothing ladylike about a woman who screamed like a fishwife. She was surprised that Harris—so soft-spoken himself—could stand it; was sure that a steady diet of that voice would grate after a few years.

Rose peeked through a gap in the hanging dresses for a better look at the pair. Mrs. Smith was wearing navy, and Claudia was in pale yellow, which accentuated her dark hair and skin. She was setting her handbag on the table and proceeding to take off her gloves. Rose watched her loosen one finger, then the next and the next, gently pulling at the soft kid leather till one hand, then the other, was exposed.

Rose adored good kid-leather gloves; had made a point of observing how the Glove Counter on Main did the fittings. The customer would be asked to rest her elbow on the blue velvet pad while the sales assistant selected three or four pairs for "Madame's consideration" from the wooden drawers on the wall behind the counter. Madame would then stand obediently while the fine leather was smoothed over her fat or thin fingers. After which, she would flex her hand, turning her wrist this way and that, giving the sales assistant an opportunity to check the fit and the give of the leather.

"A great deal to consider—" the Head of Bridal was saying. "—delighted to be of assistance. Perhaps, if you'll give me an idea of what your preferences might be—"

How sickly sweet and insufferable! Predictable, too. The women in Bridal always fawned over girls like Claudia; girls blessed with a silver spoon from day one. Silver spoons and orange blossoms; marching to the altar with each silver piece, each flower blossom, lined up like a colour party, in neat, orderly rows.

Claudia has her life to live, you have yours. So, get on with it. Make it work.

Afraid of a reprimand from Mrs. Dakin for being gone so long, and disgusted at her own self-pity, Rose hurried off.

"Rose, I'm assigning number 92 to you," Mrs. Dakin said the next afternoon. "It's tricky; there's precious little material to work with. But I'm sure you can handle it." Her voice lowered. "Important customer, this girl, Rose. Do your very best." She placed the gown on a nearby hook. "And, please, take note of the next fitting date."

It was three-thirty when Rose finished the garment she was working on and checked the assignment scribbler. Halfway down the page she found the entry. Number 92— Miss C. Smith. Ivory satin, with train. For Rose V.

Of course. It would have to be me, getting the honour of working on her gown.

There was no way out, though. Mrs. Dakin would expect her to do the assignment, no excuses. Rose put her initials in the assignment column, took the gown back to her machine, and read through the fitting lady's instructions.

Work on the gown kept her busy for the remainder of the afternoon and into the next morning. She went at it with a steely resolve, determined to blot out the snippets of Harris that hovered at the corner of her consciousness. Harris, teasing, asking for another piece of pie; Harris, diving into the water of the cove; Harris, ordering fish and chips. Kind, affable Harris; who had never given the slightest indication that he thought of her as anything more than his aunt's maid.

Stop it! ordered the logical part of her brain. Grow up.

She laboured on, fingers adjusting pins, basting needle slipping in and out of the textured fabric. All in aid of dear, buxom Claudia's wedding day. Claudia, who'd have her mother's shape by the time she reached forty; earlier, if she had managed to produce three or four little fat-ass carbon-copies of herself before then.

Got the makings of a real porker, that one. All arse and boobs. The thought struck Rose as funny, and she smiled to herself.

It was eleven when Rose hung the gown on the Completed rack. It would go back to Bridal for a fitting, perhaps require a couple of additional small adjustments, before Rose could count on being rid of it for good. It should fit well enough, come August, unless the porker gained any more weight in the course of her prenuptial frolics.

Yes, indeed, in a couple of months, Claudia would be sailing grandly up the carpeted aisle of All Saint's, standing with eyes lowered, repeating the vows. She'd accept her ring, sign the register, smile up at Harris, all without a hitch.

As for any twitches, who could say? Perhaps, by the time she was walking back down the aisle on Harris' arm, the two pins that Rose had left in the seam of the right bust dart might have worked through the fabric. *We try our best to make things perfect for our brides.* The motto was Mrs. Dakin's, not Rose's. Not for this particular bride.

New Job

A week went by, and then another. Eileen hadn't said whether or not she'd talked to her father, and Rose didn't like to ask. Perhaps Eileen's father was waiting for the right opportunity to speak to Mr. Hatfield, or perhaps he'd decided that he'd rather not get involved. So, when Mrs. Dakin asked her to stay behind for a few minutes on Thursday, Rose wasn't sure of the reason.

"Mr. Hatfield has a spot in Fabrics coming open," Mrs. Dakin said. "He told me today that he's going to put you in it."

"Me!" Rose replied, hoping she looked suitably surprised. "My goodness—when?"

"Tomorrow. You're to report to the office first thing in the morning. He'll be expecting you."

"Why, yes. Of course."

"I'll be sorry to lose you," Mrs. Dakin said grudgingly. "You were a good worker."

"Thank you," Rose replied. She couldn't say she'd miss Miss Dakin, nor any of the girls. On the contrary, she could hardly wait to be rid of them and the hot, crowded room that they would continue to slave in.

Eileen was waiting outside the staff entrance when Rose signed out at six-fifteen.

"Hi," she said. A conspiring smile crept across her face. "You got the news, I take it."

"Yes, I did. I could hardly believe it when she told me. I've been trying not to get my hopes up, in case it didn't work out."

"I knew yesterday, but I didn't dare say anything," Eileen went on. "You'll be taking my job, you know."

"Your job?"

"Yes. Mr. Hatfield's moving me up to Accessories. After you and I talked, I got to thinking that I'd like a change, too. Daddy agreed, when I explained it all out. He said he'd speak to Mr. Hatfield; and he did, too, after the Council meeting on Monday night."

So, that was how the game was played. Eileen was willing to put in a word for Rose, providing there was something in it for herself. Well, fair enough. After all, work-based friendships should only go so far. Be friendly—helpful if it suited you—but always, always, watch out for your own interests. In this instance, each of them was getting what she wanted, so there should be no hard feelings; no harm done.

They walked together to the corner, parted with a smile and a wave. There was no tram in sight, so Rose walked on, mulling over this most recent turn of events. To the world, she would be little more than a junior sales clerk, lugging bolts of fabric from the display cases to the cutting table. There wouldn't be any significant raise in pay, either. Mrs. Dakin had made that point; the store gave raises based on performance, but only after a full year of service.

The pay wasn't the important issue, however. Increased status within the store's hierarchy was worth as much as money. Getting out of the cramped and hot sewing room and into a sales position would be seen by everyone as a step up; was, in fact, a step up; no two ways about it.

She couldn't wait to tell Aunt Lettie and Ora. They could have a little drink over dinner to celebrate. Who knew where she might go next, once she'd proved herself. Children's Wear was a possibility, so was Ladies' Accessories. From there, she could set her sights on Evening Gowns, even the Bridal Salon. She had the looks, she knew that; and the brains too. And, one of these fine days, she would be modelling for the store's fashion shows.

She turned onto Lettie's walk and climbed the six steps up to the front door. "Aunt Lettie, Ora—," she shouted through the open screen. "Wait till you hear my news."

ROSE

PART FOUR

Wider World

Violet

Come hell or high water, Rose washed and curled her hair every Thursday evening. Ora, slapdash as always, laughed at her friend's self-imposed routine, claiming that, if there was ever another explosion in the city, or a tidal wave, Rose wouldn't be able to head for high ground until her hair was done to perfection. For her part, Rose simply grinned and carried on with her weekly ritual. Only Ora could get away with poking fun at her like that.

By seven-thirty, Rose had towelled off her wet hair and was combing setting gel through the damp strands when the telephone cut into the stillness of the house.

"Damn," she muttered, listening to it ring a second, then a third time. She hated being interrupted on hair night, especially to answer a phone that was rarely for her. Ora generally did phone duty, but Ora had gone out earlier with a hurried, "Ship's in; see ya later."

The phone bell was jangling for the fifth time before Rose heard Lettie's door open and her footsteps shuffling along the downstairs passageway. "Hold your horses, I'm coming, I'm coming," Lettie was grumbling.

Rose kept on with her pincurls, trying to ignore a pang of guilt at the sound of Lettie's laboured progress. She was moving much more slowly in the past couple of months; even the men had noticed.

"I have to have a talk with her about the roomers," Ora had confided to Rose. "She loves having the men, but I don't know how much longer she can cope."

"I've noticed, too," Rose had replied. "She seems so short of breath."

"Hallo," floated up the stairwell, followed by, "Yes, you're speaking to her." There was a pause, then, "Yes, course you can. Just hold on a minute."

Must be for Ora, Rose thought, winding a chiffon scarf, turban-style, around her head. Ora had probably taken off in such a hurry that Lettie didn't know she wasn't at home.

"Rosie, you up there?" Lettie bellowed.

"Yes, I'm here."

"There's a lady on the line for you."

"Me? Goodness! Tell them to wait a minute." Rose slipped her feet into her mules and threw on her robe. It couldn't be Eileen; she had choir practice on Thursday nights and she never missed. Must be Mrs. McGinn, Rose concluded. Mavis' new baby was overdue. She'd said she would call Rose as soon as it arrived.

Rose picked up the receiver, expecting to hear Mrs. McGinn on the other end of the line. "Hello."

"Hi there."

She drew in her breath. It wasn't Mrs. McGinn.

"Hello! . . . Rose . . . you there?"

Her stomach felt queer, filled with a thousand swirling butterflies.

"Yes," she breathed.

"It's me. Violet."

Violet. After all this time.

She exhaled, hardly realizing she'd been holding her breath.

"Vi . . . Violet. My sister?"

"Yes, your sister! How many Violets do you know, any-way?"

"None. I mean—just you."

Violet was back. Violet, her sister, was talking to her.

"Rose! You listening to me?"

"I . . . yes. . .What did you say?"

"I said, we need to get together."

"Sure, yes. I can't believe it's you, Violet. Where are you?"

"I'm here, in Halifax."

"Halifax," Rose repeated.

Violet, her big sister, was here, in this very city.

"Let's get together for supper," Violet said. "They tell me the Green Lantern's a good spot."

"Yes, it's fine. I don't get off till six. There'll be a line-up, but maybe if you get there early . . ."

Violet's voice, impatient, interrupted her.

"Got it. The Green Lantern. At six."

"Violet, tell me where you . . ."

"We'll talk tomorrow."

"Okay, but I . . ."

"Must run. Bye, Rosie."

Rose stood listening to the buzz of the dial tone until the operator cut in. "Madam, if your call is complete, please hang up."

Placing the receiver back in its cradle, she stared at the silent telephone, summarizing the brief conversation in her mind.

Meet Violet for supper tomorrow. The Green Lantern. Go straight from work.

It would be crowded and noisy, with a line-up clear out to the street.

How could they talk—really talk—with all that hubbub around them. Maybe she should call Violet back, suggest another place. She reached for the phone, withdrew her hand. How could she call Violet when she didn't have her number, hadn't even had time to ask where Violet was staying, or how she'd managed to get Lettie's name.

"Stupid, stupid," she said under her breath.

"Anything wrong, dear?" Lettie was standing in the doorway of her sitting room, eyeing her.

"No, no, nothing's wrong. That was my sister Violet. She's back in town. We're having dinner together tomorrow." *How strange*, Rose thought as the words came out. *Sounds as if Violet's in from the country for a day of shopping; nothing more significant than that.*

"Well, isn't that nice," Lettie said. "Haven't seen her for a spell, have you?"

"No. She's been—" Where? Rose didn't know, "—in the States."

She went back up to her room and sat on the floor with her head up against the radiator, trying to get her hair dry so that she could remove the bobby-pins. Twice she went to the window and pulled the curtains back a crack, hoping to see Ora hurrying along the darkened sidewalk. She needed to talk to Ora, to tell her about Violet's call; but she knew there was only a slim chance that Ora would be back tonight. If Jack had only a twenty-four-hour shore leave, they'd be spending it together. Shore leave was precious; every minute, every hour counted.

In the morning, Rose spent ages getting dressed, trying on three outfits before she was satisfied, and was so late leaving the house that she had to run like mad to catch her tram. At work, she fought off her nervousness, trying to focus on the customer requests for zippers and buttons and seam binding, pushing aside her fears. What if Violet doesn't show up, a niggling voice kept saying. She might be gone again, without any forwarding address.

At six sharp she was clocked out and on her way uptown, weaving around people, bumping into others on the crowded sidewalk. At the entrance to the restaurant she pushed her way to the head of the line. "I'm joining someone," she said to the hostess, eyes scanning the packed interior. When she spied Violet at a corner table, her knees went weak, and she caught hold of a seated patron's chair to steady herself.

Violet got up when she saw Rose. "Hey, little sister—" she said, holding out her arms. "Give me a big hug." With her cheek against Violet's, Rose could smell the heavy, cloying scent of perfume.

"How about you!" Violet was standing back now, looking her over. "You're all grown up."

"It's been a long time, Violet." Rose tried to keep her voice light, her movements subdued. She didn't want to put Violet on the defensive or draw unwanted attention from diners at the nearby tables.

"I know. I know. Too long. Sit down. Here's our waitress coming. I asked for menus right away. I'm famished."

Rose opened her menu. Her hands were cold and she could feel her stomach quaking. Now that Violet was actually here, there was so much to talk about that Rose didn't know how or where to begin.

"You ready to order?" Violet asked as the waitress approached.

Rose flushed. The items listed on her menu might well have been written in ancient Greek for all that she'd absorbed them.

"I . . . can't make up my mind," she said. "Whatever you're having will be fine with me."

"We'll have the breaded chops with applesauce and vegetables," Violet said, handing her own menu back to the waitress.

When the waitress was out of earshot, Rose said, "We've been so worried, Lily and I." Yes, worried was the right word. Worried sick. "Wondering where you were all this time."

"Boston for a couple of years," Violet replied, lighting a third cigarette. Rose could see two other butts, their tips red with lipstick, in the ashtray. "And after that, Montreal."

Boston. There was only one postcard from Boston.

"I couldn't write, Rose. There was too much happening; it was too hard to put it on paper."

There was the phone, Rose wanted to say. Just pick it up and ask the operator for long distance. She didn't say it, though.

"Were you alone, Violet? Were you sick? I thought you must be."

Violet's laugh sounded hard, and bitter. "Alone! If only. I'd have been better off." She dragged on her cigarette, watched the smoke spiralling over her head. "The guy I got tangled up with was a no-good jerk. I found that out pretty quick. Couldn't stay sober long enough to eat supper, let alone keep a job. I was the one bringing home the bacon. Not that I cared a jig if the jerk ever ate. But I needed grub for me and the little guy."

She'd had another baby then.

"Where is he now?" Rose asked.

"Who knows. In a ditch, sleeping it off; or, better still, dead." Violet's voice was flat, her eyes steely.

"I didn't mean your husband," Rose said. "I meant your boy. How old is he?"

A little smile played across Violet's face.

"Billy's two. He's in Boston with the old lady."

"The old lady—?"

"His granny. She's all right, though. I trust her with him."

Rose nodded. "I guess you'll be sending for him as soon as you get settled." How lovely, she was thinking. Lily and I are aunts. Our little nephew's name is Billy.

"I'll see," Violet said, looking away. "I can't be hauling the poor kid all over hell's half-acre. He's better off with her till he's older. I send money every month. He has everything he needs." She spoke matter-of-factly, as one might speak of their pet dog or horse.

Rose wanted to ask if Violet had a picture of Billy, but something stopped her. Don't, an inner voice warned. She might not have a picture. Let it be.

"I think our food's coming," she said instead.

"Good," Violet replied, stubbing her cigarette in the ashtray. "I was beginning to wonder if they were still chasing that pig around the barnyard."

"Anything else I can get you ladies?" the waitress said, setting the plates down.

"More coffee, when you have a minute," Violet replied. And to Rose, "Eat, girl, eat. And tell me about yourself."

Rose gave Violet an edited, summarized version of the events in her own life. There was no way she could tell the whole story in one sitting; and it probably wasn't necessary, or wise, in any case. A person could tell the truth without telling the whole truth. It didn't take a Philadelphia lawyer to figure that out.

"Lily's got one more year at the Home."

"God, hard to believe," Violet said when they'd finished their main meal and were waiting for the rice pudding. "I had to call there to find out where you were. Talked to a Mrs. Duffy. It was no easy task, prying your address out of her, let me tell you. She's as bad as or worse than the old battle-axe. Whatever happened to her, anyway?"

"She got married," Rose replied.

"Did she, now? Old poker-face got the real thing up her ass at last. Bet that puts a smile on her kisser."

"Shush—" Rose glanced around to see if anyone had overheard. "She married a minister."

"Well, praise the Lord and pass the ammunition. God, what a time she used to give me over seeing you two on Sundays!"

"I'll never forget Sundays," Rose said. "I hated them. They were the worst day of the week, always. It's still a big deal for Lily to come out with me. You wouldn't think it would matter so much, now that she's going on fifteen."

"The world's built on stupid rules and power games," Violet replied. "Started with the Ten Commandments and hasn't let up since. I played by them once upon a time, but not anymore." She opened her cigarette package and held it out to Rose.

"Smoke?"

"No, thanks."

"No vices, eh?"

"I never liked the taste."

"Good for you. Just as well."

Violet lit one for herself and sat back, exhaling the smoke through her nostrils.

She's got Mama's features, Rose thought, *same oval face and straight nose, same mouth. Like mine, actually. Lily's the one who looks more like Daddy.* Only the eyes were different. The same velvety brown as their mother's, but with a totally different expression. *Old eyes,* Rose thought. *Old, weary eyes on a still-young woman.*

"You remind me of Mama so much." It came out before she realized she'd said it.

Violet flashed her a smile. "In looks, maybe; but that's where it stops. I figure she'd be pretty disappointed, if she could see me now." She dragged on the cigarette, a distant expression on her face.

"No she wouldn't," Rose said quickly. "She'd love you like always. Why, she used to call you her right arm. Said you could do just about anything you set your mind to."

"Yeah, right." Violet's laugh was harsh. "Well, I guess I've lived up to that prediction."

She reached over and patted Rose on the arm. "Enough about Mama; makes us feel bad. Let's talk about fun stuff. I'll have to visit that high-fashion store of yours. Get me some new duds."

"All the summer stuff is in," Rose said. "Hemlines are shorter than ever, I swear. And you have to see our fur salon. It's glorious."

"I'll bet. I've got a fur, actually," Violet said. "I'll wear it for you when fall comes."

"Violet, don't tell me! Not a real one."

"Yeah. Raccoon; full length."

"Oh, Violet," Rose sighed. "I'd be satisfied with a fox neckpiece."

Violet shrugged. "Bit overrated if you ask me. Though mine did keep my backside from freezing off in Montreal last winter. If you're a good girl, I might loan it to you for a special occasion."

She looked past Rose, nodded to someone in the distance, and reached for her handbag. "We'd better make a move, sister of mine. The hostess is giving us the evil eye."

Violet took care of the bill. "Forget it," she said, pushing Rose's money back into her hand. "I asked you, so I pay."

Outside, Violet seemed anxious to be off. "I need to get going," she said, glancing at her watch. "I told Mrs. Mac I'd be back by eight."

"Can we go and see Lily on Sunday," Rose pleaded. "Please."

"How to make me feel bad, Rosie," Violet said with a sigh. "Sunday it is, then. I'll meet you there. Now, here comes a number eight. Isn't that your tram?"

It wasn't until she'd got on and found a seat that Rose realized she didn't have Violet's street address. "I'm sharing a place with some friends," she'd said. "Not too far from the train station."

What else had she said? She'd come down from Montreal to work for a woman by the name of Mrs. Mac. "It's a private club," Violet had offered by way of explanation. "Exclusive. For people with money. Real business-woman, Mrs. Mac. With a war on, it makes a lot of sense."

"What do you do there?" Rose had asked. "Work in the dining room?"

"Sort of," Violet had replied.

Rose studied herself in the vanity mirror when she got home. Her face, with its hint of powder and pale pink lipstick, looked pale in comparison to Violet's. Violet had chosen a much more pronounced, older look: black mascara, applied heavily, carefully plucked eyebrows, and brilliant red lip-stick. If Rose hadn't known Violet, she'd have put her at late twenties or early thirties.

Violet was attractive, though, no two ways about it. She had a gorgeous figure, one any guy would drool over; and she dressed to the nines. Tonight's outfit, a soft blue two-piece with shoulder pads that accentuated the short jacket, was the latest in chic. She wore expensive suede platforms, too, and had a bag to match.

Lily would be totally impressed when she saw Violet's clothes. She was at the age when looks mattered; had begged Rose for lipstick and nail polish, even though they were forbidden to wear it at the Home.

As for Ora, what she might have to say about Violet would be another matter entirely.

Visiting Lily

Violet made good on her promise to visit Lily on Sunday. She phoned Rose on Saturday morning to work out the details. "I'll meet you on Agricola, across from the stables. Let's make it for—say—one o'clock," she suggested.

"Be there a few minutes early," Rose warned. "The trams run on the hour on Sundays."

"I know that, kiddo. I've been away a long time, but I didn't lose my marbles."

She was waiting when Rose arrived. "You look nice," Rose said. Violet had on a tailored suit—navy, with a pleated skirt—and a darling blouse, all ruffles, with a cameo brooch pinned at her throat. She looked less showy, more subdued; she'd toned down her makeup, too. Lighter lipstick, no mascara, and only a hint of eyebrow pencil.

"First impressions," Violet said. "I wouldn't want to scare anybody off."

They caught their tram, had no trouble making their northbound connection at the transfer point, and were walking down Richmond hill at a quarter to two. "Is that Lily's school?" Violet asked, pointing to a three-storey brick structure on their right. The playground was deserted on this early summer Sunday afternoon, its swings and slides empty and still.

"Yes," Rose replied. "I went there, too."

"What grade did you get to?" Violet asked. "I forget."

"I finished Nine. Matron wouldn't send me on. Just as well; I wasn't much of a student."

"Me either. Waste of time, a lot of that book stuff. Life's the best teacher. There's more than one way to skin a cat, believe you me."

One of the older girls answered their knock.

"Hi," she said to Rose. Her eyes flicked over Violet, came back to Rose.

"This is my—our—sister," Rose said. "Violet."

"Come in," the girl replied. "You can wait there." She pointed to the waiting area across from Matron's office, and hurried off. The usual eight or ten straight-backed chairs had been set against the inside corridor wall. One man was already seated, head bent forward, seemingly intent on turning his hat around and around in his hands. He didn't look up and they didn't speak to him.

"God, this hole brings back memories," Violet said, pulling off her gloves. "Hasn't changed a bit."

Rose decided not to answer. What was there to say? It *was* the darkest part of the entire house, particularly when the four doors that led off it were closed, as they were now. Matron wasn't in her office on the weekends; there were no committee ladies in the small sitting room or the front parlor, and no girls in the sewing room at the end of the corridor.

Here was where they'd sat during those duty visits before Violet went away; Violet on one chair, with Lily perched on her lap, and Rose in the chair beside them; trying to be a family on three straight-backed chairs in a dark hallway because Matron didn't trust Violet enough to allow her to take them out for the afternoon.

Violet had told stories to pass the time—tales of shopping and movies and ice-cream floats—and had dispensed candies. Not broken pieces like you got at the store on Gottingen, next to the theatre, but individually wrapped chocolates. Sometimes she had pennies for them, as well. "Get some licorice pipes," she'd say to Lily. "And some of those yummy orange gums."

How different the house now seemed to Rose. Not that

it had become any less strict, or more loving, in the two years since she'd escaped its confines. It was still a big, rambling arc of a place, full of silly rules, unfair regulations, impossible expectations. But it was no longer her world; it had lost its place at the centre of the universe. Beyond its walls was the real world; a world of many wonderful possibilities.

Yes, that was the crux of the matter—the difference between out there and in here. This house tried to do the impossible, and in its lofty, misplaced goal, it failed. It was impossible to adequately care for—and about—thirty-plus children under one roof; impossible to see to their real needs; to see them as persons. Adversity and necessity brought them together; and a weird code of Cleanliness and Godliness kept them together; but the imposed bond was a weak one, heavy with resentment, hurt, and loss. It offered, at best, three squares a day, a few clean clothes, a bed to sleep in. Togetherness, Cleanliness, Godliness. What a God-awful, unholy trinity.

Hanging on the wall outside Matron's office was a framed verse. It had been donated by a new committee person, Rose suspected, for she hadn't seen it before.

Here Let Us Live
Life At Its Best
Here May The Heart
Find Comfort And Rest.

The words (Violet would likely call them "sentimental drivel") weren't the right fit for this house. "Life at its best" didn't add up to rows of metal bedsteads, stained enamel sinks, aluminum drinking cups, or the dozens of shoes lined up at the side door.

"Life at its best" should mean a cozy little place with lace curtains at the dormer windows, a dog on the back step, a father smoking his pipe; and a mother (very much alive) making jam tarts and lemon pies in a bright, wall-papered kitchen.

Lily didn't notice Violet when she came charging down the stairs.

"Are we going to the park?" she demanded. "There's a band concert. Greta heard it on the radio."

"Look who's here," Rose said.

Lily turned and stared, her arms dropping to her sides, as if waiting for a cue. What was that old saying? Armed and ready. Wait till you see the whites of their eyes.

Violet noticed the hesitation; Rose could see that.

"Missy mine—get over here and let me give you a big kiss," Violet said.

After that, it was all right.

Violet was insistent that they go out for the afternoon. "We can't sit here like three bumps on a log," she said, eyes flashing. "Let's find a tearoom. I think I saw a place open on our way up."

"We should check with Greta," Rose said. "She has to . . ."

"Forget Greta," Violet replied. "I'll handle her."

The little tearoom was situated on Gottingen, not far from the Base, tucked between a hat shop and a tailor's. The prices were written in chalk on a blackboard by the entrance. "Isn't it a bit expensive, just for tea and biscuits?" Rose whispered.

"Nope," Violet said. "We're only going this way once. Sit down and relax."

Lily was delighted. "It's so sweet," she kept saying. "Look at all the teapots! There must be at least a dozen of them." Three shelves of an ancient corner cabinet were, in fact, crammed with tea sets; assorted china pots, with a hodge-podge of cups and saucers; all pretty enough, but certainly not top of the line. Their waitress had covered their own pot with a knitted cozy, and the napkins were real linen.

"It'll be in the society page tomorrow," Violet teased. "Lily Morash poured."

The time flew by. Listening to Violet's stories of Montreal, a place so quaint and foreign it seemed like another country, Rose forgot about the clock until she noticed the proprietor placing a Closed sign on the door.

"We'll never get back by five," Rose said. "And we didn't get permission, either." Lily, aware of the implications, groaned. "I'll be docked points," she said. "But I don't care. It was fun."

A glowering Greta was on duty when they arrived back.

"I'm sorry, Greta—" Rose began, "please forgive—"

"Yes," Violet broke in, "—terribly sorry. But an elderly lady at the tearoom took a bad turn, and we stayed with her till they phoned someone to come and get her. Here— please accept something for your trouble."

Rose saw Lily's startled look, saw also the five-dollar bill that Violet was pressing into Greta's hand. She took a deep breath, expecting Greta to push Violet away. Nothing of the sort happened. Greta accepted the bill, folded it over, and put it into her apron pocket. "Much appreciated," she said. "Just don't let it happen again."

"I could hardly believe it," Rose said after they'd left and were walking up the hill. "I thought for sure Greta would crucify you."

Violet shrugged. "The colour of money, Rose. Best thing ever invented in this life. Keeps the world turning around. It really does."

Differences

For Rose, scrubbing the cellar steps wasn't so much a chore as a way to work off tension. There were plenty of other chores she could do on any given Saturday morning, but tackling the cellar steps was a sure way to have an uninterrupted half-hour, an opportunity to think things through in a productive way. Ora had gone upstairs to change the bed linen and to give the bathroom her weekly once-over; and Rose had seen Lettie hobbling toward the front of the house, a dust cloth in one hand and her cane in the other.

The dear old soul still tried to do her bit with the housework, but it was becoming increasingly obvious that she accomplished very little these days. Her dusting attempts were more hindrance than help, actually, consisting of whisking the dust from one table to another or onto the floor. Rose made no comment, quietly redoing the tables and running the sweeper over the carpets after Lettie had settled into her rocker. It wasn't Rose's house, after all, or her place to criticize. If there was anything to be said or done, it should come from Ora; and Ora, true to her nature, wasn't the least bit worried about a fine layer of dust over everything.

Rose set her bucket on the landing and worked her way down, step by step, her bristle brush sending soapy foam across the worn planking and up her wrists and forearms. Talk about filthy, she thought, pausing a moment to push escaped strands of hair back inside her kerchief. The rain of the last few days had turned the backyard into a mud patch—mud that the newest roomer had trekked in on the soles of his boots. Neither rain nor mud had kept him from working every spare minute on an old jalopy in the back lane; and every time he came in to clean his rags or put his toolbox in the basement, the mud had come with him.

Her hands were soon tingling from the harsh lye soap and the hot water, but Rose didn't mind. Each finished step gleamed in the glow of the overhead bulb. *Maybe by the time I get to the bottom, I'll have things figured out,* she thought.

Violet and Ora were on her mind. They'd met for the first time yesterday, quite by coincidence. Rose and Ora had finished the grocery shopping and were heading back to Lettie's loaded down with bags, when they heard someone calling Rose's name. The someone was Violet.

"Talk about a load," she said when she caught up to them. "You two remind me of a couple of pack mules."

Rose set her bags down on the grassy verge. "Don't make fun," she said, flexing her fingers and rubbing her arm. "I feel like a mule, that's for sure."

"Why don't you get a cab," Violet suggested. "Your place is a fair hike, weighed down like that."

"We can manage," Ora replied. "We're tough. A cab's too expensive, and we missed the tram by seconds."

As they stood chatting of this and that, Rose could feel an unpleasant undercurrent building. Nothing that was actually said, but a sense that each was assessing the other and finding her lacking.

They parted after ten minutes. Violet, as usual, was in a hurry to get somewhere.

"See you Sunday," she said to Rose. "I've got a nice present for Lily."

"I'm glad you got to meet Violet," Rose said as she and Ora walked on. "I've asked her to come over for a visit, but she's always too busy."

"Yeah," Ora replied. "She's quite the looker, isn't she?

What with her clothes and all. The job she has must pay well."

Rose glanced at her friend, caught by an indefinable something in her tone. For once, Ora's normally expressive face was impassive, almost closed.

"I'm so happy that she's back," Rose said.

"Me too, for your sake; and Lily's."

Ora didn't mention Violet again, leaving Rose convinced that the uncharacteristic silence spelled distaste or disapproval; probably both. Carefree, undiscriminating Ora, who liked just about everybody and everything, didn't like Violet.

When the stairs were dry enough to walk on, Rose took her bucket out to the back stoop and dumped the dirty water over the side. According to Ora, the yard had, at one time, been a delightful enclosure of perennial beds and flowering bushes. Lettie had obviously lost the energy and inclination to keep it up long before Rose had arrived; as a result, the beds had gone to seed, the bushes were overgrown, and the grass was sparse and choked with weeds. In the north corner, the frame of a wooden chair-swing had caved in on itself.

It may not be the home I want, but it's what I've got. And I don't see much change happening any time soon.

Rose had made no progress in convincing Violet that they should get a place together; that Lily could join them, once she was through school in the spring. Violet saw things differently, and made no bones about saying so.

"Rose, you should stay put where you are. It's a good set-up, and cheap. Mrs. Mac needs me with her; that's the deal we've got. Besides, anything decent costs an arm and a leg these days. Bloody highway robbery."

"But the Housing Review—"

"Don't give me that crap about the Review Board. It's just one more government outfit that's as useless as you-know-what on a bull. And I don't need to hear a sermon about being a family. We *are* family, Rose; we don't have to be in each other's back pockets to prove it. So, stop your nagging. Times are tough; there's a war on. You'll just have to grin and bear it."

Enter Ralph

June turned out to be a gorgeous month; as warm as August, with no fog, and just enough rain to speed along the early flowers and shrubs. Rose walked to work almost every day, preferring to leave a half-hour early rather than be packed like a sardine into the crowded tram car.

The last weekend was no exception; by noon on Sunday the temperature was already at seventy degrees. "Too good a day to be indoors," Lettie said to Rose after lunch. "I'm heading for the verandah. Hope you left the dishes to dry themselves."

"I did," Rose replied, stuffing a bag of bread crumbs into her satchel.

"Where you off to, dear?" Lettie asked.

"The Gardens," Rose replied. "For the band concert, and to feed the birds."

"Them birds is some lucky," Lettie sniffed. "Hitler's got the Lowlands near starved to death—people crying out for a crust or two—and we're over here throwing ours at the birds. Doesn't make sense, does it?"

"Nothing about war makes sense to me," Rose said. "Maybe that's why I like feeding the birds. They keep on flying, war or not."

"True enough. Lord knows why I get so worked up. You'd think an old lady like me would know better. But maybe that's just it—I'm too old to be alive. There's those youngsters, dying by the hundreds every day, and old girls like me who haven't got the decency to pack it in."

"Don't you be talking like that," Rose said. "You're doing your share, having the fellows here, giving them a home. They all say so."

She helped Lettie into the big wicker rocker on the porch, and then rooted for her sunhat in the box by the door. "There, I'm all set," Rose said, putting it on.

Lettie nodded, her eyes half closed. "Warm as toast, that sun. I don't plan to budge my old bones till you get back."

"Good. You stay put. We'll have a pick-up supper; it won't take long to get ready."

Rose was looking forward to the walk. The park was about six blocks from Lettie's, and the route was a pleasant one. Beyond the Willow Tree intersection, the boulevard stretched south past grand old Victorian houses much like Mrs. Browne's. Most of the front yards were a mix of flowering shrubs, late tulips, and early annuals. Weigela and crabapple had replaced the earlier lilac, and a gorgeous mock orange bush drooped onto the sidewalk, causing Rose to pause and break off a piece to take with her.

She would be spending the afternoon alone in the park. Ora was visiting her sister, and Lily was tied up with the annual Sunday School picnic. As one of the Home's senior girls, it was Lily's responsibility to keep tabs on the younger ones.

Rose wouldn't soon forget those picnics. They began at noon, with the loading of the children into the back of Superintendent Wambolt's old pick-up. Three hours of madness ensued when they reached the shore of the Arm, that narrow needle of salt water that threaded itself along the western slopes of the city. At the park, there were potato-sack races and three-legged ones, horseshoe throwing and games of ball. The ladies' auxiliary supplied sticky egg sandwiches and lime drinks; and the men brought along a great aluminum tub of homemade ice-cream, hurrying to serve everyone before it melted into pools of curdled milk and vanilla flavouring.

Ora used to adore every minute of the noisy afternoon, getting almost as excited as the little ones, but Rose found the outing tiring, with too many boisterous children running around like maniacs. Children who came home tired and cranky, with cuts and bruises that needed swabs and patches, and upset stomachs in the middle of the night.

At the hospital corner Rose paused to consider her routes. She could take the longer way round, past the ball field, or she could cut through the cemetery. She decided to take the long way, which would give her an excuse for not visiting the graves of her mother and father.

The sight of the graves saddened Rose. She'd stuck an earthenware holder into the ground to hold fresh flowers, but the bleakness of their untended plot bothered her. The two wooden crosses that Mr. McGinn had made were leaning badly, their bases rotting from the summer rain and winter snow, and she could barely make out the names that he'd so painstakingly carved on each one.

"We should have a decent stone put up," she'd said to Violet. "With Mama and Daddy's names, and the names of the two babies as well."

Violet had agreed, much to Rose's surprise. "Yeah, we probably should. Check out the prices, Rose, and let me know."

Rose did, calling two of the monument works listed in the phonebook. Their quotes turned her initial hopes into dismay.

"Jesus Murphy, girl. They want a bloody fortune!" Violet swore when Rose showed her the estimates. And then, seeing Rose's face, "Sorry, pet. I didn't mean to bite your head off. Give me the papers and we'll see."

We'll see. Rose was getting plenty used to that line.

When will we get together next?

We'll see.

Can you give Lily a call; she loves to have you phone.

We'll see.

Violet was back, but in many respects she seemed as remote, as unavailable as if she were still miles away. Rose tried to make allowances, to understand, but it wasn't easy. She found Violet very difficult to deal with, and next to impossible to pin down.

Today was a prime example. There had been no phone call; no word since they'd parted at the bus stop two Sundays ago. "I'll phone you," Violet had said. But she hadn't, and Rose wasn't allowed to call her. "Only in an extreme emergency, Rose. Mrs. Mac can't have the line tied up with personal calls."

Rose knew there was no point in arguing. It wouldn't have done one bit of good, in any case, because Violet always did what she wanted to do. Not that she wasn't kind in other respects. When she *was* around, she took them out to dinner, got tickets for shows (and not just any tickets, but the best seats in the house), bought them presents. But it was always on her terms. And if you didn't like it, you could lump it. Simple as that.

"Those birds don't care whose bread it is, do they? As long as you keep throwing it at them." The man who was sitting on the next bench sounded amused. Rose smiled over at him. He looked vaguely familiar, and she wondered where she'd seen him before. "No, they don't," she said. "That brownish-white one's a pig. Did you see how he grabbed that piece away from the grey one."

They sat watching the two birds scurry after the crumbs, pecking at each other in a ruffle of feathers and irritated squawks. The man on the bench dug into his bag and threw another handful down. "Hey, stop that. There's enough for the lot of you."

Rose couldn't help noticing the size of his hands. They were larger and thicker hands than she'd seen on anyone, including Freddie, the grounds worker at the Brownes'.

"I saw you here last week," the man said. "Sitting over there with a younger girl." He pointed to a bench diagonally across the clearing. A sailor was stretched out on it now, sound asleep.

"Yes," she replied. "I was with my sister."

So that explained why he looked so familiar. She stole a closer look at him.

He had a rugged profile, not handsome, but strong. Clean-shaven, with light-brown hair parted on the side and combed neatly back behind his ears. He wore a crisp white shirt and dark pants, and had laid his folded jacket on the seat of the bench. His expression was pleasant, and not at all bold. She couldn't tell his age. Thirty, perhaps—older, but not old.

"Guess you could say I'm a regular," she added. "I love it here."

"Me too," he said. "The flowers put me in mind of my grandmother's place. Some garden she had. Not this big, of course, but every bit as pretty." He lapsed into silence again, watching the pigeons milling around his feet.

Across the manicured lawns and flower beds, she could hear the band warming up. A piano, and then the sharp trill of a trumpet.

"Showtime," the man said, emptying the last crumbs from his bag and standing up. "You staying for the music?"

"Yes I am." When she stood, she was amazed at how tall he was. At five foot three, she barely came to his shoulder.

"Might as well sit together, then." It was a statement, not an offer. Mildly put, though; inoffensive.

"Sure, why not," she replied. He seemed very much a gentleman, and she couldn't think of a good reason to turn him down.

They strolled companionably toward the spectator benches. "This'll do," he said, stopping at a bench halfway back in the middle section. The band began, and gradually the benches filled up until there was hardly an empty spot left.

"That was great," he said afterwards. It was past four o'clock and the audience had dispersed quickly, leaving them standing alone in the shade of an enormous maple.

"Yes, it was," Rose replied.

"Must be on my way," he continued. "I've got a train waiting."

"Oh. Well, have a good trip."

"Will do."

She watched him walk purposefully toward the lower gate, and then turned and headed in the opposite direction. At the fountain in the park's northwest corner, she ran her hand through the water in the lower basin before taking a coin out of her pocket. She closed her eyes, made a wish, and, trying not to look too foolish, threw the coin into the water.

She'd never been one to search for four-leafed clovers or pull petals off daisies. It was Lily who'd started the little tradition, and Rose had been willing to play along for Lily's sake. Who knew, perhaps there was something magical in the combination of water, wishes, and copper coins. Mrs. McGinn would have said so, Rose was sure of that. She'd always been a superstitious, religious, woman; and some of it seemed to have rubbed off on Lily.

The following Sunday it rained; not a refreshing, misty summer rain, but a pelting rain; rain that lasted all day and into the night as well. Rose and Lily spent the afternoon at the show. Then, on the second weekend in July, Violet was back on deck, all fired up and insistent that they book for three o'clock tea at the hotel. It was later in July before Rose and Lily got back to the park.

"There's enough uniforms around," Lily said longingly. "I should have one of them."

"The uniform, or the guy inside it," Rose teased.

"Both," Lily replied, pouting. "I'm old enough."

"No you aren't," Rose said firmly. "Plenty of time, later."

"The war'll be over by then." Lily's pout lengthened. "And all the fellows will be wearing their boring civvies again."

"Don't say that, Lily," Rose said. "Everyone wants the war to be over. It's been too long now."

"Okay, okay, I take it back."

"Just look at that peacock," Rose said, changing to a safer subject. The bird was strutting along the grass, tail-feathers spread out in a striking fan of metallic blue and green.

"Wonder why they do that," Lily said.

"For attention," Rose replied. "It's a mating call, I think. Showoffs, aren't they?"

"They certainly are." Rose turned at the sound of the deep, musical voice. It was the man she'd talked to earlier that month. The man on the bench.

"Grand day," he said, smiling down at her.

Rose noticed that his eyes crinkled when he smiled; and that, surprisingly, she was pleased to see him. They sat together again, making small talk in-between the band numbers.

"My name's Ralph," he said.

"I'm Rose, and this is my sister, Lily." Lily, disappointed

because they hadn't sat nearer a group of American sailors, nodded and looked bored.

"How was your visit?" Rose asked.

"Visit?" he replied.

"Yes. When I saw you a few weeks ago, you said you were catching a train."

He laughed. "Oh, I guess I did say that. Didn't mean to confuse you. I did catch a train, but not as a passenger. I'm an engineer. I work for the CNR."

"He's a nice man, don't you think?" Rose said to Lily later.

"Yeah. Kind of old though."

"Lily, for goodness sake! He is not!"

"I'll bet he's thirty, anyway."

"Well, that's not old."

"In my books it is. Even his name sounds kind of old."

"His name's Ralph. What's wrong with that?"

"Why couldn't it be Alan, or Clark? They're much more romantic names."

"Oh, you're impossible," Rose said. Old and young, beautiful and ugly, remained, obviously, in the eyes of the beholder.

"I think you like that guy," Lily went on. "I bet by the next time we come, you'll be his girlfriend."

"Don't talk so foolish," Rose retorted. "I barcly know him."

First Date

Ralph phoned and asked Rose out the following week.

"I was thinking we could go to the ball game on Thursday—have a bite to eat after," he said.

"A ball game?"

"Yes. It's supposed to be a nice night. No rain in the forecast."

"Sure—okay."

What could she say? A ball game was the last thing she might have imagined for a first date.

"I'll come by at six, then," he said.

After he'd rung off, she went over the conversation in her mind. They hadn't talked for more than three minutes, tops. He'd sounded so sure of himself—sure that she'd agree, ball game and all. But then, why not? Hadn't she been hoping he would call?

The ball field wasn't far from Lettie's place. They talked while they walked the four blocks.

"How do you find working in that store?" he asked. "Pretty fancy spot. They treat you good?"

"The sewing room wasn't so great," she replied. "But I like my job now."

"Just the one sister?" he went on. They were at the Willow Tree, waiting to cross.

"Two, actually. There's my older sister Violet, too. She was away working for years, but she's back now. "

Thankfully, he didn't press her for more.

"And your folks?"

"They both died. I was only eleven. Aunt Lettie's a dear, though. I like living with her." That was as much information as she was prepared to divulge. There would be plenty of time later, if things worked out between them, to go into more detail.

"Your turn now," she said. "You work on the railway and your grandmother has a flower garden. That's all I know."

He chuckled. "Grew up in the country," he said. "My dad still farms. Potatoes and turnips, along with a herd of Jerseys, and some beef cattle too. My brother helps. He's got the adjoining property."

"Any sisters?"

"Two. One out west—her husband's got a huge spread. Doesn't get home much. The other one lives here—husband's in the navy."

"You didn't want to farm?"

"Just didn't turn out that way. Hank stayed with Dad and I went on the trains. They needed extra firemen, and my uncle put in a word for me. Life's funny—the hands it deals out."

"I guess," Rose replied. Funny, sad; she wasn't sure.

At the field, he took her hand and helped her climb to the top row of the bleachers.

"Good turnout," he said, looking around. Every spot on the bleachers was filled, and people were spreading blankets out on the grass below.

Rose nodded. She'd never been to a game before, and had no idea about turnouts. In fact, other than ice-skating, she wasn't much interested in sports. Once the game got underway, she tried to follow what was happening; asked what she hoped were sensible questions about the play.

Privately, though, she found the game too slow. The pitcher seemed to take forever to throw the balls; he bent down and squinted, took off his cap, made funny signals with his hands. The other players weren't much better. She didn't dare say so, or that she didn't much care who was on base, or which inning they were in.

"Who's your favourite team?" she ventured, when the bleacher erupted into loud cheering and clapping.

"The brewery guys," he replied. "In the orange and blue jerseys. Did you see the play that their shortstop just made. It was fabulous."

"Oh, right," she said.

"Now, let's see what this guy does. He's a crack hitter. Watch."

The other team won. Ralph was a good sport about it. "Can't win 'em all," he said. "They played well, and that's the main thing."

They stopped at a diner for tea and muffins, got back to Lettie's about ten. He talked baseball most of the way, pleased that Joey had hit a "homer."

"I'll phone you at the end of the week," he said, giving her a light hug. "I'm on the Moncton run till Friday."

Ora was upstairs, waiting, and she hooted when Rose filled her in on the evening. "What a guy, taking our Rosie to a ball game," she teased. "I'll have to straighten him out."

Rose found it amusing, too; but after she'd settled into bed, her thoughts turned serious. She'd had a good time, even though she would have preferred a dance, or a movie. There was something comforting about the scent of his shaving lotion, the feel of his jacket around her shoulders. He'd insisted she wear it on the way home. The air had turned damp once the sun had set, with fog creeping in from the harbour.

"Have to take care of my girl," he'd said. "My girl" was an expression her father used, all those years ago.

They saw each other more and more as August played itself out. He was away four days out of seven, but as soon as he got back, he'd be on the phone. Lettie delighted in shouting to Rose from the bottom of the stairs, "Yoo-hoo, Rosie! Your Ralph's on the line." She'd already told Rose that she liked the cut of his jib. "You can count on a man like that in a storm," she'd said. "Believe me."

Ora liked him too, and even Lily was won over. "He's old-fashioned nice," she conceded after he'd pitched balls in a midway stall until he'd won dolls for each of them.

"I'm glad he's finally got your vote," Rose said.

She had, as yet, no idea what Violet's assessment would be. Nor what he would think of Violet. Making her older sister out to be a companion was a stretch, and she felt a little guilty about the fib, but she half-suspected he might have put two and two together in any case. Railway men and cab drivers knew what was happening in the city; knew where the best clubs were, how to get a bottle, and a woman.

Rose had met *his* sister at one of the ball games.

"Ralph's been telling me about you," Bernice said. "Sit down and take a load off your feet." She patted on a corner of the blanket.

Rose sat, expecting the questions to fly; but, if Bernice was curious, she didn't show it. She watched the game, and smiled indulgently at the banter between Ralph and her two boys.

"I was ten on my birthday," the older one informed Rose. "And my brother's eight."

They were well-behaved little fellows, sitting quietly, legs dangling, totally absorbed in the play. The only time their eyes left the field was when the older one made entries in the Campfire notebook on his knee, recording figures in pencil-ruled columns that had headings like, "Times at Bat, RBIs, Singles, Doubles, Triples, Home Runs."

They had a cow-bell, too, which they liked to ring

when their team hit a home run. Rose had her first experience with the cow-bell the second time Ralph took her to a game. At the bottom of the seventh inning, the batter up cracked a high fly ball. Rose watched it arc out into centre field, saw the centre fielder's outstretched glove miss the catch, heard the crowd gasp.

The boys and Ralph were up on their feet, shouting as the runners on second and third came home; and, amidst the cheering and yelling, the younger boy climbed to the top bleacher, and stood shaking the bell as hard as he could.

Ora's Wedding

"What's up with you and this Ralph guy?"

Ora's question caught Rose by surprise. She'd made up her mind that she wasn't going to make a big deal of Ralph—not yet. A fellow could come in and out of your life pretty easily. The memory of what happened with Al had taught her that.

"What do you mean?" Rose replied.

"Just what I said. Lily told me you met him in the park and that it's serious."

"That's just Lily exaggerating. We're only going out a bit," Rose protested.

"Just going out, my backside!" Ora replied. She was standing at the sink, unaware that she was splashing dishwater onto the floor. "Don't think I can't smell romance," she went on. "'Fess up, now."

"Don't you dramatize, too," Rose said, wiping off the table. "It's bad enough with Lily." She set a bowl of pansies that she'd picked that morning in the centre and stood back to admire the effect.

"Have it your way, then," Ora said. "I don't mind admitting when I'm in love. "It's damn great and that's all there is to it." She dumped the dishwater out of the pan, watched it swirl down the drain, and turned to Rose.

"So, how about listening to my news." She waited a moment, and then went on. "Jack and I are getting married in two weeks. I want you to be my bridesmaid. Will you?"

"Ora—you rascal!" Rose exclaimed, grabbing her friend and hugging her. "Talk about me keeping quiet. I knew you two would be a match! I just knew it!"

"We're keeping it small," Ora said. "Just family and a few

friends. It'll mean a lot to have you stand with me. Safer, too, because no matter which one of my sisters I'd ask, the others would be mad. This way, they can't say I showed favourites."

"I'd love to," Rose said. Bridesmaid by default. It didn't matter, though. She wanted whatever Ora wanted.

"You having a church service?"

"Yeah. At St. Mark's, in the chapel. Jack's not a bit religious—he'd just as soon go to City Hall. But I couldn't do that to Pa. He expects a church wedding, with a real minister. I'm doing it to please him, really. St. Mark's is where we were all baptized, so it'll mean a lot.

There would be no white gown, however. "I refuse to pay out good money for something I'll never wear again," Ora said. "There's too much else we need."

"What about a simple street-length one—maybe in ivory," Rose suggested.

"Nope. I got my outfit already," Ora said. "Found it in a little place uptown. Come on upstairs. I'll show it to you."

The summerweight, ice-blue crepe was quite sweet, and the colour was perfect with Ora's hair but secretly Rose was disappointed. They'd had such visions, when they were twelve, playing dress-up from the boxes sent over by the church ladies. Visions of satin and lace, long veils and six bridesmaids, everyone carrying bouquets of roses and fern and baby's breath.

"Me and you will have matching corsages," Ora said. "Pink and white carnations, with a rose in the middle. It'll be my one splurge. Pa says he's paying for the cake."

There was to be no new hat either. "I hate hats," Ora said. "I only wear them for church." She was having a milliner add some veiling to a hat that she'd picked up at a rummage sale.

This is what real life is, Rose thought. *Made necessary by practicality, war, and sea-postings.* With only one week of shore leave for Jack, and more than one reason to hurry-up and get the ceremony over with, there was precious little time for romantic dreams.

Rose was not about to deny herself the opportunity for a complete new outfit. She found the ideal hat at her own store—a perky little half-moon with a forehead veil and a crescent row of rhinestones stitched across the front. The head of the hat department gave it to her at cost.

She could have used her store discount for a dress too, but instead, she decided to check out the shop that Ora had suggested. It turned out to be a funny little hole-in-the-wall, not far from the movie theatre. The warped floorboards creaked, and a curtained corner at the back did duty as a fitting room, but the amount of merchandise in the small space was impressive.

The proprietor, an ancient crone with bleached hair and rouged cheeks, waited on her. "These—for you," she said in a thick accent, producing three dresses from the crammed racks. All three looked good and fitted well, and Rose ended up trying each one twice before she made up her mind.

"This is for you," the proprietor said, rubbing the plum-coloured fabric between her fingers. "With black hair—yes. Sara knows. My customers all say so."

"Do you think the lapel will hold a corsage nicely?" Rose asked.

"Right here for flowers," the woman said, jabbing at a spot just below Rose's collar bone. "Too low not looking right."

Twenty-six people piled into the pews of the chapel on

a hot August afternoon. Ora's three sisters, their husbands and children, Lettie, a couple of cousins, and Jack's family made up the bulk of the guests. The only others were Rose and Jack's best man, a buddy from the ship.

Rose had turned down Ora's offer that Ralph could join them. She didn't yet know how to define their relationship, and didn't want him subjected to the curious eyes of Ora's family. "He'll be on the Moncton run that weekend," was her excuse, and was relieved when Ora didn't push it.

The ceremony was painfully short. There was no processional, no music at all, as it turned out. "Our organist just got the news of her oldest son," the rector explained quietly before they took their places by the font.

Ora spoke her vows in a clear, confident voice. Jack was the nervous one. His responses were barely audible and he stumbled over his own name. "I, Jack— Sorry—I, John Harold take you, Ora Pauline—"

Rose listened intently, aware that, with this ceremony, Ora was leaving her behind. Once the register was signed, Ora would be a married woman, with her loyalty and her attention focused on Jack—as it should be. They would— could—still be best friends, but it wouldn't ever be the same, ever again.

They went to Lettie's afterwards for sandwiches and cake.

"Jack's uncle has a beach cottage in Hubbards and he said we could have it for a week," Ora told them when she brought around the sliced cake on a tray. "I hope the weather's decent. I want to soak up lots of sun, and just plain relax. Lord knows, but I'll be too busy this time next year to even catch my breath."

She and Jack left Lettie's in the late afternoon. Rose had the young ones organized in a line, ready with the rice and the paper streamers.

"Hey, Jack!" the best man called out. "Remember to eat your porridge every day!"

"You got to be kidding," Jack shouted back. "I damn well plan to live on love alone."

A week later, they arrived back at Lettie's, tanned and relaxed. Rose had insisted that Ora and Jack take over the big front bedroom, and had moved across the hall. "This will suit me fine for the time being," she said. "Just fine."

"When this damn war is over, Jack and I plan to talk to Lettie about taking over this place," Ora said the day after he'd left to re-join his ship. "It's a good house for kids."

Rose couldn't have agreed more. It needed some fixing up but it was a great house and a good location. They'd end up with a brood of kids, Rose was certain of that. Ora was great with children, and had confided in Rose that the stork would be visiting soon after Christmas.

"I don't want you to move, Rosie," Ora said. "There's plenty of room for you, and Lily too, next year. We'll just get rid of the other roomers, that's all."

Rose appreciated the offer, but she knew the time would soon come when she'd need—and want—to find a place of her own.

"I think I should look around and see what I can come up with," she said to Violet and Lily the next Sunday.

"Yeah," Lily chimed in. "A nice flat, with a room of my own. I can put up my movie star pictures, and have my own radio playing whenever I want."

"Nice flats are at a premium, kiddo," Violet replied. "The

city's bursting at the seams. Let's take it cool and think this through."

Think it through; put it off. Violet's name shouldn't be Morash at all.

It should be Maybe. As in, Wait-and-See.

Decision Time

It was Ralph who brought up the subject of meeting Violet. They had gone to an early show and were waiting at the bus stop across from the theatre.

"Rosie, hon—" he said, "—it's high time I met that other sister of yours."

"Violet's pretty hard to pin down," Rose replied, hoping she wasn't sounding too evasive. "She's always so busy."

"Nobody's got a busy schedule all the time," he replied. "Anyway, no harm in asking. We could meet her for supper and a movie. We can go to the Bon Ton, if you want. You said she likes Chinese."

Rose couldn't help wondering what might be prompting his suggestion. She couldn't see his expression; he was bending low, away from the wind, trying to light his cigarette. Although he wasn't the sort of man to make suggestive comments, nor one to flirt, either, he was a man; and most men would be curious about a woman like Violet; would welcome an opportunity to meet her.

"Well, what do you say, hon," he asked, shoving his lighter and cigarette package back into his jacket pocket. "There's only two answers she can give you, aren't there? Yes or no."

"I'll ask her," she replied. "But don't expect miracles."

The next day she felt guilty for questioning his motives. *He just wants to meet your sister, not "the" sister,* she told herself crossly. *Family's family; for better or for worse.*

As it turned out, Violet agreed—with a condition. "The mysterious Ralph! Well, I guess I'm up for that. But we'll have to have an early supper and catch the first show. I'm busy later."

That's my sister, Rose thought, hanging up the phone. On her terms, once again.

They met at the Bon Ton Café. Violet looked nice—subdued and sisterly. She was wearing one of her tailored suits, with a simple cotton blouse under the jacket, and a lace-bordered hankie in the breast pocket.

"Good to meet you, Ralph," she said, holding out her hand. "I've been hearing marvellous things."

"Same here, Vi," he replied. "Let's grab a booth."

Rose was amazed to hear him call her Vi. Nobody had ever done that. It seemed to work, though, for Violet just grinned. They ordered egg rolls, steamed rice, a platter of sweet and sour pork balls, and another of chow mein noodles.

They chatted while they ate, the conversation flowing from one topic to another with amazing ease. Mackenzie King's policy on conscription got a working over, as did the situation on the European front, and General Eisenhower's leadership.

"Even with the Germans on the defensive in Italy, it's a long, hard slog," Violet said.

"Yes," Ralph agreed. "The Allies have their work cut out for them. It's a big, big job."

Rose was happy to let them do the talking. It was going better than she'd hoped. Violet was on her best behaviour—pleasant, charming, diplomatic.

Over a pot of green tea, the conversation turned to radio shows. "What's your favourite program?" Violet asked Ralph. "My little sis loves the crooners, don't you, Rose? Ten minutes with Sinatra serenading her, and she's on cloud nine."

Rose made a face at Violet, and Ralph laughed.

"To each his own," he said. I like to listen to sports and the mystery shows. "Give me a ball game and *The Shadow* and I'm one happy man."

"*The Shadow*'s a good scare," Violet agreed. "But it's still *Amos 'n Andy* for me. I got hooked when I was in the States. Nobody else makes me laugh like they do; they're crazier than loons, honest to God."

She winked at Rose when they were settling into their seats at the theatre. "Good guy," she whispered. "Hang onto him."

As the Hope and Crosby duo romped across the screen, in pursuit of their lovely Dorothy, Rose sat in the dark, thinking. *Good guy*, Violet had said—as if she'd know a good man when she saw him. Then again, perhaps Violet was the sort of woman who *would* know. Just because she couldn't—or wouldn't—pick out a rock-solid fellow for herself didn't necessarily mean she wouldn't recognize top quality when she saw it.

It wasn't quite nine when they came out into a night that had turned cold, with a raw wind that was sending fallen leaves and bits of paper scudding along the sidewalk. "Nothing like a *Road* picture to draw the crowd," Violet said, fastening the top button of her coat. Already, there was a long line waiting for the second show. It stretched from the box office clear down the block and around the corner.

"People need a good laugh," Ralph replied.

"You got that right," Violet said. She glanced at her watch. "Time goes by, you two. Must run."

"I'm glad you could come," Rose said; and she was pleased. It had gone well—much better than she'd expected.

"Passed the test, I hope," Violet replied. She gave Ralph's arm a pat and leaned toward him. Rose could see her lips moving, but her words were drowned out by the screech of the tram on its rails. It lurched around the corner, sending out a shower of sparks as the overhead cable made a faulty connection with the junction box.

"Lord, love us," Violet said over the noise. "What a bloody racket." Then, with a hurried "see you," she darted across the street.

Ralph linked his arm through Rose's, and they started off in the opposite direction.

"Well? Say something," she implored. "You wanted to meet her. You met her. What did you think; do you like her?"

"Of course I did, hon," he replied. "I liked her just fine."

She waited for him to elaborate, but he seemed content to leave it at that. *If only he'd talk more*, she thought. His quietness did test her patience at times.

"She doesn't put on any airs," Rose said.

"Nope. She's herself, out and out," he replied. "Calls a spade a spade, which is just fine in my books."

"What did she say to you, just now? I couldn't hear, with the tram and all."

"Oh that," he said. "Just a little favour."

"A favour? What kind of favour?"

She could hear his base chuckle. "No secrets, eh? Must tell my Rosie everything."

He waited for the traffic to pass, and then hurried her across the street. It wasn't until they stepped onto the opposite sidewalk that he stopped and turned to face her.

"She asked me to take good care of her little sister," he said. The teasing tone had disappeared, and she could see a little twitch at the side of his face.

"Oh," she said. And then, "What did you say to that?"

"I said I was trying to. That I'd keep trying, if you'd let me."

"I see," she said. This was, she realized, his way of proposing. Right here, in the middle of the sidewalk, with people walking, and cars honking, and a streetlight flickering above their heads.

How should she answer it? Did she need more time?

Everybody who knew him, liked him. She liked him; he was a fine man. Too fine, in fact, to keep dangling on a string.

"Sure, Ralph," she replied. "I'll let you." She couldn't kiss him, not in a public place like this. Instead, she hugged at the sleeve of his coat, felt his solidness through the fabric.

"You won't regret it, Rosie," he murmured. "We'll be a team. I'll stand by you, I promise."

"Yes, I know you will."

The wind was whipping at her coat and her hair, and she could see the tips of his ears reddening. "Can we go and get a coffee?" she said. "You're cold, and so am I."

"Right. Let's," he said.

They headed north, into the wind.

He'll be good to me, she thought. *And I'll be good back. What more can I ask, or expect.*

Engagement

"You look like Frosty," Rose said when Ralph arrived at Lettie's on Saturday afternoon. It had started to snow hard, and his cap and jacket were coated.

"I'll bet," he said, stamping his feet on the mat. "And this Frosty's taking his girl shopping. Get yourself bundled up; we're heading for the diamond mines."

"But Ralph," she said, "—we don't have to buy a ring today. It's snowing. We can wait."

"No damn way," was his reply. "We're going, and that's that."

There were no other customers at the jeweller's when they arrived. The clerk, an older man in a double-breasted brown suit and a bowtie, directed them to a counter at the back of the store. They watched while he opened the back of the glass case and selected several for their viewing. Positioning each ring on a green velvet display pad, he pointed out the features, and had Rose try them on, one-by-one. The methodical process was lengthy, and it was close to five o'clock by the time they settled on a small diamond cluster in a white gold setting.

"An excellent choice, madam," the clerk said, checking her finger with a metal ring-sizer and making notes on a blue pad. "A small hand such as yours needs something elegant, but not overstated."

He put the ring box onto a tray and placed the tray in a drawer. "A few minor adjustments are all that are required," he explained. "Our jeweller will have it ready by midweek."

"That will be fine," Ralph said.

The clerk opened his invoice book, paused, and looked at Rose. "Perhaps madam would like to view our china? We carry several of the best lines. You'll find our Royal Albert on the far wall."

It was Rose's cue to disappear while the men dealt with the terms of payment. "Thank you. I will," she said, picking up her bag and gloves. She moved away from the counter, pretended to examine the china, and the display of crystal in an adjoining case. Everything was very lovely, and very expensive, too. She knew that without having to look at the price stickers.

"Are you sure we shouldn't have found a less expensive one," she said to Ralph when they were back out on the sidewalk. Behind them, the clerk was locking the door and pulling down the blind.

"Nothing doing," Ralph said in a quiet voice that meant business. "I'm only getting married once. And now that we've taken care of that, we're going out to dinner."

"What do you want for a wedding?" he asked her over the meal.

"I always wanted white," she said. "With two brides-maids."

"Then that's what we'll have," he replied. "As long as it's you coming up that aisle, I can handle any colour—white, green, or purple."

"Now you're teasing," she said.

"No I'm not," he protested. "I'm dead serious. It's the girl that's important, not the dress. The only thing I ask is that you carry the biggest bouquet of roses we can find in this city."

Gifts

Lily was thrilled when Rose showed her the ring.

"When's the wedding?" Lily asked. "I'll be a bridesmaid, won't I?"

"Next June," Rose replied. "And, yes, you'll be a bridesmaid."

"Who else—Ora?"

"Yes, of course."

"What about Violet?"

Rose couldn't answer this question. It was an issue that she couldn't yet face.

"I don't know," she said. "We haven't decided."

"I don't know where the time's gone," Rose said to Ora the next evening. "Seems like it was just Halloween, and here we are, with less than two weeks till Christmas."

"Time flies when you're in love," Ora replied, giving the last supper plate a quick wipe and putting it in the cupboard. "That's it, then," she said. "We're done. Don't I hate doing dishes."

"You hate doing housework, period," Rose said, shaking Old Dutch onto a Brillo pad and going at the sink.

"You got that right." Ora draped her wet dish towel across the oven door and sat down at the table. "I can't wait to get this baby born," she said, easing her feet out of her shoes. "My back's killing me, and I look like a bloated cow. Good thing Jack's away and can't see me."

"Why don't you go in with Lettie for a while," Rose urged. "Put your feet up on her big hassock. I'll make us some hot drinks after a bit."

"Good idea," Ora replied. She heaved herself up from the chair and padded in stocking feet to Lettie's room.

Rose had stashed her cleaning things under the sink and was looking over her shopping list when the doorbell chimed.

"I'll get it," she called out to Ora when she went past the open door of Lettie's room. "You stay put. It's probably the new roomer."

It was a nuisance, having to keep the door locked, but the warning notice that had been issued to the entire neighbourhood was making Lettie nervous. Two German sailors off a sub had been caught near the armoury, and the police were advising all area residents to be vigilant and to take extra safety precautions.

Rose unlocked the door, opening it a crack and peering out into the gloom of the verandah.

"You going to ask me in," a woman's voice demanded. "Or will I stand here till I turn into an icicle?"

"Violet! For goodness sake," Rose stammered, feeling foolish. "I . . . it's just that I wasn't expecting you. You never drop by. Come in; come in."

Violet followed her into the front room and waited while Rose switched on the floor lamp.

"How's it going?" she asked, setting her shopping bag on the floor by her feet and perching on the arm of the sofa. "You're a busy little beaver, I suppose."

"Yes," Rose replied. "What with Christmas and all."

"And Ora?"

"The baby's due around the twenty-first; she's really big and uncomfortable. The doctor told her to keep her feet up as much as possible."

"I'll bet. Carrying them's a lot less fun than making them, that's for sure," Violet said.

Rose knew she couldn't top a comment like that, so she didn't even try.

Violet looked around the room. "Getting the place all gussied up, I see," she said. "Looks good."

"Thanks," Rose replied. She'd put wreaths in the windows and a mixture of holly, fir boughs, and silvered pine cones in the big earthenware vase on the hearth. "We'll get the tree this weekend."

Violet nodded absently.

"Something's cropped up," she said, looking directly at Rose. "Thought I should tell you in person."

Rose braced herself. Now what?

"I'm leaving tomorrow," Violet said. "For Montreal. I'll catch the late afternoon train."

If it hadn't been for the shopping bag, Rose might have thought that Violet was joking. She could see the parcels sticking up. Wrapped in red and green paper and tied with ribbon.

"But Violet—" she said, "—why now? It's nearly Christmas. What about Lily? How will I explain—"

Shut up! ordered an inner voice. *Don't whine. She doesn't like it. You know that.*

"Business is business," Violet said, looking irritated. "So perk up. It's not the end of the world, for God's sake. It's only Montreal, not Timbuktu."

She reached into her coat pocket, pulled out a twenty-dollar bill and shoved it into Rose's hand. "Here, take this. You and Lily can have dinner on me. Go some place fancy; Lily will like that."

Rose offered to make tea, coffee—anything that might help delay Violet's departure—but Violet was having none of it.

"I can't, Rose. I need to get back. There's packing to do,

and a bunch of other things to take care of." She gave Rose a quick peck on the cheek, and had let herself out before Rose could think straight; before her anger and disappointment could find release. She was still holding the twenty-dollar bill in her hand—the yardstick by which Violet did her measuring. How many things, how many people—or parts of them—could this amount of money buy? Violet would know, of course. She was the expert.

"Who was it?" Ora asked when Rose had made the hot drinks and brought them in on a tray. Lettie was dozing in her rocker and Ora had her feet up against the radiator, with Nibs, their newest adopted stray, stretched out on her stomach.

"Just an ARP fellow," Rose replied. "We're due for another drill." She couldn't deal with explanations—not tonight.

Rose had laid out her nightgown and was applying cold cream to her face when it struck her that Violet didn't know a thing about her engagement. In the midst of Violet's bombshell news, Rose had totally forgotten to share her own. The sight of the shopping bag angered her and she grabbed it, determined to stash it out of sight. Too bulky to stuff into a dresser drawer, she tried to shove it onto the shelf in her closet. It tipped sideways in the process, and before she could catch it, the top item slipped out and fell to the floor with a thump.

You clumsy thing, she thought, picking up the cloth-covered pouch with a drawstring top. It wasn't a Christmas gift—that much was obvious—so she carried it over to the bed, opened the drawstring, and dumped out the contents. Four cellophane-wrapped articles and a leaflet lay scattered on the bedspread. The leaflet bore the imprint of a woman's profile and a heading, *Your Personal Kit. Read Instructions Carefully.*

Rose looked at the diagram on the first page of the instructions leaflet, put the paper down, and picked up one of the cellophane-wrapped articles. It was an odd-shaped sponge, with two thread-like extensions at one end. It looked ominously clinical, through its protective wrapper, as did the accompanying thermometer, a longish metal object with a rubber bulb, and the two tubes of petroleum jelly. There was a note taped to the thermometer. *Rose— This kit is for smart girls, so use it. If you want a diaphragm, see Dr. MacKay on Gottingen. He's reliable, quick, and doesn't ask questions. V.*

It took a minute for the full message to sink in. Good old Violet; her big sister—never a woman to beat around the bush—was being helpful. Not only was she delivering the straight-goods message, she was delivering the goods themselves, as a worldly, helpful big sister should. Rose had been wondering how to handle this sort of thing, reluctant to talk to Ora, who would probably know what to do even if she didn't *do* it. Yes, it would be a very useful kit, indeed.

Rose took a detour to her usual route home after work the next day. She headed south along Granville, walking purposely until she reached a section of two-storey houses a few blocks away from the train station. It was after six and the winter dark had closed in, but she could clearly see the brown house across the street. There was nothing out of the ordinary about it; a two-storey box, with steps that went directly up from the sidewalk to a yellow door.

Beyond the yellow door would be a central hallway and the usual number of rooms that one would expect to find in a house of this size and vintage. In that respect, it was not unlike Lettie's place. Rose stood in the slushy snow, resisting the urge to cross the street and pound on the door until the lady of the house answered. "Why has Violet gone away?" she wanted to ask the faceless Mrs. Mac. "She's not in trouble, is she? Tell me she isn't."

She didn't move, however. Instead, she stood for five, perhaps ten minutes, ignoring the cold that was penetrating her snowboots and numbing her toes. Violet might be sick again and trying to hide it; or in some other kind of trouble. How—how—would she be able to find that out?

Rose was shivering now. She looked at her watch; it was past six-thirty. Violet's train would have left an hour ago. Rose had tried to phone Mrs. Mac's place during her noon break, wanting to talk to Violet, to ask if it was okay to go to the station to see her off. There had been no answer. "Try your call again later, madam," the operator had instructed after it had rung and rung.

She stomped her feet and flexed her gloved hands. It was silly, to be standing here in the cold, staring at a house that Violet no longer lived in. If she didn't have the nerve to knock on the door and ask questions, she might as well get on home. Violet was probably sitting comfortably in the train's dining car, having a nice meal, oblivious to Rose's whereabouts—and her confusion. In a few hours, the train would cross the border into New Brunswick, heading for the Gaspé, the St. Lawrence River valley, Montreal.

Not that Rose knew of those places firsthand. Up to now, any knowledge that she had gained about her country were from the maps at school, and from Ralph. She hoped that she might see those places for herself someday; see what lay beyond this tough little city. She thrust her hands into her pockets and trudged to the corner. She might catch a tram by the church, although you couldn't count on it. They were maddeningly unreliable at night.

Violet was gone. She might be back again—maybe.

There were no guarantees; never had been, with Violet. In the meantime, there'd be silence. Violet wouldn't write and she wouldn't phone. There were plenty of uncertain things in life, but that was one certainty that Rose could count on.

Boxing Day

"How's everything, hon?" Ralph's call came through soon after Rose got in from work on Friday evening.

"It's been quite a week," Rose replied. It was good to hear his voice—familiar, steady, reassuring.

"Busy at the store, I'll bet."

"Yes," she said. And then, because she wanted to get it out and over with, "Violet's gone."

"Gone?"

"To Montreal. She left Wednesday, on the train."

There was a short silence. *He's wondering what it's all about,* she thought. *And I don't know the answer.*

"Rose, I'm sorry," he said. "You had such plans."

"Yeah, stupid me," she replied. "I should have known better. Never have plans; not with my sister."

My sister, not Violet. She realized immediately that she was already putting an emotional distance between them, as a kind of self-preservation tactic.

"Rosie—"

"Yes?"

"It's just— Well, sometimes, people just can't give us what we want."

"I realize that," she replied.

Ora's baby arrived at noon on the twenty-second. "We got us a whopping big boy!" Jack yelled over the wire from the hospital. "Eight pounds, seven ounces."

"That's wonderful!" Rose said. "Give him a big hug from us. I'll tell Lettie right this minute."

He landed in at suppertime, with a teddy bear and two brown-paper bags.

"Is that our new Daddy?" Lettie called out from her room. "I'll bet he's beaming brighter than the Chebucto Head light."

He did have a real glow on; Rose could see that. Helped along, she was sure, by the contents in one of the brown bags.

"Have a cigar," he insisted, pulling a package of Havana Royals out of his jacket pocket. "For good luck."

"That makes my third great-grandnephew," Lettie said from the doorway. "We have to celebrate with a toast."

Jack lit a cigar for himself and Rose got three glasses from the china cabinet. "We're gonna call him Luke," Jack said. "Since he came in time for Christmas."

"How long will Ora be in hospital?" Rose asked.

"The doc says he'll let us know after tomorrow." He waved aside the glass of sherry that Rose was offering, and opened the cap on his rum bottle instead. "Ora's fine; strong as a bloody ox, and hankering to get back into the swing."

Back into the swing was one way of putting it. Rose tended to think it would be more like a merry-go-round, at least for the first few weeks. She should probably get an extra box of soap powder, and another bucket, too. Ora wasn't fussy, but Rose wasn't about to allow Ora to put the baby's things in an old bucket. It just wouldn't do.

The next day, she was able to sneak past a frazzled duty nurse toward the tail end of visiting hours. As luck would have it, Ora was sitting up, nursing Luke.

"He's a guzzler," Ora said. "They're having to bring him up every couple of hours."

Rose held him for a few minutes after he'd finished feeding. "He's a sweetheart," she said, kissing the reddish down on the top of his head, smelling the fresh newness of his skin, mingled with the scent of talcum powder and milk.

"Jack says you'll be home in a week."

"I sure hope so!" Ora said. "Jack's only got ten days leave, and I'm bound we're going to my sister's on New Year's Eve."

"But Ora," Rose protested. "What will you do with Luke? You can't leave him with me and Lettie, surely. Not for all that time."

"We'll take him with us, of course," Ora said. She had brushed her hair and was tying it back with a blue ribbon. "He doesn't need a crib; we'll just put him in one of her dresser drawers."

Rose groaned. "Oh, Ora, you can't do that to the poor little thing."

"Now don't get all in a tizzy. Mom used to do it with us, and we're still around to tell the tale."

Ralph had the two days off over Christmas. They took Lily with them to Bernice's for turkey dinner at noon. After they'd eaten, they all ended up in the backyard, having a snowball fight. On Boxing Day, he came to Lettie's in the late afternoon. Rose made supper for the three of them and afterwards they sat in her den, listening to the radio together.

"That's it for me, folks . . ." Lettie said at ten o'clock. "This old girl's heading to bed."

"We might play records in the front room for a while," Rose said, gathering up their empty teacups and the plate of leftover cheese and crackers.

"Fill your boots," Lettie replied, giving Ralph a playful wink. "Hope you brought your mistletoe."

They sat together on the sofa, talking over Christmas, with Artie Shaw playing in the background.

"Next year will be ours, Rose," Ralph said. "What with the wedding and all."

"Yes," she said. "It will."

She snuggled in closer, giggling at the feel of his fingers, playing up and down her arm. When he turned her face to his, the kiss was much longer than usual. The second was longer, deeper still.

"Rose, I wasn't planning on going home tonight," he murmured.

"Stay, then," she said.

"You sure?"

"Yes."

"Where?"

"My room."

She undressed in the bathroom, remembering too late the little bag that Violet had left for her. It was sitting, untouched, in the bottom of her bureau. *Fat lot of good it's going to do me there,* she thought ruefully. *If he hasn't anything with him, I'll have to count on the calendar being on my side.*

He was lying on his back, one arm behind his head, when she returned. She turned the key in the lock, noticing that he'd draped his shirt over the back of the chair and folded his pants on its seat. *Fastidious,* she thought.

"You looked after," he asked when she unfastened her robe and slipped in beside him.

"Yes," she fibbed. "Fine."

He'd left it to her, then. So unlike Al, who had been prepared. "Those things are standard issue for the military fellows," Ora had told her. Ralph, however, was not a military man.

"Better if this is off," he whispered. A quick tug and she felt her nightgown slither over her head.

It took a long, delicious time. Much longer than she

remembered with—Al. Ralph's large hands were surprisingly soft in their exploring, tickling, discovering.

"What time is it?" she managed sometime later. He was curled up beside her, one leg over hers.

"Two or so."

He moved his leg, rubbing his foot over hers. "Are you sleepy?" he asked.

"No."

"Good. Sleep's a waste of time."

She gasped and arched up when he turned her over. They slept again after a while, and when she awoke it was almost eight. She could hear water running in the bath room.

He wouldn't stay for breakfast. "I'm going along, hon. Can't hear any sounds down below." He dressed quickly, neatly, and laced up his shoes.

"Lettie doesn't surface much before nine these days," she said.

"Good. No questions asked, no answers needed."

He came over to the bed, bent down, and gave her a light kiss.

"You're quite the girl, my Rosie. Quite the girl I love."

Wedding Plans

There were times when Rose felt she should pinch herself. Things were coming together like the jigsaw puzzles that she and Mr. Browne used to work on at the cottage. Now, though, the pieces weren't cardboard shapes, but her life. Even the war was co-operating. The tide had turned since the Battle of the Bulge, and the newspapers were reporting that the retreating German army was decimated, in total disarray; that it would be a matter of weeks—months at most—before the war would be over.

The only fly in the ointment was the lack of a place of their own to live. "It won't happen for a while yet, hon," was the way Ralph put it. "Bernice has offered her top flat and I think it's too good a deal to turn down."

"But isn't it already rented?" Rose asked. "She can't put people out, surely; won't the Review Board squawk?"

"No worries on that score," he replied. "It's an army recruiter and his wife. They'll be posted back to Kingston."

Bernice was full of reassurances when they went over for Sunday dinner. "Be great having you two upstairs," she said.

Rose struggled to find the right words to respond. *How different she is to my sister*, she was thinking. Violet, who hadn't yet written; who seemed hell-bent on getting as far away as possible.

Bernice picked up on her silence. "Look here—" she said, leaning across the table to Rose, "—I've got no intention of nosing into your affairs. You can live your lives, and we'll live ours. But, if either of us needs a hand, we're there to help out."

"I keep thinking it's all a dream," Rose admitted on their way back to Lettie's.

"Nope," was his reply. "Just a damn good arrangement to tide us over till I have enough for a good down payment. Another year or so should do it. You can count on that."

She knew she could count on that—and on him; but she still couldn't rid herself of the niggling fear that festered just below the surface. *What if things don't work out? I should have a backup plan—just in case.*

Her insecurity was the one source of disagreement between them. He wanted her to give up her job at the store as soon as they were married. "I can support you very nicely, Rose," he insisted. "You don't need to work."

"But Ralph," she pleaded. "Mr. Hatfield told me I'm next in line for Better Dresses. I've been waiting for that. And there's more modelling, too, which I really like. Besides which, I have my store discount. I'd lose that if I leave."

She got him on her side, eventually.

"Okay, Rose; looks like you're the winner," he finally said. "I'm away a lot, so I guess it makes some sense for a while. At least till you've got other things to occupy your time."

She got his drift, of course. Till we have our first child.

"I can keep house and work too," she said. "You'll see."

Keeping house—being kept—used to be her idea of the ideal life, but a lot had happened in the years since she'd played dress-up with Ora, since she'd sat on the back steps of the Brownes' house. Harris and Violet had come and gone; so had Al.

The world was a mixed-up place, no two ways about it. There might be another screw-up in the future. Her luck might not hold. In which case—what then?

They settled on June 30th as a wedding date.

"I'll see to the licence," Ralph said. "If you look after the church stuff."

"Okay." She hesitated, weighing her words.

"Ralph, I was thinking—there's something I need your opinion on."

Ralph looked up from the sports section, saw her frown, put the paper aside.

"Go ahead," he said. "Shoot."

"It's about Violet," she began. "I'm not sure . . ."

"Not sure about what?"

"Asking her to be part of the wedding. To stand with me, in place of my mother." Once she'd said it, out loud, she felt relieved. Hopefully, a problem shared was a problem halved. She waited to see what he might say.

He didn't answer immediately. Instead, he fished a cigarette out of the package in his shirt pocket, walked over to the stove, took a match from the tin on the warming shelf, and struck it alight from the edge of the grating.

"I wonder if that's such a good idea, Rose," he said when he came back to the table. The tip of his cigarette glowed, and she watched the smoke spiral up, up, to the crack in the ceiling.

"But she is my sister; and weddings are for family." She spoke deliberately, as though it was him, not herself, who needed to hear the rationale.

"I grant you that, Rose," he said. "But Violet's made her choice when it comes to family. Don't get me wrong; I'm not criticizing. It's her life to live. But she may not be able to come. Or want to, for that matter."

It was his turn now to let the words sink in.

"I suppose so . . ." she said, pulling at the fringe on the tablecloth.

"You don't sound convinced."

"I—no."

"Well, at least sleep on it. I wouldn't want you to get your hopes up. Or have your wedding day spoiled. It wouldn't be fair."

They spent a quiet day, with the house to themselves. Ora and the baby had left for an afternoon with her sister, and weren't due back until late. Ralph stoked the furnace, fixed the kitchen tap, and, while Rose got the supper going, he took himself into Lettie's room for their weekly war strategy talk. *Seems like we're married already,* Rose thought, as she fried fish, mashed carrots, and kept an eye on the potatoes in the oven.

"Ralph and I got Hitler tried, shot, and buried," Lettie announced when Ralph helped her to the kitchen table.

"Good," Rose replied. "No less than he deserves." She was feeling better now that she'd made up her mind about Violet. She would invite her to the wedding; if she could find an address, that is; and that's as far as she'd go. Ora and Lily would stand with her, and Ora would be her matron of honour.

"I'll call the church and set up a meeting," she said when Ralph was leaving.

"Right," he replied. "Shouldn't be a big deal, should it? They must have wedding services down to a fine art by now."

He pulled his cap lower on his head and put on his gloves. "No more fretting over Violet, then?"

"No," she replied. "I'll write her, though, if you can help me find out where she is."

"I'll see what I can do."

He would. He was a man of his word.

Rose went to see the rector on her next Saturday off. He ushered her into a small book-filled study at the rear of the sanctuary. Three floor-to-ceiling shelves were packed with them, and piles more were stacked on two corners of the massive desk

Sitting in a straight-backed chair opposite him, she tried to keep her nervousness in control. He would have checked the parish list and not found her name on it; would know that she wasn't a regular in the pews. She expected that there might be a gentle reprimand over her sporadic attendance. Instead, surprisingly, he stuck to the facts.

"June twenty-sixth, you say. Two in the afternoon?" He was studying the form that she had filled out in the office.

"Yes, um . . . Reverend."

"You've been baptized?"

"Yes. Here, in this church."

"And confirmed?"

"Yes, at St. Mark's when I was fourteen. I have my certificate."

"Very good."

"And your betrothed?" the rector continued.

That was an old-fashioned way of putting it, she thought. Nobody said "betrothed" these days.

"He was brought up Anglican," she replied. "He has his certificates—if you need them."

"Excellent."

"So far, so good." She watched him make notes in the small black journal in front of him. He was an older man, with a mouth that was not overly stern, and eyes that were neither piercing nor kindly. He had introduced himself as Reverend, not Father, which in itself was a relief. Ever since Father Hanrahan, she had distrusted all priests with that title.

"I ask that you both come for instruction sessions," the

rector said. "And you must be present during Matins for the publishing of the bans. Please inform the office of the size of your wedding party. There are some restrictions regarding the placement of flowers." He put down his pen, and studied her for a moment before continuing. "There can be no Communion during an afternoon ceremony. I trust you realize that."

Rose shook his hand when she left. Whatever it takes, was Violet's motto. Rose's own motto, now. She was being a hypocrite, but she wasn't letting that small fact get in her way. It wasn't the church's blessing that she sought. What she wanted was its ceremony; an aisle to walk down, her friends gathered in the pews; a white dress, flowers, a veil. She didn't think it was too much to ask. After all, that's what most girls wanted—and got. Ora had taken a few shortcuts, in the hurry-up of last summer, but that was understandable.

In her mind's eye she could see the proceedings. Ora and Lily would walk up the aisle, ahead of her. Ralph, bless him, would be waiting at the chancel steps, with his brother beside him. They would be wearing new black suits, with roses in their lapels.

Aunt Lettie would be there, plus Ora's father and the McGinns. Perhaps Minnie May would come. Rose planned to ask her. Eileen, from the store, would be invited, as would Mr. Hatfield. As for Violet—who could predict?

Ralph would have more family, of course: his elderly parents, Bernice and her husband and boys, Ralph's sister and other brother, a couple of elderly aunts and uncles.

Choosing someone to fill the shoes of her own father had given her more than one sleepless night. "Who gives this woman" was such an important, symbolic role, and, for a while, she'd been stumped by it.

"Parents are deceased?" the rector had asked her. "Yes," she'd replied. She'd refrained from adding, "Six feet under, and for many years."

If things had worked out differently, there might have been an uncle who could have filled this role nicely. There wasn't, though. Uncle Earle and Aunt Edna had never tried to contact them again, and Rose was just as well pleased. The memory of him—his florid face and big belly, his overly hearty laugh, the Circus Rider game—made her feel a bit squeamish, even after all this time.

There had been other uncles, on her father's side, but she knew precious little about them, and nothing of their whereabouts.

"That crew! Half-drunk fishermen, every one of them—" She could hear the scathing note in Violet's voice. "Mama had no use for the lot. Daddy, either, for that matter. He was glad to get out and make his own way."

Sometimes, an older cousin could fill the bill, or a friend of the family. It hadn't taken her long to go over the short list of candidates, rejecting each of them. Mr. Browne—hardly. Harris? That would be a laugh. She could hear herself, on the phone: "Harris, could I borrow you for the day? I need someone to give me away at my wedding, and I figured you would do."

Ora's father? A dear man, who would be willing—Ora had told her so. Rose had hugged her, trying her best to explain that she so wanted someone who had known her own father, who'd been part of her early childhood. There was, ultimately, only one man left. Very dear, very Catholic. Mr. McGinn.

One Fine Night

"You're gonna have a peacetime wedding after all," Ora declared, running to greet Rose when she came in. "Lettie's got her ear glued to the radio. Hard to believe, isn't it? That it's all over."

"I know; it's wonderful," Rose exclaimed, flushed from her hurrying and her excitement. "They let us off early. There's crowds of people whooping it up downtown; climbing lightposts and stuff. I hope it doesn't get out of hand."

Ora was holding Luke, and Rose bent down and planted a kiss on his forehead. He looked solemnly at her, blew a bubble, and smiled.

"Your daddy'll be home soon, sweetheart," she said; and, to Ora, "I wonder if Ralph's heard yet."

"He'd have to, unless he's driving a train across the North Pole. The radio's full of it. He'll probably call you later."

Rose laughed. The image of Ralph on an iceberg was too ridiculous.

"Let's head over to the Hill after supper," Ora said. "There's a victory concert planned. They've been announcing it on the radio every fifteen minutes."

"Okay," Rose agreed. "We'll have something quick; maybe that leftover ham and potato salad."

"I'll get it ready," Ora said. "You go in and see Lettie. She's got the sherry bottle out—her way of celebrating. You don't need to pour me one, though. I had a couple of snorts with her at three o'clock."

The concert was in full swing by the time they picked their way through the crowds to a spot halfway up the southwestern slope. Rose spread their blanket on the grass, and Ora parked Luke, asleep in his stroller, beside it.

Around them, people with cameras were snapping pictures of the crowd and of each other. Rose wished Ralph were here, partly because the evening was so special and she wanted to share it with him, and partly because he was so good at taking pictures.

Ora nudged her side, pointing to a couple sitting nearby. The young fellow with them—a kid brother, perhaps—was kneeling in the grass, his camera aimed at their faces. "Kiss her, Sid," the young fellow was urging. "Give her a great big smacker." The fellow obliged, and then leaned forward, into the camera lens, doing a perfect Churchill Victory V with his fingers.

Somewhere close by, a woman with a rich contralto voice began to sing. In minutes, everyone around them had joined in. Rose listened to the voices rising into the night sky. Her own throat felt strangely tight and she had difficulty getting the words out.

The thistle, shamrock, rose entwine
The Maple Leaf, forever.

They had sung the same song, six years earlier, on this very hillside. She was an excited fourteen year old then, standing with Ora and Lily and the other kids from the Home. One of thousands of happy people—many of them schoolchildren—waiting for the King and Queen's motorcade to pass by.

They had waved their Union Jacks on that summer's afternoon, cheering the lovely Queen, in her powder-blue dress, and the dignified King, decked out in a naval uniform trimmed with gold braid and rows of medals. Both their Majesties, as well as the men in the colour party, had worn white gloves. Rose would always remember those white gloves; gloves that waved and saluted; that shook hands; gloves that never seemed to be at rest.

She and Ora—and Lily, too—had grown up since that summer's afternoon. The war that had raged all these months and years had succeeded in turning the world into a much nastier place; had dirtied, bloodied thousands of gloves, hands, faces, legs; had blown away forever the people who had worn them.

Looking over the seemingly happy crowd, Rose suspected that much of their merriment was, in fact, a false kind of cheer; play-acting. Happy wasn't a simple thing, ever; it always came before, or after, sad. Ora hadn't talked about her brother, Joe, for ages, and Rose hadn't mentioned Al, either; but the memories were there still, flickering, haunting. It would surely be much the same for others in this crowd. Awareness and memory, tucked under the protective layers of rollicking song and dance. Buried deep, under the guilt and heartache and sorrow.

They dragged themselves away at nine-thirty. Luke had been good, sleeping through most of the noise, but, as they worked their way down through the throng, with the band still going full blast, he awoke and started to fuss.

"Soaked, I imagine," Ora declared, trying to pacify him with a bottle. He pushed it away, squirming and crying even harder.

They were approaching the Commons corner when they came up against the first of the roadblocks. "What's all this?" Ora demanded of a policeman standing guard. Behind him, a Detour sign had been attached to a barricade. "I've got a child to get to bed," she complained. "We can't be running around hell's half-acre to get there."

"You got that right, ma'am," he growled. "You can't. Curfew's being imposed. I'd hustle, if I was you." He wouldn't elaborate any further. "Read about it in the paper tomorrow," was the most they could get out of him.

They followed a path that led north, with Rose pushing the carriage and Ora walking ahead. In the distance, they could hear a steady rumbling and what sounded like the occasional crack of gunfire.

"It's a little weird, don't you think," Rose began when Ora motioned for her to stop. "For God's sake, will you look at that?" Ora said, pointing across the street.

Rose peered into the darkness and spied the two men, on the far side of the street.

From their uniforms, she could see that they were sailors, and very drunk ones at that. They were carrying a large, plush-covered sofa, staggering every few steps, both from the weight and the effects of the drink. When they came abreast of an elm tree, they stopped and lowered the sofa to the ground. One man took the opportunity to relieve himself against the tree trunk; the other, swaying slowly back and forth, pulled a bottle out of his jacket pocket, uncapped it and took a swig.

"What on earth are they doing?" Rose muttered to Ora.

"Taking a leak and a swig, I'd say," Ora replied with a little snort.

"No, I mean the sofa. What's that all about?"

"I wouldn't want to guess," Ora said. "But you can bet your boots there's a long story to it. Not to mention hell to pay. I suppose we'll read all about it in the paper. Isn't that what the copper said?"

ROSE

PART FIVE

New Nest

The Big Day

Ora groaned when Rose showed her the patterns for the bridesmaid's dresses. "I'll look like the dickens in that fitted style, with all the weight I've gained since the baby," she said.

"You won't look like the dickens at all," Rose assured her. "You'll look like the dear you are, just you wait and see. Here, take a look at these swatches. Eileen and I spent the whole noon break going through new bolts. I like the crepe best—it's softer. What do you think?"

They settled on the crepe—mint green for Ora, and pale yellow for Lily. For the next two weeks, the upper alcove at Lettie's was strewn with scissors and tape measures, spools of thread, and pieces of dresses in various stages of assembly.

"I can't believe I'm going to be a bridesmaid and start work, all in the same month," Lily exclaimed. Although Lily was only fifteen past, Matron had obtained approval for her to leave school to take a job. Ora had put in at work for her at the plant; and, as of the middle of the month, Lily was happily installed in the small bedroom at the back of Lettie's house.

She and Rose were sitting in the front room, basting furiously, when Ralph arrived to take them out.

"How's it going?" he asked with a wink at Lily. "With the Germans defeated and young Lily preparing for her bridesmaid debut, I doubt life could get much better."

"Don't tease," Rose chided. "We're having a terrible time with some of these tucks. We'll need another half-hour before we finish this bit."

"Okay by me," he said in his calm way. "I'll read the paper." He went to the kitchen and came back with the morning's edition.

"What colour are you wearing, my Lilybelle?" he asked, sitting down. "I'm partial to red polka dots."

"Stop being silly," Lily replied, sticking out her tongue at him. "It's a secret; I can't tell."

Ralph opened the Saturday sports section. "Well, I wouldn't want to interfere with state secrets," he said. "I'll keep quiet and read. Let me know when you're ready."

"Aren't you the least bit excited?" Lily demanded. "Or don't men get that way?"

"I don't know about that," he said, folding the paper over twice. "I got the tailor making me a nice black suit; and that sister of yours sent me out for a new pair of shoes. Why, I might even have a shave and a haircut for the big day."

"There's no use being serious with you at all," Lily said. "I can see that."

"Lily," Rose interrupted. "Hem while you're talking—please! I'll be right back. I need to press this sleeve piece, now that it's stitched."

"Tell me about your new job," Ralph said to Lily. "There's been so much wedding talk lately that I've hardly had a chance to hear about it."

"They put me in the cutting department," Lily said. "It's where everybody starts out. It's hectic, but I don't mind it. Ora says that if I'm fast and meet the quotas, I'll get moved into piecework. That pays better."

"You're a lucky girl, to have Ora and your sister," he said with a smile.

"I know," she replied.

She was silent for a moment. "There's just one thing I don't understand, though."

"What's that?"

"Something Rose said."

"Which was—"

"She said that, with you and her getting married, it would be a new start for all three of us; that we shouldn't be looking back; only ahead."

"Not bad advice," he replied. "I don't see what's so hard to understand."

"It wasn't that; it was the promise she asked me to make."

"Promise?"

"I'm not to mention the Home, ever again. If anybody asks, I'm supposed to say we lived with Aunt Lettie after Mama and Daddy died."

"And did you promise?"

"Yes, she did." They both turned to see Rose, standing in the archway, the pressed sleeve piece in her hand.

"I still don't understand why, though," Lily said.

"You don't need to understand why," Rose replied. "You just need to keep the promise."

"I will. I said I will."

"Good. That's the end of it, then."

"Yes," agreed Ralph. "It is."

Rose couldn't have asked for better weather for her wedding day. When she raised the blind and looked out just after seven, the dew had already evaporated, and the birds were in full song. She raised the sash higher, breathing in the scent of the lilac, directly below her window, before gathering up her wash things and heading for the bath.

No one else was up when she finished bathing and dressing, so she made tea and took her cup out to the back stoop. From next door she could hear the clink of milk bottles and a woman's voice calling, "Myra. Myra! Get down here! You're slow as cold molasses."

In front of Rose, a robin hopped on the skimpy grass, searching for worms. After a few minutes, he picked up a twig and flew off. *Reinforcements for his nest*, Rose thought.

After the reception, she and Ralph would be in their new nest. They would spend the night at the flat and leave by train for The Pines in Digby at noon the next day.

She was thinking about their flat and the gifts that had arrived, when, from the window above her head, Ora's voice interrupted.

"Lily, where the devil's that sister of yours?"

"I don't know," Lily was saying. "But I need her. The white shoe polish isn't covering the smudge on the heel. What am I going to do about it?"

The morning sped by in a flurry of shoe repairs and pin-curls and dresses and flowers. At noon, after a hurried bowl of soup and crackers that only Lettie was interested in eat-ing, Ora's sister arrived to take the baby.

"You're a lifesaver," Ora said to her, through a mouthful of bobby pins. "I can't deal with him and pin veils at the same time." She had barely finished securing Rose's head-dress when Ralph's cousin was pulling up outside.

"Holy smokes, the car's here," Ora exclaimed. "You ready, Rose—Lily? God, I can't believe it! Where did the time go?"

Rose surveyed herself in the hall mirror one last time. "Is my veil falling over my shoulders all right?"

"Yes, yes, it looks great," Lily said. "Here, take your flow-ers." She lifted Rose's bouquet carefully out of the florist's box and passed it to her.

"Hey, you gals," Ralph's cousin called from the verandah steps. "Anybody getting married? Tin Lizzie's all shined and polished. All she needs is a bride."

He had done a fine job on the car. Every bit of chrome gleamed, and he had decorated it too, tying pink and white streamers to the aerial and pompoms on each of the four handles.

"Ready, set, go, Rose," Ora said, giving her a light hug. "You look wonderful in that dress, and the locket Ralph gave you is darling."

"Thank you, Ora—for being such a friend."

She was following Lily down the verandah steps when a young fellow on a bike wheeled to a stop at their walk.

"One of you Rose Morash?" he called out. "There's a telegram for her."

"Here, I'll get it," Ora said. She signed the slip and dashed back to Rose.

The message was short and to the point, as telegrams always were.

Congratulations on your marriage. Stop. Best wishes for every happiness. Stop. Gift following. Stop. Violet. Full Stop.

Rose folded the yellow slip and slid it back into its envelope. Ralph must have found out the address and written to her. She wouldn't have known otherwise.

Waiting in the vestibule, Rose wasn't at all nervous. The massive inner doors were open, and she could see the guests, arranged in proper order in the front pews. Ralph's family was on the left. His mother, frail but very alert, was pointing to the stained-glass window above the altar table. Next to his father sat Bernice with her husband and the two boys. Behind them were Ralph's older brother and his wife; his other sister, Vera, and two of the elderly aunts who'd come down from Folly Mountain.

Rose's people were seated on the righthand side. Aunt Lettie, sitting in the second pew between Jack and Ora's father, was so bent over that Rose could only just see the top of her head. Minnie May—bless her—was sitting further back, with Eileen and her fellow. Mr. Hatfield from the store was next to them.

Mrs. McGinn was in the front pew, seated beside Mavis and her husband. Behind them were Bridget, no longer a baby but a sturdy girl of eight, and the twins. Only the two oldest boys were missing. Paddy, an infantry soldier, was still in an army hospital in England, and Tim, the oldest, was living in St. John's, Newfoundland.

"We don't need to bring the whole brood, Rose," Mrs. McGinn had protested when Rose was making up the invitation list. "It's too many."

Rose had insisted. "I only have Lily, and she's in the wedding party," Rose pleaded. "I want you all to come. Please; it means a lot."

"You're a picture, you are," Mr. McGinn whispered when the organ sounded the first notes of the processional. "Wish your father was here, instead of me. He'd be so proud, Bill would."

As soon as Lily and Ora had started up the aisle, Rose counted to ten, as they'd worked out in last evening's practice, breathed in, once, and tightened her hold on Mr. McGinn's arm. The walk (eight paces behind Lily) seemed to take hours. As she approached the front pews, she had a brief glimpse of Mrs. McGinn, beaming, and of Bernice, wiping at her eyes.

Although she'd intended to pay attention to every word of the ceremony, she hadn't counted on the little distractions: the slight touch of Ralph's jacket against her shoulder; Ora's lace-gloved hands, holding the flowers (her own nosegay and Rose's bridal bouquet—deep pink sweethearts, dotted with fern and lily-of-the-valley); the minister's long fingers turning the pages of the prayer book; the toes of her own satin shoes, peeking out from under the hem of her dress.

They stood on the steps afterward, smiling for the photographer. "I like to take four at the church," he'd said when Rose called for a quote. "And two at the reception, with the couple cutting the cake."

Rose had agreed to the six formal shots. "I want two full-length views, so that our gowns show up well," she'd said.

After the pictures, they walked the short block from the church to the hotel.

"A telegram came from Montreal as we were leaving the house," she said in a low voice to Ralph. "How did you get the address?"

"Don't ask questions, Mrs. Ralph Varner," he whispered. "Just be happy."

The hotel's small but elegant banquet room was all that Rose had hoped for—the rich, embossed wallpaper and burgundy draperies, the linen cloths and Regency place settings (she knew all the patterns from studying the Birks catalogue), the fresh flowers in the dainty milk-glass vases on each of the tables.

She was glad that she'd settled on a sit-down meal, rather than tea and little sandwiches in the parish hall. Ralph, in his usual style, had left the final decision to her. "It's the bride's day," he'd said. "The groom just goes along for the ride."

Ora was impressed. "This is some posh place," she said, giving one of the gold tassels a yank as they took their seats. "I'll have to make sure I don't goof and use the wrong fork. I can't guarantee how Pa will fare out, though; it's all a bit too elegant for him, I'd say."

"That punch bowl looks damn lonely," Jack said with a wink at Rose. "I better get over there and make its acquaintance."

"You'll be bosom buddies by the time this party is over, if I know you," was Ora's good-natured retort.

When it was time for the toasts, however, Jack did an excellent job.

"Ladies and Gentlemen," he called out. "I propose a toast to this fine couple. To Rose—the first lovely bloom of summer."

"To Rose," everyone murmured, clinking their glasses.

"And to Ralph," he continued. "There's a man who knows how to pick 'em."

Later, at Ora's insistence, Rose agreed to throw her garter as well as her bouquet. "You have to, Rose. It'll be such a hoot, watching Ralph take it off your leg."

Everyone clapped and cheered when Lily caught Rose's flowers, and howled when one of the twins caught her garter.

"Let that be an inspiration to ya, sonny," Jack said with his arm around the grinning teenager. "Start young, I say. And get yourself a collection."

"Sure you don't want the garter back, dear?" Mrs. McGinn interjected. "It should be your keepsake."

"No," Rose protested. "I'll have flowers from my bouquet; Lily's going to press them for me. And I'll save two pieces of the cake. I want him to have it. For good luck in love; for the future."

A week later, when they returned from their trip to their newly furnished upper flat, Bernice had a hot supper ready and waiting.

"Two more gifts arrived," she said. "I left them in your front room."

There was a vase of fresh flowers from Lily on a table in the small foyer. "See you after work tomorrow," she'd said to them downstairs. "I'm staying with Bernice overnight. You'll want time on your own, to get settled in."

"She's growing up, isn't she?" Rose mused.

"Indeed," Ralph agreed. "She'll do okay; you'll see."

He took care of the luggage, carrying both suitcases into their bedroom. Rose wandered about, turning on lamps, running her hand over the tabletops, straightening the pictures on the walls.

The front room furniture was new, but the bedroom suite had come secondhand, from a buddy of Jack's who was heading West. "Hardly slept in it, honest to Christ— what with me at sea most of the time, and the wife at her mother's." He'd winked at Ralph when they were settling up on the money. "Make good use of it; you hear?"

In the kitchen, Rose looked in the icebox. It was cool enough, with a new slab in the tray. Bernice had obviously had the ice man come by within the past day or so. Such a messy business, fooling around with ice, but there was no choice but to put up with it for now. Ralph had put their names on the list for a fridge at Simpson's, but that had been two months ago, and they were still waiting.

"Every factory is way behind schedule," the salesman had told them. "The whole country wants new kitchen appliances. You'll just have to be patient, that's all I can say."

"Want to come and see what's in these two packages?" she called to Ralph when she returned to the living room. "I'm dying to open them."

"You go ahead," he replied. "I'll be along in a few minutes."

The first gift, a crystal fruit bowl, was from the Brownes. It was obvious that Minnie May had told them the news. Her own gift—a set of kitchen knives—had already been put away in the knife drawer.

"I don't mean to be cutting the bonds of friendship," Minnie May had told her at the reception. "But every kitchen needs good knives. You can't keep house without them."

The second gift was an oval tray—silver, with fluted edges. On its card, *My sincere best wishes to you for every happiness. Harris.*

"Who's he?" Ralph asked, having emerged from the bedroom to peer over her shoulder. "Their son?"

"No," Rose answered. "Their nephew. It was good of him to remember us."

"Remember you, you mean," Ralph replied mildly. "He doesn't know me from a hole in the ground."

Rose said nothing. Harris had written "my" best wishes and "to you." She supposed she could make a lot of it, if she wanted; but she was determined not to. Harris was in the past. He had his life to live, and she had hers.

She mailed the thank-you cards on Monday. On each she had written: *We wish to thank you so much for the lovely and thoughtful wedding gift. We shall use it often. Sincerely, Rose and Ralph Varner.*

She would use them, too—every single one of the gifts that people had sent; and she would gather more lovely things as the years rolled out. There would be birthdays and Christmases; anniversaries and baptisms. It was important to have nice things in your home; given to you by special people on special occasions. That's what life was about. A home, with the things and people who meant so much to you in it.

If she'd written down that thought in sentence form, she may or may not have noticed the order; *things*, then *people*. Perhaps the sequencing was significant; perhaps not. There was little to no point in overanalyzing. Life was to be lived; the best way that you could. Period.

Baby

Rose has pulled the curtains closed in the baby's room. She's left the window open, though—just enough. Although the autumn afternoon is a warm one, she doesn't want to risk a draft.

Across from her, sitting next to the dresser on a hooked mat, the rocking chair hasn't yet come to a full stop. She can see the ever so slight back-and-forth movement of the runners, gradually coming to rest. Ralph has painted the rocking chair white, to match the crib and the dresser. Rose likes the clean, fresh whiteness of the furniture. A lovely blend to the pattern she's hooked into the mat: Bo Beep in pink, two white sheep on green grass; a blue, blue sky.

She likes the curtains, too; a cotton print with tie-backs: little girls, in pastel pinafores and bonnets, sprinkling clumps of shasta daisies with their watering cans.

Against an inside wall stands the crib. Lord, the hours she's spent, getting it ready! Days and weeks of hours. Applying Mother Goose stencils; sewing coverlets, shirring the edges of the miniature pillows.

She creeps over and stands beside the crib. Two teddies—one dark brown, one golden—sit quietly, obediently, in the two lower corners. The child is sleeping on her back, mouth open, one tiny hand curled under her chin. A damp, curly wisp of dark hair sticks out above her ear. Rose bends down and smoothes the wisp back. The child's fingers flex for a moment, and then close again.

Two thoughts register. *Her mouth is like Mama's.* And, *She'll sleep for another half-hour.*

Already, Rose is confident of the routine. The baby is a

good little soul. She hadn't expected her to be this easy; not after such a rocky start. Things seemed to be falling nicely into place now, though. Finally. After the nervous months of worry and uncertainty.

By rights, she should be exhausted from all the upset. Instead, she feels exhilarated, optimistic. This little girl—Barbara—holds such hope for Ralph and her. What's past is done with. "Put it to rest," Ralph has said. "No more looking back." Rose has hung pictures on each of the four walls: a little girl hugging her dog; two kittens frolicking in a basket of yarn; a floppy-eared rabbit munching on a lettuce leaf; and Cinderella, waving from the window of her pumpkin coach. All happy scenes. Fitting for a now-happy house.

Two of the pictures were gifts—the kittens scene from Eileen, at the store, and the rabbit from dear old Aunt Lettie. Bernice presented them with a silver mug and spoon (now arranged on a shelf of the dining-room hutch). Lily sent a complete knitted layette. And, from Ora, the ever-practical one, a mound of flannelette diapers, plus two cozy blankets—one yellow, the other white.

What a dear, that Ora! And so funny, too, as always. She'd had several ladies in for a teatime baby shower, just two weeks ago. "I had no intention of giving you anything pink, or with bows on it, Rose," she'd said over a piece of banana loaf. "Even if you do have a mania for them. What if you'd got a boy, instead of little missy, there. Why, the poor tyke would have had a bow tied to his dink till he went to school—no word of a lie." Crude, of course, but very funny. How they'd all laughed!

Rose smiles to herself again. "Better mileage out of a pint of laughter than a gallon of tears." Ralph's favourite saying. He was right, too.

Yes, good riddance to the tears. They'd been buried, for

good. In the ground, with the tiny boy who wasn't meant to live more than one day. As for the other two misses, she was keeping the vow that she'd made to herself: "Forget that they ever happened."

Rose bends and kisses the damp-warm forehead of her new daughter, pulls the coverlet down—ever so slightly—and tiptoes from the room.

Bless you for coming to us. We'll have happy times together. We've waited so long, you see.

ROSE

PART SIX

The Home
1997

The Royal Visit

"It's so hot. Are you hot as me, Ora?"

"Course I am. And parched, too. My tongue's practically stuck to the top of my mouth."

"If only we could have a drink of lemonade. Or water, even. Why don't they bring around a water bucket and a dipper?"

"Yeah. We might faint from the sunstroke. Then they'd have to call for the ambulance."

"It would never get near in this crowd. A person would be dead by the time it got through."

"I wonder how many people are here."

"Must be thousands."

"Look, those Guides and Scouts have flags. That's not fair—we should have flags, too. Who gave them their flags, I wonder?"

"That soldier, I'll bet. See? He's got some in his hand. I'm asking for two—one for you and one for me."

"Excuse me, sir. Two flags, please. Thanks."

"Here's yours, Rose."

"These flags will be our souvenirs. I'm putting mine under my mattress—I don't care what Matron says."

"Me, too. I'm not pinning mine up on the playroom wall. It wouldn't be my souvenir anymore. It would just be anybody's."

"Oh, Ora, listen! The lady with the mouth organ is tuning up the choir. See?"

"Those girls are picked specially, aren't they? I'll bet they're rich, too. You can tell, just by looking at them."

"Rich and snotty."

"Oh Ora! Rich kids don't get snotty."

"I don't mean runny nose snotty. There's more than one kind, you know. My pa says so."

"Aren't you glad you're here, even if it is hot. When we get old, we can tell our grandchildren all about it."

"Grandchildren! Don't be a goose."

"Listen! The band's playing—'God Save The King!'"

"Look—look! There's the car. The King's waving."

"Oh, Ora, just look at her dress and hat. I knew she'd wear blue. Oh, the car's stopping; they're getting out!"

"I know, I know. I got eyes. I can see."

"I wonder who the little girl with the bouquet is."

"Dunno."

"Don't you wish you could be her?"

"Maybe. If she's got lots of toys and games and her own room."

"Just imagine! Giving flowers to the Queen! Why, your picture would be in the paper. Everybody would see it. You'd be a star."

"You'd be in the Star *Weekly, too."*

"Hey! The choir's singing!"

"Let's you and me sing, too."

"Okay."

In days of yore / From Britain's shore
Wolfe, the dauntless hero came,
And planted firm / Britannia's flag
On Canada's fair domain;
Long may it wave / Our boast and pride
And join in love, together
The thistle, shamrock, rose / entwine
The Maple Leaf – forever!

"Rose, Rose—wake up. Had a little doze, haven't you? I think I heard you singing."

Rose stares at the woman. What on earth is she gabbing about? It doesn't make a bit of sense.

Her head feels heavy with fatigue and disappointment.

Where is Ora? There is no sign of her, or the other children. Oh dear. Perhaps they went back to the Home without her.

"I should get you changed," the woman says. "Keep that pretty dress nice for tomorrow. It's a sweet one to wear to the fashion show downstairs. Your daughter tells me she's taking you."

Who is this woman? And why is she holding out two paper cups? Rose can see water in one, and coloured pills in the other. That's it, then. She must have fainted, waiting on the hill for the King and Queen, and the ambulance has brought her to the hospital. That's why the grassy slope has disappeared, and she is lying in this bed, covered with a sheet.

"There you go. I'll just raise your bed a little. Soon be time for supper; but first, some pills for the lady." Rose opens her mouth and swallows the pills; lets her head drop back on the pillow. Supper? The Royal Couple will be seated at the banquet by now. The Queen will have changed from her lovely blue day frock into an evening gown; the royal blue sash across her chest, and a tiara on her head.

After two attempts, Rose finally gets out the words. "Did you see all the people?" she whispers. "Did you hear the band?" Goodness! How faint and laboured her voice sounds.

The woman in yellow isn't listening. Instead, she is standing at the foot of the bed, unzipping a long gown. Rose brightens. Perhaps she's going to the banquet, too. Eating pheasant under glass; and, for dessert, Baked Alaska. Yes, she thinks. The perfect menu—fit for Royalty.

"And what would my lady's second choice be?" The woman in yellow is smiling down at her. "I'm not sure there's any Baked Alaska today. Some chicken potpie, I do believe. And I think I saw butterscotch pudding on a tray."

Rose scowls. What's wrong with the cook, anyway? Doesn't he know how important these visitors are? Chicken potpie, indeed.

"I hate potpie!" The voice—someone's—comes from a long way off.

"Okey-dokey, Rose," the woman says. "Stay in your pretty dress, then. But don't blame me if you spill something on it at supper."

Rose watches the woman toss the empty pill cup into the wastebasket.

Her head feels so strange. If only she could make the woman understand. She needs—what does she need? Someone. Barbara, that's it. She needs Barbara to help.

"Could you phone her? My daughter, Barbara. She'll drive me down to the hotel. Her number's in the book in the kitchen drawer."

There is no reply. Irritated, she pushes at the bedclothes. You can't rely on maids these days; not like when she worked for Mrs. Browne. It was different back then. Maids did what they were supposed to do.

Evening Fog

The pills. It's the pills she's giving me, that yellow-haired wench. Doesn't she know I can see through her? I'll have her dismissed, that's what. Stupid girls are a dime a dozen; everyone knows that.

Why do I care? Why try to remember; most things are best forgotten; kept under wraps.

Barbie doesn't know. She doesn't need to. I don't want her to.

The fog's thick tonight. Thick and grey. Odd, how we say that. Fog isn't thick at all; it's wispy-thin. So thin I can put my arm through it. See?

It comes from the ocean, fog; starts way out beyond the mouth of the harbour, creeps along the shore, sneaks up on me when I'm not looking. Oh, I know! You can't fool me. I can see it from my window, watch it drifting in. I try to keep clear of it, but it doesn't give up. It keeps drifting, drifting, up and up, hiding me, hiding everything.

Brain fog. That's bad, too. It makes you so murky. Turns you into a wreck.

No! Not a wreck; a shadow. It rises up inside you, clouds of it. Terrible. What shall I do?

No point going on. Enough's enough. I need to die. Nothing ever worked out the way I wanted, anyway. All those secrets I had to keep.

My Ralph knew some. Not all, though. Dear Ralph! Rosie, he called me. "Just let me steer, Rosie. I'll get us there okay."

Except that he didn't. He should have, but he didn't. I wonder if he remembered saying so. At the last—before the crash.

Life goes off the rails sometimes. His did. Tumbled into a gully, in a smoking, horrible mess. His going left me alone, again. I didn't want to be. I hate being alone.

I hear her coming; the one with the pills. I'm foggier than ever after I take them. They like it that way, though. Gives them a chance to sit back and relax. I know their tricks. I wasn't born yesterday.

She never pulls the drapes at night. Sloppy, lazy girl. Ora didn't pull the blind down, either. But she was different. I loved Ora.

George's Island will be shrouded in grey tonight. Swirls and swirls of grey.

I'll be shrouded too, before long. But I won't swirl. I'll be stiff as a poker, with my eyes shut tight. Shipping out, like those big hulks, pulling away from the jetty. Sliding out, drifting out. Grey on grey.

I'm grey on grey, too. Invisible. I always was. Of little consequence. My destiny.

"Jean, I just wanted to let you know that Mom's had another episode. The Home just called to tell me."

"Oh, dear goodness," Jean replies. "And me, over here, trying to do for my mom. I'm no help whatsoever. Makes me feel so bad."

"Please don't. You can't do anything. I just wanted to keep you up to date."

"Are you in Halifax?" Jean asks.

"Yes. And I'll be staying—at least, for a while."

"And you, with work and all."

"No worries. I can get Family Leave for this."

"What does the doctor say?" Jean asks.

"He's not hopeful. This is pretty much the home stretch."

"Barb—I can't come now, but I'll be there when the time comes," Jean says. "I love Aunt Rose. Will you tell her that?"

"I'll try. And I'll keep you posted."

Last Dream

The house is enormous. It stretches out before her, above her, below her. On and on, room after room, window upon window. The stairs go up and up, turn into dark, echoing corridors, climb again. Up and up, to where the ghosts of the little ones, whimpering for their burned teddies, hover; where the blind rattles, back and forth, back and forth, sending wavering shards of light into the darkened rooms.

More stairs. Down and down they go, past a heavy metal door that hides the dull rumbling, the roaring flames, the sickening heat, of the firebox. Stairs that descend into heavy mustiness. A massive timbered door, an echoing corridor, a cold clammy chamber. Moss sprouts from spidery cracks on the damp walls, wispy triangles hang from the ceiling corners, and trickles of water spread slowly, forming pools in which drowned spiders float.

She is so tired, but she must keep on. She needs to collect her things, put them safely away. They belong to her, and she must retrieve them. The little girl needs them, too, for her hope chest.

If only she could remember the girl's name. She knew it, once. But it's slipped away, elusive, hiding from her, just like those *things* she's come for. Once she's gathered them all, she'll feel better. She'll wrap each one separately, in tissue paper, and pack them all in her valise. The girl can take them, for safekeeping. You can't trust anyone with your things, not around here. You need to attend to them yourself, properly. She prides herself in knowing how to do things properly.

The flap of the valise opens. It is stuffed with small, flat, neatly wrapped packages. Slowly, methodically, she takes out each package, unwraps it, places the contents on the tabletop. How lovely they are, lined up in a row! Such rich colours, such fine stitching. She wants to admire them, but they won't stay put, on the mahogany tabletop. As she watches, stunned, one by one, they take flight and float away, up the staircase, along the dark corridors.

"Come back here," she tries to call out; but her tongue is swollen and no sound emerges. Frantic, she scrambles out of the chair, hampered by a terrible numbness in her arm and leg, and hobbles after them. The *things* glide ahead of her, beyond her reach. She stumbles awkwardly from room to room in the deepening gloom, her eyelids growing heavier.

If only she could find the light switch! Her fingers grope the wall beyond the doorjamb, feel only the smooth cold-ness of plaster. Cold as death, she thinks, recoiling from the touch. She hears Ora's voice: "Look up, silly goose. It's not a switch; it's a chain."

Of course. If you stand on your tippy-toes, you can grab it; if you pull hard enough, the gloom retreats to the shadowy corners, waiting, scheming for another chance to pounce.

So many shadows. Too much darkness.

Trust not thy neighbour, nor thy Lord
For each will forsake you.

The cross-stitched warning has been fitted behind the glass of a little painted frame. There is another, blue-bordered, hanging above the dresser in the spare room:

One crow sorrow
Two crows joy
Three crows a wedding
Four a baby boy.

Downstairs, as chatter of no substance is being served in china cups, another warning, embroidered on the corner of a linen tea napkin: *In a world of strangers / We walk alone.*

A weak afternoon sun filters through the fan light above the front door. A framed *Thursday's child has far to go* hangs above the furled umbrellas in their stand. *Yes*, she thinks, numbed fingers trying to stick a hat pin through her old navy felt. *It might be a long trip. I should take an extra sweater. And a five-dollar bill, folded over, inside my shoe. Just in case.*

BARBARA

Solo Act

Funeral

The last notes of the processional fade and the priest moves into place at the top of the chancel steps. Barbara feels a momentary fluttering in her stomach. What nerve she had, going ahead with this, a full funeral Eucharist. It was her mother's doing, she tells herself—in that final rally of energy, before the end.

"See that you give me a proper send-off. The same as I did for your father." Her mother's voice was heavy from the medication. "Dress me nicely; and don't forget my wedding ring."

Seventy-two hours later, Barbara finds herself honouring both requests. The old adage holds: it's the least a person can do.

The priest has finished the Opening Collect, is beginning the first lesson. He seems a decent sort; had asked her preference as to the prayer book, and when she'd looked at him with a blank stare, had been quick to come to her rescue.

"Perhaps the old book," he'd said. "People of your mother's era much prefer it."

"Yes, thanks," she'd mumbled. How was she to know there was a new book; she, who hadn't set foot inside an Anglican church for years.

The Homily is short, based on the passage from Corinthians. *"Now we see through a glass, darkly; but then, face to face; now, we know in part; but then shall we know even as we also are known."*

Barbara's mind wanders. She thinks of the Johari Window theory that they'd studied in a second-year Psychology course. That Johari bunch sure did get plenty of mileage out of their windowpane metaphor. Trinities and quadrants were all the rage, for a while. In their case, four windowpanes. Pane One was things known to self and to others—stuff that the whole world was in on. Blindspots was the second one: those things known only to others. The third all about secrets—things known only to self. Last up—number four—was all the unknown crap that lurked below the surface of the consciousness. Plenty of baggage under there to make every shrink in the land big-time wealthy.

She stifles a sigh. She shouldn't be thinking about Johari windows, not at her mother's funeral service. It's irrelevant—and irreverent. Beside her, in the front pew, cousin Jean sits comfortably, seems to be listening.

The rest of the Homily's message is—she searches for the right word—appropriate. Enough of the universal, not too much of the specific. No doubt, these priests have handy reference books in their studies; with chapters titled, "Homilies for Parishioners You Don't Know Very Well."

From the pew behind her, a woman coughs. Must be her cousin's wife; the one married to Aunt Bernice's younger son. They'd travelled down last evening, were staying overnight at the Delta. That was it for her father's family. Aunt Bernice had died five years earlier, and Uncle Cy, her father's brother, was too feeble to make the trip. As for her mother's side, there was only Jean to represent them. Poor Aunt Lily was very unwell, and Jean's husband, Len, had stayed home to care for her.

Barbara's thoughts drift in another direction. She'd attended Sunday School at this church for one year, coaxed into it by a Grade Two friend. She hadn't cared for it much, had gone home crying after an upset with one of the teachers.

"Shame on you, Barbara! You mustn't make crayon marks in the Bible."

Her mother had been annoyed—at Barbara, for being out of line, and at the teacher, for making a fuss. "You won't do that again," she'd said to Barbara. "Because you're not going back. I'll buy them a new Bible to shut them up, and that will be the end of it." Even after all this time, Barbara can hear the disapproval in her mother's voice.

Beside the pew, right *there*, is her mother's casket, draped with the Pall. She could reach out and touch it if she wanted; if she dared. Her mother can't stop her; not now. Barbara clasps her hands together, holds them tight in her lap. She must behave herself; make up for all of those childhood times when she didn't.

Afterwards, from the portico steps, Barbara watches the white-gloved hands of the Undertaker's assistant lifting the casket into the back of the hearse. He sets the floral sprays down beside the oak casket, shuts the hearse's door, looks in her direction.

She nods her approval, lets out a long breath. Her hands and feet are cold. Not as cold as those of the body lying below the lid of the box, though. That entire body is cold; without breath or blood.

"Not a breath of air in here." Is that her mother's voice? "Open a window, for God's sake, or I'll faint."

At the interior door, both Jean and the priest are greeting mourners. Jean is pleasant, her manner comforting. The priest's voice and manner are calm, reassuring. In control. But then, he should be. Weddings, christenings, funerals— the milestones—are his specialty.

Barbara tries to copy their act. "Thank you for coming," she says. "So kind." She's not comfortable in the role, however. Her words are wooden; her body stiff. She's not used to hugs, the brush of cheeks against her own.

"Barbara—" Jean is holding the arm of a ruddy-faced

woman in a black cape, "—this lady is Mavis. She's Mrs. McGinn's daughter."

"Mavis—" Barbara tries to place the name.

"We were neighbours," Mavis says. "Your mother and Lily lived with us for a while."

"Oh! Of course."

"And your mother . . . ?" Barbara ventures. Would—could—the elder Mrs. McGinn still be alive?

"Ma's gone nearly twenty years," Mavis replies. "She and your mum used to keep in touch, though."

"Yes, I remember," Barbara says. "I appreciate your coming today."

"It'll take a while, getting used to your ma being gone," Mavis adds. "Look after yourself, now."

Ora's two daughters each kiss her, and then help their father maneuver the steps. A handful of neighbours murmur their sympathy. The other mourners include a volunteer from the Home, a woman from the store where her mother had worked, and, of course, the Lodge ladies. They linger, wanting—needing—to reminisce.

"Your mother was so talented. I still have the evening dress she made for my installation."

"Dear, dear, Rose. She was such a special person."

Finally, thankfully, the line trickles.

"All set, then?" the rector asks, buttoning his trench coat. He hasn't noticed the lone man, leaning heavily on his brass-headed cane.

"My sincere condolences," the man begins. Barbara takes in his white hair, brown tweed overcoat, and silk scarf. This is a patrician gentleman, no question

"The name is Dunlop—Harris," the man says. "I've known your mother for many years. A very fine lady, Rose. I shall truly miss her. Forgive me if I don't attend the committal, but my legs aren't up to it." He moves away and is gone, his cane tapping on the wooden ramp outside.

"A fitting service," Jean says when she and Barbara are seated in the back of the limo. "The minister did a fine job."

"Yes. It was—he did," Barbara replies absently. Ahead of them, a delivery van makes a sharp left, to avoid the cortège.

Five minutes later, the car is entering the cemetery. The driver proceeds slowly, avoiding the worst of the ruts. Off to the right, at the end of a narrow lane, the mourners stand waiting, braving the November cold.

When the car comes to a stop, Barbara gets out as gracefully as she can, determined to wrestle down a sudden stab of panic. Scene three, act three. In ten minutes, it will be over. She will leave her mother here, in the cold ground. Nothing about the service—not the sentences, the prayers, the Homily—have convinced her. Yes, she'd put the coins in her mother's handbag two nights ago (a crazy, stupid idea). No matter. She still didn't believe in all that business about the hereafter.

Graveyards represented endings, not new beginnings. Lonely places of earth, mold, decay. A bit of grass, a few flowers, yes; the flowers soon wilted and died, however; leaving only the granite stones, and the bones, behind.

Clearing Out

Barbara sees Jean off the following afternoon.

"Of course you must get back," she says for the tenth time. Jean, hovering at the open car door, looks worried and guilty. "I understand," Barbara repeats. "I'll be fine; and I'm coming to see you and Aunt Lil as soon as I get things seen to here."

Jean nods, gets behind the wheel, turns on the ignition. Deep down, Barbara is relieved that Jean isn't staying longer. She's weary of talking, reminiscing; of saying the right things. Jean means well, but she bloody well talks a dozen blue streaks, plus.

She lies down after Jean has gone, sleeps for over two hours. When she wakes, it is dark, and she's hungry. She heats a plate of the beef casserole Jean has left, eats it and two of the tea biscuits. Half of Jean's lemon pie is in the fridge, too; as well as a container of sliced chicken, and another, unopened, of fish chowder.

No chance of me starving, Barbara thinks with a wry smile as she cuts a wedge of the pie. *Jean has seen to that.*

Tomorrow morning, she will call the real estate agent. Getting the house on the market before she returns to Ontario is a priority. She'd like it to sell quickly, though the market lately has been soft. Its sale will, of course, be a total, final step. With the house gone, her ties with Nova Scotia will be completely severed. *You can't go home again.* Wolfe was right, muses Barbara. Placing flowers on a grave is its own ball of wax.

Which is another item for her "to do" list. She must arrange to have her mother's name added to the headstone. What a lot of work, leaving this life! Perhaps ashes in an urn would have been easier. Her mother wasn't having any of that, though. "I have no intention of being burned to a crisp," she'd informed Barbara years earlier. "I'll go in the ground next to your father, thank you very much."

That night, Barbara sleeps for nine hours, awakes early, re-energized. She throws on jeans and a T-shirt, eats a piece of toast, takes her second cup of coffee and a notepad into the front room. Placing several sheets of paper side-by-side on the dining-room table, she prints headings at the top of each one: Furniture, Dishes & Silver, Ornaments, Books and Albums, Linens, Kitchen and Bath, Clothes. Under each heading she adds these columns: Keep, Sell, Give-away, Garbage.

She has given herself three weeks to empty the house. By month end, she will have everything sorted, sold, boxed, or tossed. Everything.

Taking the sheet labelled Clothes, she heads up the stairs, places a package of garbage bags and an empty carton on the bedroom mat and surveys the interior of her mother's closet. Each hanger, every inch of shelf space is filled with dresses, suits, belts, bags, shoes, hats. She must paw though the lot, make considered decisions, somewhere between ruthlessness and sentimentality.

She starts at the left side of the rack and works to the right. The task gets easier as she moves along. Few of the dresses and none of the pant suits fit her; she holds aside three or four wool sweaters, an embroidered dressing gown, a brown leather bag, and a beaded evening purse.

One garbage bag fills, then a second. She will do a drop-off at the Sally Ann and take some of the bags to her mother's Lodge president. The ladies will get a kick out of the evening gowns, shawls, and boxes of hats. Barbara knows they have "New to You" sales on a regular basis.

The shoes are last. There seems little point in trying on

any of them; her own feet are two sizes larger than her mother's, and she has no idea who else they might fit. Pulling the empty carton toward her, she begins to toss the shoes into it. One of the silver evening slippers hits the side, and a five-dollar bill flutters onto the mat. Barbara retrieves the shoe, puts the money on the bedspread.

She scoops up a second armful of shoes and places them into the carton. Her back is beginning to ache from the bending and reaching, but she is determined to finish. The last of the shoes is a pair of sixties-style black pumps. She runs a finger over the soft leather upper. The memory of her mother wearing them at her college graduation reception is a vivid one.

From under the right insole, which has come unglued, a bit of blue paper sticks out. When Barbara attempts to straighten the crooked bit of leather, it slides sideways, exposing another five-dollar bill. Something—suspicion, tinged with curiosity—sends her digging through the shoes in the carton. Sure enough, she finds a loose insole in every pair, and each right shoe contains a five-dollar bill, folded lengthwise.

Barbara counts the mound of bills that have accumulated on the bedspread. They add up to sixty dollars, total. Her mother owned more than a dozen handbags and satchels, yet she chose to stuff twelve of her shoes with Sir Wilfrid Laurier fivers, in two-toned blue.

Barbara returns the shoes to the carton, closes the lid. Three days ago, Barbara had placed silver coins into the change purse of her newly dead mother—just in case. The coins seem a paltry amount now, in light of this discovery. Not that she was surprised. Her mother had always been strategic, always one step ahead. It's little wonder that she'd insisted on being buried in her shoes. She, who prided herself in planning the details of life, had planned for this, too.

Mother's Desk

Two days later, as a wet snow begins to fall, Barbara watches the real estate agent mounting a For Sale sign in the middle of the front lawn. The flakes slide down the outside of the windowpane, dissolving into rivulets that trickle off the ledge and drip onto the blackened stalks of lobelia in the beds below.

She shivers, pulls her sweater tighter across her chest, walks over to the thermostat, hikes it up two notches. Shortly, she will tackle this familiar room. Meantime, and for a few hours yet, everything remains in its usual place: the paisley print sofa, the accent cushions, the swivel rocker, the leather hassock, the old stereo player.

"Not bad," the dealer had said to her that morning. "The price I'll give you is for a house lot. You end up better off that way." Thanks to a bit of dickering, the figure is a fair one. He's to return on Friday, with his truck and his helper.

Barbara has no misgivings at selling most of the furniture pieces. She hasn't room for them in her condo, and, in any case, they don't fit with her modern decor. Only the dining-room suite and her mother's desk will go to Ontario.

It's the smaller items that are problematic. How should she fairly, sensibly, sort and sift through the accumulation of fifty years? What is the fine line between preserving memory and clearing away clutter? Without brothers and sisters to help or to squabble with, she's "it." No one else to do the work, make the decisions, reap the benefits.

Nothing new, there. This is the way it's always been.

The previous evening she'd spent over an hour looking through photo albums; her childhood, recorded in black-

and-white three-by-five snapshots, held in place by gummed-triangle corners. Pages of her father and mother, herself between them; sitting, standing, holding hands, smiling into the camera's lens. A threesome: in winter coats, Easter hats, beach togs and sunglasses. The Varner trio, until, with the turning of a page, a threesome no longer.

The later snapshots accentuate her mother's sad eyes and strained expression. Barbara's own face—at seventeen, eighteen—is sullen and glum. Why were they always standing apart? Was it because touch reminded them of the big, kind man who'd been taken away?

At midnight she'd given up, tumbled the albums into a carton, crawled into bed with a hot water bottle. Later, from the safe distance of Ontario, she might be able to come to terms with the pictures, the remembered anguish.

By the time the snow has eased and a weak winter sun peeks through the grey clouds, Barbara is sitting at her mother's single pedestal desk. She opens the shallow centre drawer and pokes through its contents. Everything is neat. Pens and pencils, in separate metal trays; a stapler and a roll of address labels; a pewter letter opener. Barbara recognizes the letter opener; she'd sent it some years back, as a Mother's Day gift.

There's a writing tablet and a package of envelopes, a wrapper of outdated Canadian stamps, and a small black address book. Barbara flips through the address book, counts nineteen names, all told. Tucked between the last page and the back cover is her mother's Christmas card list. The book, the list, give Barbara a weird, empty feeling.

She puts the lot into a carton, tries the next drawer. It is filled with Royal Bank calendars, dating back five years. The entries—Pay light bill, Deposit pension cheque, Wash bed linen—are a record of her mother's daily maintenance routine. Each completed task—noted on the same day of each month—has been checked off with a pink marker. Barbara dumps them into the waiting garbage bag.

The bottom drawer contains bundles of sewing patterns: suits and jackets, long out of style; floor-length evening gowns; wedding and bridesmaid's dresses; a baby's christening ensemble. Barbara recognizes the wedding dress pattern. Her mother had offered to make it for her, and had been offended when Barbara had chosen a short, plain A-line from a marked-down rack at Simpson's. Barbara hadn't wanted a veil, either, much to her mother's disgust; had carried a bouquet of mixed flowers from the back garden. Just as well she hadn't gone to a lot of expense. The marriage barely lasted four years.

The patterns join the other discards.

Last is a manila folder. Barbara expects to find business papers inside it: a house insurance policy, a property tax invoice, other receipts, perhaps a safety deposit box key. Instead, she pulls out a batch of yellowed newspaper clippings and a Thank-You card, held together with a disintegrating elastic band.

The top clipping is her father's obituary. She reads it through, feels her throat tighten. She can't recall having seen the formal announcement of his passing, although she must have, at the time. With her father's death, she'd become the first girl in her class to have lost a parent in a train wreck. How she'd hated that bit of notoriety—and the sympathy that went with it.

Ora's obituary is there, too. Her mother had been devastated at Ora's death, had phoned Barbara, distraught, weeping. Barbara had taken time off work to fly down for the funeral, only to be confounded by her mother's flat-out refusal to attend the service.

The third clipping is her Aunt Lily's wedding announcement. *Lily Morash Weds Local Horseman, Chester Jardine on Saturday, September 8th, at the Freetown United Church. The groom was attended by his brother, George Jardine. The Maid of Honour was Rose Mildred Varner, sister of the bride. Lily wore a simple gown of white satin, with an overskirt of . . .*

Barbara skips the tedious fashion details. There is no mention of Violet, the other sister. She can't remember much about her absent aunt; had seen her only twice in her life. There had been a falling-out years ago, apparently; and, as a result, Violet was seldom spoken of.

The Thank-You card is an acknowledgement of sympathy.

Dear Rose: I appreciate your kind words of comfort to me at the loss of Claudia. As you know, she'd been ill for many months. Now, thankfully, she is at peace.

Perhaps, by autumn, I will be able to resume my duties at the Lodge.

Most sincerely, Harris

The name means nothing to Barbara; the card is scrapped.

She can feel a telltale throbbing at the back of her eyes, a sign that one of her headaches is coming on. She goes to the kitchen, takes an aspirin, makes herself a cup of tea, brings it back to the living room. She sips the liquid slowly, rests her head against the sofa cushion, and dozes off.

It is very late when she wakes. "Damn it all," she curses, annoyed at having lost two more precious hours of the day. She hauls one of the empty cartons over to the stereo and begins to rifle through old LPs. Al Martino, Englebert Humperdink, Frank Sinatra, Dean Martin, Tony Bennett— her mother loved listening to them all.

Loved to dance, too. After her father's death, her mother had continued to take part in the Lodge events. Barbara suspects that the draw wasn't so much the Lodge's worthy causes as the opportunity it afforded her to attend the fancy banquets and dance parties. A chance to dress up and be escorted by one Mason gentleman or another—in his installation tuxedo, his dinner jacket, or his Hawaiian summer shirt.

Barbara doesn't ditch the albums. Instead she packs them into the carton, tapes it securely, writes "Records / Toronto" on its top and shoves it to a corner of the room.

Keepsakes

The house empties, gradually, systematically. The dining-room suite and her mother's desk are covered with blankets, ready for the long-distance movers. The cartons are ready, too—eight of them—lined up against the inside wall. They contain the photo albums, the Royal Albert china set, a chest of flatware, assorted books and linens, several prints of Nova Scotia scenes.

My mother's life, in eight boxes.

On top of the blanket covering the dining-room table are four Royal Doulton figurines—convenient birthday gifts at one point in the past. Barbara has never cared for the prissy, pretty ladies, in their bonnets and bows, fur muffs and crinolines. Looking at them now, lined-up, waiting for their Prince Charmings to arrive, it strikes her that, in this instance, the four last things are not death, purgatory, heaven, hell, after all, but these four miniature ladies, decked out in their catch-a-man best gowns.

I'm getting rid of those damn dames today!

She grabs the tattered phonebook, thumbs through to the *Ls*. Ora's oldest daughter, Beth, married a Landry. Barbara can't remember the husband's first name, but she knows their street address. She's visited the old, Victorian-style house that was Ora's many times in the past: for birthday parties, Christmas gatherings, summer holidays.

She finds the number, dials, and waits.

"Beth, Barbara here," she says when Beth answers.

"Barb— How are you? I've been thinking about you. Wondering how you're doing."

"I'm okay; a little tired. Sifting through fifty years is a big job."

"God, I can only imagine," Beth replies. "It was bad enough after Mum went, and we had nothing to do, compared to you."

Interesting point, that. The degrees and complexities of a life ending. Barbara can't spend time on it now, however; not with the clock ticking.

"Are you going to be home?" she asks. "I was hoping to stop by your place. I have a package for you."

"Sure, come on over. I'll put the coffee on."

"I can't stay long," Barbara warns. "I'll aim for about seven."

She searches for the surname, Gilhen, next. *Mavis*, daughter of Mrs. McGinn. Jean had made a special note of the name from the guestbook in the church foyer. There are five listings with this unusual spelling. Barbara starts with A.J. and works down the list. She hits paydirt with call number four.

"Yeah," replies a youngish male voice. "She's here. Just a minute." In the background, Barbara can hear the clatter of pots.

He yells out, "Gram—it's for you." The clatter ceases and a moment later, Mavis comes on the line.

"By all means, come on over," Mavis says when Barbara explains herself. "We're two blocks beyond the Legion Hall—a yellow house, on the right. If you see the nursing home, you'll know you've gone too far."

Barbara arrives at Beth's place promptly at seven, as promised. Of Ora's four children, Barbara knows Beth best. They'd played together as little girls, gradually growing apart as they reached their teens. By the time Barbara had finished university, their contact had dwindled to a card at

Christmas and a brief summertime hello when Barbara was in Halifax, visiting her mother.

The last time she'd been inside Beth's house was at the time of Ora's death, four years earlier. She'd taken an azalea plant, feeling the need to explain to Beth in person why her mother hadn't attended her best friend's funeral service; hoping that Beth would understand.

"I've brought you something," Barbara says, setting the wrapped package on the coffee table. "A little memento of the friendship between our mothers. I thought maybe you could find a spot for it."

Beth unwraps the tissue, turns the figurine around in her hands. "It's so pretty," she says. "I'll think of your mom whenever I look at it." She gets up, makes a place for it on the mantel. "I remember those figure-skating lessons we took together," Beth says, returning to her chair. "I wasn't that good, but you were a natural." She takes a sip of her coffee. "Do you still skate?" she asks.

"God, no," Barbara replies. "I haven't been on ice in over ten years."

"What a shame," Beth says. "I used to be green with envy over those darling outfits your mother made for your competitions. You usually won, too. I was convinced you'd make the nationals."

Barbara laughs. "Hardly! That'd take more discipline than I ever had. I only did it because it came easy."

"Remember that doll you got—the Barbara Ann Scott one. Do you still have it? How I wanted one; but mother told me they were too expensive."

"The doll—no," Barbara replies. "I haven't seen it for years. I'm not sure what happened to it."

It's an hour before Barbara can make a tactful, gracious exit.

"Come see me when you get back East again," Beth says at the front door. "You're welcome to stay here, too. We've got lots of room, now the boys are gone."

Barbara nods, waves, and hurries down the walk. She doesn't expect she will ever take Beth up on her offer. There's no longer a valid reason to keep in touch. With both mothers gone, their bond, tenuous at best, has been broken.

The route to Mavis' house takes Barbara past the old Forum. She'd spent countless Saturday mornings here, with the skating club, practising her pivots and twirls.

Funny, that Beth would remember the doll. What grief it had caused, all those years ago. "She's too delicate to play with," her mother insisted after Barbara had opened the gift on Christmas morning. "But she'll make a sweet decoration for the top of your bureau. I'll fix it up with a white doily and a mirror—make it look like an outdoor skating rink."

Barbara had left the doll alone for weeks, finally giving into the temptation to try her out one January day after school. She'd set the doll, balanced on her imitation blades, spinning on a patch of ice in the driveway. After the doll had toppled over for the fifth time, Barbara had given up in disgust and gone off tobogganing. Her mother had found the doll the next day, lying face-down in a layer of freshly fallen snow, one skate boot missing.

"What a careless girl you are," she'd scolded. "Taking your lovely doll outside, when I asked you not to! If you had to do without, like I did, you'd act different."

Barbara had sat at the kitchen table that evening, fists clenched in her lap, torn between guilt and resentment. "It's only a doll," she'd wanted to say, but didn't dare; not when her mother had *that* look on her face.

Barbara passes the yellow house, realizes she's gone too far, shifts into reverse, backs up. The front-porch light comes on—one of those automatic jobs—as she picks her way along the walk. *Am I crazy, or what?* Barbara thinks. *Running around the city after dark with these stupid figurines. I should have let the dealer take them.*

She declines Mavis' offer of an armchair; stands awkwardly in the archway to the living room, snow from the soles of her boots making a puddle on the hall runner.

"Aren't you a pet," Mavis says, gently uncovering *Wendy* from the tissue wrapping. "Dear little lass, she is." Mavis places the china figure on a low table and stands back to admire it.

Barbara murmurs a vague agreement. She's feeling less stupid, now that the deed has been done. Mavis, on the other hand, seems totally at ease, happy to chat with Barbara, the gift-bearing stranger.

"I remember when your mum and Lily came to live with us," Mavis says. "Lily was just a little thing. I used to sing to her and hear her prayers. They shared a room with my little sister, Bridget."

"It was good of your mother to take them in," Barbara replies. "It couldn't have been easy, with so many children of her own."

"It was different times then. We were used to sleeping two or three to a bed. Always room for another—that was Ma, bless her heart. And it wasn't all that long that they were with us. Less than a year, seems to me, before they went into the Home."

"The Home?"

"Yes, the orphanage."

Orphanage. Never had her mother, or anyone in the family, mentioned an orphanage. Not even a hint. Her brain whirs, struggling to process and store this startling, new information.

"I didn't realize their stay with you was so short,"

Barbara says, choosing words that she hopes will cover her amazement. "I thought it was much longer . . . until . . ."

Until—what? This, then, must be a part of that hazy period—the years that her mother had always glossed over. Her mouth has suddenly gone dry as Barbara stands, stupidly silent.

Thankfully, Mavis doesn't seem to notice.

"Ma and Dadda would have kept the girls. It was Father Hanrahan who said they couldn't; and Ma would never go against a priest. Never."

"Did they see you again, afterwards?"

Why is she asking? Who cares? Ancient history; lived, over and done with.

"Oh yes. Your mother ran away once. Came to our place, looking for the older girl. Ma had to take her back that night; but she used to go and see them. Once a month it was; on Sunday afternoons. After your mum got out on her own, she'd come down every so often and have supper with us. We used to meet up in the Gardens, too. Listen to the band concert together."

Barbara needs time to absorb all of this, but Mavis has no mercy. She talks on, pleased with the opportunity to reminisce.

"Ma was so happy when your mum got married. Dadda gave her away, since she didn't have anyone of her own. I was at the wedding. We all were."

Ah. This bit puts her on firmer ground. The wedding photos exist, in one of the albums. Mavis would have been one of the younger ones, standing on the steps of the church. Barbara had never thought to ask the names of the guests, or who had walked her mother up the aisle. It was, after all, in the "before" time. She could pick out her aunts—Lily and Bernice; knew Ora and her husband, Jack. As for the other people, they didn't really matter.

The House at Night

Barbara drives slowly, peering at the unfamiliar street signs through the swish of wiper blades. During her youth there had been no reason to venture into the far north-end. Her own life and travels seldom took her much beyond the shopping district on Gottingen, or the bridge approach at the bottom of North Street.

After two wrong turns, she sees the correct sign, shifts into second gear, follows the street down, down, toward the harbour. "It's big and kind of on its own," the young fellow at the service station had told her. "Vacant lots on both sides. You can't miss it. There's a sign over the door."

She spots the house in a dip of ground on the far side of the boulevard, pulls over to the curb, cuts the motor and rolls down the window. The young fellow was right. Big it is; a dark rectangle against the night sky; four stories high, with a flat roof, and rows of tall, narrow windows.

The entrance is flush with the sidewalk, as imposing as some of those on the heritage buildings in the central part of the city. Double Greek columns flank a massive wooden door. The frame itself is bordered with glass insets, and set over its arched top is a stained-glass fanlight.

Not an easy house to get into, or out of. The thought troubles her.

At one time there certainly would have been three or four brick or flagstone steps leading up to the door; but the steps have been removed, or are hidden now by an ugly wooden ramp. The architect would turn over in his grave if he saw that, Barbara muses. "Wheelchair accessible" is the concept behind these ramps; a modern-day requirement for all public buildings. No longer can anyone—man, woman, or child—be denied their rightful access. Or exit.

The sign above the door announces to the world that this dwelling is a community centre, set up to serve a new generation of the city's needy. These days you didn't dare write "bring us your widows, your orphans, your destitute and we will provide." This sign, however, amounts to the same thing.

Barbara has lived in many houses over the years: duplexes, condos, flats, apartments. None have been particularly memorable; none worthy of either secrecy or pride. She used to joke about her pads. "A place to hang my hat. Keep the rain off my head."

Her mother's experience had been, obviously, a quite different one. Barbara peers upwards, scanning the darkened windows of the second floor. Should she come back here tomorrow and inquire; try to fill in some of the missing details? There would be records of the children who had passed through the system over the years. Here, still, in boxes; or sent for safekeeping. Perhaps at the provincial archives.

She can't remember when the city's orphanages closed their doors for good. In the sixties most likely, part of the sweeping social policy changes of that era; her own cohorts bulldozing anything that didn't fit their vision of the "just society": railway stations, ethnic neighbourhoods, church-run schools, houses like this one. The high road to the future, they'd told themselves. What a laugh.

She won't like you prying. You know what she was like. Still waters and all that.

The thought nags. Her mother wouldn't spend time rifling through old registers and yellowing files; not when there were more pressing tasks awaiting. Like a house to close out; a lifetime to dismantle.

"Right. I should get back."

Barbara eases the car from the curb, edges around the boulevard's median, coaxes the car back up the hill. She passes the gas station that she stopped at earlier, can see the young fellow inside, leaning on the counter by the till. He won't get much more business tonight, she thinks. He should close up and go home.

She reflects on the meaning of *close*. Modern-day psychology stresses the importance of the "closure" process. Considers it a vital way to bring things to completion. A way to heal, to achieve the emotional space needed to move on. Barbara isn't sure she buys in. It seems to her that precious little this side of death is ever completely finished. Few straight lines exist, and fewer new beginnings. Plenty of loose ends, though. An abundance of the old weary, recycled threads.

At eleven o'clock, in the four-poster canopy bed her parents bought for her when she was thirteen, she tosses and turns. She drifts off finally, sleeps badly, dreams of a winter moon shining its cold light onto a massive, silent building. Moonlight filters around the sides of the pulled blinds, plays over the faces of the sleeping children. Children whose mouths are taped shut with white bandages.

She wakes before six, bedclothes tangled and her nightgown damp from sweat. She changes into a clean one, pulls on a terry robe, goes down to the kitchen to make coffee. In the rising steam of the boiling water she can almost hear her mother's voice.

"Daddy called me Rose because I was born in June. He carried me out to our back garden and stood in the arbour and christened me."

Barbara has heard that story many times, often with a change of detail.

"I was just a few hours old."

"I was three days old."

"Mama said that Violet cried. She wanted to take me back."

When is a story not a story anymore but a legend, or a lie? Something beyond itself in the telling.

Barbara had never known her maternal grandparents. Both were gone long before she was born. What little she did know, she'd gleaned from muddied details and a couple of faded photos. Grandfather Bill, a pleasant-faced man in an old-fashioned suit, had suffered a heart attack when the three sisters were quite young. And Grandmother Katherine, a pretty woman in a flapper dress and a triple string of beads around her neck, had succumbed to pneumonia not long afterwards.

Barbara's mother and two sisters had been cared for by a neighbour until Aunt Violet, the oldest girl, was able to take over. Or, that's the story Barbara had accepted as truth. Until this evening, when Mavis had set her straight.

Barbara sips the hot liquid in her mug. Her mother's disinterest—even resistance—at talking about, delving into the past, makes much more sense, now.

"A waste of time," her mother had replied when Barbara had asked to see old documents and pictures for a first-year Sociology project. "The past is over and done with. You young people need to be looking ahead," her mother had said. Disappointed, Barbara had changed topics, doing her project on "Courtship Rituals in New Guinea" instead.

She gets up, makes a second cup of coffee, warms her hands on the mug. Risky business, playing the sleuth. The process called for resilience as well as ingenuity. Once you discovered, uncovered, new facts, you could never undo the knowing. The burden, the responsibility of the knowledge, remained.

Researching other peoples, other societies, was definitely the safer, easier way to go. No emotional attachments, no dark secrets unearthed, no skeletons tumbling out of musty closets.

No war of wills, either. Which is what it boiled down to. Two sides, each with their own agenda. The "Rightful Access" troops, advancing carefully, strategically; probing, uncovering. Pitted against the "Just Privacy" Brigade, who were entrenched, determined not to be heard, seen, or disturbed.

Aunt Lil

It is early afternoon when Barbara turns into the lane that leads from the red mailbox to Jean's house. The ploughed fields and pasture lie under a blanket of early snow, but otherwise the property looks the same as ever to Barbara. The creek where she and Jean used to sail birchbark boats, the gabled house, the linden trees, the two huge silos, the cattle barns, are just as they have always been. Only the new tractor shed is different.

She pulls up behind Len's four-wheel drive and cuts the engine. Jean is waving, smiling, from their back door. "Lunch is waiting," she calls out as soon as Barbara steps from the car. "Come on in. Len'll get your bags later."

After bowls of stew and the requisite biscuits, she leads the way upstairs. "Mom may not know you," she warns. "She's so forgetful these days." At the landing, Jean stops to catch her breath. "Steps will be the death of me," she says. "I bet I'm up and down twenty times a day."

"Why don't you put Aunt Lil in the little room off the kitchen?" Barbara asks. Jean's colour isn't good, and she is carrying too much weight for her small frame.

"I should," Jean replies. "But I keep putting it off. She'll be more confused than ever if I do."

She taps on a door mounted with a sign, Mom's Room, and they enter. Lily is dozing in a chair by the west window. Never a big woman, Lily looks more diminutive than ever in the big La-Z-Boy rocker, with an afghan over her knees and a shawl around her shoulders.

"Wake up, dear," Jean says, picking up her mother's hand and rubbing it gently. "You've got a visitor."

Barbara squats beside the rocker and puts her mouth close to Lily's ear. "Hi, Aunt Lil. It's me, Barbara."

Lily's pale blue eyes stare at her. Barbara waits a moment, and then tries again. "Aunt Lil," she repeats. "I'm Barbara. I drove over from Halifax to see you."

"Barbara."

"Yes."

Lily's hand creeps out from beneath the shawl, finds Barbara's sleeve, rests there. "Violet's girl," she whispers.

"No, dear, not Violet. Rose. Your sister Rose." Barbara speaks deliberately.

"Rose died," Lily says.

"Yes she did. Her funeral was last week."

Lily looks past Barbara, her brow furrowed. "What about Violet? Where is she?"

Jean leans over Barbara's shoulder. "Mom, Violet's gone. Remember?"

Lily pays no heed. Her grip tightens on Barbara's arm.

"Go get Violet. Hurry. Before she gets away again."

The bony fingers dig in and Barbara winces. She eases her arm out of Lily's grasp, stands up, and walks over to the window. A trail of smoke rises from the chimney of a farmhouse across the fields, and, closer in, a flock of barn swallows rises from behind the silo, and makes for a copse of firs on the northern rim of the property. The birds fly in formation, descend, disappear into the cover of green.

They're smarter than we are. They know where they're going— and why.

From the window, Barbara watches as Jean brushes her mother's hair. Jean hums as she strokes: "Rock of Ages." The cadence of her voice, together with the steady motion of her hands, seems to have calmed Lily. Her sparrow face has lost its agitated expression, and the arm that had grasped at Barbara's wrist now rests quietly in her lap.

Seeing Lily in such marked decline is upsetting for Barbara. She had so liked Lily's quiet, unassuming ways; had enjoyed coming to the farm during her summer holidays. Her aunt's laid-back style was a refreshing change from Barbara's more critical, driven mother. Barbara had loved to help with the chores, happily scrubbing the men's work overalls in a big tub, stoking the woodstove, getting the bread ready for the oven, searching for eggs in the hen-house.

"Why doesn't Aunt Lil have clothes like yours?" Barbara had asked her mother. "Why does she wear lace-up shoes and a bib-apron over her housedress?"

"Because we're different," was her mother's answer. "She's a farm woman and I'm a city lady."

That evening, after an evening meal dominated by Len's analysis of the island's potato-marketing troubles, Barbara and Jean linger over their third cup of tea. Jean appears touched at the keepsakes: a silver tray, a cut-glass vase, and the two remaining figurines.

"Your mother had such good taste," Jean says, wistfully.

"Yes. She liked her home, her things."

"She was so fashionable, too," Jean continues. "I liked to peek in her closet when I was visiting you. I'll never forget how elegant she looked the day of your father's funeral, in her black suit and the veiled hat."

"The things that stick in our minds," Barbara says. She has no recollection of the outfit her mother wore on that terrible day. What she does remember is the feel of the damp grass on her shoes at the gravesite, the solemn faces of the railway men, and, later at home, her mother's dry-eyed silence.

Deliberately, she changes the subject. "Jean, I've just found out about the orphanage. It was a real shocker, I must say. I had no idea—did you?" She watches Jean's face, hears a tinge of apology in Jean's voice.

"Well . . .yes, I did. Not till I was older, though. Mom said not to talk about it; that Aunt Rose didn't want you, or anyone, to know."

"Did she tell you any details; what life was like there?"

"Not much. Only that it was big and crowded; and that they were fed okay. The special occasions were best, she said—Christmas, Halloween, Valentine's Day—when they got treats and gifts. She said she didn't hate it, but she was glad when she was old enough to go out to work. She lived with your mother till she married Dad."

"What about Aunt Violet? Where was she?"

"I don't . . . really know," Jean replies, hesitating. "She was always the black sheep. My mother forgave her, years ago, for deserting them. She said that Aunt Rose never did."

"I only ever saw Aunt Violet twice. She used to send gifts, though. Lovely dolls and clothes; from Montreal."

It's Jean's turn, now, to switch topics. "We'll keep in touch, won't we, Barb? You and I don't have any other cousins."

"Of course we will," Barbara says.

"You're welcome to stay longer," Jean adds. "I wish you could."

"I know that. But it's a long drive, and I'd like to make Montreal by tomorrow night," Barbara replies. "I've been away so long as it is."

They watch the late-night news together. Barbara waits while Jean turns off the lights and shuts the cat in the kitchen.

"There's an envelope for you," Jean says. "It's in Mom's cedar chest. Old letters, I think. I'll give it to you in the morning. Don't let me forget."

The Envelope

Barbara awakes in the middle of the night, parched. The spiced scallops that Jean served at supper have left an aftertaste. Craving juice over tap water, Barbara gropes her way along the upper hall and down the stairs.

At the landing window, she peers out into the darkness. There is no moon or stars, making it difficult to tell where the sky stops and the earth begins. Barbara shivers; she shares her mother's distaste of the country at night. "Too black and lonely," her mother had always maintained. "Give me the city any day. You can see where you're going, and there's something to do when you get there."

Making it to the kitchen without tripping or slamming into furniture, Barbara is greeted by a faint meow. She feels the cat's tail against her leg when she opens the fridge door. She pours a glass of juice for herself and refills the cat's saucer with milk. The milk pitcher is an old crockery one, with a chipped spout and a cluster of bright purple grapes painted on one side. She drinks the juice in three gulps, refills her glass, and, fully awake now, decides to read for a while.

The cat accompanies her into the front room, jumps onto the piano stool when Barbara switches on the floor-lamp. "Were you Chopin in one of your other lives?" Barbara asks, watching him sniff at the keys.

The top of the old upright is crowded with photos of Jean and Len, their boys, the grandchildren. There are several older ones, too; Lily, in her fifties-style wedding gown, holding the arm of a grinning Chester; a small, framed snapshot of a teenaged Lily with Rose. In the background, a sailor leans over the rim of a fountain, suggesting that it had been taken in the Gardens in Halifax.

It's Barbara's theory that family picture collections arranged on tops of pianos and mantels are deliberately deceiving. The milestone events—weddings, christenings, graduations—show the viewer hairstyles and fashion trends, but little else. For the real story, you needed to analyze the dozens of photos pasted in the albums; or, better still, the rejects that didn't make the album and were stashed away in a box under the eaves.

The last picture in this group is a casual shot of the two sisters—Lily and Rose—standing in front of a barn. Lily, with perm-frizzed hair and wearing her trademark housedress, looks frumpy beside her glamorous older sister. The faces in the old snapshot are not at all crisp, and Barbara holds it under the lamp for a better look.

That can't be Mom, she thinks. Her mother had never worn her hair in a beehive, never owned a pair of hoop earrings. No, that must be the other sister, Violet. Certainly, her mother and Violet did look very similar, especially in photos; same nose and eyes, same oval face and trim figure.

Their differences appear to have been their distinctive personalities, their approach to life. Barbara's mother had been stylish in an understated, classic way, never stepping out of the house unless her makeup and hair were perfect. Aunt Violet, on the other hand, had been the flamboyant one. In this shot, she is wearing a miniskirt, an off-the-shoulder blouse, and white boots.

Barbara puts the picture back in place. The house will be waking up in another hour or so, but she doesn't feel a bit sleepy. *I'll try a crossword puzzle,* she says to herself. *There must be one in the local newspaper.* She finds yesterday's paper, folded neatly, on a corner of the kitchen table. Propped beside it is the envelope that Jean promised to put ready.

Barbara takes the newspaper and the envelope to the living room, finds the cat asleep in the middle of the sofa, makes a space beside him, and sits down. She works on the puzzle until her eyes begin to feel heavy. The envelope's old letters can wait until morning.

The sound of a truck engine starting up wakes her. She can hear a man's voice, shouting out to someone above the roar of the engine.

Barbara gets up and reaches for her robe. The room is chilly in the way old houses can be, and she is dying for a cup of coffee. Peeking out into the hall, she can smell the combined aroma of frying bacon and perked coffee. She wishes she could sneak her first caffeine fix of the day up to the bedroom. Hotel coffeemakers have been one of the greatest inventions, as far as she's concerned. The first coffee of the day should be hot, black, and, most importantly, solitary.

Propping two pillows against the headboard, she picks up the envelope and stretches out on the bed. It has been well sealed, and she needs her nail scissors to cut through the layers of tape. Inside is a sheaf of papers, tied together with a red ribbon.

By now, she is weary of old papers; is looking forward to her return to work, and her high-speed Internet. Whatever these papers are, she knows they aren't her mother's will. She'd found it, and a copy of a cancelled life insurance policy, from the tinbox that her mother had kept on the top shelf of the linen cupboard.

She unfolds a single sheet of flimsy gold paper. *Division Registrar's Certificate of Birth* is printed below a scrolled border. On the top line is her name, Barbara Ann Varner.

Barbara has never seen her original birth certificate. When she was applying to universities for scholarship money, her mother had given her one of the laminated, wallet-sized cards. Barbara keeps it, with her Baptism Certificate and passport, in a leatherette writing case that she won in a Bingo game.

Her father's name—Ralph E. Varner—appears as *Father of Child and Registration Applicant*. The attending physician was a Dr. G. Wiswell. Barbara has no idea who he was. The gruff old fellow who had seen her through measles, tonsillitis, and a broken arm had been Dr. Tomkins.

The form is a very comprehensive one, including a line at the bottom for racial origin. *Name of Mother* is halfway down the page. Barbara looks at it, blinks, and looks again. How very odd; her mother's first name has been entered incorrectly. Typical of government, though. In her father's opinion, if anyone could mess up a simple form, it was a government worker. She can hear his deep voice, even now. "Most of 'em don't know their arse from their elbow."

A queer, unsettled feeling is beginning to form in the pit of her stomach. She lays the certificate on the bed beside her and unfolds a piece of pink notepaper. It is a letter, addressed to Lily. The paper emits a faint aroma of Yardley's Lavender, her mother's favourite scent.

Dear Lily —

This is in haste, as there seems to be so much to do. Am sending the certificate and lawyer's papers by registered mail. Ralph agreed, finally, though I know he thinks I'm being overly cautious. I'm so relieved that everything is finalized, and that you will keep the papers locked up over there.

Violet left on the 16th. I don't expect to see her again for a good long while. She promised, so I can only hope she keeps her word. Everyone off to a fresh new start, so to speak.

The baby is so good. Sleeps through the night already and takes

*her bottle like a little pig. She's got my colouring, thank goodness,
and the same eyes . . .*

Barbara skims the rest, unfolds the accompanying document. She reads the document slowly, deliberately, as if
trying to decipher a hidden code in the pages of legalese.
After she finishes, she folds the document, runs her finger
over the creaseline.

One of Lily's samplers hangs on the opposite wall: *God's
in His Heaven. All's right with the world.* Browning, of course.
Only a Victorian would have such simple faith.

*I should have known. Why didn't I know? Somebody should
have told me.* The nervous, hollow feeling that had begun in
her stomach is rising, spreading through her.

You're blind, silly. And besides that, you don't see so well. An
old schoolyard taunt.

Her feet are like ice; her hands, too. She pulls the quilt
up around her neck. Her head feels dull, thick. She is thick.
Stupid. So totally stupid.

When she was five or six, Barbara had complained that
she needed a brother or a sister. "Why can't I have one?"
she'd insisted. "Other kids have them."

Aunt Bernice had taken her aside that day. "Don't go on
like that," Bernice had said. "It makes your mother feel bad.
You had a brother once, but he died when he was just two
days old. Your mother was sad for a long time. And then,
when she got you, she was happy again."

Got you. That was exactly the way Bernice had said it.
As if she'd been ordered from the baby section of the Sear's
catalogue.

Blinders

Barbara is eight when she meets her Aunt Violet for the first time. It is summer and she waits excitedly on the front porch. Her aunt from Montreal has called from the train station, is on her way over in a taxi.

Barbara sees the cab turn into their street, watches it pull up.

"Mom, she's here," Barbara calls through the screendoor. "Aunt Violet's here."

Her aunt is as pretty as Barbara has imagined her to be. Her dark hair is set in waves that curl around her ears. She is wearing dangling earrings, a beaded choker, and a full-skirted dress. And her shoes! High, high heels, with open toes, and straps that buckle at the side of each ankle.

"Hi there, sweetheart," her aunt says when she nears the steps. "Here I am, all the way from Montreal to see my special girl. Come, give me a big hug."

Suddenly shy, Barbara gets up slowly, allows herself to be pulled into her aunt's embrace. The smell of perfume is strong—a bouquet of flowers, mingled with another, sickly-sweet scent. Cough medicine, perhaps, or the sherry that her mother serves the ladies when they come for Lodge meetings.

Aunt Violet has brought her a present. It is a leather shoulder bag, with tassels on either end. Inside the bag is a change purse with two silver dollars in it. There's a little mirror, too, and a tail-comb that fits into a slot on the inside flap.

"I really like my bag," she says to her aunt at the supper table. "It's just like a real lady's one."

Aunt Violet laughs. "Guess I've got a pretty good eye for what girls like—and the boys, too, for that matter." Her father smiles. Her mother gets up and goes into the kitchen for the teapot.

While they are eating, her aunt tells them stories. Sometimes she says things in a funny accent. Her father tells Violet that her pig French isn't half bad. Barbara doesn't know any pig French, but she does know pig Latin. She and her friends talk in pig Latin at recess. If a new girl wants to join their skipping circle, they test her out. "Ou-say ou yay onna-way ip-skay op-ray?" If she can answer back correctly, she's in.

Aunt Violet has been on lots of trips. She tells them about Boston, and New York, and Niagara Falls. She also shows them a picture of her son, Billy. He is older than Barbara; through at school and learning to be an electrician.

Barbara protests when her mother tells her it's time for bed.

"Can't I stay up longer?" she pleads. "It's Sunday tomorrow."

When her mother insists, Barbara flounces out of the room.

She lies awake for ages, listening to the rise and fall of their voices below her. They are talking loudly, almost as if they are arguing. Surely, they aren't mad at each other. Why would they be?

She isn't yet asleep when she hears her bedroom door open. Through half-closed eyelids, she can see Violet framed in a band of light from the hallway lamp.

Her aunt moves quietly around the end of her bed, sits down on the quilt. She is humming a tune that is not familiar to Barbara. After several minutes, the humming stops and Barbara can feel her aunt's face, close to her own, can smell the sweet odour of her perfume.

"Sleep tight, *chérie*," Violet whispers. "I'd take you back if only I could." There is a moist touch of lips against her cheek, a rustle of clothing, and then the band of light narrows and the door closes.

Barbara turns on her side and pulls the blanket over her face. Maybe her aunt will invite them to Montreal next summer. They can go on the train—her father has a family pass—stay at Violet's house, go shopping in the toy stores, see the animals at the zoo.

The next day Violet treats them to lunch downtown. "I won't take no for an answer," she says to Barbara's mother. "We're going, and that's that. Call it a family celebration."

Violet lets Barbara place her own order; and, after she's eaten all of her sandwich, she is allowed to select a chocolate eclair from the dessert cart.

After lunch, they walk in the Gardens and feed bread to the ducks. "Almost like old times," Aunt Violet says. Barbara's mother seems tired, looks constantly at her watch. "We'd better not be late," she says. Late for what, Barbara wonders.

They take Violet to the train station, wait while she stands in a long line-up at the ticket counter. "Can we go to Montreal next year?" Barbara asks.

"No," says her mother. Her father says, "Maybe. Someday."

"Be happy, Rose," her aunt says to her mother after she gets her ticket. "You've got the family you wanted. It's more than a lot of us can manage." To her father, Violet says, "Thanks, Ralph—for being you."

They don't kiss goodbye. Barbara wishes they would. All around them, people are kissing and hugging, crying and laughing.

"Well, she's off," her mother says when Violet has gone through the gate. "We should head home."

They drive back in silence. Barbara is disappointed that Aunt Violet didn't say a word about them visiting Montreal. Maybe she could write her aunt and suggest it. Her mother has notepaper and envelopes in her desk. Barbara has seen an address book in the drawer, too. She can look in it for Aunt Violet's street number. Barbara knows the rest: Montreal, Quebec, Canada.

The room is quiet, so quiet. She can hear the tick of her travel alarm, and her own heart, beating, beating.

She hopes Jean doesn't knock on the door. She can't deal with her—with people—at the moment. She's not *herself*. Ha! That's a laugh; a sick joke.

I deserve to have known, she thinks. *I should have known.*

Yesterday was so uncomplicated. She'd dealt with her grief, her new reality as a midlife orphan. A draining experience, yes; but one that she shared with countless other people.

Now—this. Her own history in tatters. Shot to hell.

Barbara. Daughter of Rose. By adoption; a transfer process.

Little girl of Ralph. A dear man, but unlikely to have been her genetic father. She will, of course, never know for sure. They now had the technology to conduct DNA testing, but he died such a long time ago. Nor did she have fingernail clippings, a lock of his hair. Nothing. Zip.

After a while, she showers and dresses, anxious to get breakfast over with and be on her way.

Jean presses her to have bacon and eggs. "No, please, not for me," Barbara says. "Just plain toast and coffee."

"You're as bad as your mother was; she never ate enough to keep a bird alive."

Your mother—

Barbara manages a small smile.

"Mom's a bit brighter this morning," Jean says. "I do hope you've got time to see her again before you go."

Brighter. Duller. Opposite ends of a continuum. Life staggers and stumbles onward, heading, in its bleary-eyed drunkenness, toward a gaping, black hole.

Jean brings the plate of toast to the table, sits down. "One of these days, I'll have a trip up to Ontario to see you."

"That will be great," she replies. "We'll do all the high-lights. See a Jays game at the SkyDome if you like."

Jean grins. "I'm not much for baseball. What I'd really get a kick out of would be a ride on the subway."

Barbara laughs outright at this. Mothers, baseball games, subway rides; weird, the things people wish for, keep hidden. In most cases, the reasons are inexplicable, the motivations highly suspect. A ride on the subway, for God sake! Barbara can't tolerate subways; hates the smells, the crush of too many bodies in too small a space.

After she's brushed her teeth and packed her cosmetic case in her overnight bag, she goes in to her aunt. Jean has positioned the rocking chair at a window that overlooks the front yard and the driveway.

"I'm going now, Aunt Lil," Barbara says. "I came to give you a goodbye kiss."

"Going? Where?" Lily asks.

"To Toronto," Barbara replies. "Where I live."

"What a trip!" Lily exclaims, looking up at her. "You'll be tuckered out by the time you get there." She shakes her head, wags her finger at Barbara. "Remember me to your mother."

"My mother died," Barbara says. "Rose died."

"Oh, Rose died. And Violet, too?"

"Yes, they both died."

"Oh." Lily was silent for a moment. Barbara plants a kiss on her forehead and turns to leave.

"Tell her to call me," Lily says from her chair.

"Who?"

"Your mother, that's who. Violet."

Downstairs, Jean is fretting over the latest weather report. "I'll make Montreal before dark, and push on in the morning," Barbara says. "I'll phone you when I arrive—promise."

"I've never been to Montreal," Jean says. "Always wondered what it's like. Mom went, years ago, to see Violet."

Violet had kept in touch with Lily; the pictures on the piano said as much.

"When did Violet die?" Barbara asks in an even voice.

"Fifteen years ago, last February. It was cancer. Mom missed her; they'd got quite close. But she still had your mom, so that helped."

Barbara cannot tell what Jean is thinking, or holding back. Perhaps nothing, though Barbara finds this hard to believe.

At the end of Jean's lane, Barbara pauses to let a tractor lumber past. She follows it until it turns right, onto a narrow clay road.

A few miles ahead, the bridge that spans the Strait will take her across to the mainland. She will drive to Aulac, turn north, follow the highway to Sussex. Up and up she will go, past Fredericton, Edmundston, into the St. Lawrence River valley. Heading west, heading home.

For Ontario is her home; has been for a long time. Her heart is there: with her friends, her work; and, lately, Knut. The sun is in her eyes, and Barbara pulls the visor down.

The years since moving to Toronto have been good ones for her. She has a well-established life there; and a view for the future. It's too late to consider having children, but she's come to terms with that. Just as well, actually. She never liked babies, or keeping house; is content with her career-woman role. With it comes a decent salary, nice clothes, restful vacations, jazz concerts, dinner with friends.

Violet had a son, don't forget. Your half-brother. You could probably find him, if you wanted to.

The past has, as with everyone, shaped her in many ways. And, now—this new layer of family history has come to light. It need not warp her, though, or trip her up. Cousin Jean is the only person who might know the story, and Barbara is certain that Jean won't blab.

Mothers and aunts. Secrets and silences. Barbara considers the implications of her new knowledge; and whether it would be wise or foolish to try and locate the half-brother who is out there, somewhere. She shall tread carefully; will take her time.

Now that the blinders are off, she will just have to see.

– End –

ACKNOWLEDGEMENTS

For their input during the research phase, I wish to thank Lillian Lohnes, Helen Fostaty, Flo Trillo, Colleen Wambolt, Pearl Gregory, and Georgia Jordan. Thanks also to the Public Archives of Nova Scotia, the Director of Veith House, and to various members of the Northwood Community Centre.

For their critique time and talents, a special thank you to my mentor, Carol Bruneau; readers Helen Cook and Cynthia French; Gwen Davies, Mary Jane Copps, and other members of the Oxford Street Writer's Group; Kim McArthur and her staff; editor Pamela Erlichman; agent Nick Harris.

For their continued support and belief in this project, thanks and love to Keith, David, and Charles Cameron.